The Husband Gambit

L.A. WITT

ISBN: 9781730708893

Copyright Information

This is a work of fiction. Names, characters, places, and incidents are either the product of the author's imagination or are used fictitiously. Any resemblance to actual persons living or dead, business establishments, events, or locales is entirely coincidental.

The Husband Gambit
First edition
Copyright © 2018 L.A. Witt

Cover Art by Lori Witt
Editor: Leta Blake

ISBN: 9781730708893

THE HUSBAND GAMBIT

L.A. WITT

Chapter 1
Hayden

"Whoever wrote that ad is either a serial killer or someone making pornos," Luis declared without looking away from the TV.

My other roommate, Ashton, snorted. "That, or he's a serial killer making pornos."

I laughed and rolled my eyes. "And that's different from any other ad, how? This is Hollywood, babe."

Luis frowned. "I'm serious. That's not a normal ad. Not even in this town. It's fucking weird."

"Oh, it is." I peered at my laptop and the ad I'd incredulously read aloud to my roommates. "But I won't lie—I am curious."

Luis just shook his head, still frowning.

"I'd be curious too," Ashton said. "How come no one ever offers to be my sugar daddy?"

"Because you're straight, stupid," Luis said with a laugh. "You need a sugar mama."

"Hey, look, I'm broker than both of you. I won't

discriminate if someone wants to pay my bills." Ashton, lounging beside me on the battered old sofa, craned his neck to look at my screen. "Does it say being gay is a requirement? Or could a straight guy—"

"Oh, no you don't." I turned my laptop away and shot him a playful glare. "I've got dibs."

"But…" He pouted, then huffed. "Fine."

"That's what I thought."

Luis blinked. "Hayden, please tell me you're not actually going to respond."

"No, I'm not *going* to respond." I started typing. "I'm responding right now."

He shook his head and turned back to the TV show we'd all been ignoring. "Enjoy making serial killer porn."

I chuckled, but didn't say anything.

In the email, I wrote:

Hello, I saw your ad, and I'm interested. Could you please contact me with details?

It was a benign enough email. The same generic response I'd send to any ad I'd found, but as I hit Send this time, there was an odd flutter in my stomach. Equal parts curiosity, amusement, and… jitters? As if the person on the other end might reply to me, and something might come of this besides them having a good laugh because someone had fallen for it? I couldn't put my finger on it.

But the response was sent, and all I could do now was wait.

I closed the email, but there was still a browser tab open to the ad, and I couldn't resist reading it one more time.

Marry me for 1 year.
Payment: $1.2 million.

I'm a man looking for a temporary husband. $100K per month. Cohabitation, legal marriage, and NDA are required. Sex is not. Contact for more info.

Okay, so I could totally see why Luis thought it was weird, but I mean, $1.2 million was $1.2 million. That would pay off student loans for all three of us and still leave enough for, I don't know, a trip to In-N-Out for burgers or something.

It was probably a prank. Or a phishing scheme. I had no doubt just signed myself up for thousands of spam emails. That, or a team of hackers was, as I sat here, breaking into my financials and bleeding me dry. Joke was on them if they were. I hoped they liked In-N-Out, because that was all they were getting with my hordes of riches.

Ugh, I hated being this broke. Why had I let someone talk me into going to school again? Oh, right, because without a college degree, I'd spend the rest of my life pathetic, broke, and living with two roommates in a tiny apartment in a shitty neighborhood. Wait...

But hey, at least our shitty apartment had five degrees on the wall—all of our bachelors' degrees, plus Luis's MBA and my Masters in Theatre Arts that had totally not been a waste of time or money. Another few months and we could add Ashton's MBA to the wall of shame too. After that, we could all celebrate by adding some actual seasonings to our ramen and toasting with whatever store-brand soda was on sale that week.

So, yeah, to be honest, serial killer porn wasn't as unappealing as you might think.

As long as there were no clowns involved. I was desperate, but a man had to have some standards.

We were halfway through an episode of The Big Bang Theory—oh my God there was *nothing* on today—when my email pinged. I jumped like someone had shocked me, and sent up the same prayer I always did when I had a new email: *please tell me Carmen landed me another audition.* That well had been discouragingly dry lately, but hope sprang eternal.

As soon as I'd opened the window, my teeth snapped together so hard I almost bit my stupid tongue. The email was not from Carmen.

Sender: guest_user
Subject: re: Marry me for 1 year.

I had to force back an excited announcement to my roomies that the mystery sugar daddy had responded. Better to see what he'd actually said before I made more of an ass of myself.

Holding my breath, I opened the email.

Thanks for the response. Are you seriously interested?

I swallowed, then wrote back: *I need details, but yes.*

If I hadn't been curious before, I was now. If he asked for my bank details, then I'd block the hell out of him, but so far he hadn't mentioned anything about being a Nigerian prince. Not necessarily promising, but definitely intriguing.

The next reply came in seconds:

Would you be willing to meet? I would prefer not to discuss this via email.

Serial killer porn was sounding more and more plausible. On the other hand, if I was going to be "marrying" this guy for a year, it probably wouldn't hurt to see him face to face and make sure he wasn't… like…

A serial killer porn star?

I cleared my throat. "So hey, remember that sugar daddy ad?"

Both my roommates turned to me.

I gestured at the screen. "He responded. He wants to meet to talk details."

Luis made stabbing motions and mimicked the shrill music from *Psycho*.

Ashton leaned closer, peering at my screen. "Did he give you any more info?"

"No, he just said he doesn't want to discuss it via email."

Right then, my Nigerian prince of sugar daddy serial killer porn wrote back. The email contained the name of a restaurant, an address, and a time.

Tell the hostess you're here to meet James.

I quickly googled the restaurant, which turned out to be an insanely exclusive high-dollar place in West Hollywood. "Holy shit. I probably can't even afford the tap water at this place."

Ashton whistled. "No kidding. So are you going to go?"

Some part of me thought the smart answer would be "Uh, no," followed by deleting the email, closing my laptop, and never speaking of this again. But in some way, every step I took down this rabbit hole made me curiouser and curiouser. Who was this guy? What was his deal? And who the hell needed to hire a husband—an actual, legal husband—anyway? Was this some sort of romcom sitch where he had to get married in order to stay in Daddy's will?

"I think I'm going to do it, yeah," I said.

Luis huffed. "Dude. If this guy's rich enough to pay

someone a million bucks to marry him, doesn't that tell you that maybe there's a reason nobody's been willing to marry him for free?"

"Shut up," Ashton hissed. "Hayden's about to get rich."

"Or murdered."

"I'm not going to get murdered." My hands hovered over the keys, though, and I cut my eyes toward my roommates. "But, um, could one of you hang out close by? Just in case he does turn out to be Pennywise the Porn Star?" Oh Christ, there really would be clowns, wouldn't there?

Luis shook his head. "No way. I'm not having any part of this."

Ashton rolled his eyes. "I'll go. My car will actually get you out there without breaking down, too."

He… wasn't wrong. My poor clunky beater was one sudden stop away from going to the big parking lot in the sky, but Ashton's ancient Honda was still puttering along somehow. Seriously, that car was immortal.

"Okay. Thanks. I'll see if I can smuggle out some breadsticks or something."

Ashton groaned. "Oh my God. Yes *please*."

I chuckled and turned my screen. With a little trepidation, a lot of curiosity, and maybe a pinch of excitement, I wrote back:

See you at 8.

"I'm here to see James." I felt stupid as hell saying those words to the bow-tied hostess at the restaurant's podium. It reminded me of one of those ads on the radio where they said you're supposed to "tell them Bob sent you" or whatever, and nobody ever actually did because even as broke as I was, a dollar off was not worth the momentary humiliation.

The hostess didn't miss a beat, though. "He's waiting for you in the VIP section. Right this way."

The VIP section? Whoa.

As if this place wasn't already gleaming right out of my price range. It was dimly lit, and everything that would have been paper in a restaurant that might have hired me—yeah right—was linen, and every surface that would have been smudged in fingerprints or grease was immaculately polished marble, faux gold, or some other shiny stone or metal that my trash ass could never identify. There was a bar that looked like it only served top shelf, and between that and a fireplace, an *actual string quartet* wore tuxes and played soft music.

As I followed the hostess past all this class and style, I self-consciously glanced down at my button-up shirt and slacks, and quickly scrutinized my hair in one of the many shiny surfaces. Did I look remotely suitable to be in anything marked VIP? Should I have worn something else? Did I look like a million dollars? Because I was here to convince a man I was worth a million dollars.

Oh, sweetie, some voice inside my head tsked. *You look like twelve bucks in wrinkled bills.*

Great. This felt like every audition and interview I ever did—blown before I walked through the door.

There was still time to hightail it out of here, right? It wasn't like anyone knew me, so—

The hostess opened a door with VIP in gold letters, and she waved me inside. "Your party is in here. A server will be along to get your drink order."

"Oh. Um." I cleared my throat. "Thanks."

She shut the door, and I was in the VIP lounge, and there was only one other person in this room, and James was... oh my Lord, James was *not* what I had envisioned.

Between reading the ad and walking into this room, I'd painted a mental picture of him that involved scraggly gray hair (assuming he had any left), fucked-up teeth (assuming he had any of *those* left), and a skin-crawly perma-leer. I mean that wasn't technically fair, but it was hard to ignore Luis's comments about what kind of guy was loaded and still had to *buy* a spouse. It hadn't taken long for my imagination to build a James with Mafia ties, dragon breath, and some serious toenail fungus. Clown hat optional.

So I was utterly unprepared to walk in and see someone *that* gorgeous looking back at me.

Sitting at a small booth, leaning back against the leather seat with a half-empty glass in his hand, was a tall white man who belonged on a magazine cover. His light brown hair and fair complexion brought out the startling blue of his eyes, and a dusting of five o'clock shadow framed gorgeous full lips. There was no expression on his face—he was studying me intently, but I couldn't have guessed what was on his mind.

He'd worn a gray button-up shirt that wasn't any fancier than the cranberry one I'd worn. That made me feel better about being underdressed, at least until I noticed the two-tone Rolex peeking out from his cuff. I wasn't a watch connoisseur or anything, but my brother had been given a similar one by his coach after he'd qualified for the Olympics the first time, and I knew at a glance that was a ten-plus thousand dollar watch. So much for not feeling underdressed.

James cleared his throat, and I realized with no small amount of mortification that I'd been just standing there staring. As he rose, so did my pulse, and when he extended his hand, I almost forgot what to do with it. "You must be Hayden?"

I swallowed, and mercifully remembered how to shake hands. "Yeah. I assume you're James."

The expressionless façade broke, and I was again startled, this time by a soft laugh that sounded... shy? Really? "James isn't my real name. Just a name I use for..." He waved toward the door.

"So like a code name?"

"Kind of, yeah." He met my gaze, and a smile lingered on his lips. "My name is Jesse."

"Oh. Okay."

We locked eyes for a moment, and then Jesse gestured at the table. "Have a seat. We can order drinks and discuss—"

"I'm pretty sure I can't afford more than water in this place." I glanced around. "Might not even be able to spring for that much."

His smile warmed. "I'm buying."

"Are... are you sure?"

"You answered my ridiculously cryptic ad, and made it past all the emails that probably sounded creepy." He chuckled self-consciously. "After all the cloak-and-dagger, the least I can do is buy you dinner."

"Oh." I blinked. "Okay. Sure." My stomach growled, though I hoped it wasn't loud enough for him to hear. After months of eating whatever garbage I could afford, I was getting dinner in a place like this?

Well, hell. Bring on the serial killer Nigerian prince clown porn.

Chapter 2
Jesse

I'd posted the ad because I hadn't known how else to find someone for this arrangement, but I hadn't had high hopes about getting a response. It was true that in Los Angeles—land of dreams and disappointment—people would do a lot of things for money. Wave six figures in their faces, and most reservations evaporate. Make it seven, and, well, that was the only explanation I could think of for why certain actors took certain roles.

So I guess I wasn't really surprised that someone responded. I just hadn't expected... *him.*

As Hayden slid into the booth opposite me, I stole a moment to drink him in. He had to be an actor or a model. No one in this town was that pretty and didn't get in front of a camera. Maybe he was a struggling one—after all, he was considering my offer—but I didn't imagine his big break was far off. Unless he was a terrible actor or something. But even then...

I shook myself and shifted my attention to the menu

I'd already read a dozen times. I'd never been able to pull off acting either, but the prospect of pretending to be this man's other half wasn't what I'd call daunting. He was just... my God, he was gorgeous. That was a face that would never need my professional assistance to look good on camera. Contouring would be overkill on cheekbones that high. Mascara would be redundant on lashes that long. He had sun-kissed skin that wasn't overcooked or sun-damaged and would probably be perfect on-camera without any help from me. Eyebrows that were flawlessly shaped, lips I could stare at all damn night, meticulously styled dark hair—I could think of a dozen casting directors who would take one look at him and have him lined up with work until he was ninety.

Pretend I'm married to him for a year? Yeah, I can swing that.

But there were some details we needed to work out first. As silly as my proposition had probably seemed on the surface, it was serious for me, and I wasn't taking chances. So, after the server had come and gone with our orders, I reached for the manila folder sitting on the bench beside me. "Okay, before we go any further, I need to have you sign the non-disclosure agreement."

Hayden's eyebrows climbed. "Um. Okay?"

I slid the document across the table. "I need everything we talk about to stay between us. There's a bit too much on the line for me to take anything for granted."

His eyes widened, and he drew back just slightly. I could practically hear the second thoughts banging around in his head.

"You're not committing to anything," I said. "Just that whatever we discuss doesn't leave this room."

Hayden considered the folder for a moment. Then he

opened it, and silence hung between us while he read it over. Smart man—he didn't just sign a document without reading it. Not even with a cool million on the table.

After he'd gone over it, he quietly asked, "Do you have a pen?"

I handed him one, and he scrawled his name at the bottom of the NDA. I put aside the papers and pen, and looked at him across the table. "All right. With that out of the way, I guess we should start with a rundown of what I'm doing."

Hayden nodded. "Okay."

I sipped my iced tea, then folded my hands on the table and took a deep breath. No one had gotten this far yet. A few nibbles via email, but Hayden was the first to meet me face to face and the first to sign the NDA. He'd be the first to hear this, and I was suddenly terrified of how it would sound to an actual person.

No time like the present to find out.

"Are you familiar with Isaac Ambrose?"

Hayden tensed. "People living under rocks are familiar with Isaac Ambrose."

That was the God's honest truth.

I shifted, staring down at my folded hands. "Okay. Well. He's my father."

Hayden made a sound like he'd choked on air, and when our eyes met this time, he was staring at me like I'd just told him I'd had sex with the Pope. "You're... you're Isaac Ambrose's *son*?"

I nodded, and said with a bitter laugh, "One of the sons that *isn't* an A-lister, which is probably why you haven't heard of me."

Hayden gulped, but said nothing. Now that I thought

about it, it was entirely possible he had heard of me. Dad occasionally mentioned me in passing in interviews, and my name sometimes drifted into those lengthy multi-page articles about him in Vogue, Vanity Fair, and People. Kind of ironic considering I was the only one of his five kids who'd been nominated for an Oscar *and* an Emmy, but as far as Dad was concerned, the hair and makeup categories didn't count. He sure as hell wasn't going to make a big deal about his *son* being nominated in *those* categories.

Clearing my throat again, I sat back against the seat. "The super condensed Cliff's notes version is that my father is planning to run for governor next year. On a liberal progressive platform."

"So, what?" Hayden thumbed the edge of the leather placemat. "He wants a happily married gay son to push his whole 'family man' image?"

I snorted. "No. If I marry a man, he'll disown me."

Hayden froze. "Um. Come again?"

"He portrays himself as this progressive, pro-equality liberal because let's face it—that's what Southern California voters want these days."

"Yeah, I guess so, but I always thought he was pretty conservative."

"He is. He's *very* conservative. But most Republicans see him as a member of the Hollywood liberal elite, and he's managed to alienate the rest by being staunchly pro-choice. They're not interested in him."

Hayden laughed dryly and rolled his eyes.

"So, he's been carefully painting himself as someone liberal voters will back, but behind closed doors?" I shook my head. "A few journalists have tried to show who he really is, but honestly, there aren't many media outlets left that'll butt heads with him unless there is indisputable evidence to back up anything they say."

Hayden's eyebrow rose. "I feel like that answers my question about why you haven't just done a tell-all instead of, uh…"

"I tried. Believe me. And some industry rivals and estranged family members have tried in the past, but it always blows up in their faces. Half the time they're pulling it out of their asses, and the other half, Dad has some kind of dirt on them and a bulletproof defense for himself, and it winds up reflecting a hundred times worse on them than him." Sighing, I shook my head. "It would be a lot easier, believe me, but there's no way anyone will listen to me."

"Damn."

"Right?" I rubbed my forehead. Just talking about this exhausted me. "Doesn't help that he's put extra effort into looking like the liberal he's pretending to be. He's always putting on bullshit fundraisers for everything from AIDS research to feeding starving children."

Hayden shifted, eyeing me warily. "He's… he's not funneling that money into something else, is he?"

"No, no." I shook my head. "But he's very quietly funneling his own money into things like preventing queer people from adopting kids. He told any camera he could find that he supported marriage equality, but I know for a fact he donated tens of *thousands* to campaigns to ban it."

"Aren't political donations public, though?"

"They're supposed to be, but if you run the money through enough shell companies and anonymous channels, tracing them back is almost impossible."

Hayden whistled. "Wow. I mean, I guess I shouldn't be surprised someone that powerful is corrupt, but…"

"Everyone in Hollywood is corrupt," I grumbled. "Especially the ones who go into politics."

"Yeah. You don't say." He took a drink and rolled it around in his mouth for a moment. "So, does he know you're gay?"

"He does. And..." I hesitated, wondering if I should tell Hayden the whole story now or later. I decided he deserved to at least hear the pertinent parts, and made a mental note to pour myself something strong as fuck when I got home tonight. I sat up a little and folded my arms on the edge of the table. "I came out to the family when I was fifteen. Dad was ready to cut me off and throw me out that day."

"When you were fifteen?" Hayden sputtered.

"Yep. My mom stepped in, thank God. She convinced him that booting me out like that would do some serious damage to his reputation. Which... I mean, it was almost twenty years ago, so he might have gotten away with it, but Mom could see that society was shifting. Even if he got away with it at the time, it would come back and bite him in the ass later."

"So he kept you in the family because he wanted to protect his reputation?"

I half-shrugged. "Hollywood."

Hayden nodded and gave a quiet grunt of understanding. Amazing how much a single word could explain to anyone who'd spent any time in this city and its deceptively glittery industry.

"Anyway, the end result is they came to an agreement that I could stay in the house, and they'd tolerate me discreetly dating men, but Dad would cut me off if I ever got married."

Hayden's eyebrows quirked with confusion.

"It was..." I sighed, waving a hand. "Dad needed to have some kind of line so he'd still be in control—so he'd still *win*—and Mom figured I'd never be able to get married anyway, so she agreed to let that be the bar." I sat back, fatigue pressing down on my shoulders after mentally reliving that hellish week of tense negotiations between my parents. "We all kind of figured it was settled, you know? But then Canada legalized gay marriage, and I happened to be seriously dating someone at the time. My mom pulled me aside and told me not to even *think* about it. She said if I wanted to go quietly elope or something, fine, but don't tell my father, don't wear a wedding ring around him, don't change my name..."

"So she thought he was serious. That he really would jump at the opportunity to kick you out, even all those years later."

I nodded slowly as I swallowed bile. "She knows he is, and he confirmed it, too. The day marriage equality became law in this country, he told me that everything from when I was fifteen still stood. I marry a man, he will disown and disinherit me. It's the only way he feels like he's in control of the situation. He's a man accustomed to having his way no matter what, and he has zero tolerance for defiance. Especially from his own kids. Honestly, the line in the sand could have been anything as long as he could use it to control me. It just happened that mom suggested marriage and he agreed to it."

Hayden's lips parted. He watched me for a long moment, then moistened his lips and took a breath like he was about to speak, but before he could, his phone beeped. "Shit. Excuse me a second." He took it out, and as he typed, added, "My buddy was waiting outside in case you ended up being a creeper." Beat. "No offense."

"None taken." I liked that he was this cautious. He'd read over the NDA instead of just signing it, and he had a backup plan since he'd had no idea about me before he'd come in here. That was encouraging—this was someone I could expect to take things seriously and go in with both eyes open.

"Okay. Sorry." He pocketed his phone. "Just needed to check in with him so he didn't think you were chopping me up in a back alley or something."

I laughed. I could have made a joke like "not in this part of town" or "we haven't even had dinner yet," but that didn't seem appropriate right now. Hayden had every right to be wary of me and my intentions, so I kept the wisecracks to myself.

"Anyway." Hayden folded his hands on the table, mirroring me. "So, are you saying you want to pretend to be married so your dad will disinherit you?"

"Yes. If California decides they're okay with a governor who will disown his gay son, then…" I shrugged. "There isn't much I can do about that. But they should know who he is before they vote."

"Jesus." He paused. "Then… why is the contract for a year? Wouldn't it be enough to just show him a marriage certificate? Or even just tell him you're engaged?"

"I wish." I took a deep swallow from my drink. Not that it helped. "He's smarter than that, though. And… um…" I dropped my gaze. "He'll definitely be suspicious because it's me doing this."

"Meaning?"

"Meaning I've tried to out him as a homophobe

before." I watched my nails tapping on the table, then finally looked at Hayden through my lashes. "I've tried to get him to say something incriminating in front of people. Encouraged a journalist I knew to ask him certain questions. Acted out in front of important people in ways that I hoped would get a reaction. That kind of thing."

Hayden ran his finger around the rim of his glass. "So he knows it wouldn't be below you to do something like this."

"Exactly. Which is why it has to be a long game. Dad is absolutely going to be suspicious of any move I make that involves my sexuality and could be interpreted as an attempt to provoke him. If I say I'm planning to marry a man, he'll take it as an act of rebellion at first. Just something to push his buttons. He'll hold out until he's convinced it's real. So I need it to *be* real long enough to convince him. And when he *is* convinced it's real, he won't be able to laugh off or ignore my defiance of his red line, and then he'll act. He will not, under any circumstances, let me 'win'."

"I can't decide if that sounds more like a staring contest or playing chicken."

I managed a laugh. "Probably a little of both."

He folded his hands on the table and stared at them for a moment. "Okay, so, let's say he takes the bait, decides you're serious this time, and he disowns you. He doesn't have to actually put that in the... I don't know, whatever papers he issues, right?"

"No, he doesn't. But I know him. He can't stand when someone—especially an underling or one of his kids—defies him, and he'll make sure *I* know this is why he's cutting me off. He won't put it on paper, but he'll get me one on one, and he'll say it."

"And you'll be recording it when he does, won't you?"

"You better believe it."

Hayden drummed his fingers on the table. "And you've tried recording him? Just getting him to say... *something*? That has to be easier than going through getting married and all that shit."

"I've tried." I exhaled hard. "Enough that he figured out what I was doing. Like I said, though—he's too careful. He's got a lot of practice being careful what he says too—all it took was one reporter recording him and then leaking some scoop about a new film, and he learned to keep his mouth shut. Even around family members, and especially now that smartphones are a thing. The only way he's going to let his guard down and say something like this out loud is if someone *really* provokes him."

"Like if his son marries another man."

"Exactly. I need to push him hard enough to lose his temper and say out loud that he's kicking me out of the family, and why, and given the warnings from both my parents over the years? This is the best weapon I have to make that happen." Hayden's expression screamed skepticism, so I added, "Trust me. He'll make sure I have a piece of paper declaring me disowned, disinherited, and cut off from any and all of his financial resources. He'll tell me verbally—not in writing—exactly why he's doing it. All I have to do is make the papers and the recording public." I hoped. There was every chance my father would use his political smooth-talking to tell me why without outright telling me why, but I hoped in the heat of the moment he wouldn't be able to resist absolute clarity.

"And you think it'll be enough to convince voters to

reject him?"

"If they care about queer rights, it will be. If they don't…" I trailed off because that was a reality I couldn't let myself think about. I had no control over what people actually did with the information I was turning my life upside down to give them. All I could do was show them who my father was and hope that wasn't who they wanted.

Hayden was silent for a long moment, and I didn't push. This had to be a lot to process for someone who hadn't spent his entire life marinating in Ambrose dysfunction. I chewed the inside of my cheek, worrying he might be having second thoughts about this whole arrangement, so I was unprepared when he finally said, "Do you think a year is long enough?"

Oh thank God. He's still in.

I cleared my throat. "I hope it is." I unfolded and refolded my hands on the table, wondering when they'd started sweating. "If it isn't, we might need to renegotiate." I paused, then quickly added, "'We' being whoever agrees to this. You or whoever."

"Right." Hayden shifted, avoiding my gaze. "Wow. Jesus." He started to say something else, but right then, the lounge's door opened and our server entered with our meals. Neither of us spoke while the plates were arranged in front of us, but I swore I heard a groan of pleasure escape Hayden's lips at the sight and probably smell of his richly-seasoned and garlic-filled pasta. When he took a bite, he looked like he'd just tasted the most amazing thing on the planet.

"Like it?" I asked.

"Oh my *God*, yes." He twirled some sauce-drenched noodles around his fork. "I've been basically living on ramen and cereal since forever, so…"

"You have?"

He met my gaze, and after he'd swallowed the next bite, he dabbed his lips with his napkin. "Look, you seem like a nice guy and all, but I'm not gonna lie—it was the $1.2 million part that made me respond, not the 'marry me' part."

I laughed. "I figured it would get people's attention."

"Mmhmm. It did." He inclined his head. "That part wasn't bullshit, was it?"

"No! No. Definitely not bullshit." I chased a piece of cauliflower around in the marinade from the chicken breast. "Also a bedroom in my condo, a car if you need it, paid travel if we go anywhere together, and any other expenses that come up."

Hayden nearly choked, and he stared at me incredulously. "Holy shit. Don't tell me there's medical and dental too."

"Um, actually—"

"Dude, I was kidding."

"Okay, but I'm part of a union." I shrugged. "If you're married to me, you'do qualify for benefits."

He blinked. "I… really?"

I nodded.

He arched a perfectly-shaped eyebrow. Then he cast a slow, sweeping glance around the room, his mouth working as if he were tonguing one of his molars.

"What?" I asked.

"There have to be cameras," he whispered. "This has to be a reality show joke." He faced me again. "If I'm being punk'd just tell me now so I can—"

"You're not being punk'd."

"I'm not?"

"No." I put down my fork and looked him in the eye. "Hayden, I need someone to help me prove who my father really is before he gets enough power to start fucking people over."

"And you're sure he will?"

"I'm positive. This isn't a personal vendetta for me. I know what he's capable of and where his loyalties lie. I'm asking someone to pretend to be my husband for a year to stop him from ever being in a position to work his bigotry into laws. Whatever makes that worthwhile for the man who's helping me…" I waved a hand. "I'll spare no expense."

"What'll it do to you financially, though?"

Now there was a thing I'd thought about, but didn't really enjoy thinking about, so I plastered on a smile and waved a hand. "It'll hurt, but I have savings and a job."

"Oh." He swallowed hard, and he studied me for a long moment. "You're serious about this whole thing?"

"All of it. Including the dental benefits."

He put his fork down too, and released a long breath as he sat back. "Whoa."

"You don't have to make a decision tonight. If you need some time, then—"

"No." He met my gaze again, and the shock had vanished in favor of sheer determination. "No, I'm in."

I straightened. "You are?"

"Fuck yeah. If it'll get me out from under my student loan debts, get me out of that godforsaken apartment, *and* keep a homophobic jackwagon from getting voted into office where he can shit all over my rights?" Hayden nodded emphatically. "You're damn right I'm in."

A relieved breath rushed out of me, and I smiled. "Awesome. I was honestly afraid I wouldn't be able to find anyone to take me up on this."

"Please." He picked up his fork again and speared a piece of shrimp. "For *that* price? Someone was bound to come along."

"Yeah, but I like the enthusiasm for the cause."

We exchanged smiles, and we both continued eating.

After a while, Hayden looked at me again, some renewed nerves in his expression. "So, um, about the non-disclosure?"

"Mmhmm?"

He fidgeted. "My roommates know about the ad. They don't know anything we've talked about, but they know I'm here talking to someone about an ad for a temporary husband. Once we start, uh, dating or whatever, they'll put two and two together. Maybe not *why* we're doing it, but that it's not real."

"Hmm." I chewed thoughtfully for a moment, then swallowed. "Honestly? As important as this is for me, I'll pay them each to sign one too."

"You… you will?"

I nodded. "How many roommates do you have?"

"Two."

"Okay. Ten large apiece if they'll keep it under their hats."

Hayden's mouth fell open. "Seriously?"

"Like I said." I half-shrugged and started cutting off a piece of chicken. "This is important."

"Yeah, I… I get that. It's just… that's a shitload of money." He paused. "I mean, for us it is. I'm pretty sure we have two hundred dollars between us until next Friday, so…"

"Really?"

"Uh-huh." He shot me a good-natured smirk. "Not all of us come from Hollywood dynasties."

"You're luckier than you think, believe me."

I totally expected an eyeroll followed by some comment about how horrible it must be to live such a privileged life. I probably deserved it, too—I had no idea what it was like to stretch two hundred dollars between three people for days on end—but the financial security I was currently gambling with only did so much to alleviate the toxicity of the world I'd grown up in.

To my surprise, Hayden nodded. "Yeah. I've heard the rumors."

I was the one to roll my eyes. "Let me tell you—it's awesome having your family's business in print all the time. That… that might happen to you, by the way. I'm not really on the press's radar like my older brother and sister, but if this turns into an actual scandal…"

He waved a hand before dragging a piece of shrimp through the creamy sauce. "Eh, my brother had the press on his ass for a while, and they were always looking for dirt on the rest of us just for a dramatic story. Been there."

"Your brother?"

Hayden popped the shrimp into his mouth. After he'd swallowed it, he said, "My brother is Brian Somerset."

I furrowed my brow. "Why do I know that name?"

"He was a figure skater. Went to the Olympics twice."

"Oh. Right. I remember reading about him."

"Exactly. So… I'm not exactly a stranger to the press. It was mostly focused on him, but they did some stories on us too. And a few times people thought I was him, so…"

"Hmm, yeah, you do look a lot like him, now that you mention it."

"I would hope so." He winked. "We're identical twins."

"*Oh.*"

"Which… now that I think about it, don't be surprised if someone sees us together and thinks you're dating him."

I laughed. "Eh, I guess I could think of worse things for them to say about me."

"Well, except he's married with a couple of kids, so unless you want to be the sidepiece of the married ex-figure skater who everyone knew *all along* was gay like his twin brother?" He raised his eyebrows.

"Okay, point taken. But you have to admit—it would get my dad's attention."

Hayden snickered. "Yeah, but sweetheart, I don't think you want my sister-in-law thinking you and Brian are dating. Trust me." He grimaced, but it was a playful expression, so I didn't imagine there was any actual hostility between him and his sister-in-law.

"I'll take your word for it."

He gave a soft laugh, but then sobered again. "So your dad, though. This, um… you really think he'll bite?"

"I know him. He might put up with it for a few weeks or maybe a few months, but the minute he thinks my"—I made air quotes—"'husband' and I are in it for the long haul, he'll drop the hammer. He won't be able to help himself. Not after a slap in the face like this. Because believe me, he'll take this as a slap in the face."

"Jesus fuck."

"Tell me about it."

"Wow. I'm…" He stared, then shook himself. "I'm sorry. I'm just so amazed that a parent would be so…"

"Vindictive? Toxic?" I reached my drink. "Welcome to the Ambrose family."

Chapter 3
Hayden

"Hold up, hold up." Ashton glanced at me from the driver's seat as he drove us home from the restaurant. "This dude's going to pay me and Luis ten Gs to keep our traps shut?"

"Yep. Cash."

"Well, damn. So when's the wedding?"

I laughed. "No objection at all about signing a—"

"Man, he waves ten grand in front of my face, I'll say I've never seen *you* before."

"What? Is that all my friendship is worth to you?"

He shrugged. "Times are tough, amigo. A man's gotta do what a man's gotta do."

I elbowed him and chuckled. "Asshole."

He laughed too, but didn't say anything. In fact, neither of us did for a while. Ashton seemed unusually preoccupied, and I couldn't blame him. On the way to the restaurant earlier, we'd been comparing notes on which gas stations were the cheapest right now, and if it would be worth coughing up the cash for the Sunday paper to get the coupon circular, or if this week's coupons would be as worthless as they'd been last week.

Three hours later, Ashton was one signature away from ten thousand dollars in cold, hard cash that he might not even have to mention to the IRS. His mind must have been reeling now, trying to comprehend that much money and mentally stretch it as far as possible. Fix his car? Maybe replace it? Textbooks and tuition? Put a dent in his student loans? Sock some away for some actual savings? For any of us, even a windfall of five hundred bucks would have been like something coming along and pushing the iceberg out of the Titanic's way.

So Ashton was probably trying like hell to make sense of that much money dropping into his lap.

And me? Oh, I could relate. Holy shit, could I relate.

$1.2 million.

Plus a room in a condo in a high class West Hollywood neighborhood.

Plus travel and expenses.

Plus a car.

Plus medical and goddamned *dental*. I might actually be able to do something about that precariously loose filling in the back of my mouth. Something besides always chewing on the other side and just praying the damn thing didn't fall off.

I stared down at the folder in my lap. In it was a copy of the NDA I'd signed, plus a longer and more detailed agreement spelling out every inch of the arrangement. I hadn't signed it yet. Hadn't even read it yet. Jesse had insisted that I take it home and sleep on it, and we could finalize everything tomorrow.

I didn't see any scenario in which I didn't sign this thing. Unless there was something tucked in there committing me to watch Jersey Shore on loop 24/7 or give up Diet Coke for the rest of my life, I—oh hell, who was I kidding? Take my Diet Coke and show me to the TV because hello a million fucking dollars and basically everything I needed.

So yeah, I'd sleep on it, but I was signing the damn thing.

Ashton pulled into the parking lot below our building. He put the car in Park and shut it off. It gave a shudder and made some noises it probably wasn't supposed to. He didn't unbuckle his seat belt, though, and neither did I.

For the longest time, he just stared straight out the windshield at the dilapidated building we'd called home for the last six months. Our last place had been nicer—fewer six-legged roommates, not quite so many smells of unknown origin—but the rent had finally climbed to the point we'd had to choose between staying there and keeping our cars insured. We'd even floated the idea of taking the risk and letting insurance lapse, but with the way our luck had been going, one of us would've been cited for driving without insurance, one would've been rear-ended in a parking lot, and one would've had the engine block and wheels stolen. Probably all on the same day.

So that hadn't been an option. And anyway, Luis commuted to work and sometimes had to drive to job interviews. Ashton needed to drive between work and school. I needed to drive to auditions (haha yeah because those happened so often) and spend the rest of the time delivering pizzas. We needed insurance, cars, and gas.

We'd finally given up on Mediocre Heights or whatever that complex had been called, and we'd moved into this little slice of hell on earth. We obsessively clipped coupons. Drove out of our way to save a dollar on gas. Put off oil changes. Bought the cheapest imaginable version of everything even though we knew they'd fall apart. Hell, the dress shoes I was wearing? Twelve bucks. This was the third time I'd worn them, and they were already coming apart on the inside. My sneakers were even cheaper and I was pretty sure if they ever came untied, they would literally disintegrate. But what was I supposed to do? Buy a three hundred dollar, good quality pair with… Monopoly money, I guess?

Now, sitting in Ashton's seventeen year-old Honda, wearing thrift store clothes and carrying the skinniest wallets ever because all our cash went to rent and loans… things were about to be different.

I could barely get my head around ten thousand. In Ashton's battered old Chuck Taylors, I'd have been in shock too.

But I wasn't getting ten thousand.

I was getting a million.

A million fucking dollars.

Plus most of the things I worried the most about paying—rent, a car, medical stuff—were covered. I was one signed agreement away from not having to worry about money, and I literally had no idea how to process that.

Ashton was the first to speak. He was still staring out the windshield, and he sounded almost drunk: "I've never even *seen* ten thousand dollars."

"Neither have I."

"And you're going to be seeing…" He turned to me. "Shit, was he serious about what he's paying you?"

I nodded. "Yep. He's serious."

"A million dollars? Just to fake like you're married to him?"

Another nod, but I couldn't speak. And why the hell did my eyes sting?

Beside me, Ashton sniffed.

I surreptitiously wiped my eyes. "You're not crying, are you?"

"Shut up. So are you."

Yeah. We cried. We sat in his junk-ass car in the parking lot of our craphole apartment, and we goddamned cried because we wouldn't have to stretch two hundred dollars between three people until next Friday, and we wouldn't have to do it next pay period either.

There was no way Jesse could understand why sleeping on this was a moot point. The Ambrose family had been richer than God since Jesse's paternal grandmother had been a star in the 30s and 40s, and his mom's side hadn't exactly been shopping at Goodwill either. Poverty was as foreign a concept to them as being rich was to us.

It was funny because a lot of people thought my family was rich too. After all, my brother was a famous skater. You didn't go to the Olympics and come home poor, right? Yeah, turned out that training someone to be an Olympic athlete was stupidly expensive, and it had pretty much bankrupted my parents. There'd been a brief taste of hope that things would finally pay off, but when the world heard Brian's knee shatter after that disastrous triple lutz landing, my family had heard an investment of hundreds of thousands of dollars going down the toilet. Now my brother was trying to make it in real estate, my parents would be working until they were dead, and I was in Los Angeles delivering pizzas until my mythical big break finally happened.

At least, that was what I'd been doing three hours ago.

Now I was agreeing to fake-marry Isaac Ambrose's middle son, and I'd have all the trappings of the Ambrose life for a year. Longer if I kept up my painfully frugal habits and saved the hell out of every penny he paid me.

Sleep on what? Show me where to sign, damn it.

Ashton and I finally pulled ourselves together and went inside. Luis was dressed for his security job, and he did a double take when he saw us.

"Uh." His eyes darted between us. "Have you two been…" He squinted. "Have you been fucking crying? What the hell happened with that rich dude?"

"Oh. Man." Ashton wiped a hand over his face.

"You going to be home tomorrow?" I asked Luis. "Around noon?"

Luis nodded. "I'll be asleep, but yeah. Why? What does that have to do—"

"Because my new 'husband' is coming by to have you two sign non-disclosure agreements." I swallowed. "So you don't talk about the ad or what he and I are doing."

Luis's eyebrows shot up. "You're fucking doing it? You're marrying this guy?"

"Yep, and he's paying you each ten grand to keep your mouths shut about it."

"Ten—" Luis blinked. "You're… like ten thousand *dollars*?"

"No, idiot." Ashton smacked his arm as he walked

past him toward the couch. "Ten thousand coupons for putt-putt. Yes, ten thousand dollars."

Luis stared at Ashton. Then at me. Then at Ashton again. "You guys are bullshitting."

"No, we're not." I gestured with the folder. "I'm signing the agreement with him tomorrow, and he just wants the two of you to stay quiet about it."

"For ten grand?"

"For ten grand."

Luis's mouth worked like a fish's. Then, slowly, he looked around our shitty living room. Pretty much around the entire apartment—the bathroom, Luis's bedroom, and the bedroom I shared with Ashton were behind closed doors, but the rest of the place was out in the open. We kept it clean because none of us liked piles of dishes or trash, but you could only polish a turd so much.

Luis seemed to be taking in our polished turd for the first time. Slowly, his shoulders sagged. His knees kind of buckled, and he sank into the crappy recliner he'd been dragging from apartment to apartment. More to himself, he murmured, "Ten thousand."

I knew as well as they must have that ten grand wasn't going to last forever, but it was a huge, almost incomprehensible amount of money for people in our situation.

Finally, Luis looked up at me. "So you're really gonna do it. You're really gonna marry this guy."

I nodded.

"Is he at least, like, nice?"

"Yeah, actually. He's a lot nicer than I thought he'd be." I grinned. "A lot hotter too."

Luis chuckled, still sounding a bit dazed. "Good.

That's good." He paused, and seemed to sober a bit. "I mean, you're not doing this so we get paid, are you? Because that kind of cash is great, but not if it means you're going to be—"

"It's not a bad arrangement. He seems like a good guy, and it isn't like he's making me his sex slave or anything." Though I supposed it wouldn't take much for him to convince me to very enthusiastically and voluntarily join him for some sex. I cleared my throat. "I'm okay with it. All of it."

My roommate studied me for a moment, then nodded slowly. He turned to Ashton, who looked like he'd been thrown on the sofa. That was kind of his natural state, but tonight he seemed wrung out and exhausted. Like he was going to fall asleep at any moment and stay that way until noon. Couldn't say I blamed him.

"Who the fuck is he, anyway?" Luis asked me.

"Uh. Well." I cleared my throat. "Turns out he's Isaac Ambrose's kid."

Luis's eyes bugged out. "Seriously?"

I nodded.

Luis scowled, and he didn't have to elaborate. The three of us had had many conversations about Luis's distaste for that asshole's movies. That, and there'd been a few think pieces in the last few years suggesting Isaac's filmography had, at best, racist undertones. His movies weren't on-the-nose overtly racist in ways that white guys like Ashton and me would instantly recognize, but in the more subtle, insidious ways that made Luis's skin crawl. Lily white heroes and brown-skinned villains. Ensemble casts dying in order from darkest to lightest, with the pristine Caucasian leads surviving to the end. *So* many white saviors.

Isaac always deftly avoided the accusations in interviews. He'd destroyed a few screenwriters' careers by throwing them under the bus, but usually just shrugged and innocently said that he filmed the world as it existed.

"*When you see racism in my pictures,*" I'd never forget him saying, "*it's because that's what exists in the real world. When the real world changes, so will my films.*"

I shuddered as if I could feel his sliminess on me right then. "I can't fill you in on everything until you've signed the agreement, but basically you get ten grand to keep quiet while I help his son fuck him over."

"Well, shit." Luis laughed dryly. "If I'd known that, I'd have driven your ass to the restaurant tonight." He leaned forward, elbows on his knees, and released a long breath as he rubbed his hands over his face. "Wow. This is nuts, you guys."

"Right?" Ashton said. "I mean, can you imagine buying textbooks and groceries in the *same week*?"

"And paying rent?" Luis sat back again. After a moment, he frowned. "You're sure he's not yanking your chain, right?"

Okay, so I had no way of knowing if Jesse would actually show up tomorrow with the cash and NDAs, but after my long conversation with him tonight, I believed he would. He seemed genuinely committed to his plan, and my roommates' silence was important.

So I nodded. "Yeah. He'll be here."

~*~

Our complex was anything but quiet, and I was anything but asleep.

While Ashton snored in the other bed a few feet away, I stared up at the water spots illuminated by the too-bright mercury vapor lights outside. There were cars going by because nobody ever slept in this town. Someone's TV was on loud enough I could tell they were watching an Avengers movie. There was a couple fighting somewhere, but I couldn't quite decide if they were real or on TV. Somewhere in the distance, there were sirens because this was Los Angeles and of course there were sirens.

Hands laced behind my head, I was wide awake, but not from the noise.

Jesse and I had talked a lot about the arrangement over dinner, and I'd read the agreement twice since I'd come home. It was fairly straightforward and didn't seem to have any weird loopholes. I'd legally marry Jesse, and we'd stay married until a year from the day we signed the contract, regardless of when Isaac actually took the bait. After that period, we'd quietly divorce and go our separate ways, understanding there was still an ironclad non-disclosure agreement in place. If I broke the NDA or bailed on the marriage, I was liable for everything Jesse had already paid me, any other costs that had accumulated, and "damages to be determined at arbitration," which sounded hellishly expensive. If Jesse bailed for some reason, or he violated the NDA, he was on the hook for the full $1.2 million, plus expenses and damages. Basically it was a sweet deal and in both of our best interests to stick to the script.

Now that I'd had some time to think about the whole thing, more questions worked their way into my whirring mind. Exactly how committed was he to making this look real? Was there going to be an actual wedding? Or were we eloping?

And if we did the actual wedding instead of eloping…

My heart sank.

Could I really stand up there at an altar, hold hands with this man I didn't know, exchange rings, and vow (sort of) to love him (on paper) until death (or not) do we part…

…in front of my family?

I cringed at the thought. My mom had been beside herself when marriage equality passed because it meant I could someday have a real wedding and not a commitment ceremony. She thought commitment ceremonies were beautiful, but she was literally in tears over the idea of me being able to legally get married and have all the rights straight couples did. She told me once she'd lost sleep for months after reading an article about a man being kept from his partner's side in the hospital, and she was more relieved than I was that there were now legal protections in place that could mostly prevent that.

So how would she feel if she came to my wedding to Jesse, and she found out later it had all been a farce? And how would I feel keeping the truth from her? No matter how good our intentions were, that had to be crossing some sort of line.

It wasn't like I could *not* invite my mom. Even if Jesse wasn't one of Isaac's more famous kids, it was a given that some high society article would be written about the lavish wedding, or a tabloid column would have something to say about billionaire director-producer-politician Isaac Ambrose's son getting married in front of the justice of the peace. Marriages were public records, and I didn't believe for a second that my mom didn't google me and my brother every now and then just because.

If I married Jesse, my mom would know about it. End of story.

And she wouldn't be the only one. People in the industry would definitely know, and those who wanted to stay in Isaac's good graces were going to be cautious as fuck when it came to me. If he faked that he was happy with his son's marriage, acting opportunities might open up. But if he let it show that he was pissed at me or about this marriage, those opportunities would instantly dry up. And from what Jesse had said… well, it was a safe bet that whatever pitiful shot I had at an acting career would probably be history as soon as I signed this agreement. No one even needed to know that my marriage to Jesse was a sham. If Isaac wanted to push back on Jesse's defiance, to rev the engine on their game of chicken, all he had to do was let it get out that he disapproved of our marriage for non-homophobic reasons and no one in Hollywood would want to touch me with a ten foot pole.

So once I signed that thing, I could kiss acting goodbye. And to my surprise, that didn't bother me all that much. In fact, it was kind of a relief. I was trading a career that might never have happened anyway for a degree of financial stability I'd barely been able to fantasize about. Suddenly there was no pressure to get *this* audition right or score *that* role because it could finally be my big break. I hadn't even realized how much pressure I'd been putting on myself to make this thing happen until, lying here in my bed in the darkness, I made the decision to let it all go. Letting go of a dream was supposed to be heartbreaking, not liberating. Maybe that meant it hadn't been a good dream for me after all.

And even if acting really had been my dream, my conscience wasn't going to let me pass up this opportunity just to keep reaching for that star. Sticking with it and saying to hell with taking down a homophobic politician was weirdly reminiscent of letting a career dominate the lives of people who wanted nothing to do with it. Like, say, when an entire family's life is at the mercy of one son's shiny, glamorous skating career, whether they want any part of it or not. Maybe I was just tired and overwhelmed, but it seriously felt like I'd be doing to the California queer community what my brother's career had done to my childhood. Nope. Couldn't do it.

And speaking of my brother…

It occurred to me that I *should* want to tell my brother the truth about this marriage, but I was oddly indifferent about lying to him. I supposed that drove home just how wide the chasm was between me and my twin. A long, long time ago, we'd been as close as everyone expected identical twins to be. One roller coaster of a skating career and a whole lot of bitterness later? Brian and I were so far apart we bordered on estranged. I didn't feel as guilty keeping this arrangement from him as I would from my parents, and that—more than anything had in a long time—made me realize how much I missed that closeness with Brian. His ego and my resentment had driven us apart, and nothing—not even his unexpected early retirement—had closed that distance. We'd have to work on that because right now, it bothered me how *little* it bothered me to keep my brother—my *twin*—in the dark about this marriage.

For the time being, though, my primary concern was lying to my parents. I could make peace with my brother later. I actually *liked* the idea of finding something to do besides acting. But… Mom and Dad.

So the question was—would Jesse let me tell them the truth?

And if he said no…

Then what?

Chapter 4
Jesse

I was nervous pulling into the parking lot of the apartment complex where Hayden lived. Not because this was a rundown part of town or I felt unsafe or anything, but because I was worried he'd had time to have second thoughts. Even with a chunk of change as incentive, this wasn't exactly a small favor I was asking. That was why I'd offered so much money in the first place.

I parked in a guest spot, picked up the folder off the passenger seat, and got out. As I headed up the stairs toward unit B, I slipped two small envelopes from the folder and tucked them into my back pocket. Hopefully the men who'd be getting those envelopes wouldn't have second thoughts either. Or want more cash. I mean, I could get more cash if it came down to it, but I really wasn't looking to get extorted if I could help it.

At the door of unit B, I stopped, and I glanced down. Instead of a Welcome Mat, there was a faded black mat with a crudely drawn skull and dirty white lettering that read *Abandon All Hope Ye Who Enter Here.*

I laughed as I reached up to knock. Though I'd only known Hayden for a matter of hours, I was somehow positive he wouldn't be able to blame his roommates for the mat. Not entirely, anyway. To think, I'd been worried about "marrying" a man who'd want to redecorate the condo. With taste like this, Hayden could do whatever he wanted to the place.

There were footsteps on the other side. Then a chain rattled, a deadbolt clicked, and the door opened.

And there he was.

Hayden was dressed down from last night, trading the pressed shirt for a Pittsburgh Penguins jersey and a pair of jeans. His hair was still flawlessly arranged, but seemed a bit more finger-combed than painstakingly styled, and damn it now I wanted to be the one finger-combing it.

I coughed as warmth rose in my cheeks. "Um. Hey."

"Hey." He smiled and stood aside. "Come on in. Just, you know, keep your expectations low."

I stepped into the apartment. It was small but neat, though I couldn't blame Hayden for wanting to get out of here. While he and his roommates were obviously tidy, the place hadn't been well-maintained. There wasn't a speck of dirt in sight, but the ceiling had water stains on top of water stains, and the distinct smell of mildew nearly made my eyes water.

Who the hell makes people live like this?

"So." Hayden shut the door behind me. "This is the place, and these are my roommates, Ashton and Luis. Guys, this is Jesse."

The two men on the sofa stood, and we shook hands and exchanged murmured hellos. "So, um, you guys don't mind..." I held up the folder.

"Naw, man." The one called Luis put a hand on Hayden's shoulder. "If you're gonna take care of our boy, we won't talk."

Hayden smiled fondly.

"You're gonna take care of him, right?" Ashton shot me a pointed look. "This whole thing you guys are doing, it's kind of weird, but he'll be—"

"You won't have to worry about a thing. I promise."

"Okay, well." Luis nodded toward Hayden. "Just don't get cute or this fucker will kick your ass."

"Luis!" Hayden rolled his eyes. "Oh my God."

Ashton laughed. "He ain't lying, man. Don't you remember?" He gestured emphatically at a scar on the left side of his forehead.

"Oh come on. You put ice on my back while I was asleep on the couch, and I came up swinging." Hayden buffed his nails on his shirt. "Not my fault you didn't move fast enough." They glared playfully at each other, then chuckled, and Hayden turned to me. "You have the things for them to sign?"

"Yep." I held up the folder. "Right here."

They took them, and like Hayden had last night, they both carefully read over the non-disclosure agreements.

"So like..." Ashton looked at me over the top of the page. "I can tell people I know you two are a couple, right? Just not the fake part?"

"Of course."

"Oh. Okay." He set the agreement on the TV stand and quickly signed it. Then he held it up to me. "No problem. My lips are sealed."

"Mine too." Luis signed his agreement and gave it to

me as well.

"Perfect. Thanks." I took the two envelopes from my back pocket and handed one to each of them.

As they took them, their eyes widened, probably from the thick contents, and they both suddenly looked shell-shocked. Like I'd just handed them each a letter saying someone had died, not an envelope full of cash.

Shit, were they going to ask for more money? Should I have offered more?

I cleared my throat. "Um, is there a—"

"No problem," Ashton said quickly. "Just, um…" He looked into the envelope and exhaled. "Shit. That's a serious wad of cash."

Luis looked into his too, and he murmured something I didn't understand as he thumbed through the bills. They exchanged wide-eyed glances, then pocketed the money and faced Hayden and me.

"So yeah." Ashton laughed. "My lips are *sealed*, man. No worries."

"Same," Luis said with a nod. "We're good."

Hayden chuckled. "Good, because I have loads of dirt on both of you, and that shit will be all over Facebook if—"

Ashton snorted. "Uh-huh. You post a word about that shit, and I'll post on *your mom's wall* about the time we busted you blowing—"

"Dude!" Luis smacked Ashton's arm. "Not in front of the man's husband. Show some respect, pendejo."

"Hey, I'm just saying." Ashton shrugged. "He opens his mouth, I'll open mine." Instantly, he cringed, and Hayden and Luis snorted. I laughed too, and Hayden started giggling uncontrollably.

"Oh my God," Hayden howled. "Did you really just say—"

"*Hush.*" Ashton covered his eyes and swore. "Fuck my life…"

Luis snickered. "Don't you mean fuck your mouth?"

Ashton groaned and flipped both of them off.

Still giggling, Hayden turned to me. "I'm sorry. This, uh, happens sometimes."

"Don't stop on account of me," I said. "I mean, he *did* walk into it."

"Hey!" Ashton glared at me. "What the fuck, man?"

I shrugged. "You kinda did, dude."

It was my turn to get the bird from him, and that prompted another round of laughter from everyone in the room, including me.

As we started to collect ourselves, I turned to Hayden. "So, um, if you have some time, do you want to come by and check out the condo?"

His eyes lit up. "Hell yeah. I…wait, do I have time?" He frowned at his phone. "Oh yeah, I have time. I don't need to be at work until seven."

"At work?" Ashton rolled his eyes. "Why the fuck would you go back to that place now?"

"To quit, for one thing." Hayden gestured at the short hallway. "Let me just get my wallet and stuff, and we can go."

I nodded, and he left the room.

Instantly, his roommates shifted their attention to me.

"We ain't joking, man." Luis's voice was stern but not actually threatening. "Hayden's our boy. Take care of him."

Ashton didn't speak, but his expression echoed

53

everything Luis had said.

"You have nothing to worry about," I said. "He's doing me a huge favor by going through with this. I'll make sure he's taken care of."

A moment later, Hayden returned, sliding his wallet into his back pocket. "Okay. Ready?"

"When you are"

We said goodbye to his roommates, and we'd only made it two steps from the door before I heard, "Ten grand. Holy shit, ten grand!" from the other side.

Hayden glanced back and chuckled. "You made their day, believe me."

"Yeah. Sounds like it."

We walked down to the parking lot, and after I'd unlocked the Porsche, Hayden slid into the passenger seat. "Wow. This is a sweet ride."

I smiled. "Yeah, I like it." As I started the engine, I asked, "You want one?"

Hayden laughed, but then did a double take. "Wait. Really?"

"I told you a car was included if you needed one."

"Yeah, but there's a car…" He gestured at the others in the parking lot. "And there's *a car.*" Another gesture, this time at the console between us.

"Uh-huh." I backed out of the space, glancing at him as I did. "I mean it, though. Whatever you want."

He squirmed, the leather upholstery creaking with the movement. "Maybe not something quite this fancy."

"Your call."

"So, a souped-up one-of-a-kind custom Lamborghini with—"

I shifted gears. "Don't push your luck."

He chuckled. "Honestly, I'll just be thrilled with something that fucking *runs*." He pointed out the window. "Unlike that piece of crap."

I craned my neck and found a battered red Nissan with bald tires and a crooked bumper. "Oh. Yeah, I think we can upgrade you a little."

"Thank God," he muttered.

We drove in silence for a while. Until the complex was no longer visible in the rearview, anyway.

"So, you and the guys. Your roommates." I glanced at him. "Sounds like you have a pretty good arrangement with them."

Hayden's smile returned. "Oh yeah. We've all been living together since we started college. Luis moved out with a girlfriend for a while, but after they broke up, he came back."

"Oh, so he's straight?"

"Mmhmm. They both are. Luis and I were roommates in college, and we met Ashton during our sophomore year. After we graduated, none of us could afford a place, so we got one together."

"You've been living together ever since?"

"Aside from Luis living with his girl for a while, yeah."

"And it works for you? All of you?"

"Couldn't ask for better roommates."

"Wow. Huh. Now I kind of feel bad breaking up what you guys have going on." I glanced at him. "To have you move in with me."

"Nah, don't. It isn't like we're going to another country or something. Right?"

"Well, not to live."

He eyed me. "Huh?"

"I mean, we might go on a vacation or something somewhere."

"A vacation? To another country?"

"Sure, why not?"

Hayden looked out the windshield again. "Whoa."

"Is that… is that okay?"

"Oh, yeah. Totally. I just…" He sighed. "Look, I'm going to be honest with you. Last night we had dinner at a restaurant I couldn't afford to *steal* food from. I haven't quite gotten my head around the idea of, well, any of this, so being able to jet off to some other place is… It's a lot, I guess."

I didn't know what to say.

After a moment, gaze still fixed on something outside the windshield, Hayden quietly said, "The money you gave Ashton and Luis—that's going to make a huge difference for them. Like *huge*. So, thanks."

"You're welcome. I just… I don't know. Felt like it was better than just asking them to sign it."

"Well, they won't talk. I know them. They'd have signed it for free, but the money…" Hayden exhaled, pressing back into the seat. "I don't think you realize how much money that is for someone like them or me. I mean, the truth is the only reason we still live together is we've all been too broke to get by on our own. We're great as roommates, but none of us want to do this forever. Maybe now we won't have to."

I definitely didn't know how to respond to that. Most of the people I worked with on film and television sets were in similar boats, if not to the same extent, but it was admittedly difficult for me to fathom.

Though if our arrangement worked out the way I

predicted, I supposed I'd become acquainted with the concept soon enough.

I tamped that thought down, and kept driving. Clearing my throat, I tapped my thumbs on the wheel. "Well, I'm glad it's helping all three of you. God knows you're all helping me." I glanced at him. "Especially you."

"Keep thanking me all you want, but I'm pretty sure I'm getting the better end of this deal."

"Guess we'll find out after we've lived together for a while."

Hayden just laughed.

"So." I flipped the switch beside the front door, and my twelfth floor condominium was immediately bathed in warm light. "This is the place."

"Oh, wow." Hayden surveyed the living room, kitchen, and dining room, which were one big space lined with floor-to-ceiling windows on two sides, and showroom lights on the ceilings and walls.

I smiled. Admittedly, I was proud as fuck of this place. It wasn't huge, but it was gorgeous and it was mine. Especially now that I was done remodeling the kitchen, it looked great.

"*If you hire professionals,*" I could hear my father saying a year ago, "*you won't have to live in a mess like this for months on end.*"

Maybe he was right, but having my condo turned into a construction zone for six months had been a small price to pay for the tile work I'd meticulously installed on the floor and backsplash. It would have been done sooner, but right about the time I'd started putting in the cabinets, I'd gone to New Zealand to work on a film. And yeah when I'd gotten home, and I'd been jetlagged out of my head, the construction zone had kind of made me want to burn the whole place down, but once I'd recovered, I'd finished the job, and I loved the results.

I watched Hayden taking it all in. "What do you think?"

"It's amazing." He sighed melodramatically. "Except I mean I kind of expected my husband-for-hire gig to land me someplace in Beverly Hills, but I *guess* this will do." He glanced at me and winked.

I laughed. "Eh, those big places are overrated."

"Yeah?" He wandered toward the kitchen, glancing back again before checking out his surroundings. "I've never been in one, so I wouldn't know."

"I mean they're gorgeous." I followed him into the kitchen and leaned over my hands on the granite-topped island. "My older siblings both went the mansion-in-the-hills route, but those places always seem too big and empty for me. I don't want to live in a giant box I'd have to fill with stuff I don't give a shit about."

"Hmm, yeah, I can see that. Moving is a pain in the ass even when you don't have much stuff."

"Exactly. Besides, this place is walking distance to like half a dozen of my favorite restaurants, and places actually deliver to me." I smirked. "Not that I ever rub that in my brother's face when he complains that no one will deliver to his compound in the middle of nowhere."

"Ha! And restaurants—now you're speaking my language." He looked at me over the island. "You'll have to show me the good places around here."

"I will. You like kebab?"

"Pfft. Are you kidding? Of course I like kebab." He sniffed indignantly. "What kind of Philistine do you take me for?"

I chuckled. "Hey, I'm just checking. My ex couldn't stand the stuff."

"Well I can see why he's an ex." Hayden grimaced. "I mean… uh. Sorry. I…" He cleared his throat as his cheeks colored. "Not much of a filter anymore, I guess."

"It's okay. He's ancient history."

"Okay good. So, um, there's good kebab near here?"

"Three places, all within a five-minute walk."

Hayden made a happy noise and I swore he shivered. "Oh my God I'm in heaven. If you tell me there's a place nearby that makes good paninis, honest to Christ I will marry you for real."

"Please." I waved a hand. "As if any neighborhood in this town wouldn't have a few dozen places like that."

He swooned, and his smile was adorable as he said, "I'm gonna get so faaaat…"

"Yeah, just wait till you see the burger joints. Anyway, come on. I'll show you the rest of the condo." I gestured at the hallway beside the living room, then started toward it. "Bedrooms are down that way. Aside from mine and the third bedroom, the whole place is yours."

Hayden followed. "Which room is mine?"

I stopped at the first door on the left. "This one. Mine's across the hall, bathroom is at the end, and the third bedroom is next to yours." I pushed open the door and switched on the light. "This one's yours. It's been my guest room, so if you want to change the furniture or something, that's—"

"Are you kidding?" He stepped into the room, looking

around like he'd just walked into a museum hall full of priceless artwork. "This is great. And it's…" He met my gaze again, a puzzled expression on his face. "You're serious? This is *my* room?"

"Well, yeah." I cocked my head. "Did you think I was going to have you sleep on the sofa?"

"I, um… no. But this is just so…" He looked around again and murmured, "*Nice.*" Then he shook himself. "So what's in the third bedroom?" He flashed me a mischievous grin. "Is that where you keep the sex dungeon?"

I laughed. "Yeah, right. Come on, I'll show you." I took him across the hall to the other room and opened the door. "This is where I store everything I use for work." I gestured at a light-framed mirror with a dummy head sitting in a chair in front of it. "It's also where I practice sometimes."

"Where you—" He looked around, brow furrowed. "Are you a makeup artist or something?"

"Yeah. My father's second biggest shame besides me being gay."

Hayden blinked like he wasn't sure if he should laugh at that. When I cracked a smile, he allowed himself a quiet chuckle. "He really doesn't approve?"

"Never has, never will. In fact, the first time I told my parents I was going to learn how to do makeup, he lost his mind and said if I did that, then people would *know* I was gay." I smirked. "I mean, I don't think he could have pushed me harder into this career if he'd gone out and bought all my gear."

Hayden laughed. "You went into this to spite your dad?"

"Well, no, but when I realized going into it *would* spite my dad, it didn't do much to discourage me, you know?"

"Oh, you are a man after my own heart. Just ask my parents—the best way to get me to do something is to tell me I can't or shouldn't, or that people will talk." He frowned. "They've actually used that to their advantage a few times, the bastards."

"How so?"

Hayden huffed melodramatically. "When we were living in Colorado, my dad convinced me that I shouldn't be the one to shovel the driveway because it was just too much work for a kid my size. Maybe next year."

"And you fell for it?"

"Uh-huh. In my defense, I was eleven."

"Hmm, well. I guess we'll let it slide."

Hayden laughed. Then, gesturing around the room, he asked, "So how long have you been doing this?"

"Almost ten years. In fact I'm finishing up a film this month."

"Wow." He moved to the wall where I'd put up some framed photos of stills from films I'd worked on. "Oh my God. You made up Lorna Collins in *Risen Star*?"

I smiled. "Yeah. I've worked with her a few times actually. She, um, requests me now."

"No shit?" He turned to me, eyes wide. "That must look sexy as hell on your résumé."

"It does. Mostly because it means I can put up with her."

"Oh yeah? Is she really that hard to work with?"

"Jesus, she's *awful*. She pitched a fit one time because when everyone reviewed the dailies after a shoot, she looked terrible. I was like, don't yell at me! Yell at the photography guys who didn't tell me they were using blue fucking gels on the lights." I groaned and rolled my eyes. "I'm telling you, they just did it to screw with me, because Lorna's makeup aside? Those gels didn't do that scene *any* favors."

"Ugh. But she blamed you anyway?"

"Of course. Don't you know everything is makeup's fault?"

"Well, someone has to be the scapegoat."

"Yeah, maybe not the person in a position to stab you in the eye with a mascara wand," I grumbled.

Hayden burst out laughing, then clapped a hand over his mouth, but it didn't help. "Holy shit, now I'm picturing you going all"—he made exaggerated stabbing gestures—"with a mascara wand and…" He collapsed into giggles, murmuring "I'm sorry" but not really doing much to collect himself.

I laughed too, mostly because his amusement was infectious. Last night, he'd been nervous and things had been a bit more businesslike, but now he was starting to relax. Watching him banter with his roommates had been cute, and seeing him laugh uncontrollably was… hell, it was fucking adorable. He had the most gorgeous smile anyway, and the blush in his cheeks and the crinkles at the corners of his eyes were enough to make me weak in the knees.

Pretend to be married to this *guy? Yep, still I think I can swing that.*

Hayden finally pulled himself together, and cleared his throat. "So. Um." Another muffled cough. "Is your job always that exciting? Or does it get boring like everyone else's?"

"It's kind of a mix. It does get kind of boring to spend six *hours* applying special makeup and prosthetics for the same character every single day over the course of months."

And just like that, we were lost in conversation about makeup and filmmaking and the drama that happened whenever someone with an ego showed up on set. He listened intently as I told him about how tedious prosthetics were, and how yes, some makeup jobs really did take *hours* every single day. I laughed sympathetically as he told me about trying to do a commercial without tearing up or squinting because the makeup artist had accidentally gotten some powder in his eye. He stared in slack-jawed horror when I told him how one production came to a screeching halt because the lead actor suddenly developed an allergy to a chemical in either the makeup, the prosthetic material, or the adhesive.

After a while, the conversation reached a natural lull, and I realized we'd been standing in my storage/practice room for a solid hour.

"Well. Anyway." I cleared my throat and gestured around the room. "It's not really off limits, but it's probably not a room you'll be using unless you need some storage space."

"Or unless I want you to give me some pointers?"

I thought for a second he was joking, but his expression suggested he wasn't. Not completely, anyway. "Really?"

"Why not? When I find myself newly-divorced, I'm going to want to hit the club to dance my sorrows away." He winked. "Might as well be looking hot when I do?"

You already look hot, I somehow kept myself from

saying out loud.

Jesus, Jesse. Don't make things weird.

"I'm sure I can offer a few pointers, yeah." I gestured up the hall. "For now, should we get all our paperwork taken care of?"

"Oh. Right. Yeah I guess we should."

I led him back into the kitchen where I'd left two copies of our agreement. "You read it last night, right?"

"Twice."

"Okay good. Anything you want to change?"

Hayden's gaze shifted to the agreement sitting on the kitchen island, and he chewed his lip, brow creasing with what seemed like sudden nerves.

"Something wrong?" I asked.

He eyed the agreement, but didn't speak.

"Nothing's signed," I said. "It's still negotiable."

"I know, but there's…" He rubbed the back of his neck and didn't look at me or the unsigned agreement. "Before we do this, there is one thing that's giving me second thoughts."

Oh shit. I knew it was too easy. Please don't bail—I need this.

"Okay?" I pressed, keeping my voice gentle.

He was quiet again, this time for longer, and finally took a deep breath. "I really, really need to be able to tell my parents the truth."

I shifted my weight. "The more people know, the more likely it is someone's going to let it slip. Even unintentionally."

"I know, but…" He kept his eyes down. "If there was absolutely no way for her to find out, it would be one thing. But with the internet and the media, and…" He hesitated. "I mean, how exactly are we getting married? Some big shindig? Or eloping?"

"I, um… figured we could work that out between us."

"Okay, so, if we do the big shindig, it's going to look weird if my family isn't there, right? And if they are there, but they don't know what's really going on, I…" He looked in my eyes. "Listen, I'm onboard and I want to do this." There was a note of pleading in his voice as he whispered, "But don't make me lie to my mom about getting married."

Shit. I didn't want this getting out to more people than absolutely necessary, and I'd even been a little uneasy about Hayden's roommates knowing what was going on. On the other hand, while I couldn't care less about lying to my own mother about something like this, it was obviously not something Hayden could do.

I swallowed. "All right. How do you want to play this?"

Hayden jumped like he hadn't expected the answer. "How do… play this? What do you mean?"

"I mean, you know your parents. Do you want to talk to them on your own? Or do you want us to talk to them together?" I hesitated. "And yeah, I would want an NDA here. I feel so paranoid, asking for those at every turn, but I—"

"No, I get it." He folded his arms loosely, and his eyes lost focus. "I don't know. I need to think about it, but maybe we should go see them together. Before anything leaks to the press, and so they can get a feel for you and don't think you're some kind of creeper."

I was nodding as he spoke. "Sure. However you want to do it."

"Okay." He slowly relaxed. "Thanks."

"Don't mention it." I hand-wrote "*okay to discuss with Hayden's parents with signed NDAs*" on both copies, and we both initialed beside the addendums.

Then we both signed the agreements.

"All right." He laid the pen down on top of his copy and smiled uncertainly. "I, um, I guess this means we're getting married."

I laughed, extending my hand. "I guess we are."

We shook on it, both chuckling.

"So, um." He drummed his nails on the granite countertop. "I'll talk to my parents. See when is a good time to visit. Or I mean, we could do it via Skype or something."

"It's your call." I gestured at the wall calendar beside the fridge. "My work dates are all on that."

"Old school, huh? Handwritten on a calendar?"

I laughed. "Eh, old habits die hard. But anyway, if I'm working it's on there."

Hayden nodded. "Okay. I'll check with them. And then…" He chewed his lip, gaze fixed on my calendar instead of me, though I didn't get the impression he was trying to read my terrible handwriting.

"What's wrong?"

He pulled his attention from the calendar to the papers on the counter between us. "Still trying to figure out how to tell them. Probably because I haven't quite gotten *my* head around it."

"Do you need some time? We don't have to tell them tomorrow."

Hayden searched my eyes. "You wanted to get things moving, though, right?"

"I do, yeah. But this is a long game. We'll still need to tell my family too, and God knows when Dad will be able to pencil us in."

Hayden eyed me like I'd said something utterly ludicrous. "Pencil... he has to pencil in his son?"

The laugh burst out of me before I could stop it. "Are you really surprised?"

"Huh. I guess not. But... Jesus."

I wasn't sure how to follow that without scaring him right out of this agreement, so I quickly changed the subject. "Well, um, now that we've signed everything..." I opened the manila folder again, withdrew a smaller envelope, and slid it across the island. "This is yours."

Hayden opened the flap, and he stared at the cashier's check inside, eyes huge with the same disbelief his roommates had had when I'd paid them. More to himself than me, he whispered, "Holy shit."

"It's, um..." I checked my watch. "It's only 2:30. The banks are open if you want to deposit it. I'd be happy to go with you in case they want to give you any grief about whether it'll clear."

He lifted his gaze, shocked expression still firmly in place. "Really?"

"Yeah, sure. What bank do you use?"

"Uh." He swallowed. "SoCal Credit Union."

I did a quick search on my phone. "There's one about three blocks from here. You want to walk over now?"

"Um. Yeah. Okay." He looked down at the check again, and nodded. "Yeah, we can do that."

I smiled. "I'll get my keys."

Chapter 5
Hayden

$100,048.47.

I stared at my bank balance. It was like I could literally see both of my lives right there—the old one where I was praying some bill didn't come out too soon, and the new one where the numbers actually included a *comma*. That was a punctuation mark I was used to seeing on my student loan statements, not... not on my *bank balance*.

But there it was. Forty-five minutes after Jesse and I had walked into the credit union branch a few blocks from his—our?—condo, the teller handed me the receipt, and there it was. It had taken a little extra time, some patient but don't-bullshit-me words from Jesse, and a phone call to his bank, but the manager had agreed to release the funds. Now the money was right there in my account.

$100,048.47.

Holy. *Shit.*

"Hey." Jesse nudged me, and I realized we were still standing at the counter.

"Oh. Um." I cleared my throat, apologized to the teller who was looking at me like I'd lost my mind, and I made a quick escape while she called out "Next in line?"

"You okay?" Jesse asked as we started walking back toward the condo.

"Yeah. Yeah. I'm... I'm good."

I think?

It wasn't until that moment that I understood just how much my financial insecurity had consumed me for the last several years. Ever since my brother's endorsements had evaporated and the "we're not going to be able to pay for your college after all" conversation with my parents had happened, money had been a constant source of stress. One that had settled itself deep in my bones and permeated every thought. Even if I wasn't actively thinking about my financial situation, the stress was there in the tension in my neck, in the perpetual growling of my stomach, and in the compulsive mental calculations that happened any time I drove, ate, turned on a light, took a shower, threw food away instead of just scraping off the mold...

And now it was all gone. I imagined this was what it felt like to hit the ground after going skydiving—that sudden stop of not only motion, but fear. I wasn't falling anymore. I wasn't one fraying cord away from disaster. I was on the ground, my parachute settling at my feet, and my brain was this close to short-circuiting. The fact that I could literally afford to go skydiving for real was not lost on me. Not that I would ever do that, but Jesus fuck, yesterday I'd been mentally tallying whether I could afford to eat lunch. Now I could pay someone to throw me out of a plane for fun.

"Hayden?"

"Sorry. Sorry." I shook myself. "I think this whole thing is going to take some getting used to." I laughed, rolling my eyes. "God, I sound so ridiculous. Like I need to cope with the fact that I'm not day-old-ramen poor anymore."

Jesse smiled. "Well, if you need me to do anything to make it easier, just say so."

Bruh, you just rattled a bunch of cages to make the bank release a hundred fucking grand into my account right now instead of waiting twenty-four hours.

I sobered a little and dropped my gaze. "No, you're fine. But I do need some time to sort things out with my roommates and my job. I... wouldn't feel right quitting without two weeks' notice."

"Sure. Okay." He shrugged. "Where do you work?"

Heat rushed into my face. "Um. Mario & Antonio's."

He glanced at me. "As in, the pizza chain?"

I nodded, too embarrassed to meet his gaze.

"Man, I haven't eaten there in ages," he said. "I love that place."

This time I did look at him. "Really?"

"Yeah." He shot me a playful look and dropped his voice to a conspiratorial whisper. "Any chance you can smuggle out some of their recipes before you quit?"

I barked a laugh, as much from surprise as relief that he wasn't being a twatwaffle about me being a lowly pizza guy. "Maybe. No promises."

Jesse just chuckled.

I cleared my throat. "So that's okay? If I keep working there while we're... um..."

"Well, yeah." He paused. "I mean, you don't have to.

You probably won't need the money."

"No, I know, but I don't want to burn bridges."

He shot me a puzzled look.

I shrugged, dropping my gaze again. "Hey, I don't know how things will play out in the future, you know? What if I'm stupid and blow all the money you give me?" I made myself look at him. "I'd rather leave some bridges still standing in case I need them again, you know?"

He blinked as if he couldn't comprehend that I would ever need to deliver pizzas again. Maybe it wasn't something a man could comprehend when he'd been rich since he was a fetus, and maybe I wouldn't ever need to deliver pizzas again, but I knew how quickly money could disappear. My brother had been on top of the world and on the verge of some seriously lucrative endorsements when he broke his leg. Within a year, the only people calling the house had been bill collectors chasing down their chunks of his numerous surgeries.

I stopped, and when Jesse did too, we faced each other on the sidewalk. "Look," I said, "I just need to make sure I'm not screwing myself over. It's a lot of money, and I think I can be smart with it, but even if I am, life happens. So I just want to make sure I have things to fall back on."

"Okay. That makes sense." Jesse's voice was soft, and he added with a placating gesture, "I'm asking you to turn your life on its head for me. Whatever you need to do."

"You don't think it's weird?"

Jesse held my gaze. "I don't have a frame of reference, to be honest. I figure you know your life and your situation better than I do, so I'll follow your lead."

"Thanks." I smiled. "I really appreciate it."

~*~

So, I gave Mario & Antonio's my two weeks' notice. When I turned it in, I even resisted the urge to write "*I hereby give my notice to you slave-driving asshats that I will be leaving your stupid bullshit company effective two weeks from today. And even though I don't need to give you a reason, I am, just because I want to see the looks on your smug bastard faces when you find out I'm getting paid a million fucking dollars to be some guy's arm candy for a year. P.S. I hate this place. Peace out, bitches!*"

I resisted. Honest, I did.

Okay, I technically did write it, but only so Ashton, Luis, and I could laugh our heads off over it before I wrote up the boringly professional real one. While I was at it, I'd written to our landlord to have my name taken off the lease, and I'd paid six months of rent—the full rent, not just my part—to give Ashton and Luis some cushion.

And now I lived in this weird temporary Twilight Zone where my busted-ass car and I would go deliver pizzas, and at the end of the night, I'd go back to that gorgeous sunny condo with my "fiancé." I still took shit from customers who wanted to be dicks, I still got stiffed on tips, and I still had to pray to the car gods a few times when my engine acted up, but then a few hours later I'd be lounging in a bathtub the size of Orange County. With actual hot water. *Clear* hot water. After the place I'd been living with Ashton and Luis, that was legit a novelty.

In a week, I'd be done with the pizza delivery gig, and the condo-and-bathtub life would be my reality. For a while, anyway. *Weird.*

Today, I was meeting up with Luis at a mall near the

apartment for an early dinner before we headed off to our respective jobs. We picked out a reasonably priced bar-and-grill style restaurant beside one of the anchor stores, and before he sat down, Luis set a handful of shopping bags on the far end of the bench.

"Blowing your wad?" I asked.

He laughed, shaking his head as he slid in beside the shopping bags. "Naw, man. I came here the other day and got an awesome pair of work boots." He gestured under the table. "I can wear 'em like sneakers, and they don't fall apart. So I figured while I still have the money…" He nodded at the bags. "Get another pair so when these finally do crap out, I'm still good."

"Ooh, they're that good?"

"Hell yeah. And I don't know what kind of voodoo they used on the sneakers Ashton just bought, but man, he said his back and knees haven't been hurting or anything."

"Nice! They'll actually last a while, too, right?"

"Yeah, that's the best part." Luis grinned. "My coworkers always told me you're better off blowing a shitload of money on a solid pair of shoes because they'll last."

"Pfft. Like any of us ever had the money for the *cheap* shoes."

"Right?" He proudly patted one of the shopping bags, which contained a large shoebox. "But I got 'em now— pair and a spare."

"Awesome." It really was, especially with how sore he and Ashton always were after their shifts. Ashton's back had been killing him for over a year, and Luis's knees and ankles were probably twenty years older than he was by now. The shoes wouldn't magically fix everything, but they'd help.

Luis flipped open his menu. "So how's this thing going with... what's his name?"

"Jesse. And it's going good so far. He's a nice guy. I mean, I haven't seen much of him because he works during the day and I work in the evenings, but when we've talked, he's pretty nice."

"He works?" Luis cocked his head. "I thought he was loaded."

"He is, but he's a makeup artist for one of the film studios." I grinned. "Man, you should see some of his work. He has a few pictures up in the condo, and he's *good.*"

"Yeah?"

"Oh yeah. He could probably make you look datable."

"Hey! Fuck you."

We both laughed and continued perusing the menu.

As I skimmed over the options for burgers, pointedly not looking at the prices for once in my goddamned life, I said, "The weirdest thing is whenever I go looking for something in his kitchen, I find like a million other gadgets. There are things in his kitchen drawers that I swear are torture devices."

Luis laughed. "They might be. You never know."

"Right? But I..." I could feel myself blushing, God knew why. "I kind of want to try actually cooking. I mean, he has every possible utensil and appliance, so it's not like I'd have to improvise the way we always did. Plus with as much as he's paying me, I could buy literally anything from the grocery store. Name brand and everything."

"Why not?" He shrugged. "You've got the money and the gear. Good time as any, right?"

"Yeah it is."

The server came, and we ordered, and after some hemming and hawing, decided to splurge and order some nachos too. Entrees *and* an appetizer? Whaaat?

When the drinks and nachos came, we dug in. As I scraped a piece of jalapeno and a glob of sour cream onto a chip, I said, "You know, you should come by the condo one of these nights. We could try out some of your mom's recipes, except this time you'd have actual sharp knives and an oven that works."

Luis nodded vigorously. "Hell yeah. We gotta bring Ashton too—he'll never speak to me again if I cook when he's not there."

"Obviously. Because he'll be making his mom's salted caramel carrot cake for dessert."

"Ooh, awesome." Luis tilted his head. "Your man won't have a problem with that, will he?"

"I don't think so. He's said he doesn't mind me having people over, just as long as I'm not throwing house parties or something."

"Aww. But can we at least have Magic nights at your place?"

"Fuck yeah we can have Magic nights at my place." I huffed as if that was the most ridiculous thing ever because it totally was. "In fact, we should do that soon. He might as well know what kind of closet nerd he's marrying."

Luis laughed, but then his expression turned completely serious and he spoke in a discreet voice. "Okay, money and swanky-ass condo aside... I mean, you're *marrying* him, dude. Are you still sure about all this? Pretending to be this guy's husband?"

"Yeah. Why not?" I tugged a chip from the plate of nachos. "You've met him. He's not a creeper."

"Neither was Ted Bundy," Luis muttered.

I rolled my eyes as I crunched on the chip. "Dude, he's not a serial killer. He's actually pretty chill. Pretty easy to live with, too."

"Except you don't see him very often."

"Well, not at the moment. But like I said, when I do see him, it's all good."

"Okay. But you know me and Ashton got your back if shit goes south, right?"

"I know. I appreciate it."

"Good. Don't stick with something shitty even if the money is good, you feel me?"

"I won't." Though admittedly the thought of walking away from this kind of cash was… well, I was pretty sure Jesse would have to be an actual serial killer who moonlighted in Nigerian prince clown porn for me to jump ship.

Luis and I continued catching up over lunch, and after we'd finished, the server brought our bill. Luis put some cash into the folder for his half, and with my customary knot of trepidation in my stomach, I slid my debit card in and put the folder on the edge of the table. I silently sent up the usual prayer—*please don't decline, please don't decline*—and tried to act casual after the server came back to pick it up.

A moment later she returned, and she smiled as she put it down. "Thank you, gentlemen. We'll see you soon!" Then she was gone.

I sighed with relief. Okay, the card hadn't declined. Awesome. After I'd given Luis back his change so he could figure out a tip, I mentally calculated the tip on my end, filled in the receipt, and signed it.

Luis and I said goodbye outside the restaurant, and I headed to my car. The moment I was alone, I did the same thing I always did after I'd used my card—I logged into my bank account. I was certain to the point of nausea that some bill had come out early or the cable-internet-phone company had added some stupid fee like excessive consumption of cat videos, and between that and whatever I'd just spent, I was overdrawn.

Whenever I did this and my balance still showed positive, the relief was almost orgasmic. Maybe I was still broke, but I wasn't over-fucking-drawn.

Today, when the balance appeared, the panic vanished, but I just stared in shock at the screen.

There was still money in my account.

There was still *a comma* in my balance.

I could buy stuff. Stuff I needed. Maybe even some stuff I wanted, but especially stuff I needed and had been needing for a long time.

Stuff like, say…

I glared at the dash of my clunker car. The engine was making weird noises again. I was pretty sure the only reason my check engine light wasn't on was that it had actually burned out. Something didn't feel right whenever I turned, and the transmission seemed wonky on the rare occasion I dared take this death trap on the freeway.

My gaze slid back to my phone.

To the balance on my bank account.

To that goddamned comma.

I was still driving Shitty Shitty Bang Bang, why?

My heart and my stomach did weird fluttery, jumpy,

jittery things. I could literally leave this parking lot right now, go to a car dealership, and buy something brand new. *In cash.* Well, with my debit card, anyway. But no payments, no loans, no credit, nothing. Straight up walk in, say "I want that car," and drive away.

I released a long breath. It wasn't reckless or frivolous. I needed another car because this one was pretty much in its death throes. A car was a practical, reasonable thing to buy, and it was something I could *afford* to buy. Today. Right now. In cash.

Jesse had said a car was included in our agreement if I wanted one. He'd offered to get me one like the Porsche he was driving. The smart thing to do would be to take him up on the offer, but the reality that I could afford to buy a car on my own was too sweet to ignore.

So, twenty minutes and four hundred million second thoughts later, my piece-of-shit beater rattled and clanked its way into the parking lot of a gleaming Ford dealership.

The sales people seemed pretty divided about what to do with me. Half of them took one look at my car, then basically decided I didn't exist. The other half came at me like Great Whites who smelled blood. I insisted I was just looking, so they let me be for now, but they hovered in the wings as if they knew I really did intend to buy. Which, I mean, there was no guarantee my car would live long enough to leave the premises, so yeah, it was a pretty safe bet that I was here to buy. Or at least try to, anyway.

I wandered through the rows of shining vehicles. The SUVs were nice, but the mileage... eh. No. A Mustang could be fun. Oh, but the Focus was like five thousand less than the Mustang, and it got way better mileage.

I closed my eyes and rubbed the bridge of my nose.

Why was I stressing so hard about this? I had the money. There was more money coming soon. I'd signed a contract with Jesse, and as long as I didn't bail, that contract guaranteed me $100,000 per month for twelve months, even if we ended up divorcing sooner. So aside from what I still had in my account now, I had a cool million coming my way over the next year. In three weeks, I'd have another $100K.

But financial security was a foreign concept to me. Jesse's promise wouldn't be worth the paper it was printed on if he suddenly lost all his money tomorrow. Until the next payment landed in my account, I had to assume that what I had now was all I was getting. This money had to last.

My car, however, wasn't going to last, so I could at least accept that buying one was a reasonable thing. The question was how much did I spend? Where was the line between doing a practical adult thing and splurging on something ridiculous? And even if it was a practical adult thing, could I actually go through with buying a car and not like throw up or something? Because I'd had palpitations just buying textbooks when I was in college. I couldn't even look at the balance on my student loans without dry heaving. Dropping five figures in one go? Oh my Lord.

"Anything catching your eye?" A salesman with Eric on his nametag appeared beside me, grinning broadly.

"A few, yeah." I scowled at the car I'd been staring at for the last ten minutes. "I like the Focus. I'm just not sure about the price."

"Well, we have some low mileage pre-owned Focuses over here." Eric motioned toward the other side of the lot.

"Why don't we have a look?"

We did. Oh Lord, the used cars really did mean a lot less sticker shock. This price range I could totally cope with. In fact, it didn't take long for me to settle on the perfect car—a three year-old cobalt blue Focus with about thirty thousand miles on it. It handled nicely, didn't make any weird noises, and didn't have any mystery smells like fried electronics, burning oil, or the stale remnants of a demonic ritual. It was also like half the price of the new one, so hell yeah, sign me up.

Of course my parents hadn't raised me to be gullible, and of course I haggled with the guy. Halfway through, I almost broke into hysterical laughter at the realization that I was haggling on a car I could afford a few times over. It wasn't an attempt to get the payments down to where I could scrape together enough money each month to keep up—just trying to negotiate the price down so I didn't pay more than I had to. This whole "suddenly having money" thing had been one strange experience after another, and "haggling over a car I can 100% afford" was definitely in the top five. This was my life now? *How?*

Oh, and the best part—I would never in a million years forget the look on the salesman's face when I handed him my debit card.

"Um." He cleared his throat. "How much did you want to put down?"

"It's not a down payment." I smiled, feeling giddy and kind of queasy at the same time. "It's for the whole thing."

"Oh. I, um… I see. Okay, let me just get that squared away for you."

He took my card, and I swallowed the bile in my throat.

I just bought a *car*? With my *debit card*?

Yes. Yes, I had.

It took a while to process everything, especially since the credit union had to call and confirm that it really was me putting the entire price of *a motherfucking vehicle* on my debit card, but then it was done. They took my old car for a trade-in, which I mostly cared about because I wanted the stupid thing gone, and then Eric the sales dude handed me the Focus's keys and title, and sent me on my way.

Numb and kind of in shock, I got into the car—my car—and left. I drove a block or so from the dealership, then pulled over because I needed to adjust the seat again. Before I started driving, though, I just sat there for a moment. Hands on the wheel, gaze fixed on the dash, listening to the healthy idle of the engine, I had to work hard to swallow.

This car was mine. This gently used cobalt blue Ford Focus with 32,646 miles and air conditioning and a sunroof that worked was *mine*. Free and clear. No payments. No loans.

Because this was real. This was my life now. Two weeks ago, my roommates and I had pooled our resources and still been sweating over whether we could afford dish detergent on that shopping trip. This afternoon, I'd held my breath when the waitress had taken my card because I was sure it would be declined like it had been so many times before.

And tonight, before heading to the job I didn't actually need anymore, I'd bought a functional, nice-looking car from a real dealership.

I'd paid cash. I had cash left. If I wanted to, I could go back to the dealership and buy *another* car and *still* have a five-figure bank balance. I wouldn't, but I *could*.

Exhaling hard, I let my head fall back against the seat, not sure if I was going to laugh or cry. Maybe both. I didn't have to pinch pennies anymore. I didn't have to cross my fingers and hope someone made a mistake on a pizza and my coworkers and I could eat it ourselves. No more praying for my car to wheeze and sputter through just *one* more paycheck that wouldn't be enough anyway.

Sitting there on the side of the road, the reality sank in completely. Answering Jesse's ad had changed my life in a matter of days. Everything I'd been sweating over and losing sleep over was just… it was gone. My two best friends could finally breathe too.

I was going to be okay. They were going to be okay.

And as I sat there in my newly-acquired car, I'm not ashamed to admit it.

I cried.

Chapter 6
Jesse

My hands were *killing* me.

It kind of came with the territory of my job, though, and I had plenty of icepacks and ibuprofen at the ready. After I'd eaten something so I could take the ibuprofen, I put on my super stylish beige wrist braces and settled onto the couch with an icepack and the remote. I'd checked my email earlier to see if there was anything I needed to deal with right away, but everything could be put off until tomorrow, so I left my phone and tablet on the coffee table. Time to give my hands a much-needed break.

After I'd settled on an episode of Lucifer that I'd seen a hundred times, I gingerly arranged braces and the frozen gel pack so I could get... well, not comfortable. Not with the relentless ache in every moveable part of my hands and arms. Since I'm left-handed, my left hand hurt worse, so I put the icepack over it and just kept the brace on my right to give all the muscles and tendons a break.

Eventually, I had everything arranged so I could start

to relax… and that was the exact moment I realized I'd left the ibuprofen and my drink on the kitchen island.

"Seriously?" I muttered. When the universe didn't choose that moment to bestow telekinesis on this pitiful, aching makeup artist, I swore, tossed the icepack aside, and got up.

With the ibuprofen in my gullet where it belonged, I dropped onto the couch again. I glared around the room suspiciously, making sure I hadn't forgotten anything else. Then I settled back down, at which point the joke was on me because I'd paused my show and—naturally—left the remote on the coffee table.

I let my head fall back on the couch. Was there such a thing as too exhausted to relax? Because I was pretty sure that was where I was right then. I loved my job, and I was excited to see how this current film turned out, but tired? *Oh* yeah.

Closing my eyes, I tried not to think about my aching hands and how long it would take the ibuprofen to do its thing. My mind wandered through tomorrow's shooting schedule. It was a lighter day, at least where my department was concerned. Not so many fine details. Not so many prosthetics. One character had a number of large scars, elaborate tattoos, and fresh wounds for a huge portion of the movie, but tomorrow's scenes were flashbacks to her pre-scar and pre-tattoo days. She'd need some extra work to make her look quite a few years younger, but that didn't take much. Just leaving off the ink and injuries made her seem younger anyway, so… easy day for me. As long as my hands cooperated tomorrow, I'd be fine.

Then I need to do an inventory because I'm pretty sure I'm running low on a few things, so if I order them tomorrow, they'll be here by—

A key in the door made me jump so hard, the icepack tumbled onto the carpet.

What the—

Oh. Right. I live with someone now.

I had just enough time to grab the icepack and regain some of my dignity when the front door opened. Hayden walked in, still wearing his red, white, and green uniform from Mario & Antonio's, and tossed his keys on the counter.

I got up to refill my drink. "You're home early."

"Slow night." He shrugged as he put his wallet beside his keys. "They always cut some of the drivers loose if— oh God, what happened to your hands?"

I glanced down at the braces and the icepack. "Oh, it's just tendinitis. Today's job involved a lot of really fine detail and some prosthetics. My hands and wrists get a little tired sometimes."

He frowned. "It's not carpal tunnel?"

"No, no. I've been to the doctor half a dozen times to be sure, but he says it's just some inflammation. Ice and ibuprofen usually help." I flexed my fingers, which were getting stiff from being still for so long. "Occupational hazard."

"Wow. I never thought about makeup artists having that much strain, but I guess it makes sense."

"Yeah, I didn't either. But it's something you learn real quick in this line of work."

"I bet." He flexed and straightened his right wrist. "Hell, I was getting sore for a while just from cutting pizzas. You wouldn't think it would do that much, but..."

"Repetitive strain is repetitive strain." I paused, realizing I was still holding my empty glass. As I went through the motions of refilling it, I said, "Have you eaten? Do you want anything?"

"Ugh." Hayden wrinkled his nose. "Anything I eat right now will taste like garlic." He tugged at his shirt and sniffed it. "And I fucking smell like garlic too. I think I'm going to change and grab a shower. Then maybe I'll think of something."

"No hurry."

He was right—in the twenty minutes it took for him to shower and change, he'd decided something from the kebab place down the street sounded good. Fine by me. There would never be a time when I didn't want something from there. Good thing, too, because I'd just gotten the Blue Screen of Death on my brain. Not because I was tired from the long day on set, though. No, it was because Hayden had casually come strolling out of his bedroom in a pair of blue gym shorts and nothing else.

Holy. *Shit.*

He hadn't even lived here a week yet, and he'd already mentioned a couple of times that he was worried about putting on weight. Having access to food on a regular basis was a new thing for him, and he wanted to be careful. I didn't think he had much to worry about. If anything he struck me as too slim; putting on some weight would do him good. He wasn't emaciated, just on the thin side, and he still looked damn good. He was a little shorter than me, definitely built narrower, like someone who would always be long and lean.

He had a faded tattoo of Garfield the cat on his pec, and there was a freckle on his left shoulder blade that was mesmerizing for some reason (most likely because it gave me an excuse to stare at his bare back). Probably without even realizing it, he walked like someone who knew he had an ass to die for, and he was right. What I wouldn't have given for a handful of that gorgeous butt, not to mention a chance at holding onto those narrow hips and—

I pulled my gaze away from…

From my…

Oh, fuck my life.

This wasn't my roommate or some guy who'd just come over to hang out. No, I was marrying him. I would literally be this man's husband in the very near future—on paper, but not in bed.

Son of a bitch. Where were all the guys this hot when I wanted to marry someone for real? Or at least hook up and fuck each other senseless?

No, I had to find God's gift to the male form, and make a business arrangement with him that pretty much guaranteed this was the last man on earth I'd ever have sex with. Because let's face it—Hayden was in this for the cash, I was in this to torpedo my dad's political career, and none of that exactly set the mood for a passionate roll in the hay. Not without making things unbearably weird, anyway.

"Jesse?"

I turned around, eyebrows up. "Hmm? What?"

He cocked his head, looking oddly amused as if he'd seen right through to all the chaos he'd stirred up in my head. Gesturing with his phone, he said, "I asked if you wanted me to order anything else."

"Order—oh, um. No. No, I think that's enough."

"You sure?"

Was I sure? Did I want anything more? Since when did this kind of shit require that much thought? Oh, right, since my painfully hot husband-to-be moved in.

I cleared my throat. "I'm good. Just let me know how much it is." I grabbed my wallet off the counter and started thumbing through some bills. It was something to do.

Hayden finished placing the order and put his phone in his pocket. "They said forty minutes, so they must be busy tonight."

"That place is always busy. Trust me."

"Eh. I can wait." He drummed his fingers on the counter. "So, um..." He swallowed, suddenly... uneasy? "I bought a car this afternoon."

"Did you?" I straightened. "What did you get?"

"Nothing crazy." Blushing, he dropped his gaze. "But it runs, and it's nice, so..."

"Can I see it?"

He met my eyes again. "You want to?"

"Sure. Why not?"

"Okay. Well." He hesitated, then picked up his keys. He didn't bother putting on a shirt, but paused at the door to slip on a pair of flip-flops, and then we walked to the elevator.

In the parking garage, he grinned shyly as we walked past a row of cars, and then with a proud smile, he pressed the button on the remote in his hand. Three cars down in a row of Mercedes, Lexus, Porsches, and one gleaming Maserati, the lights flashed on a small blue Ford. It was compact enough to slide in comfortably between a wide Mercedes and a badly parked H3. I loved the color, but I was admittedly surprised he'd gone for something so plain.

I looked at Hayden and tilted my head. "This… you didn't want anything… I don't know—fancier?"

He eyed me, the grin vanishing. "This is all I need."

"Well yeah, but I told I'd buy you something, right? You could've gone for a new one or—"

"It's *all* I need." There was a hint of a growl in his voice. A warning.

"Okay, but I mean if you really want something new, there's no reason you can't—"

"*Hey.*" He glared at me. "This may seem like a piece of crap to you, but it is literally the biggest thing I've ever bought for myself besides my damned degree. Maybe it's not good enough for someone as high up the food chain as you, but it's more than I saw myself ever getting at all."

"What? No, I'm just saying—"

"I really don't care, Jesse," he snapped. "Listen, you see a car like this and wonder why the fuck anyone would get something so crappy and cheap. Or why I'd buy one myself—even if it's with money you paid me—instead of letting you buy me something better. You know what I think? That I've spent the last few hours losing my mind over how amazing it was to drive all the way to work, on all of my delivery runs, and all the way home without worrying once that some piece was going to fall off or explode." He pointed sharply at the car. "It works, it's nice, and it's fucking *mine*. You've been up in your ivory tower way too long to *ever* understand what a novelty that is."

He didn't wait for a response, turned on his heel, and stalked toward the elevator.

I stood there, rooted to the spot and speechless. Why was he so upset? There was nothing wrong with the car, but my God, why would he sell himself short when he could get something so much better? Or when I'd happily buy it for him?

I looked at the little blue Ford again. There really was nothing wrong with it. I didn't know much about the particular model, but it *was* a hell of an upgrade from what he'd been driving this morning.

My own words from the other day echoed in my mind:

"*I have no frame of reference.*"

My heart sank.

Shit. I should've listened to myself. I honestly had no frame of reference for Hayden's situation, so it hadn't occurred to me that something like that might upset him. I still didn't quite understand why, but something told me that didn't make me any less of an asshole.

"*Christ, Jesse,*" I could hear my father saying with a condescending laugh. "*Have you seen how little those makeup people are paid? You don't have the chops to act, but you could earn ten times a makeup salary as a producer.*"

I grimaced in the empty parking garage. Wow, yeah, I got it now. I was mortified to realize my father's voice had come out of my mouth, and I definitely needed to make this right with Hayden. Like, now.

I hung back in the garage to wait for our food to arrive. I was, after all, just a bit of a coward, and wasn't sure how to approach Hayden without some kind of peace offering. Fortunately, the kebab place had, as usual, overestimated the delivery time, and it wasn't long before I was sheepishly heading up to the condo with our food.

The smell or the crinkle of plastic bags must have signaled to him that dinner had arrived, because I was just putting everything on plates when he quietly came into the kitchen. He glanced at me, but quickly cut his eyes away, and he refused to look at me as we arranged our food on plates.

Before he could escape to his bedroom or something, I cautiously said, "Can we talk?"

He stiffened. Staring down at his food, he didn't speak, but he also didn't leave.

"I'm sorry," I said. "I… I didn't mean to insult you, but I realized afterward I sounded like a dick."

He chewed the inside of his cheek.

Sighing, I shook my head. "Listen, I meant what I said the other day—I don't have a lot of frame of reference for this kind of thing. So I just thought…"

He narrowed his eyes a little.

I swallowed. "It doesn't matter what I thought, honestly. I don't know what it's like to walk in your shoes, and I'm sorry I was a dick about the car. I'm… I'm really glad you got something you like and that will work for what you need."

He watched me, suspicion keeping his features taut for a moment, but slowly he began to relax. Dropping his gaze again, he said, "We come from really different worlds. I don't expect you to understand mine, but… just trust me that I know what I need, okay?"

"I will. I'm sorry. I really am."

"I know." He looked at me through his lashes, and a smile gradually came to life. "I guess just consider yourself lucky."

Usually, it grated on me when someone reminded me of my family's mountains of money, and how I should be thankful for it instead of complaining about, well, anything. This time? He had a point.

"I do," I said. "I'm well aware that growing up in my family means a lot of wealth and privilege. I'll be the first to cop to that. But I've spent a lot of time wishing I grew up in a different family."

He searched my eyes, some more of the hostility slipping out of his expression.

"Look at why we're doing this whole marriage thing." I sighed, plucking a fry off my plate. "People from healthy, functional families don't need to fake marry so their dads will disinherit them."

Hayden exhaled. "Yeah. That's true."

"Still, it doesn't excuse being an asshole. So I mean it—I'm sorry."

"I know." The smile came back with some more feeling this time. "Just part of working out the bugs, I guess."

I studied him uncertainly. "So… we're good?"

Hayden nodded. "Yeah. We're good."

I exhaled. "Okay." Laughing self-consciously, I added, "Can't imagine why I'm still single, right?"

He chuckled. "Oh come on. You're a nice guy. We just come from different worlds. That's all." Before I could respond, he motioned toward the living room. "Want to find something to watch while we eat?"

"That sounds perfect."

"Dude, you can't block my Mirrorwing Dragon!" a voice exclaimed from inside my condo. "It's flying *and* it's unblockable because it's enchanted by Cloak of Mists."

I frowned at the door, pausing with my key in mid-air. Huh?

"I'm not blocking it, jackass," Hayden replied. "I'm taking the damage, and then using a Simulacrum to divert the damage to my Drudge Skeletons, which regenerate, because fuck you."

The other voice muttered something I didn't catch, though it sounded suspiciously like a defeated "son of a bitch."

I unlocked the door and stepped inside to find Hayden and his former roommates hunched over the coffee table, colorful cards laid out in front of them.

"Oh hey." Hayden flashed me a quick smile before returning his attention to his cards. "How was your day?"

"Um, it was all right." I hung up my keys. "Usual craziness on a movie set."

"How are your hands?"

I flexed them and shrugged. "Eh."

"I picked up some more ibuprofen." Without looking up from his cards, he gestured at the kitchen. "You said you were almost out, and Luis and I were at the grocery store earlier."

"Oh. Thanks." I glanced around and found the bottle sitting beside the microwave. Same brand I always used and everything.

While I was at it, I realized my kitchen was spotless except for a covered casserole dish on the stove and some kind of cake on the counter. The air was warm with spices I didn't recognize, and my mouth watered.

"Hope it's cool that we used the kitchen," Hayden said. "Luis and Ashton made dinner, so we—"

"Mind?" I chuckled. "Mi casa, su casa. Whatever it is,

it smells great."

"There's a ton left," Luis said. "Help yourself."

I was about to decline, but my stomach was grumbling and the food really did smell amazing. "You don't mind?"

"Nah, man. Have at it. There's—" Luis huffed. "Motherfucker, what did I tell you about killing my creatures?"

Hayden cackled. "That's what you get for playing those stupid dragons." He waved a hand at the cards laid out in front of Luis. "Go away, dragon. Shoo."

Luis grumbled something, picked up a card, and put it aside, adding a much more audible, "Asshole."

While they continued playing, I helped myself to some of the food they'd made.

"We're not in your way, are we?" Hayden asked. "We can move to the island or the dining room table if you want to sit in here."

"Nah, it's fine." I pulled a Diet Coke from the fridge. "Do you guys mind if I watch you play?"

He smiled. "Not at all."

I sat on the armrest of the sofa, balancing my plate on my knee, and put the soda on the end table. The coffee table was a little closer, but I didn't want to risk one of us knocking the can over and soaking their cards.

As I ate and they played, I couldn't relax as much as I needed to. My work day was over. I was in my own home. I had something to eat. I needed to just chill, for God's sake, especially since I had to be on-set at the crack of dawn tomorrow. I should've been winding down, not getting more wound up. What the hell?

As if I didn't know.

While the guys played, I stole a surreptitious glance at

Hayden. He was focused on his cards right then, frowning at the ones in his hand and the rest laid out in front of him, his expression one of intense concentration.

Just by sitting there, innocently playing cards with his buddies, he was stressing me the hell out.

It had been a few days since that incident in the parking garage. Ever since, he'd seemed perfectly pleasant, but I'd been on edge whenever we were in the same room. While he casually went about his business like he didn't have a care in the world, I was tense, waiting for the other shoe to drop. Waiting for him to suddenly whirl around and snarl about what I'd said about his car.

So far, nothing. He hadn't given me a single indication that he even remembered or cared about that evening.

I knew this game, though, and I knew it well. Fight. Settle things a bit too easily. Let them simmer for a while until the other person let their guard down. When the time was right, let fly and tear the other person a new one.

To this day, I got sick to my stomach if my mother was being chillier than usual. Even if I knew there was nothing for her to be pissed at me about, that didn't mean she wouldn't flip her lid at me before she finally had it out with whoever had crossed her.

My dad was ten times worse—he could let things like this go dormant for months or even years before finally bringing it up, usually in front of people. Like the time he'd been furious at me for refusing to attend a premiere of his latest film. I'd calmly explained that I really didn't want to see yet another movie where the only gay character wound up dying alone for no apparent reason. He'd been angry because it wouldn't look good for the filmmaker's gay son to boycott his movie, and what kind of ungrateful asshole was I, anyway? He'd finally put a queer like me onscreen and I couldn't even be bothered to attend the premiere? We'd both coldly walked away from the conversation, and it didn't come up again. Stupidly, I'd thought that was the end of it.

Fast forward almost five years later, my first major film was premiering, and the producers had all but begged me to invite my parents. Having Isaac Ambrose attend a premiere was a huge stamp of approval, even if he was just there to support his makeup artist son.

My parents regretfully said they couldn't make it.

The next day, though, Dad had announced he was throwing one of those *"you'll show your face if you value your place in the industry"* parties.

The same night as the premiere.

Of course everyone who was anyone attended, including every A-lister who'd been invited to the premiere and every relevant columnist, reporter, or film reviewer who might have given us a desperately needed boost.

Dad called me the next day to ask how it had gone, and I'd admitted it had been pretty lackluster. He'd chuckled and calmly said, "Well, next time might I suggest showing your face when *I'm* premiering a film?"

From then on, I'd been wary of any conflict between us, knowing it would come back and bite me when I least expected it. It was part of why I knew my arrangement with Hayden had to be a long game. Dad was much too patient and calculating for me to come at this any other way.

And damn it, that meant I didn't do well with unresolved conflicts and lingering tension. Especially since I didn't really know Hayden. Not well enough to know how this would come out once it had festered long enough. It would eventually. Always did. But when? And how?

Fuck. No wonder I was so wound up.

I kept the worry and tension beneath the surface as much as I could, and just quietly watched Hayden and his friends playing cards while I ate my dinner. After I'd finished eating, I took my plate back into the kitchen, rinsed it, and took an ibuprofen. Then I picked up my wrist braces and went back into the living room. The game was still going on, and getting intense apparently. Luis had already been eliminated, and the trash-talking between Ashton and Hayden had been escalating by the minute.

As I tugged on my wrist brace, Ashton dropped a card on top of Hayden's cards. "And *that* is seven points of damage, but *you* only have four life points left." He grinned triumphantly and waved at Hayden. "B'bye!"

Hayden groaned, tossed back Ashton's card, and started collecting his own into a stack. "Next turn, you'd have been dead."

"Don't matter." Ashton started on his own cards. "Next turn didn't happen, and *you're* dead."

Hayden flipped him off. Then he looked at me. "You want to play?"

"Um. You'd have to walk me through it because I have no clue how."

"That's fine." He smiled warmly. "I taught these idiots to play."

"Oh." I grinned. "So then I'll probably win?"

He rolled his eyes as his friends laughed. "All right, smartass."

I adjusted the Velcro strap as I watched them clearing

away the game. "What are you guys playing, anyway?"

"Magic: The Gathering," Hayden said.

"Oh, *this* is Magic?" I craned my neck to look at the cards. "I've never actually seen anyone play it."

"Never?" Hayden slid over and patted the cushion beside him. "You're welcome to watch if you want to. Or I really could teach you to play."

"Seriously?"

"Sure." He grinned up at me. "We're always game for fresh meat."

I laughed nervously and sat beside him, keeping some comfortable distance between us on the couch. I was still guarded and edgy, but hell, why not? Maybe the game would distract me from everything tumbling around in my head. Or make it worse considering I was now even closer to Hayden and still had no fucking idea what was going on in *his* head.

"Step one." Hayden plunked a thick deck of cards down in front of me. "Shuffle."

I glanced down at my wrist braces. "Uh…"

"Oh. Shit." Hayden jumped, then grabbed the cards again. "Sorry."

"What happened to your hands?" Ashton asked.

"Just some tendinitis from work."

"Ugh. That sucks." Luis shook his head. "My job used to fuck with my ankles really bad."

Ashton nodded. "Same. And my back too. Those boots you bought me made a huge difference."

"The boots—what boots?"

"With the cash you gave us," Luis said. "To keep our mouths shut."

"Oh. Right. Glad it's helping." I gingerly flexed my

fingers. "Not a whole lot I can do about this except ice and immobilize. Stupid body parts."

Ashton chuckled as he started shuffling his own deck. "What do you do anyway?"

"I'm a makeup artist," I said.

"Like for movies, right?" Luis asked.

"And TV, yeah."

"You guys should *see* his work." Hayden glanced up from shuffling. "This guy is a fucking magician."

"Yeah?" Luis put his neatly stacked cards on the table and reached for his drink. To Ashton, he said, "We should look this guy up on IMDB. See if we've seen any of his stuff."

"You should show them your other room," Hayden said. "I didn't want to take anyone in there since it's your space, but they've probably seen a ton of your movies and shows."

I could feel myself blushing, and laughed. "Maybe another night. I've been up to my eyeballs in work today, and…" I waved a braced hand.

"Oh, I get that, man," Luis said. "Work stays at *work*."

"Says the guy who comes home and spends an hour bitching about his job." Ashton plunked his deck down on the table. "So we playing or what?"

Hayden slid closer to me, and I tried not to let it show when my breath hitched as the warmth of his leg met mine. "So. You start by drawing eight cards…"

The game wasn't overly complicated, but I admittedly had a tough time remembering all the finer points. What could I say? It was hard to concentrate when I had Hayden's thigh pressed up against mine, and it was even worse whenever he leaned in to tell me what to do. It had been way too long since I'd been laid, and the man casually touching me now was way too hot to be anything but distracting. And hey, touching him was *almost* enough to distract me from the Sword of Damocles. That was what I told myself, anyway. Much easier than figuring out how to deal with being both maddeningly nervous about him and ridiculously attracted to him.

You're so damn hot.

And you're also still pissed at me.

Would you just say something already?

"Jesse." Hayden elbowed me gently. "It's your turn. Draw a card."

"Hmm? What. Oh. Right." I took a card off my deck. There was a picture of black horse with a fiery mane, but the words under the picture didn't make much sense. I wasn't sure how much that had to do with my lack of familiarity with the game, and how much was because of the guy sitting next to me.

He was perfectly relaxed, and I was pretty sure that was going to drive me insane. I hated the feeling that someone was playing it cool just to let me twist in the wind until they finally decided to let me have it. Fuck. If I wanted this kind of crap, I'd call my mother. My older brother was pretty good at it too.

I had a solid poker face, though, and made it through the game without anybody catching on that I was losing my shit.

I thought, anyway.

When I got up to get another drink, Hayden came into the kitchen too, and as soon as we were relatively alone, he turned to me. "Hey. What's up with you?"

"Hmm? What do you mean?"

Hayden's brow furrowed. "You've been kind of, I don't know, weird the last couple of days." He paused. "Is this about the thing with my car?"

"You tell me."

"What?" His whole body tensed. "Wait, you think... you think *I'm* upset?"

"You're not?"

He shook his head. "Jesus, no. I... is *that* what's been bothering you? That you thought *I* was upset?"

"I... well..."

"Jesse, we settled this the other night. Why would I still be upset?"

"So... you're not?"

"No!" He touched my arm, eyes sincere. "I'm serious. We're cool. If we weren't, I would have said something."

I watched him, not sure if I should take the words at face value.

Hayden's expression softened and he stepped a little closer. "Hon, if there's one thing you should know about me, it's that I don't let things sit. If I'm upset, you're going to know about it. I promise."

I swallowed. "Really?"

"Well, yeah." He looked at me like it was the dumbest thing I'd ever said. "Why would I stress myself out and make myself miserable when I could just come talk to you and sort it out?"

"That's..." I blinked. "Uh..."

He tilted his head. "Is that really what you think I was doing?" Before I could answer, his lips quirked. "This is another way your family is super dysfunctional and you totally think it's normal, isn't it?"

"Um." I cleared my throat and very nearly asked in

disbelief, *"You mean it isn't normal?"* but stopped myself and went with, "It's kind of starting to sound like that, yeah."

"Jesse." Hayden shook his head. "Oh my God. Those people…" To my surprise, he stepped closer and hugged me. To my even bigger surprise, I needed it. Especially from him.

I hugged him back, and after a moment, I quietly asked, "So, we really are good?"

"Yes, of course." He let me go and looked in my eyes. "You apologized and told me where you were coming from. I told you why it bothered me, and you understood." He half shrugged. "What else is there to say?"

Besides you finding some way to throw this in my face when I least expect it?

I shook my head. "I don't know. I guess I'm just not used to things being resolved and not coming back up later."

He laughed humorlessly. "With as toxic as your family sounds? Yeah. Not surprised." He gave my arm a squeeze. "I promise, though—we're good, and if we're ever not, I'll tell you. Just promise me you'll do the same."

"Of course. Yeah." I nodded. "I kind of like this whole approach where we don't let things fester."

"I know, right? Healthy communication. What a novel idea."

It is for someone from my world.

"So, we're good?" Hayden asked. "With this?"

"Yeah." I smiled, relaxing for the first time in days. "Yeah, we're good."

"Okay. Now let's go kick my friends' asses at Magic."

We returned to the living room and settled back in to keep playing. I was slowly getting the hang of the game, and wonder of wonders, I was absorbing way more of the rules now that I wasn't sweating bullets over Hayden. At this rate, I might even sleep tonight.

"So, uh." Ashton's eyes flicked back and forth between us. "You guys told your families about all this yet?"

My stomach flipped. Hayden and I exchanged uneasy looks.

"Not yet," he said. "We're... Jesse was giving me some time to settle in, finish up with my job—"

"Put off the unpleasantness," I grumbled.

"Yeah. That too."

"It's not gonna get any more fun if you keep putting it off," Ashton said without taking his eyes off his cards. "Just tell 'em."

"Easy for you to say," Hayden muttered. "You just want to watch the fireworks."

"If I wanted to watch fireworks, I'd go to Disney. Don't be stupid. Just *tell* 'em."

"I'm with Ashton," Luis said.

"Yeah, I've always suspected that," Hayden deadpanned.

Ashton threw a pillow at him, narrowly missing me.

Hayden snickered. "Hey, now. Don't be a homophobe."

"I'm not a homophobe. If I were gay, I'd just have better taste in dudes."

"Hey!" Luis smacked Ashton's shoulder. "Fuck you."

"Nope," Ashton replied. "Told you—better taste in dudes."

Luis rolled his eyes. "Anyway. Let's not change the subject." He wiggled a finger at Hayden and me. "You guys gonna tell your families or what?"

Beside me, Hayden sighed. "He's got a point. We really should do that sooner than later."

"It's up to you." I shrugged. "Whenever you're ready to tell your family."

"You ready to tell yours?"

"I'm never ready to talk to mine about anything, but the sooner I drop the hammer, the sooner I can force Dad's hand."

Hayden watched me for a moment, chewing his lip. Then he released a long breath, his slim shoulders sagging. "Okay. I'll give my mom a call."

So much for sleeping tonight.

Chapter 7
Hayden

"Could you run all that by me again?" My mom's voice was faintly tinny though the computer's speakers, but her puzzled frown came through loud and clear on Jesse's laptop screen.

I glanced at Jesse, who was sitting beside me, close enough to make sure we both fit in the frame. To my parents, I said, "We're getting married so that—"

"So that your father"—my dad gestured at Jesse—"will out himself as a homophobe and not get elected."

Jesse and I both nodded.

"And you really think he'll disown you?" Mom asked. "His own *son?*"

"I know my dad," Jesse said with a mix of bitterness and resignation. "Trust me—he'll do it."

My mother stared at us in shock.

Dad was pretty stunned too, but he wasn't as mute as Mom. "And what exactly is our role in this?"

"Basically we just need you to play along," Jesse said.

"Come to the wedding, don't say anything about—"

"Come to the wedding?" Mom's eyes widened. "You want me to attend my son's fake wedding? I... honey, this just seems..." She grimaced, glancing at Dad, who looked equally uneasy. "I mean are you sure you have to actually get married to do this? You can't just tell him you're thinking about it?"

Jesse shook his head. "My father won't buy it unless he thinks we're doing it for real."

"But what about after all of this?" Dad asked. "Once he's... well, disowned you, I guess?" He winced like it was painful to even discuss a father disowning his child. "Then what?"

"We divorce," Jesse said. "Hayden keeps all the money, we check 'irreconcilable differences,' and we move on."

My parents were quiet for a moment, as if absorbing everything. Finally, Dad asked, "Are you sure you want to do this, Hayden?"

I was already nodding before he'd finished the question. "Yeah. Jesse and I have discussed all the particulars, and... yeah. I'm onboard. I just didn't want to lie to you guys about it."

"We certainly appreciate that, but I still..." Dad exhaled hard. "I just hope you've both thought this through."

"We have," I said. "I promise."

Beside me, Jesse nodded, but didn't speak.

In a quiet voice, Dad asked, "What about your brother?"

I winced. Jesse glanced at me, his expression inquisitive. Avoiding his gaze and my parents', I cleared my throat. "I'd, um, rather not tell more people than we have to."

Mom released one of those sighs that made my conscience hurt. "Honey, I really wish you and Brian would resolve things. You're adults now."

"I know. I know." I rubbed the back of my neck. "And we will. But I'm just telling you and Dad about this, okay?"

My parents didn't look thrilled, but they didn't argue. God knew we'd all butted heads over my sour relationship with my twin, and it was a dead horse no one enjoyed beating. Brian and I were civil. We could be in the same room and have conversations. We just didn't go out of our way to be involved in each other's lives. Which, yes, it fucking hurt, and I didn't like where things stood with him, but one thing at a goddamned time.

"So it's just us and the two of you?" Dad asked. "No one else knows?"

"Us and my roommates."

"All right. So. That's all you want us to do?" Mom asked, her tone flat. "Just play along and come to the wedding?"

"And don't talk about it, right?" Dad held up some papers, which I assumed were the NDA they'd signed, scanned, and emailed us earlier.

"Yes." I wrung my hands in my lap. "Look, I know we're asking a lot. I know this is… it's weird for me too. But Isaac knows what to say to win people over, and he's starting to get really popular among progressive voters. If he gets elected, he's going to be awful to people like us." I gestured at myself and Jesse.

Both my parents straightened a bit.

"You really think he'll be able to cause that much harm?" Dad asked.

"I don't know," Jesse said. "But in this day and age, I'm not taking anything for granted. What I do know is that he'll *try* to do that harm, and that's enough for me to do everything I can to stop him."

My dad nodded, his expression grim. "That I can understand. You can't be too careful. What is his big hang up with you being gay, though? I never realized he was a religious man."

"He's not." Jesse's voice was sour. "But he has very rigid beliefs about how men should behave. It's…" He quirked his lips like he couldn't quite find the words.

"So he's a poster child for toxic masculinity," I said.

Jesse snapped his fingers. "*Yes.* That. Absolutely that."

"Oh." Mom rolled her eyes and groaned. "We know people like him."

"You do?" Jesse asked.

"Are you kidding?" Dad sniffed. "Our son was a figure skater."

"Ah. Gotcha. Enough said." Jesse shifted beside me on the couch. "So you get it. And in Dad's case, it doesn't help that when a relative's lavender marriage was outed in the fifties, it did some serious damage to the Ambrose reputation. My grandfather was incredibly protective of the family's image after that, and my dad was raised to be the same way."

"And they had a gay scapegoat." Dad was nodding as he spoke.

"Exactly." Jesse exhaled. "So it's a bunch of messy family history, decades of indoctrination, an obsession with the family's image, and…" He waved a hand. "You wind up with my dad. In his mind, there is nothing in the world you can do that's worse than staining your family's name, and no worse way to stain that name than to be queer."

Dad inclined his head. "How does throwing his own son out of his family stack up in the list of sins?"

"Not as high as you'd think," Jesse said.

"He obviously has issues with gay people in his own family," Mom said. "But does he feel that way about them outside the family?"

Jesse nodded slowly but emphatically. "*Oh* yeah. Back before he started being careful what he said around me in case I was recording him, he was incredibly open behind closed doors about how conversion therapy should be not just legal, but mandatory. I only escaped going through it myself because by the time he'd learned about it, I was of age and he couldn't force me to go. He's told me more than once that's one of his biggest regrets in life too."

"Oh my God," my mom said, her voice filled with horror.

"Yeah." Jesse rolled his shoulders, probably trying to hide a shudder. "Plus he thinks all queer marriages should be annulled. He's… I mean, the bottom line is that Dad is *not* a friend of the LGBT community. Let's put it that way."

"Jesus. Well." Dad glanced at Mom, then back at us. "You have my support."

Mom hesitated, but then she also nodded. "Mine too. I don't like it, but under the circumstances, I think you boys are doing the right thing. Just let us know if there's anything we can do to help."

A minute later, we exchanged goodbyes, and I

disconnected the call. As soon as the screen went dark, Jesse and I both released sighs of relief as we sagged back against the couch.

"Well." I let my head loll toward Jesse. "That was more painless than I thought it would be."

He nodded slowly, looking dazed. "Yeah. Yeah, it was."

"So, now what?"

"Now the fun part." Jesse grimaced and met my gaze. "Telling *my* parents."

Was I really going to Isaac Ambrose's house?

My stomach knotted as I slid into the passenger seat of Jesse's Porsche. We weren't even on the road yet and I was already starstruck, and if I thought too hard about the fact that we were going to tell him we were getting married, I'd probably throw up all over the Porsche's leather interior.

"So. Um." I cleared my throat and managed to croak, "Where does your dad live, anyway?"

"Out in Joshua Tree."

"Joshua Tree? Isn't that like two hours from here?"

"Two and a half to his front door, yeah." Jesse started the engine, and the roar echoed through the parking garage. "Might be a bit over three if there's traffic."

As he backed out of the space, I resisted the compulsion to look up the gas mileage on the Porsche and compare it to my Focus. I mean seriously, Joshua Tree was like a hundred and thirty-some-odd miles from here. That was like... *come on, math*... almost five gallons of gas each way in my car, and I doubted the Porsche was prone to sipping instead of guzzling.

But since I was already sweating bullets about making a first impression on the most powerful man in Hollywood who, oh by the way, was about to be my temporary father-in-law, I decided not to add "what will he think of my pitiful little car?" to my list of things to obsess over.

So I settled back in the extra comfy passenger seat, basking in the cool rush of the AC while Jesse pulled out onto the road. "Why Joshua Tree, anyway? I mean, doesn't your dad mostly work in LA?"

"He's got a house in Beverly Hills too." Jesse said it casually, as if the perfectly logical answer to a long commute was a crash pad in one of the most exclusive neighborhoods in Southern California. Which, given the world Jesse came from, maybe it was the perfectly logical answer. While lowly people like me were practically starving ourselves to make one-third of the rent on a crumbling shoebox, the elite bazillionaire jackwagon on top of the food chain had a spare house in Beverly goddamned Hills. Of *course* he did.

"Oh," was all I said.

"He lived in Palm Springs for a while when I was a kid," Jesse went on. "But I guess he kind of fell in love with Joshua Tree. He likes being a bit more isolated." There was a note of bitter amusement as he added, "I think what he really likes is having everyone drive clear out there for his parties and shindigs."

I nodded wordlessly. If the Isaac Ambrose who appeared in magazines and interviews was the real deal, then Jesse was probably right. He'd always seemed like the kind of person who thought he was above everyone else.

A god among mortals. He'd won Oscars for Best Director and Best Picture a few years back, and I swear to Christ, his second speech remained the single most smug thing I'd ever heard in my life, and that included that time when my brother was considered one of the top skaters in the world and let it go to his seventeen year-old head. When you can out-smug a full-of-himself teenage Olympian, that says something.

Isaac Ambrose, building a place a hundred plus miles out of Los Angeles and compelling people make a pilgrimage to his remote mansion to kiss his ring if they knew what was good for their careers? Sounded about right.

"Must be nice," I mused. "Having the power to make everyone in Hollywood drive that far to bow and scrape."

"I know, right?" Jesse rolled his eyes. "But as my mom always points out, my father wouldn't be who he is if he didn't have the ego to think that was who he should be."

"Never thought of it like that."

He grunted, but said nothing. In fact, he didn't say much at all after that. I hadn't known him long, but we'd gotten the hang of casual conversation pretty quickly. Plus we were still getting to know each other, so there was no shortage of things to talk about.

But for the three hours it took to get from Los Angeles to Joshua Tree—yay, traffic—he didn't say much.

To be fair, neither did I. Was he as nervous as I was? Maybe not for the same reasons. I literally had the worst case of stage fright I'd ever experienced, and I'd puked onstage once and during auditions twice, so I *knew* what stage fright was. There was also that horrible jittery fear of meeting a new boyfriend's parents. Which kind of seemed stupid since Jesse wasn't actually my boyfriend. Okay, on paper he was technically my fiancé and would soon legally be my husband—whoa, that was still so weird to think about—but we weren't *actually* a couple. We slept in separate rooms, lived separate lives, and were just performing as a couple in the name of taking down a supervillain before he got too powerful. Or, well, outing Jesse's dad as a homophobe before he got elected, but the supervillain thing sounded way cooler.

So I got why I had stage fright. It was stupid to be nervous like I was meeting my real soon-to-be in-laws, though.

Eh, at least that thought gave me something chew on for all those uncomfortably silent miles. Because I wasn't going to lie—I was terrified of meeting Jesse's parents. I would have been even if we'd been a normal couple happily announcing our normal engagement. Isaac fucking Ambrose, man. Seriously. How was this my life now?

Because apparently this was what happened when I answered weird and cryptic ads on the interwebs.

The silence followed Jesse and me all the way past Palm Springs and into the town of Joshua Tree, and continued as we headed out into the wide open country just outside of town. There weren't many trees out here, of the Joshua variety or otherwise (not that I could identify a Joshua tree to save my life). The landscape was a lot of scrubland and rocks and open space. Which… Southern California. Kind of to be expected. We just seemed to be getting further and further out into the middle of nowhere, leaving the gleaming skyline of Los Angeles miles and miles behind us as we got closer and closer to La Casa de Ambrose. Oh shit.

Eventually, Jesse pulled off the highway onto a two-lane road with barely visible stripes. From there, it was a few more miles until we were well and truly out in the middle of nowhere, and then he turned again, this time onto... cobblestones? Whoa. There was also a broad metal gate with a gleaming gold cursive *A* hanging above it, because fuck subtlety.

Jesse stopped, took a keycard from his wallet, swiped it, and entered a combination. A second later, the gate began a slow inward arc, opening but taking its sweet time about it as if to make sure we knew that no one was in any rush to let us in. A passive-aggressive gate. Nice.

The gate finally opened enough to let us in, and Jesse continued up the drive, which was significantly newer and nicer than the crumbling blacktop on the road we'd come in on. After a solid half mile, we crested the top of a small hill, and...

Oh sweet Jesus.

I decided immediately it was a good thing we'd brought his car instead of mine. That enormous, decadent house probably would have become sentient and tried to smite my unworthy little Focus before it got close enough to taint the flawlessness of the sprawling estate.

I'd actually seen pictures of this place before because God knew it had been featured in a million articles. In person, though? Holy shit. No wonder he just had a crash pad in Beverly Hills—he needed the space of Joshua Tree to *fit* this beast of a house. I mean, it was a palace. A fucking *palace*.

At the center was a mansion in and of itself, gleaming white in the afternoon sun. Attached to either side was another wing that was easily as big. So it was like three full-size mansions squashed together to make a mega-mansion. Two more and they could come together and be Mansion Voltron or some shit. I'm so not joking—this was unreal.

The driveway circled around in front of the central part of the house, and a gigantic marble fountain stood in the middle. I couldn't help sneering at it. There was probably an enormous swimming pool in the backyard, and I swore rich people in California had fountains and pools just as a *fuck you* to everyone else.

"*Look at me!*" they said with water spraying all over the desert. "*I'm so rich I don't have to* care *that there's a drought!*"

Jesse parked in front of the stairs leading up to the front door (who needs a door *that* big? Seriously?). We both paused to make sure our cell phones were charged and recording. Then, as we got out of the car, a Hispanic kid in a uniform that looked way too hot for this weather came jogging toward us. Jesse offered him a smile and handed him the keys, then gestured for me to follow him inside.

I didn't move. I needed a second. I mean, who the hell had valet parking at their house?

The Ambrose family, apparently. People who worked on Isaac Ambrose's films struggled to get by even on union-demanded wages, and the man had valet parking *at home*.

"Hayden?"

I shook myself, and as the valet drove the Porsche off to parts unknown, I followed Jesse up the stairs. Another staff member pulled open the immense door, and—look, I'm not kidding. The door was like three stories high and wide enough to pull a small plane through it. Does that seem excessive to anyone else?

I swore then and there that, in-law harmony be damned, if it turned out he was keeping a Cessna in his living room, I was going to have to strike a up a conversation about wealth distribution and oppressing workers.

"Good afternoon, Mr. Ambrose," the staff member said with a smile. To me, he just said, "Good afternoon, sir."

I smiled back. "Good afternoon."

We stepped inside, and the cold air was jarring after the heat outside. Naturally my brain immediately started trying to calculate how much it would cost to keep a place this big this cold. Turning on the AC in our apartment had required intense negotiations and precise budgeting, and this foyer alone was bigger than that apartment.

And when I say the foyer was bigger than my apartment, I don't mean it was bigger than the little box I'd shared with Ashton and Luis. I mean it was bigger than the building. Like someone could literally pick up the three-story six-unit building, plunk it down in this foyer, and probably not even disturb the crystal chandeliers hanging over the winding staircases.

Speaking of the staircases—the place naturally had those sweeping stairs that curved down from either side so someone could make a grand entrance. Everything was immaculate white and trimmed in shining black. Even the paintings on the walls were monochrome, and it was all elegant and gorgeous and—

No, really, someone could bring a *plane* in through those fucking doors or fit my *apartment* right here in the foyer. What. The hell.

I stared slack-jawed at everything. I'd already felt out

of my element living in Jesse's mind-blowing West Hollywood condo and riding shotgun in his Porsche. This was… it was unreal.

Footsteps turned my head, and I looked up to see a man descending the left staircase. His face took a second to register, but then it did.

Oh God.

Oh God.

Oh God.

That was Isaac Ambrose.

Isaac motherfucking Ambrose.

Isaac "I make and break actors' careers like a freaking Mafia don" Ambrose.

Isaac "I have more Oscars than you have brain cells" Ambrose.

And I was instantly a tongue-tied sweaty-palmed mess, and please, Jesse, introduce me because I don't remember my name and *holy shit it's Isaac Ambrose*.

As Isaac joined us on the ground floor, Jesse stood beside me. He stiffly shook hands with his father, then put a hand on the small of my back. "Dad, this is Hayden." Beat. "My fiancé."

My throat tightened so suddenly I nearly squeaked. Jesus, he was getting *right* to the point, wasn't he? No "*oh hey by the way now that you've chatted with him a bit, guess what?*" Nope. Right to the rings.

Isaac turned his gaze on me, and oh yeah, it was a hell of a lot more intimidating in person than it was on camera. Or maybe that was because he'd just found out two nanoseconds ago that I was about to be his new flaming gay son-in-law, and he was probably trying to Force choke me. He might have been succeeding, too, because I couldn't breathe.

"Your fiancé, hmm?" Isaac looked me up and down. Then he cut his eyes toward his son. "And when did this happen? Last I heard, you were still seeing Craig."

"Chris," Jesse corrected through gritted teeth. "We broke up a year ago."

"I see. So when did this"—Isaac gestured at the two of us—"start?"

"About six months ago."

I nodded. We'd spent last night getting our stories straight—how we met, how long we'd been dating, who'd proposed and when and how, the details of a handful of anecdotes we'd conjured up to sell the whole charade. As long as we both stuck to the script, we had an airtight timeline of the relationship leading up to our engagement.

Isaac opened his mouth to speak, but a set of determined high-heeled footsteps turned all of our heads toward the second floor. A moment later, a woman started down the right staircase, and I instantly recognized her. Even people living under rocks recognized Isaac Ambrose at a glance, and they also recognized his wife.

Carolyn Sherer-Ambrose was, like her husband, Hollywood royalty, and she had been even before she'd married Jesse's father. She'd come from one of those old acting dynasties with a family tree full of scandalous affairs, secret abortions, love children, lavender marriages, and more than a few people dying long before their time. Everyone who was anyone had known who Carolyn was long before she'd taken the Ambrose name.

From far away, she looked exactly like the woman who appeared on magazine covers. On-camera, she always looked decades younger, but in person, especially as she came closer, I could see how time, tragedy, and the California sun had taken their toll. She was gorgeous, but there was a touch of fatigue in her eyes that made me wonder if living in all this luxury was really worth it.

She offered her son a stiff hug, then stood beside her husband and looked me up and down, the scrutiny making my spine prickle. Demurely offering her hand, she said, "And you are?"

"Hayden." I shook her cool hand, flicking my eyes toward Jesse.

Jesse cleared his throat. "Hayden's my—"

"Were you aware that our son was engaged, dear?" Isaac sounded both bored and annoyed.

"Engaged?" Carolyn's fingers twitched in mine, and she gave me another down-up before letting go of my hand and looking at Jesse. In her eyes, there was a hint of alarm so subtle, I was amazed I'd even caught it. "I hadn't realized you were dating anyone."

Jesse smiled tightly. "We've been dating for a while. Just got engaged."

"I see." Carolyn shifted her attention to me. Then she wagged a long finger at me. "You look familiar. I swear I've seen you before."

"You've probably seen my brother. Brian Somerset."

"Brian—oh, the figure skater?"

I nodded. "We're identical twins, so I get mistaken for him all the time."

"Did your parents manage to have *any* straight children?" Isaac asked flatly.

"Darling," Carolyn growled. "Don't be rude to our guest. He doesn't know your sense of humor yet."

Sense of humor, my ass.

"It's okay." I smiled sweetly. "My brother has a wife and two kids."

I won't lie—I got *so* much satisfaction from the startled confusion on Isaac's face.

Jesse coughed, almost smothering the laugh. Carolyn seemed a bit confused, but she didn't say anything more.

Isaac scowled down at his watch. A diamond-studded gold Rolex, to the surprise of precisely no one. As he tugged his sleeve back down, he looked at Carolyn. "We still have some time yet before dinner. Why don't you give Hayden here a tour of the house? Maybe introduce him to everyone else?" He cut his eyes toward Jesse. "I'd like to have a word with my son."

"Of course." Carolyn eyed Jesse uneasily, then schooled her expression and smiled at me. "Let me show you around."

"Uh. Sure. Thanks." I looked at Jesse. He wasn't looking at me—his narrowed eyes were fixed on his father's.

After an uncomfortable second or two, he turned toward me. "I'll meet you in the dining room." He flashed a weak smile, and I didn't think I'd ever seen him so nervous. The smile only emphasized the tautness in his features and the worry in his eyes.

I was suddenly overwhelmed with the urge to take his hand, drag him out to the car, and get him the fuck away from this toxic place.

But my soon-to-be mother-in-law took my elbow, and Jesse didn't look at me as he started following his father up the stairs. Well shit. Maybe this was going down right now. Maybe we wouldn't be have to go through with the wedding after all. Hell, maybe we wouldn't even be here long enough for dinner.

As Carolyn gave me the grand tour of the immense house, I should have been gawking at the sheer size and opulence of the place, but none of it registered anymore.

I was too busy worrying about Jesse.

L.A. WITT

Chapter 8
Jesse

Walking into my father's study for a one-on-one conversation had always been unnerving. Well, not always. As a kid desperate for attention, these summons had been small victories. I'd finally done something that registered on his radar. Even getting chewed out and punished had been better than being ignored. Sure, I might walk out without my car keys, with the pieces of a cut-up bank card, or on occasion, a throbbing bruise from one of his rings connecting with my cheekbone, but at least for a few minutes, I'd been the center of my father's world.

I'd been well into high school before I'd finally figured out that more than just my face hurt after those encounters. The punishments, I could live with. The yelling, I was used to. The bruises had given me a reason to learn the art of makeup. It wasn't that bad, I'd told myself a million times.

But maybe I'd overestimated my capacity to hear what

a useless burden I was and how he had far more important things to attend to than the hopeless failure that was his son. And that was to say nothing of the barbs he'd never failed to throw in after I'd come out to him.

To this day, my father bragged that his tough love approach was what had straightened me out and turned me into an A student. In a way, I supposed he was right. Shame he never mentioned all the damage he'd done in the process.

Dad shut the French doors behind us, and he said nothing as he walked to his desk. We stood in silence for a moment in this room that was burned into my childhood memories. It was a big room just like every room in the house. Most of them seemed smaller now than they had when I was a kid simply because I had grown and my perception of space had changed. This one room, however, had stayed cavernous and intimidating. Or maybe it was just because I couldn't walk in here without feeling small. I couldn't even be around my father without feeling small, but the effect was amplified in here because this was the place where *talks* happened.

I willed myself not to tremble. Not my knees. Not my hands. Definitely not my voice. It was a challenge, though. No matter how much I'd mentally prepared for this or told myself it was worth it because my cell phone was recording every sound we made, I wasn't looking forward to it. There were things no man wanted to hear from his father, and I was here to provoke him into saying more of them than I was certain I could handle

Oblivious to my thoughts or the hot mic, Dad took off his glasses and looked at me as he released one of his customary long-suffering sighs. "I'm sure you're aware I'm going to start actively campaigning soon."

Gritting my teeth, I nodded. The election was still months away, but for candidates and their doting, loving families, the festivities started well in advance. "Yes. I know."

"Of course you do. There will be fundraisers and events coming up."

It took some serious effort not to ask why he needed fundraisers. Yeah, yeah, yeah, I knew how it worked—candidates who got the most contributions usually won. But who the fuck was going to donate to someone who probably paid more for landscaping every month than most people made in a year? Politics were weird.

The silence dragging out between us was weird too. Dad was watching me. I was watching him. The phone was silently recording, but we weren't giving it anything to record.

Finally, Dad said, "I need the whole family involved in the campaign. Voters want family unity, so it's all hands on deck."

"I know. We've talked about this."

"Mmhmm." Dad eyed me coldly. "We have. We've talked about a lot of things."

More silence. Long, loaded silence that wouldn't mean a goddamned thing to anyone listening to this recording.

After a solid minute, Dad spoke in a voice that was equal parts bored and annoyed: "I assume your wedding won't create a conflict."

I tongued the back of my teeth. Again, nothing damning if someone listened to the recording, but there was so much subtext there that only an Ambrose would pick up on. He was being careful about what he said. But he knew I heard his real meaning: "*You're not going to use this farce of a wedding to interfere with my campaign, are you?*" He couldn't use the threatening tone he wanted to use either. He was holding back, but I could feel it in the air and see it in his eyes—Dad was pissed. The way he stared at me—it was the same look of cold contempt he'd given me when I'd come out, and again when my high school boyfriend and I had been busted having sex. It wasn't quite hatred; in fact, it was almost worse. In some weird way I couldn't explain, it would have been easier to swallow if my father hated me than it was to stand here in the crosshairs of his icy dismissiveness. Knowing that while he hadn't said it out loud or put it to paper yet, Dad had already written me off. I was as good as disowned. An Ambrose in name only.

"*No son of mine is a*—" I shut off the echo of his voice before he got to the slur he'd flung at fifteen year-old me. His voice and his intent had been ugly enough: *If this is what you are, then you're not my son.*

Come on, Dad, I wanted to beg. *Just say it so we can be done with this and move on.*

He tapped his fingers on the edge of his desk like he often did when he was bored. "We've discussed this in the past, Jesse. This business of you marrying another man."

My stomach somersaulted. This was it. This was what I'd aimed for with my marriage gambit. This was why Hayden and I were here, and why my phone was surreptitiously recording from inside my pocket. So I set my jaw and refused to let my nerves show. "Yeah. We've discussed it."

We stared at each other. His eyes were hard like always, and the set of his jaw echoed that hardness. It reminded me of those moments just before he lost his temper. The calm before the storm. "But you're still going through with this."

"I want to marry Hayden." I shrugged as flippantly as I could. "If you and Mom don't want to be there, just say so, but I love him, and I'm marrying him." It didn't come out quite as defiantly as I'd hoped. My nerves slipped in more than I would have liked. But the words were out. The gauntlet had been thrown. The phone was recording.

Well, Dad. Ball's in your court.

He watched me for an uncomfortably long moment before he asked, his tone cold and flat, "Why now?"

"Why—" I laughed at the absurdity of the question. "Why *not* now?"

His icy features didn't budge. "You knew when my campaign would be starting. It couldn't wait until after the election?"

"I don't see why your campaign should have anything to do with it."

We locked eyes, and his jaw seemed as tightly set as mine, especially as he growled, "You can't have known this man for very long."

"You only knew Mom for three months."

"That's different."

"Is it?"

Dad glared at me. I thought he'd press, but instead, he checked his watch. As he tugged his sleeve back into place, he met my gaze again. "Well. I suppose we should join the family for dinner. Your brother and sister can't stay late."

Panic knifed through me. No, no. We had to do this now while I still had the courage to face him. "You don't want to talk about this?"

"Not here." He gestured casually toward the door.

"Seems like it should be a family matter, don't you think?"

My throat was suddenly sour. On one hand, I wanted witnesses in addition to the electronic one in my pocket. On the other, I looked forward to seeing my elder siblings about as much as I looked forward to seeing my parents. Even if the outcome of the next hour or so was exactly what I'd been aiming for, the process wasn't going to be any more pleasant than doing this one on one with Dad.

"All right," I croaked. "Let's go join everyone else."

Neither of us spoke as we left the office, and a moment later, Dad and I walked into the dining room to find everyone else already seated. Mom. Hayden. My sister Amanda and her husband, Mark. My brother Carson and his wife, Vanessa. Pity my younger sister lived in Atlanta. At least she and I got along okay. The only one of my siblings I could honestly say I was close to was my younger brother, Alex, and he was in New York. Not that he'd be here anyway since he'd been an ex-Ambrose for almost five years.

As I came around the table to take the empty seat beside Hayden, his expression was hard to read, but seemed to be equal parts "*are you okay?*" and "*please get me the hell out of here.*"

I attempted a reassuring smile as I sat beside him, and I gave his arm a squeeze. "You've met my siblings?"

He nodded, as did my brother, sister, and their spouses.

"So you're actually getting married," Carson said flatly. "Never thought I'd see the day." Something in his tone and the look he shot me added an unspoken, "*Are you really this fucking stupid?*"

I smiled as genuinely as I could. "Well, you know how

it is." I nodded toward my sister-in-law. "When you meet the right person."

The three of us exchanged sour looks. Carson's wife, Vanessa, was a stunningly gorgeous and talented actress with a family so connected and influential, they impressed *my* family. Dad had raved about her and encouraged them to get married, and even now he bragged about what a gorgeous "power couple" they were.

All it took was five minutes in their company for someone to figure out Vanessa and Carson *hated* each other.

Admittedly, I felt guilty for the barb. It wasn't like I reveled in my brother's misery. I felt sorry for both of them. But snide remarks, backhanded compliments, and petty digs were about the only way my siblings and I knew how to communicate with each other.

My father cleared his throat. "So. Since Jesse and…" He narrowed his eyes at Hayden. "Tell me your name again?"

"Hayden," I growled, knowing damn well that was a game Dad played to make sure someone knew they weren't worth remembering. "His name is *Hayden*."

Beside me, Hayden shifted so subtly I doubted anyone else noticed. I put a hand on his knee, as much to reassure him as to passive-aggressively remind my father that, yes, we were a couple. Hayden put his hand over the top of mine, his fingers and palms damp with sweat. Jesus, he must have been nervous as hell.

I owe you so big for this.

"Hayden. Right." Dad folded his hands on the table. "Have the two of you decided when you're getting married? And where?"

"Not yet." Hayden glanced at me, and he smiled nervously. "The sooner the better, right?"

I smiled back, squeezing his hand. "Definitely. We might as well do it ASAP so it doesn't land in the middle of the campaign."

Dad's expression hardened, and I held my breath, waiting for the hammer to drop. This was it. This was what I'd come here for.

Say it.

Say it in front of Mom, Carson, and Amanda.

Say *it, asshole.*

He reached for his glass. Everyone was still while he took a deep swallow of wine, and no one moved when he set the glass back down with a near-silent clink. Then he turned to my mother, and they exchanged looks I couldn't have read to save my life. My mom had a poker face that was second to none, but uneasiness was coming off her in waves like a bad perfume.

Finally, he took her hand on the table and turned to the rest of us. "Well, since it's become somewhat of a family tradition, I propose you use the house for your wedding."

The ripple of tension would have been undetectable to anyone not familiar with the subtleties of the Ambrose family. The way my brother's spine stiffened. My sister's lips thinning into a nearly invisible line. My mother's smile that meant she was only smiling to keep up appearances but would be having *words* with someone later.

Hayden glanced at me, probably wondering what the hell was going on and why my hand had suddenly tightened on his leg.

And suddenly everyone was watching me, waiting for

a response.

I cleared my throat, but that didn't work, so I took a gulp of wine. "Uh. Really? You're going to let us use the house?"

"This, or the one in Beverly Hills." Dad shrugged, smiling thinly. "We'll just need some time for preparations, but your mother has some event planners who can probably handle everything."

My mother's smile warmed as much as it ever did. "What about a honeymoon? Have you two thought of where you'd like to go? Hayden, where would you like to have your honeymoon?"

Beside me, he was stiff as a board, his thigh muscles suddenly hard as diamonds. "Um." He did the same thing I did—a quick drink followed by a muffled cough. "Hadn't... hadn't really thought that far ahead yet."

"Well." She sipped her own wine. "Give it some thought and let me know. I can make the arrangements."

"Mom, you don't have to do that," I said.

"No, I insist. Your wedding and honeymoon are on us, sweetheart." She glanced at Dad, who'd reddened slightly and set his jaw. Then she looked at Hayden. "Unless of course your family wants to contribute something. I don't want to step on any toes."

For fuck's sake, only my mom could turn a grand offer into a slap across Hayden's face.

Hayden cleared his throat again. "I, um..."

"We appreciate it, Mom." I returned her thin-lipped smile. "Thank you."

"Yeah," Hayden whispered. "Thank you. That's... that's amazing."

Mom just smiled, but when her eyes met mine, they

said nothing if not *"what are you doing, you idiot?"*

As dinner was served, I had no idea how I was going to get anything down, never mind keep it there. So it was on. My parents knew about our "engagement," and apparently we really were in this for the long game. Dad wasn't going to make a big move until he was sure I'd put my money where my mouth was.

Offering up the house for the wedding *and* letting my mother give us a honeymoon? That was a move I hadn't anticipated.

I didn't buy that it was a show of support. No, this was a calculated move, much like mine, and I'd need to think long and hard before I made my next one.

"Jesse, sweetheart." My mother put on one of those smiles that just made her eyes look chillier. "Could I borrow you outside for a minute?"

I glanced at Hayden. We'd settled into the living room with my siblings after dinner, and while nobody was being outwardly hostile, I couldn't say the conversation was exactly comfortable. I wasn't so sure about leaving Hayden alone in shark-infested waters. "Um…"

"It's okay." He gave my arm a reassuring squeeze. "I'll be fine." He almost sold it, too. If not for that faint hint of *please don't stay out there too long* in the creases of his forehead, I might have bought it. No wonder he'd been an aspiring actor. He sure as shit had the chops for it.

"All right." I patted his leg, then rose off the gigantic sofa. "I'll just be a minute." That wasn't a lie— conversations with my mother were nearly always short and to the point. She didn't like to give us a chance to rally and turn anything she said back on her.

Hayden's smile nearly masked his nerves, and he took a deep swallow from his wineglass. At least he was smart enough to drink. That was about the only way to make a visit with my family go down smoothly. Or keep you from giving a shit if it didn't, anyway.

Though I didn't have nearly enough booze in my own system for the exchange that was probably waiting for me, I followed my mother out to one of the many terraces along the backside of the house. With her back to me, she didn't see me take out my phone, make sure it was still recording, and pocket it again.

Alone on the terrace, we faced each other while my phone collected every sound we made. It was cooler out here now that the sun had gone down. Cold enough to make my teeth want to chatter. Or maybe that had more to do with the way my mom was watching me with hard eyes, her jaw set and her posture stiff.

She took in one of those long, deep breaths that meant she had something to *say*. "Jesse. I need you to be straight—" Beat. "I need you to be *honest* with me."

On any other day, her Freudian slip might've made me laugh. Not today. "About what?"

She folded her arms and glared at me. "I know how you feel about your father's politics. And he and I both know you're not happy about him running for governor."

I nodded, but didn't speak.

"Is this some kind of game you're playing with your father?" She inclined her head. "This marriage to Hayden?"

Yes, Mom. It's a game called chess. And it's a two-player game, so stay out of it.

I swallowed. "Is that what you think? That the only reason I could possibly find a man who wants to marry me is if I'm playing some sort of reindeer games with Dad's political career?" Wow, now that I'd said it out loud, that was kind of sad.

Note to self—when this is all over? Try for a slightly less pathetic existence.

Mom's lips thinned until they were nearly invisible, and her eyes narrowed until I could barely resist the urge to fidget. Finally, she said, "Whether it's a game or not, you know your father. Don't test him, Jesse."

"So you think he'll stick to his guns? About—"

"Don't be stupid," she snapped. "Of course he will. Even if he magically turned into a rainbow-flag waving supporter of people like you, he isn't going to back down from his word." She stepped closer, and even from an arm's length apart, her whisper barely reached me. "Do you have to marry Hayden? Can't the two of you just… well, if you must make it official, can't you do it discreetly? There can't be anything gained from a marriage to him that will make up for everything you'll lose once your father puts his foot down." She stabbed a long finger at me. "And you *know* he will."

I gulped, hoping the expression came across like I was second-guessing my engagement to Hayden. That I didn't look like someone nervously watching my plan go forward exactly the way it was intended to.

Or maybe she could see the hurt digging deeper as this conversation went on, because holy hell, this was painful. Over the years, I'd gone back and forth trying to figure out if Mom was my ally or not. She'd been more or less supportive when I'd come out. I'd never had the impression she was particularly thrilled about it, but she'd convinced my father not to kick me out by telling him how good it would make him look to his industry—and for his future political ambitions—if he accepted his gay son. A manipulative play, sure, but it had kept a roof over my scared fifteen year-old head, so I'd accepted that the end justified the means.

She took a deep swallow of wine, then looked in my eyes. "You need to think about what you're doing. Not just to yourself, but to this family." She threw up a hand. "For God's sake, I fought hard to get him to let you stay, and I compromised on marriage as the line in the sand because I assumed that even if it ever became legal, you wouldn't be this stupid. Do you really want to challenge him? Do you think he'll suddenly soften his stance just because there's an election coming up?"

I avoided her eyes. Oh, yes, I did want to challenge him and I was betting everything I had that he hadn't softened his stance.

"I fought hard for you," she growled. "Why did I even bother if you're just going to go ahead and jeopardize your place in this family anyway?"

"Because I was fifteen and needed my parents to not throw me out on the street," I threw back. We both jumped, probably equally shocked that I'd said it.

She deflated suddenly, as if she'd been trying to telepathically talk me out of this wedding, and had realized she was failing. "For God's sake, Jesse. Don't be an idiot." Her voice shook just slightly. "Don't do this and cut yourself off from everyone and everything you've ever known. It's not worth it."

Eyes locked on hers, I steeled myself. "Hayden's worth it." Destroying Dad's political ambitions? *Totally* worth it.

She sighed heavily, dropping her arms to her sides and shaking her head. "All right. All right. Do what you want to do. But don't say I didn't warn you about the consequences."

"I know what I'm getting myself into."

She studied me, then gave her head another shake and headed for the door.

"Mom."

She paused.

"If you and Dad are so against it, why the wedding? And the honeymoon?"

"You're our son." She half-shrugged as if it took all the effort in the world. "What kind of mother would I be if I didn't?"

"But you'll let him cut me off."

"Do you think I can stop him?"

"Would you try if you could?"

Our eyes locked for a long, silent moment. Then she continued back into the house.

Once she was gone, I turned off my phone's voice record function and made sure the file was saved. It wasn't enough, but it was something. More than I'd gotten from him, anyway. On its own, Dad could easily downplay it by claiming my mother was hysterical or delusional. Wouldn't be the first time. I needed something from him before any of this stuck.

Admittedly, I felt kind of guilty for recording my mom like that, but whatever. It wasn't like she was going to stop him, so why should I feel bad about using her words to bury him?

Exhaling hard, I leaned against the terrace railing. I didn't *want* my mom to stop him. Not this time. I needed him to cut me off, ideally as loudly and publicly as possible.

But I wasn't going to lie—it hurt to get confirmation that he'd go through with this.

And it cut to the bone to know that when he did, my mother wouldn't stand in his way.

Not a moment too soon, my father's slowly closing front gate disappeared in my rearview mirror, and I released the longest breath I had in hours.

Beside me, Hayden pressed his elbow against the window and rubbed his forehead. "Well that was an interesting way to spend an evening."

"Always is." I tapped the wheel and glanced at him. "By the way, I'm sorry about what he said about you and your brother."

"Oh. Pfft." Hayden snickered. "Just be glad I didn't tell him the truth."

"The truth?"

"Yep. Brian *is* married to a woman, but—" He cupped his mouth and added in a stage whisper, "He's bisexual."

"What?" I dramatically put a hand to my chest. "Say it isn't so."

"It's so. But I kind of wanted to see the look on your dad's face when he realized my brother isn't gay. Just a little white lie, you know?"

"So Brian isn't out?"

"Oh, he is, but by the time he came out, the media had

pretty much forgotten he ever existed. Like 'yeah, yeah, you like dudes, but can you still skate? That's what we thought.'"

"Brutal."

"The skating world is brutal, sweetheart." Hayden settled back against the seat. "He actually came out to me a long time before that. In fact there was this one night after his first trip to the Olympics? Back when we were still kind of close? He got hammered and decided to be a bit, uh, candid. I was DD that night, so I was sober, which means I remember *everything*. I swear on all that's holy there is not enough brain bleach in the world to cleanse my mind of all his stories about Olympic Village."

"I thought that was all a myth."

"Are you kidding? They literally have condom shortages at Olympic Villages." He chuckled. "It makes sense if you think about it. A bunch of young, hot athletes in peak physical condition after training like hell? You don't think they won't get naked and blow off some steam?"

"Man." I whistled. "I really shouldn't have dropped out of snowboarding."

Hayden chuckled. "Nope. Then maybe it would be *you* telling me about a sweaty threesome with a couple of Scandinavian speed skaters instead of my goddamned brother."

That got as much of a laugh out of me as I was capable after a visit to my parents' house. And I was admittedly kind of curious about his twin and why they weren't close anymore, but now didn't seem like the time to bring it up. Instead I said, "I'm afraid I don't have any stories like that."

He huffed melodramatically. "You're no fun."

"Do you have any?"

He thought for a second. "Well, none that involve Scandinavian speed skaters, no, but I have a few."

"Oh yeah?" I glanced at him. "Do tell."

"You going to share any of your dirty little secrets?"

"Depends on how dirty yours are. So, you first."

Hayden clicked his tongue. "Fine. But so help me, if yours is just some boring story involving missionary in the dark…"

I laughed with some actual feeling this time. "I can come up with something a little more scandalous than that. But like I said, you first."

He huffed again. "Okay. Well. There's no way to prove it, but my friend and his wife are pretty sure I was partly involved in the conception of their baby."

"What?" I shot him a puzzled look. "How can you be 'partly' involved?"

"I was fucking him while he was fucking her. He came, and nine months later…"

"Wow." I chuckled. "Were they, um, happy about this?"

"Oh yeah." Hayden gestured dismissively. "They'd been trying for a while anyway, and when she finally got pregnant, the timing was hilarious. His wife joked about renting me out to couples who were having trouble conceiving, but none of her friends' husbands were willing to try the ol' take it up the ass and knock up your wife method."

"Gee, I can't imagine why."

"Straight guys, am I right?"

"So right."

He chuckled. "Okay. Your turn. Tell me something scandalous."

I thought about it, tapping my thumbs on the wheel and wondering if anything in my sexual history could compete with banging a guy while he knocked up his wife. There were a few, actually, but some had baggage attached that I didn't really want to think about tonight. It was weird, realizing just how many of my sexual escapades were less "*let's do something wild and memorable*" and more "*how about a literal fuck off*" to some authority figure in my life. That was a depressing train of thought, so I didn't go there.

"Well." I cleared my throat. "I guess if the theme is threesomes…"

Hayden perked up, and I could hear him grinning as he said, "Mmhmm?"

I laughed. "Perv."

"Guilty, honey. Now fess up."

"Okay, okay." I paused to overtake a slow-moving truck, and as I eased back into my lane, continued. "About five years ago, I was at a club with my boyfriend at the time. We ran into my ex, and I don't know if it was sheer coincidence or if that area's gay scene was just that small, but it turned out he was my boyfriend's ex too."

"No way." Hayden thumped the console between us. "You're lying."

"It's true! I swear!" I said. "Zach dated Marco about six months before Marco and I started dating, and then Zach and I met a while after Marco and I split."

"I can't decide if that sounds really fucked up or kinda hot."

"Don't know." I flashed him a grin. "But the rest of

the night was pretty damn hot."

"Yeah?"

I nodded, and couldn't help shivering at the memory. "None of our relationships ever worked out, but all of us had been seriously compatible in bed. There was still tons of chemistry between all of us, so after a couple of drinks, we ended up going back to Zach's place that night." I whistled. "Holy fuck. One of the hottest nights of my life. Hands down." Even now, the memory of being naked with both those men threatened to give me a hard-on, especially while I was still imagining Hayden having a threesome with a guy and his wife. Good thing the sun had gone down; if I could keep from obviously adjusting myself, then maybe things wouldn't get weird.

"Man." Hayden squirmed beside me, which didn't help. "I haven't had a threesome in ages. Used to have them all the time when I was dating my ex."

"Really? Why's that?"

"His best friend was with a guy who was ace and wanted absolutely nothing to do with sex, but the other guy had a really high libido. So, they all had an arrangement where my ex and his friend could have sex, and that included whoever my ex was dating at the time. So…" He spread his arms. "Me!"

I laughed. "That must have been a fun arrangement."

"Oh my God, yes. They're probably still doing it, and quite honestly, that's about the only thing I miss about that relationship."

"Yeah, I've had those. Where you hang on longer than you should just because the sex is great?"

"Yes! God. I've done that so many times." He groaned, probably rolling his eyes. "I have wasted so much time on utter jackholes just because they were good in bed."

"You and me both." I *almost* mentioned how much I'd been itching to get laid recently. The comment very nearly slipped out because for a moment, I'd forgotten that Hayden wasn't my boyfriend or even a friend who I could be unabashedly candid with. Somehow, mentioning to the man I was about to marry (sort of) that I was horny seemed... like it could complicate things. So I kept my mouth shut.

We drove in comfortable silence for a couple of miles, my mind whirring with memories that I'd probably be thinking about after I'd gone to bed later tonight. I was curious what was on Hayden's mind after our conversation, but I was afraid to ask.

After a while, he broke the silence. "Can I ask a really stupid question?"

"Shoot."

Hayden turned toward me. "Why the hell is your dad's front door so big?"

I barked a laugh. "You noticed?"

"Uh, yeah? It's kinda hard to miss."

"Yeah, that's kinda the point."

"Is it?"

I nodded. "Okay, so, before they moved to Joshua Tree, my parents lived in Palm Springs, and the place there had a big door on the front. Huge fancy thing. Then one of my dad's friends built something in Malibu with one that was like a foot bigger. My dad went to his place for a party, and my mom says he spent the whole night complaining that his friend did it on purpose to one-up him. Six months later, he and Mom were putting together plans for the place in Joshua Tree—"

"Oh my God. You're not serious. He did not ask for a bigger door than his buddy's."

"He did. He absolutely did."

"That's…" Hayden started giggling so hard he could barely speak. "I thought it was like the house equivalent of a big truck. You know, compensating? But now you're… you're telling me it really was… basically a dick-measuring contest with someone else?"

His giggling was contagious. "I never thought of it like that."

"Oh God…" He wiped his eyes. "When they make… when they make a biopic on him someday?" He snorted and let his head fall back against the seat. "They should call it Door Wars."

We both howled with laughter. I almost had to pull over, but I managed to stay between the lines, and as I started to calm down, I realized how completely bizarre it was to be laughing right now. The drive home from my father's house usually involved clenching my teeth until they ached and gripping the wheel so tight my hands hurt. But no, we weren't even past Palm Springs yet and Hayden had gotten a real laugh out of me. He'd distracted me from everything by swapping scandalous sexcapades, and then he'd made me laugh for real over my dad's ridiculous door.

The drive continued like that for a while—shooting the shit, talking about random things, laughing as if we hadn't just spent a few miserable hours in my family's company. And like it always did, the conversation eventually hit a lull.

"So. Um." Hayden shifted in his seat, the leather squeaking softly. "Okay, I have another question."

"All right?"

"Is your dad just fucking with us? Or is he actually onboard with this?"

Annnd there went my good mood. Gripping the wheel tighter, I gritted my teeth. "He's bluffing. He thinks I'm doing this to get a reaction out of him—"

"Which you technically are."

"Which I technically am," I acknowledged with a nod. "But he probably doesn't think I'll actually go through with it, so he's—as you put it—playing chicken with me. Which I expected."

"Did you expect him to let us get married at his house?"

I gnawed the inside of my cheek. "Well. No."

"So it's possible he's—"

"No, he's bluffing. From the conversation he and I had in his office?" I shook my head. "There's no way he's onboard with this. I suspect he just wants to be sure I'm really doing this before he actually makes a move. Maybe give me enough rope to hang myself." I paused. "The thing is, Dad is the kind of chess player who doesn't try to win via the fewest moves. He'll seem like he's letting you win, and by the time you realize he's been steadily knocking all your pieces off the board, you're two moves away from checkmate." I stared at the road ahead and made a conscious effort to loosen my grasp on the wheel before my hands started hurting too much. "Dad plays the long game. So that's what I have to assume he's doing now."

"What's his angle right now, do you think?"

"Wait until I let my guard down, make me believe I'm winning, and then get a charge out of stomping me into the dirt."

"Whoa." Hayden was quiet for a moment. "What if he *isn't* bluffing, though?"

"He is."

"Humor me. If we've landed in some parallel dimension where the sky is green and every day is Taco Tuesday, and your dad really does support his son marrying another man—then what?"

I swallowed hard. *Then maybe I'll believe my dad actually loves me.* "Then I guess we go through the motions, same as we'd planned. You'll still get paid. We'll still get divorced."

"But what about the election?"

My heart sank. I was out of cards where my father's political career was concerned. "I don't know. If this doesn't work, then... fuck, maybe this was a mistake. I'm sorry. I shouldn't have pulled you into—"

"Hey, hey." Hayden put a hand on my knee. "It's not a mistake. I'm not bailing on this and neither are you. I just wanted to know what Plan B is."

"That's the problem." I swallowed. "There *is* no Plan B."

"Well." He squeezed my leg and withdrew his hand. "Then I guess we'd better make sure Plan A works."

I nodded, but said nothing.

Yeah. We'd better make sure Plan A works.

Because if it doesn't, I've got nothing.

L.A. WITT

Chapter 9
Hayden

So, apparently Jesse and I were getting married. This was happening. Families had been informed, tabloids familiar with the Ambrose family were sniffing around—though there were enough political and celebrity scandals lately that we didn't warrant much attention—and preparations were underway. Suddenly it wasn't just a plan on paper. We were going through all the motions, putting up all the decorations, and filling out all the paperwork, which meant our lives were suddenly consumed with planning. Okay not that we would be the ones physically putting up decorations and crap since Carolyn insisted on hiring people for everything short of wiping the wedding party's asses, but we did have to make all the decisions about all the details. And holy fuck, why were there so many details?

"*Christ.*" I dropped the binder onto the mile-high stack of similar binders on the kitchen island. "I didn't do this much prep the first time I bottomed."

Jesse choked on his coffee.

"Sorry," I said.

"No you're not." He coughed a couple of times.

"Yeah, you're right." I suppressed a smirk. Sort of. "You okay?"

He flipped me off, so I took that as a yes. Once he'd recovered enough to speak, he said, "We could just leave it in my mom's hands and let her plan it all." He scowled. "Except then she'd call every five minutes to make sure we're okay with whatever overpriced eccentric scheme she's thought up this time."

I wrinkled my nose. "Ugh. Do you think your parents would take it well if I said I wanted to use paper streamers from the dollar store and print the invitations on an old Dot Matrix?"

Jesse eyed me. "I dare you to suggest it. And keep a straight face."

I returned the challenging look. "Don't tempt me, darling, because I will absolutely do it."

He laughed, shaking his head. "Now that you mention it, I believe you. Completely."

"And I guess we need to make it look like a real posh Ambrose wedding if we're going to sell this."

"Unfortunately, yeah." He grimaced. "Sorry."

I grunted softly. "But I'm all for shortcuts where I can find them. Pity it's considered gauche to print out address labels. We're going to have to handwrite all of these goddamned envelopes, and my handwriting is terrible, so I nominate *you*."

A second too late I remembered the wrist brace he was wearing, but before I could back pedal, he shrugged.

"Oh, don't worry about the envelopes. Mom's hiring a calligrapher."

"She's hiring…" I turned around and peered at him. "Wait, those exist?"

"Um, yeah?" He eyed me like I'd just ask if shoes or supermarkets existed.

"You rich people live in a different world. And holy fuck, a calligrapher sounds archaic and expensive, so I'm just going to sit here and be grateful that your parents are footing the bill. Otherwise everyone would just get emails. Or Facebook invites." I groaned. "*God*, wouldn't it be awesome if we could do this whole thing via a Facebook event?"

Jesse laughed and playfully nudged me with his elbow. "Keep dreaming, sweetheart."

"Fuck you. And why am I doing all of this? What are *you* doing?"

He shot me a look. "Besides handling all the calls and texts from"—his phone vibrated on the counter—"my mother?" As he snatched the phone up, he muttered, "There's a whole other stack of those binders next to my bed if you get bored."

"Hmm, yeah. No. I'll pass."

"That's what I thought." He put his phone down and looked at me plaintively. "So, as long as I'm not working today, how would you feel about doing some of the preparations we can't do at home?"

"Such as…?"

"Getting fitted for tuxes? Picking out rings?"

"Oh." I glanced down at the binder in front of me, then shut it with a heavy thunk. "Sure. I could use a break from all this." Butterflies went wild in my stomach. Tuxes?

Rings? Oh, wow, this was getting… well, as real as this wedding was going to get.

On the way out, Jesse started to take his keys off the hook, but paused. "Do you, um, want to take your car?"

I narrowed my eyes, searching his expression for sarcasm. "Why?"

"You just got it, and I haven't ridden in it yet." He shrugged. "It's up to you."

"You don't mind slumming it in my little used piece of shit?"

He frowned. "Come on. I apologized, and I meant it. I know that car means a lot to you, so…" He gestured at the door.

I didn't move.

Jesse sighed. "I'm trying here. I know I said something stupid. But… I really am trying."

"I know. But I mean, you don't have to humor me. If you don't like the car, we can take yours."

"I like it just fine. And you obviously do too." He took my keys off the hook and tossed them to me. "Also, yours gets better mileage."

That got a laugh out of me, even if it was a slightly uncomfortable one. "Oh, now the truth comes out."

"Uh-huh. I'll pay for gas since we're taking your car."

Well, I wasn't going to say no to gas money, so I shrugged, pocketed my wallet and phone, and followed him out of the condo.

Down in the parking garage, I slowed down on the way to the car. "You really don't mind taking mine?"

"Not at all." He didn't sound patronizing. In fact he sounded pretty genuine. And he had apologized after the way he'd responded to seeing my car for the first time, so maybe I should give him a little credit. Or a little room to tip his hand and reveal that, yeah, he was a dick about things like this.

So, without a word, I unlocked the car.

As we got in, he said, "Damn, this thing *is* pretty nice."

"You sound surprised." And I sounded bitchier than I should have.

He exhaled. "Look, I'm sorry about what I said. And, hell…" He looked around at the car's interior. "Maybe you're smarter than I am because my car doesn't really have anything this one doesn't aside from a fancy name." Pulling on his seat belt, he added, "You paid for a car. I paid for a brand name. Now who's the smart one?"

I laughed quietly, relaxing a bit as I started the engine. "They're both upgrades from the hooptie I was driving before, so we'll call it even."

"Fair enough."

"So, where to?"

"First stop—tuxes."

In my head, I'd imagined us going to one of those tux rental places where kids went before prom. I suppose I shouldn't have been surprised when that turned out to be wrong. Jesse's directions took us to a high-end tailor shop with Fittings By Appointment Only etched in snooty cursive on the tinted glass door.

I glanced at Jesse. "Uh, do we need an appointment?"

"We have one."

"We do?"

"Yeah." He gestured with his phone as he reached for the door with his other hand. "I texted Steve in the car."

Steve. We were on a first name basis with the tailor. All right then.

I followed Jesse into a warmly lit showroom with a handful of flawlessly cut tuxes and suits on display. Soft classical music played in the background, and there were a few framed photos on the wall of celebrities in what I assumed were clothes they'd bought here. Somehow I wasn't surprised that one of those pictures was of Isaac. He was standing on a red carpet, his arm around Jesse's mom, both smiling brilliantly for the cameras.

"Jesse!" A white-haired man with a measuring tape hanging over his shoulders stepped out from the back, arms out. "It's been ages!"

"I know, I know." Jesse hugged the guy. "Thanks for squeezing us in on short notice."

"Squeezing you in? Pfft. I've always got room in the schedule for an Ambrose."

A grimace flickered across Jesse's lips, but he schooled his expression and gestured at me. "Steve, this is Hayden. My fiancé."

Steve turned to me and looked me up and down as he extended his hand. "Great to meet you, son. And what a surprise—I had no idea you were even seeing anyone."

Jesse smiled thinly. "We've kind of managed to stay off the press's radar, even with the cat out of the bag. Guess we're just not that interesting."

"I could think of worse things, kiddo," Steve said with a big smile. "All right. Let's get you both measured. Have you thought about what style you want? Are you thinking black or white?"

"Black is fine," Jesse said. "Might as well get something we can wear again."

My head snapped toward him. "Wear again? We're not... are we *buying* these?" They both looked at me incredulously, and I added, "Do I really need to buy one? I mean, when am I going to wear it again?"

"At any number of my dad's black tie parties?"

I wrinkled my nose and stuck out my tongue. "You're really not selling this, hon."

He laughed. "Seriously, it doesn't hurt to have one."

"I'll take your word for it."

The tailor turned to me, pen poised over a wrinkled notepad. "Are we also doing groomsmen?"

"No," Jesse said. Fortunately, that was one of the many things we'd already ironed out. There was too much pressure for Jesse to have his older brother as his best man despite their shitty relationship, some drama involving his younger brother, and no one else he really wanted to have *instead* of one of his brothers, so the most painless solution had been to skip groomsmen altogether. That was fine by me. I'd never be able to choose a best man between Ashton and Luis, and *not* asking my own brother would cause some serious tension. At the end of the day, I didn't want any hurt feelings.

Except my roommates, dad, and (presumably) brother *would* be at the wedding, which would be one of those Ambrose black-tie affairs. So even if they weren't standing at the altar with me, they needed tuxes.

"Okay, at the risk of sounding completely clueless..." I chewed my lip. "I really want Ashton and Luis to come, and my family's going to be there. I'm not sure if any of them can afford..." I motioned toward a display of designer jackets. "Are they going to stick out like sore thumbs if they're wearing rentals?"

"They don't have to." Jesse shrugged. "If Ashton and Luis can come in here and get measured, and your dad and brother email their measurements, we'll put their tuxes on the tab."

I blinked. "Wait, you're buying them tuxes too?"

"Considering everything they've put up with?" He nodded. "Hell yeah."

"Oh. Okay. I'll, um… I'll text them and let them know."

~*~

After we'd finished getting measured and picking out tux styles, it was time for the next stop on the epic journey to fake marriage—the jewelry store.

Naturally, it wasn't one of those chain places in a mall. No, this was one of those fancy-ass free-standing joints with armed security out front who had to buzz our asses in.

I very nearly balked at the heavily guarded entrance. Years of being painfully poor had made me avoid places like this out of some irrational fear that my debit and credit cards would decline the second I walked in. I wouldn't even have to buy anything. Just walk in, and all the computers would start spitting out DECLINED messages and everyone would look at me like *get the fuck out, riffraff.*

Yeah, I know, it's irrational. Shut up. Being stressed and hungry makes you think irrational things. Don't judge me.

Anyway. Giving the jewelry store my customary wide berth wasn't an option today, and as we walked in, the security guards didn't try to stop me, no one gave us dirty looks, and no computers loudly announced that we had no business there. Right, because I was there with Jesse von

Richdad, and not only were they not turning him away, they greeted him. No, not like that. Not the "*hi, can I help you find something and oh by the way in between pressuring you to spend money I'm also going to follow you around the store so you don't steal anything*" greeting.

No, I'm telling you, a sixty-something lady in a black pantsuit stepped out from behind the cases, extended a hand that was dripping with gold and diamonds, and exclaimed, "Mr. Ambrose! It's wonderful to see you again!"

And then she shook his hand and hugged him, and he did one of those fake cheek kisses that rich people do for some reason, and then he turned to me. "Debbie, this is Hayden, my fiancé."

"Fiancé?" Her eyes were instantly huge, and she extended her hand to me. "Oh congratulations, honey. Hayden, right?"

"Yes, ma'am." I shook her hand.

"Ma'am." She laughed and patted my arm. "So polite. How did you get mixed up with this one?"

"Hey!" Jesse said with a laugh.

She winked. "Well, if you're here with your lovely fiancé, you must be in the market for a couple of rings."

"Yes, we are," Jesse said.

"Wonderful. Come with me." She led us over to a brightly lit glass case, and as she went around behind it, she said, "Have you given any thought to what you want? Gold? Platinum? Diamonds?"

I stared down at the assortment of rings. Platinum? *Diamonds?* My brother and my dad both wore slim and somewhat battered plain gold bands. That seemed like enough to me.

"I don't have anything in mind." Jesse put a hand on the small of my back. "What about you?"

"Uh." Christ, now he was touching me, probably to sell the whole act of loving fiancés, and it was scrambling what was left of my brain. "N-no. Hadn't, um, hadn't thought of anything yet."

"Well, we have plenty of options." She reached into the case and withdrew a small rectangular pad containing a dozen rings. "These are bridal sets, but just ignore the ladies' rings. If you see a men's ring you like, we can certainly sell it separately."

I eyed the selection warily. They were thick bands—some gold, some platinum—and there were diamonds. Like... *diamonds*. Not little diamond crumbs, but fat sparkly boulders that could blind someone in the right light. Or straight up put an eye out. I was kind of terrified to touch any of them, especially since I might jostle them enough to see the price tag, and I was convinced any one of these rings cost more than my car, and I don't mean the dying one the dealership took off my hands. And, like, I'd just *bought* a car. Now I was supposed to get one of these things too?

Not surprisingly, Jesse wasn't as intimidated, and he pulled a ring from the pad. It was a wide platinum band with five diamonds set snugly into a channel. He put it on, and of course it fit perfectly.

"Good thing you wear your watch on your right arm," I mused. "That plus the ring, and you wouldn't be able to stand up straight."

He laughed. "You're probably right. It's seriously heavy."

"Platinum *is* heavier than gold," Debbie helpfully

supplied.

"Hmm. Maybe gold is better, then." Jesse slid the ring off and gave it back. As he peered at the other options, he rubbed his hand gingerly and his lips pulled into a wince.

Debbie put the tray back into the case. "You know, I just remembered we got in some new pieces this week. They aren't even out on display yet. If you gentlemen will wait right here for a second, I'll go get them out of the vault."

As soon as we were alone, I whispered, "Your hands bothering you?"

He glanced at me, then at his hands, and as he faced me again, he slid them into his pockets and smiled. "Nah, they're fine. Probably just need another ibuprofen when we stop for lunch."

Wait, stop for lunch? We're going to buy tuxes and rings and still have money left over for lunch?

Whoa. I guess we are. Being rich is weird.

"Are you sure?" I asked. "We don't have to do this today."

"It's okay. They're just flaring up a bit, but I might as well try on rings while my fingers are puffy. Make sure I can still get the damn thing off."

"And then have it fall off when your fingers aren't swollen?"

He pursed his lips. Finally, he shrugged. "I'll just take it off when my hands are swollen. And, you know, hope the press doesn't notice I'm not wearing my ring."

I gulped. "Are the paparazzi actually going to care about us?"

"Maybe, maybe not." He shrugged like it was the most inconsequential thing ever. "Depends on how many other scandals are going on, I guess."

"So we're a scandal?"

He shot me a wicked grin that actually made me forget about everything else for a split second. "You don't think we're scandalous?"

I managed to laugh. "Great. That'll be my claim to fame in Hollywood—half of a scandalous marriage."

"There are worse ways to get your name out there."

I couldn't even argue. Knowing what I did about this business, he wasn't wrong. Maybe it wasn't so bad, giving up on that acting career that probably never would have happened anyway.

Debbie returned a moment later with another pad of rings, and Lord help me, they were bigger and sparklier than the others.

"Wow." I cautiously plucked one from the pad. "Are we getting married or winning the Super Bowl?"

Jesse laughed. "I know, right?" He took an even bigger one and slid it onto his finger. "Christ, that's heavy."

"So's this one." The ring I'd picked was thick white gold or platinum—hell if I could tell them apart—with several large diamonds. The rocks were square and caught the light enough to make me flinch.

Debbie gestured at the ring with her pen. "Those are princess cut, so they're going to catch the light differently."

I snorted. "Figures I'd go right for the princess cut."

"Uh-huh." Jesse took off his ring. "You said it, not me."

"Yeah, yeah." I slid the glittering monstrosity onto my hand. My left hand. On the third finger.

Whoa.

Gigantic or not, princess cut or otherwise, this was a

wedding ring. A real, honest to God, till-death-do-us-part wedding ring.

For a bald-faced lie of a marriage to a man I barely knew in the name of thwarting a politician who could make my life and my friends' lives a living hell. I was doing it for a million bucks and at the cost of whatever shot I might have ever had in Hollywood. No pressure or anything for this to actually work.

I opened and closed my fingers. Why was my throat suddenly tight? And had someone suddenly dimmed the lights in here, or was I passing out?

Oh right. Breathing is a thing that's important.

As subtly as I could, I exhaled, then breathed in deeply, and big shock, my vision started clearing again. Still, I held onto the case for balance, but jerked my hand away because I was going to leave fingerprints on the glass and the polished chrome edges.

"Shit. Sorry. I'm…" I tried to wipe smudges away, but only made them worse.

"Oh don't worry about the glass." Debbie smiled. "How does the ring feel?"

The ring. The wedding ring. The wedding ring that was currently on *my* hand.

I stared down at it. The thick band would definitely take some getting used to. As I turned my hand a little, the diamonds sparkled under the showroom lights.

Could I really sell this? I thought I was a damn good actor, but who the hell was going to buy my broke ass suddenly strutting around in a new car—okay, new*ish* car—and a diamond-studded wedding ring as if an Ambrose heir would ever have to scrape the bottom of the barrel for a husband? The rags-to-riches thing was romantic on the screen, but this was real life, and everyone was going to assume I had dirt on him, or that he was marrying me to piss off his father. Which… technically…

I thumbed the band.

The only way I'll ever have any of this is if someone's faking it.

"I…" Damn it, my throat was getting tight again. And the ring felt all wrong, and everything about this suddenly felt wrong, and—

"Hayden?" Jesse asked.

I quickly pulled the ring off and put it back on the pad. "You know, I could really go for something to drink. Any chance we could take a break?"

"Of course." Debbie smiled. "I'll just keep these behind the counter for you."

Jesse nodded. "Okay. We'll be back shortly."

I couldn't get out of that place fast enough, and as soon as we were outside and out of that surly-looking security guard's earshot, Jesse stopped me with a hand on my arm. Brow creased with undeniable concern, he asked, "You all right?"

I exhaled, my shoulders sagging under an invisible weight. "I don't know."

"What's wrong?" He touched my shoulder, his hand somehow lightening that weight. "Talk to me."

"It's just weird, and I guess it's sinking in a little. What we're doing." I met his eyes, praying I didn't look or sound as pathetic as I felt. "Like, I know what the deal is, but we're… I mean, we *are* getting married. Even if it's just for show. And I… I guess I'm kind of having second thoughts about that."

I cringed inwardly, fully expecting him to remind me that I'd signed a contract and I was legally obligated to go through with this unless I wanted to pay back every penny he'd given me so far.

But Jesse's expression softened. "What's bothering you?"

"Just…" *The fact that you never would have given me the time of day if you didn't need a stand-in husband?* I swallowed, struggling to hold his gaze. "Don't you think all this"—I gestured at the shop—"is a bit excessive?"

He cocked his head, brow furrowed. "What's wrong with it?"

"We just need a couple of rings, right? Do they need to be so fancy? I mean, I'd be perfectly happy with a couple of sterling silver bands from Hot Topic that say *We're so Metal* or something."

"What? Not even plain gold bands?"

I shrugged. "I don't know. I mean, it's supposed to be about the marriage, you know? Yeah, I know, ours is…" Sighing, I waved my hand. "I guess I've just always imagined having a ring that says I'm not in this for the jewelry."

Jesse blinked.

Breaking eye contact, I rolled some tension out of my shoulders. "I know. There's no reason to get sentimental about this because it's all fake. But it feels wrong. And if we want people to believe we're doing this for real, then… I mean, call it method acting or something. I don't know. But I feel like there should be some element of reality to this, and I don't think anyone will ever believe someone like me wearing something like *that*." I nodded toward the shop again.

"Someone like you?" Jesse's face was the very picture of confusion. "What do you mean?"

I thought for a moment. "Someone like me who basically wins the lottery and buys a used car. As soon as I put on a ring like that, I don't feel like me anymore. It just doesn't feel right."

"Okay, well, what would feel more like you?"

"Something simple, I guess? A plain gold band?"

"Is that really what you want?"

I laughed nervously. "Since I doubt you'd go for the *We're so Metal* silver bands, I think it's a good compromise, isn't it?"

Jesse chuckled. "I'm perfectly fine with a plain gold band."

"You are?"

"Why not? At least then I won't be afraid of losing a diamond or something."

"That crossed your mind too?"

He made a face. "You think?"

I laughed. "Okay good. So it's not just me."

"No. And even if I wasn't paranoid about losing a diamond, this is your decision as much as mine."

I sobered, avoiding his gaze. "Except it's kind of not."

"Hayden."

I looked in his eyes.

"I know this is all really overwhelming. There's a reason I'm paying you as much as I am—I'm asking a *lot* of you, and I promise I haven't forgotten that. So if there's something you want or something that's not sitting right with you, just say so."

"Really?"

"Of course." He touched my shoulder again, and I was startled by how much I liked the casual contact. "Whatever I can do to make it easier for you, say the word, because none of this is going to work without you."

"So, no pressure, right?" I laughed halfheartedly.

He grimaced. "I'm sorry. I know it's a lot of pressure."

"It is, but I'm still onboard." I put my hand over his. "And… thanks. I'm trying not to overthink all of this, but it's a lot."

"I know it is. And thank *you*. If this works, we're going to save the state of California one hell of a homophobic politician."

"Yeah. No pressure."

"I know, right?" He glanced at the jewelry store. "Listen, do you want to do this another time? It doesn't have to be today."

I considered it, but shook my head. "Nah. Let's just get it done. But plain gold bands, right? We're agreed on that?"

"Totally agreed." He gestured toward the door. "After you."

L.A. WITT

Chapter 10
Jesse

It turned out that Hayden's preference for a plain gold band made the whole process of buying rings a hell of a lot simpler. Debbie was clearly disappointed we weren't going to drop a wad of cash on something slathered in diamonds, but Hayden seemed much happier, and I really liked the thick, smooth band I'd picked out. We didn't even have to wait for them to be sized because they had our sizes in stock, and before I knew it, we were on our way out with our wedding rings in a black and gold shopping bag.

"Lunch?" I asked on the way to the car.

"Definitely. You know this area better than I do, so wherever you want to go."

We settled on one of those family restaurants with a wide menu and loud décor. The lunch rush had apparently died down, though, and the place wasn't super crowded. After we'd been seated at a small booth, we perused the menu, ordered, and settled in to wait for our food.

"Oh, just got a text from my dad." Hayden read it, then laughed and put his phone down. "He sounds pretty thrilled to be getting a new tux."

"Yeah?"

Hayden nodded. "He has one, but he hasn't worn it in a while, and he's lost some weight. So he definitely doesn't mind a new one."

"Well good." I paused for a sip of my drink. "So, your family seems pretty close."

"We are now. My parents and me, anyway. During my brother's skating years, things got a bit rough."

"How so?"

Hayden sat back, absently running his thumb through the condensation on his glass. "My brother and I *kind* of get along now, but we *hated* each other for a long time. Which sucks because we're twins and we used to be really, really close."

I cocked my head. "What happened?"

Hayden released a long, tired sigh. "Basically, he was all wrapped up in the spotlight, and I was jealous of all the attention he got because he was this star athlete and potential Olympian—and God, it got so much worse the first time he went to the Olympics. He was seventeen and full of himself, and… you can imagine the ego, right? And he couldn't stand me because he thought I was trying to pull the spotlight away from him. Which… I was." He sighed, shaking his head. "I mean, we're twins, but I might as well have been the middle child. My parents were laser-focused on my brother and his career, so I always kind of did things on my own." He laughed self-consciously. "And I was the kid who was always doing things to get attention."

"Oh yeah? Like what?"

"Being *just* enough of a class clown that my teachers were always calling or emailing my parents." Hayden laughed again, this time with a note of mischief that did wild things to my pulse. "Don't get me wrong—I wasn't a *bad* kid. But that kid who heckled substitute teachers? Encouraged other kids to bend the rules? Tried to do physical stunts that got me stitches and *maybe* a broken arm? That was me."

I laughed too. "I haven't known you very long, but for some reason I can absolutely picture this."

"Should I be offended by that?" The playful glare suggested he knew the answer.

"No, no, definitely not." I smiled. "You just don't strike me as the type to quietly fade into the woodwork."

Hayden snorted. "Oh God. No. Not me. At least when I discovered drama in middle school, I finally had an outlet. Maybe I couldn't pull my parents' attention away from my brother for more than five seconds, but I could damn sure demand a spotlight and get a crowd's attention. It's really no wonder my brother and I stopped getting along."

"But it's better now?"

"Eh. We're civil. Ish. The fact that I didn't tell him what you and I are doing should tell you something."

I grimaced. "Whoa. And that's unusual for twins, isn't it? To be…"

"To not be joined at the hip, share a language, and practically share thoughts?" Hayden nodded, lips quirked. "Yeah. It is. And I miss having that with him. Which I guess should tell you how much damage we did to our relationship."

"Do you think it'll get better?"

"I hope so, but I don't know." He frowned. "God, that makes me sound pathetic, doesn't it? Letting things get so bad with my brother over getting attention when we were kids?"

"Not really, no. My siblings and I are a mess, and believe me, we did all kinds of stupid shit to get attention."

"Such as?"

"Oh…" I thought back, wondering where to even start. "I mean, it takes a bit more than acting up in class to get my dad's attention, so…"

Hayden's eyes widened. "Oh God. I can't even imagine. Do I even want to know?"

I laughed uncomfortably. "If we were getting bad grades or not turning in homework, my mom would just call and convince the teachers to look the other way. So if we actually wanted to get attention, that took things like snorting coke in the school bathroom, wrecking a car, getting busted having sex over a teacher's desk…"

His jaw fell open. "Did you do all of those?"

"No, no. I never did coke, and I've never wrecked a car."

"And that other thing?"

Heat rushed into my cheeks. "Yeah, I might have done that a time or two."

"A time *or two?*"

"Uh-huh. And I may have been bent over the hood of my dad's Bentley the first time I bottomed."

Hayden blinked. "I'm assuming it wasn't just because you happened to feel horny when it was the nearest flat surface?"

"Nope. And we didn't get caught that time." I took a deep breath. "But then when I was a sophomore, I was dating… well, I won't name names, but he was in kind of the same boat I was. A-list parents, desperate for attention, looking for a way to lash out after his family didn't take it well when he came out."

"Oh God. That sounds like a perfect storm of queer teenage rebellion."

"Plus our school was, shall we say, not exactly queer friendly. They didn't like anyone being out, and our parents had warned each of us to stay in the closet because of what it would do to our families' names. So we were cutting class to make out behind the bleachers, and long story short, we got it into our heads that we could say 'fuck you' to our parents, our school, and our family names." I chuckled at the memory of how arrogant and stupid we'd been. "So when my teacher walked in right before fifth period English, I had my boyfriend bent over the desk."

A laugh burst out of Hayden, and he clapped his hand over his mouth. "I'm sorry. I'm sorry. That's… I should be horrified, but I'm just picturing the look on her face, and…"

I laughed too. "It was pretty epic. Now, the aftermath…" My humor faded. "My mom was pissed, but my dad was just… I mean, he was pissed and he was disgusted, but then he kind of snickered and told my boyfriend's dad, 'Well, at least mine wasn't the girl.'"

Hayden's eyes were instantly huge. "Are you serious?"

"Yeah. Which… should probably explain why we got busted the *second* time."

"Oh. Yeah. Gotcha."

I sighed. "At the time, it was a way to get the attention

we were so desperate for. If I could go back and tell teenage me not to do it, I would."

"Yeah?"

I nodded. "Especially since I'm pretty sure it didn't end well for my boyfriend. Our parents yanked us out of that school and sent us to separate private schools, and he stopped responding to my emails." I dropped my gaze, guilt settling deep in the pit of my stomach. "He's married now. To a woman. Has a couple of kids, and…" I sighed. "I just can't help thinking his family did something to him. Threatened to disown him, maybe even sent him to conversion therapy or something. God knows my family threatened me with it if I embarrassed them like that again. Whenever I see pictures of him with his wife, or even see him in interviews or something, he looks like he isn't even there."

"Wow." Hayden exhaled. "Wait, so your parents actually threatened you with conversion therapy?"

"Obliquely, yeah. And my dad will never say it publicly, but he's determined to roll back any bans or even restrictions on conversion therapy in California. Shame I was never recording when he said *that* out loud."

Hayden's eyes were immediately filled with horror. "Holy shit. No wonder you're willing to…" He gestured at himself, then me.

"Exactly. I know it's a hell of a Hail Mary, and it might not even work, but there's no way I can let my dad get that kind of power without at least *trying* to stop him."

"No, definitely not," Hayden breathed. "Your family really puts the 'fun' back in dysfunctional, don't they?"

I laughed halfheartedly. "Yeah. They kind of do. And the fucked-up thing is it took me until I was in my teens to realize we were messed up at all."

"What made you realize it?"

"Coming out to my dad, for one thing," I muttered. "But it was mostly because my uncle started self-destructing when I was in middle school. Looking back, I think that was the one of the few things that kept me and my younger siblings from really fucking up."

Hayden stiffened. "Oh yeah, I remember reading about that. What..." He hesitated. "What *was* the real story? Like I've heard how the tabloids spun it, but something tells me the reality isn't quite the same."

"It's closer than a lot of people realize." I took a deep breath and slowly released it. "The real story is that even though my dad thrived in Hollywood and he loved being part of a famous, powerful family, my uncle hated it. The more he rejected it, the worse it got because he couldn't escape it. Nobody lets you forget when you're an Ambrose, and I think it was literally driving him insane."

"Wow. Poor guy."

"I know, right?" I sighed. "So since he couldn't physically escape, he did everything he could to *mentally* escape. I think some of the stories about him have been exaggerated a bit just because the family wants to make it sound like he was the problem, not them, but the gist of it is that he started stealing alcohol when he was eleven or twelve, and by fifteen, he was a full-blown cokehead. By the time he realized the drugs weren't actually helping, and that it just made everything with the family a million times worse, he was in too deep. Rehab didn't help. Even that seemed to make things worse."

"Jesus."

"Yeah. So it was just one train wreck and rehab stint

after another for a long time. He finally got on an even keel in his thirties, and he stayed that way for… I don't know. Six, seven years?" I scowled, shaking my head. "Right up until someone wanted to make a documentary about the family."

"Oh no."

I sat back, stomach knotted as the memories came rushing in. "I mean, the guy had finally straightened himself out, and a huge part of that was because he kept his distance from the family. And he was adamant they keep their distance from him. But then this filmmaker starts hounding him, and he guilt trips my uncle. 'Don't you want the world to know the ugly truth about the Ambrose family?' Which… he did. He hated how the whole world acted like the Ambrose family was the most glamorous, amazing family that ever lived." I rolled my eyes again. "So he caved. He did the interviews. That brought all the shit back to the surface, and he started spiraling down again. And *then* when the documentary actually came out, they'd edited it to make it sound like he was just a black sheep who couldn't live up to his name."

"Ugh." Hayden shook his head. "Amazing what they can and will do with some creative editing. It's like they don't even care they're talking about real people."

"I know right?" I sighed. "So, after that, he got himself so fucked up it's a miracle he could stand, and got it in his head to drive out to Joshua Tree and have it out with my dad."

"That's when he got in the wreck, isn't it?" Hayden asked softly.

I nodded. "No one knows if he passed out, if he was hallucinating, if… I mean, it doesn't really matter. He crossed the yellow line and killed five people." I swallowed. "Six, including himself."

"I remember reading about that." Hayden blew out a breath. "Jesus."

"Like you said, we put the 'fun' back in dysfunctional." I lifted my glass in a fake toast. "Hooray for a family that's governed by money, power, and reputation."

Scowling, Hayden nodded. "I can relate. Not on quite the same scale, but I had a little taste of it."

"Yeah? It was that bad?"

"Not *that* bad, but having your life run by someone else's career and reputation? I get that part. My brother's skating pretty much dictated all our lives since I was in second grade. I knew most families didn't have full-time athletes like that, but I think I was in college before I realized just how much his career ran everything. And how normal that wasn't. But we came out of it… not great, but okay, thank God."

"You're lucky," I whispered. "I think anyone can get consumed by a career, but once power and money start going to people's heads…"

"I believe it." He swallowed. "So, you really think this will work? What we're doing?"

It has to work. I don't know what to do if it doesn't.

"It'll work. Either that or Dad really has had a change of heart, in which case, I guess…" I hesitated, then exhaled. "I still wouldn't say it'll be good for him to get elected. He's got plenty of, um, views that don't need to be influencing legislation. No more than he already does by rubbing elbows with politicians, anyway."

"Good call." Hayden fidgeted. "And there's really no

plan B if he doesn't take the bait before the election?"

"Hopefully we won't need one."

"Hopefully not. But if we do, let me know how I can help."

"I will. And thank you."

He just smiled, and I sent up a silent thanks to the universe that Hayden had been the one to answer my ad. With him onboard, we *would* see this through.

I hoped.

Chapter 11
Hayden

It had been over two weeks since I'd turned in my last timecard, and I still wasn't sure what to do with myself. For the last few years, any time I wasn't at work—especially if I had the day off—I was sick with guilt and worry because I needed money. Now I didn't have a job and I had money. No reason to worry. No reason to feel guilty. How did people *do* this?

Well, for tonight I'd start with making myself a sandwich and getting online to check out Masters programs. I already had an MFA, but as long as I was flush with cash, and especially since I was letting go of my acting aspirations, it didn't seem like a bad idea to look into a more useful graduate degree. Maybe an MBA, even if Luis's hadn't opened as many doors as we'd expected and just the thought of sitting through the courses made me want to keel over and die from preemptive boredom. Business classes were the biggest snorefest on the planet.

Which I supposed made them the perfect way to prepare for whatever equally exciting job I might get with an MBA.

But boring classes and boring jobs were a lot more fun than the exciting roller coaster of destitution, so I'd suck it up and be a damn grownup. Whine.

I had just finished my sandwich and was settling in to check out grad programs when the condo's door buzzer went off. I shot it a wary look. Who the hell...?

Maybe it was UPS or something. Jesse might have a delivery on its way. I was pretty sure he'd been ordering some makeup supplies the other day, and the package might need a signature.

I pressed the button on the intercom. "Hello?"

"It's Amanda. Is Jesse home?"

My gut clenched. He hadn't said anything about his sister coming over. I cleared my throat and pressed the button again. "He's still at work."

"Oh. Do you mind if I come up?"

"Um." I didn't want to be rude to Jesse's family. Okay, that was a lie. I totally wanted to be rude as fuck to all the assholes he shared DNA with, but they *were* his family, and I didn't want to cause World War III between him and his siblings. And if working in food service and retail had taught me anything, it was how to be perfectly sweet and polite to people I desperately wanted to take outside and curb stomp.

So, I buzzed her in, and when she arrived at the door, I plastered on an Oscar-worthy smile. "This is unexpected."

As she stepped past me into the condo, her smile was as frosty as mine was fake. "I just thought I'd drop in and say hi to my brother." She plunked her gigantic bag on the kitchen island. A Birkin, because of course it was. "Maybe get to know my new brother-in-law, too."

My artificial smile almost faltered, but years of theatre training and food service kept it in place. "Well. It's just me for a while." I shut the door and motioned toward the living room. "Do you want something to drink?"

"I'm fine. Thank you." We moved into the living room, and she sat primly on the sofa. Her gaze went to my open laptop. "Oh. Did I catch you in the middle of something?" She didn't sound like she actually gave a shit.

"I was, um…" I closed my laptop and took a seat on the opposite end of the couch. "Just looking into some graduate programs."

"Graduate programs?"

"Yeah. I've got a Masters, but I'm thinking I should get one that might actually help me get a job." I laughed nervously.

Amanda's expression didn't budge. "That sounds expensive."

I cocked my head. It was an odd comment anyway, but I mean, she was the daughter of a literal billionaire, and she was an A-list actress who commanded eight figures per role. The rock on her left hand probably cost more than a Masters degree. Textbooks included.

"Well," I finally said, "it's not cheap, but it'll open some doors."

She eyed me skeptically. After a moment, she folded her hands on top of her knee. "So how did you and my brother meet?"

"Grindr."

Her spine straightened and her features tightened. "I see."

"I'm joking." I plastered on another fake smile and winked. "Jesse told you—we met at work. I was an extra on a film he was working on."

"Which film?"

I tried not to fidget under her scrutiny. Jesse would be home soon, right? I wouldn't have to entertain her by myself for much longer, would I?

Schooling my expression, I said, "*Due East with a Tailwind.*"

"Hmm, see, that's interesting." The corners of her mouth lifted slightly, turning the frosty smile into a smug one. "Because our older brother knows the producers of that film." Her eyes narrowed into icy slits. "No one there had ever heard of you."

I arched an eyebrow, pretending I didn't feel a cold sense of panic welling in my chest. *C'mon, Jesse. Where are you? A little help here?* But Jesse wasn't here, so I was on my own. "Okay. Okay. You got me." I showed my palms. "I do work as an extra sometimes, but I didn't meet Jesse on-set."

"Mmhmm. That's what I thought. So how did you meet him?"

I deflated with a slightly exaggerated air of resignation. "Look, we came up with that story because we didn't think anyone would be comfortable with the truth. Neither of us figured any of you would care enough to check our story."

"So then what *is* the truth?"

"I told you." I shrugged as flippantly as I could. "Grindr."

The slightest twitch of her lips almost drove a laugh out of me.

I just sighed, though. "It doesn't make for a very

romantic origin story, you know? I mean, what are we supposed to tell people? We hooked up twice before we knew each other's names, then finally stopped screwing long enough to have a conversation and realize we liked each other?"

Oh. Yeah. I was enjoying Amanda's discomfort *way* too much.

Sorry not sorry, lady. You started it.

"Well." She set her jaw. "I suppose that's, um, one way to meet someone."

I smiled sweetly. "Worked for us."

"Mmhmm." She studied me for a moment. Then she sat back, draping her arm across the back of the couch, probably in an effort to look relaxed. She failed miserably, which wasn't surprising. While her older brother was a solid actor, Amanda Ambrose's career was proof that nepotism was alive and well in the industry. I swear she had all the acting chops of a corpse. I'd seen disembodied fish heads with more range of expression. When she had to interact with other actors, it was enough to give me secondhand embarrassment. You know when someone is totally not a kid person, and someone else shoves a baby into their arms, and they look totally horrified and have no idea what to do? That was Jesse's sister onscreen with other people.

And yet they pay you $12 million per lead role, and I'm lucky to get a callback for a background role in a deodorant commercial.

Ugh. Good thing I'm ditching this biz. Merit-based economy, my ass.

"So how is it living with my brother?" Her tone was a bit less hostile, but I didn't buy it. "Does he still snore like used to?"

I laughed despite my nerves, and thought fast. "I wouldn't know. I'm out cold the second I hit the pillow, and I sleep with earplugs in anyway."

"Lucky you. He and Carson shared a room until they were teenagers, and I thought Carson was going to smother him with a pillow." She absently played with the hem of her blouse. "What do you do, anyway? What's your job?"

"Well, I *do* act."

"Is that right?"

I fidgeted uncomfortably. What was I supposed to do? Say out loud that I was quitting acting to save her dad the trouble of blacklisting me? "I'm still working on establishing myself."

"I see." She leaned forward, forearms crossed on top of her knee and eyes focused intently on me. "And how do you pay your bills while you're 'establishing yourself?'"

I studied her. "You want to tell me what you're angling for? Because this doesn't feel like a casual little chat."

She narrowed her eyes at me again, dropping her pleasant pretense completely. "I just want to know who the hell this random person is that my brother suddenly wants to marry."

"Random person? Gee, thanks."

"What can I say?" Her shoulder lifted in a tight half shrug. "Out of nowhere, Jesse's getting married to someone no one's heard of. I'd just as soon not watch him get taken by a gold digger."

"A gold digger?" I barked a laugh. "Oh. Honey." Okay, so she was technically right, but it wasn't like I'd gone looking for him and his money. "No. Just no."

"Yeah?" She mirrored me, folding her arms, and glared down her nose at me. "Prove it."

"Prove—how the fuck do I prove that?"

"You tell me." She shrugged. "What do you do? How much money do you have?"

"How is that any of your business?"

"It's my business because I think you're just another in a long line of assholes who want to loot my family."

"Loot your family?" I laughed. "Is that what your husband did?"

Her expression hardened even more, and I was shocked I didn't hear her teeth grinding. "My husband had money of his own."

"Mmhmm. I'm sure he did. And I'm sure he wasn't after any Ambrose family prestige or that nepotism that keeps you employed?"

Her lips parted. "I beg your pardon?"

"Oh, don't act offended." I waved dismissively. "You don't get to come in here and start throwing around accusations, then act like I'm the bastard when I—"

"My husband has nothing to do with this," she snapped. "Jesse is the idiot who keeps getting reeled in by assholes who just want access to either my family's fortune or have my dad hook them up in the industry. I'm not about to watch him marry one of you."

"Two things, honey." I sat up and inclined my head, looking her right in the eyes. "One, you don't have to watch him marry anyone. Feel free to skip the wedding if you can't stomach it. Two, I'm not some asshole trying to get money. I love Jesse, and I—"

"Bullshit. You love his money."

"Are you suggesting that's the only reason anyone

could love him? Because he's loaded?" I laughed dryly. "What a lovely sister you are, having so much faith in your brother and his judgment."

Her glare darkened. "I'm suggesting that my brother is a hopeless romantic who keeps getting lured in by—"

"For fuck's sake. Fine. *Fine.* You want to see how much of a gold digger I am?" I got up and headed for the kitchen. "Follow me." I snatched my keys off their hook, opened the door, and stared at her like, *well? You coming?*

She got up, pausing to straighten her blouse as if to make sure I knew we were doing this on *her* time. In tense silence, we left the condo and rode the elevator down to the parking garage. Then I led her down one of the rows, the sharp clomp of her high heels echoing through the concrete structure. At my parking space, I stopped, glared at her, and gestured grandly at my little blue car. "Ta da— the gold digger special. A used goddamned Focus that already had thirty thousand miles on it when I drove it off the lot. Happy?"

To my great satisfaction, she stared incredulously at the Focus. "*This* is your car?"

"Yes. And yes, your brother bought it for me. He said I could have any car I wanted, including a Porsche like the one he drives." I pointed at the car again. "*This* is what I wanted."

She was quiet for a moment, and I thought she might have gotten the point, but then she narrowed her eyes at me. "So you admit you're spending my brother's money. He's bought you a car, he's letting you live here, and now you're going to sign up for a stupid college degree you probably don't even—"

"A stupid degree?" I snorted. "Please. The only money

I've wasted on education was my other Masters, which I got in theatre." I pointed emphatically at her. "Though after seeing your last couple of movies, maybe you should think about getting one, sweetheart."

Her gasp of horror made it ridiculously hard to keep my poker face solid, especially when she followed it with "*Excuse* me?"

"You heard me," I growled. "You don't get to come strolling into my house and—"

"Your house?" She laughed sharply. "That's my brother's house. Not yours."

"Community property, honey. Soon as we're married, it's half mine."

"So you are a gold digger."

I rolled my eyes. "Yes, Amanda." I poured on the sarcasm. "I'm scamming your brother out of all his money so I can have a whole fleet of used Fords and a stack of degrees." I rolled my eyes. "Do you hear yourself? Why in the world would I bother getting a degree if I'm a gold digger?"

She glared at me, but said nothing.

And I decided I was done. The nerve of this woman. Seriously? Fuck this.

"You know the way out," I grumbled, and stalked toward the elevator.

"Excuse me?" she shouted at my back. "Don't you dare walk away from me."

"Or what?" I called over my shoulder without even slowing down. Thank God the elevator hadn't left, and as soon as I hit the button, the doors opened. As I stepped into the elevator, I heard her heels on the concrete floor. She was trotting toward me, calling after me, but I jabbed the close doors button until they finally obeyed, and they closed just before she could jam her hand between them.

I requested the twelfth floor, then sagged against the wall. Well that was a fun little twist my evening had taken.

At the condo, I let myself in, then kicked the front door shut and turned the deadbolt with an emphatic click.

And stay *out*.

Seriously. The *nerve* of that lady. What the actual fuck? Coming in here and trying to make me slip up somehow? Accusing me of being a gold digger? Uh, no. Not happening.

In the hallway, the elevator dinged. Aww, shit.

Then I realized Amanda's Birkin bag was still sitting on the island. Probably had her wallet, keys, and all, along with like the Hope Diamond or whatever rich people hauled around with them. I grabbed it off the island, and I was heading for the door when she started banging on it.

"Open this door!" she demanded. "You're not throwing me out of my brother's condo, asshole. My father owns this place and he'll—"

"Yeah, yeah, I'm sure he will." I turned the deadbolt, carefully planted my foot so she wouldn't be able to open the door farther than I allowed, and pulled it open enough to shove her bag through. "It was nice to see you, Amanda," I said with another bucketful of sarcasm. "Have a good night."

She looked at her bag, then at me. After a second or two of stunned silence, she laughed humorlessly. "We're not doing this out in the hall. Let me in."

"Um, no. We're not doing this at all." I jiggled the bag. "Would you take this please? We're done here."

She folded her arms. "Let me in."

For fuck's sake. I was not playing her games. I released the bag, and it hit the floor with a satisfying thunk.

"What the hell?" she squeaked. "I'm not—"

I shut the door and turned the deadbolt again. She was still yelling, but... fine. She could talk to the door all she wanted.

I sat down on the couch where I'd been earlier, put in a pair of earbuds, and let some European techno drown out my enraged soon-to-be sister-in-law. Time to get back to looking into Masters programs like the gold-digging bastard I was.

Slowly, though, horror crept in.

I turned my head toward the door, and realized... I had locked Jesse's sister out of his condo.

I mean, she was being a colossal jackass and seriously deserved to stand there and listen to me tear into her for an hour or three, but... was kicking her out, like, crossing a line? Especially right after I'd flat out told her she was a terrible actress? Shit. I'd never had in-laws before, and aside from some intense sibling rivalry, I'd never been part of a toxic family. I didn't know how all this worked. I needed a goddamned manual for dealing with the complications of marrying into the dynasty of dysfunction that was the Ambrose family.

Groaning, I covered my face with both hands. Amanda was probably texting Jesse right now, and he'd probably flip out at me when he got home.

Christ, what did I just do?

Chapter 12
Jesse

My house key was difficult to maneuver with my wrist braces on, but I managed. Ugh, my hands were killing me tonight. And I needed a drink. It hadn't been a bad day, just a long one, and I was drained and wound up and—yes, a drink sounded amazing.

Bourbon on the rocks with an ibuprofen chaser, please.

As I stepped into the condo, Hayden got up from the couch.

"Oh hey." He smiled, but it was an uneasy smile. "How was your day?"

"Eh." I hung up my keys. They fell off the hook, but... whatever. Wasn't like they were going anywhere. "Long and chaotic. Typical day on set."

"How are your hands?"

I groaned.

"Ouch. Sorry to hear it."

"Nothing a drink and some ibuprofen won't help." I opened the cupboard. "You want anything?"

"Sure. I'll have whatever you're having. In fact, why don't you sit and I'll take care of the drinks? Give your hands a break." He was oddly eager, and something about that didn't sit quite right, but I didn't argue.

"All right. Let me go change clothes. I'll be back in a minute."

I returned a moment later in sweats and a T-shirt, and my bourbon on the rocks was on the coffee table beside an opened bottle of ibuprofen.

"I wasn't sure how many you take," he said. "But I figured you didn't need to be messing with the childproof lid."

"Thanks. I really appreciate it." We exchanged smiles—his still kind of nervous for some reason—and I threw back a couple of ibuprofen before settling against the couch. "So what about you? How was your day?"

Hayden stared into his glass. "Um. It was all right. Just, you know, getting used to this whole being unemployed thing." He laughed quietly. "Except I guess I am technically employed, right?"

"Technically, yeah." I sipped my drink.

"I also looked into some Masters programs." He gestured at the laptop charging on an end table. "The MBA programs sound excruciating, but the degree will open some doors, so..."

"I thought you had a Masters already."

"Mmhmm. And that degree in theatre arts has doors swinging *wide* open." He rolled his eyes and muttered into his drink, "What the fuck was I thinking?"

"You want to work in the industry, right? Seems like a

good degree to have."

"Well, I did. Now things have changed, so it probably wouldn't hurt to come up with a plan now that I have the money to pay off my loans *and* go back to school." He paused. "And that's even before you consider what taking part in this"—he pointed at each of us—"will do to my acting prospects."

I winced. "Yeah. Good idea."

We drank in silence for a moment, but it didn't take long for Hayden to finally crack. He shifted nervously, fidgeting like a little kid working up the courage to admit he broke Mom's vase. "So, um, your sister came by earlier."

I tensed. "Which one?"

"Amanda."

"Oh. That's... wow." Though I guess it made sense, considering my younger sister didn't even live in California and hadn't met Hayden. I hadn't seen her myself in quite a while. "That's weird. She never just drops by."

Hayden shifted nervously. "Yeah, I, uh, I don't think she was here to see you."

"How do you figure?"

"Well." He folded his arms loosely. "Either she was here to see us, or she was her to see me, and she was seriously sniffing around for dirt."

Horror slowly swelled in my chest. "What kind of dirt?"

"She was here to bust me for being a gold digger, I swear." He took another swallow of bourbon. "She kept trying to get me to trip up. Like asking about you snoring, and how we met, and..." He waved his hand, nearly dumping his drink in the process. "I kind of got sick of her shit, and I *may* have kind of convinced her to come down to the parking garage with me to prove I wasn't a gold digger, and then I *might* have, um…" He cleared his throat and looked at me through his lashes as he sheepishly mumbled into his glass, "I *might* have told her she was a terrible actress right before I locked her out your condo."

I snorted and clapped my hand over my mouth. "You're joking."

"No." He grimaced. "Are you mad?"

"Not at you, no."

"You sure?"

"Dude." I shook my head. "My sister came around and started interrogating you about shit that's none of her business." I motioned toward the door with my glass. "By all means, show her ass out."

"Okay. Okay good." He was fighting a smile and losing. "Do you think she'll reject a friend request on Facebook after that?"

I just laughed.

"Oh, and um…" Hayden cleared his throat. "Also we have a new *how we met* story now."

"Do we?" ·

"Yeah. Apparently your brother got in touch with some of his people and figured out no one who worked on *Due East with a Tailwind* had ever heard of me."

I groaned, rolling my eyes. "Jesus. Seriously?"

"Uh-huh. I mean either that or she was bluffing."

I thought about it, then shrugged. "Could be either, to be honest. So what's our new cover story?"

"Grindr."

"Seriously?"

"Well yeah." Hayden folded and refolded his arms. "If

they're going to go all amateur sleuth on us, I figured I'd keep it simple."

"So, you kept it simple? Just 'we met on Grindr'?"

His lips quirked.

"Hayden…"

"Um. Well." He tried and failed to hide a smirk. "I figured if I gave her a bit TMI, she'd be horrified and quit asking. So I said we hooked up twice before we knew each other's names, and then finally stopped fucking for five minutes, had a conversation, and figured out we liked each other."

I laughed, imagining my sister's disgusted expression. "How did she react?"

He made a face that wasn't far from what I'd pictured on her.

I snorted. "Nicely done."

He smiled faintly, but it faded. He chewed his lip, then looked at me again, and he was absolutely serious now. "Listen, I know this thing we're doing isn't exactly a long term thing, but we've got a wedding coming up and family obligations, so maybe now would be a good time for you to fill me in on your family. Like, more than you already have so I kind of know what I'm up against."

I pushed out a breath. "I guess that's fair." Was there enough booze in the house for this? I supposed we'd find out. "So besides what I've told you, how much do you know about the Ambrose clan?"

Hayden blushed. "Are you asking how much of my time I've wasted on tabloids and gossip sites?"

Chuckling, I shrugged. "Something like that."

"Well, I know the tabloids say the family is a dysfunctional snake pit that would be too over the top on a soap opera." He grimaced. "No offense."

"None taken." I pressed the cool glass against my forehead. "What you see in the tabloids... it's not even the half of it."

"From what you said the other day, I believe it. But how bad *is* it?"

"Oh, hell. Where to start." I lowered my glass. "The whole thing with the door wars, as you called it?"

He smirked, but quickly sobered. "Yeah?"

"That's kind of how we were raised. If someone else was doing something, you had to do it bigger. You could never be second. Top of the class. First in the race. Best in show." I waved a hand. "I mean, three of Dad's five kids—including me—have been nominated for major awards, but if we don't win, he'll make sure to remind us of that at every turn. My brother's been nominated for three Oscars, and every time someone mentions it, Dad says, 'and does anyone remember or care who was nominated against Gone With the Wind?'"

"Seriously? Even getting nominated for an Oscar isn't good enough for him?"

"If you don't win, who cares?" I rolled my eyes. "Not that it would matter if I won because I'm just the makeup fairy as far as he's concerned."

Hayden made a disgusted sound. "What a charmer."

"Right? So nothing is ever good enough for him, and my siblings and I have always been groomed to compete against each other. On top of *that*, from the time we were little, he drove it into our heads that our loyalty was to him. Not each other. Not our mom. *Him.* In fact, I'll never forget..." I paused for another much-needed swig of bourbon. "When I was seven, I saw my older brother break a decorative plate. Threw a baseball and shattered it. Carson was terrified of getting in trouble—we were all scared shitless of Dad's temper—so he begged me not to tell. And I didn't."

Hayden watched me, the crevices deepening between his eyebrows as he hugged his knees to his chest.

I went on. "Dad grilled all of us about who did it. Of course I denied that my brother had done it." I pushed out a long breath. "After a week, Dad finally told us he'd known all along that it was Carson. And he knew I'd lied to him to cover for my brother. Since I'd done that, I not only got the same punishment as my brother as if I'd been just as guilty, but he took one of my favorite toys and made me throw it away."

Hayden blinked. "That's... wow, that sounds mean."

"Yeah. And believe me—especially at that age, shit like that leaves an impression. From that point on it was every man for himself because no one wanted to be punished for covering for each other. So now my siblings and I don't trust each other any further than we can throw each other. And I would bet my fucking car that my father put Amanda up to coming here to see if there's anything hinky between you and me."

"Do you think she knows what we're doing?"

"Don't know. But my dad's probably covering all his bases and making sure he's not being played."

"Wow." Hayden drained his drink. "I think I need more booze for this." He started to get up. "How about you? Need a refill?"

I looked into my glass. Damn. Empty. "Yeah, I should get one." I started to stand, but he waved me back.

"Sit. I'll get it."

"You sure?"

"*Sit.*"

I sat.

Hayden returned a moment later with two refilled glasses, and he sat down on the couch again, tucking his bare feet up under him. "I still can't get my head around how fucked up your family is. It's just... it's mind-blowing."

"Tell me about it." I took a deep swallow of bourbon, then lowered the glass and looked in his eyes. "In fact, to tell you the truth, if what we're doing pays off, my financial situation is going to be, uh, very different."

Hayden's lips parted. "What do you mean?"

"I mean, it's not just my inheritance that'll go." Slouching back with my drink cradled carefully in my hand, I sighed. "The thing is, Dad set up trust funds for all of us kids. *Huge* trust funds. But he keeps a tight rein on how much of it we actually have access to. When he dies, all the money will be turned over to us along with our portion of his estate, but while he's alive?" I shook my head.

"So he gives it to you, but doesn't *give* it to you."

"Basically. As far as he's concerned, it's called a trust fund because he's trusting the money to be enough incentive for all of us to toe the line. That, and if he's showering us with cash, we can't say anything negative about him without looking like spoiled brats." My shoulders sagged. "That's why I couldn't just do a tell-all article or something. No publication or journalist will touch it without proof because they've all been burned by vindictive, spoiled heirs before, and they don't want to be on Dad's shit list."

"So it's not that everyone believes he's benevolent and perfect—"

"No, no, just that they'd better have *proof* before they claim he isn't. Unless of course they want to get sued. Especially when he can show that he showers his family with money and favors."

"*Does* he shower you with money and favors?"

"Oh, he gives us each…" I rolled my eyes. "He gives us each a fucking allowance every month, like we're damned kids. What we do with that, he really doesn't care. But if we want more, like when I wanted to buy the car or the condo"—I gestured around us as if he might have forgotten where we were—"then we have to come to him for it. Plead our case. Justify the expense. If he thinks it's worthwhile, he'll arrange for us to get the money, and make sure anyone who listens knows that *he* bought the car, the house, or whatever." I scanned the room and sighed. "And that includes the mortgage company."

"Wait, what?"

Avoiding his eyes, I said, "Dad's name is on this place, not mine. Ditto with the car."

"Why would he do it that way?"

I laughed bitterly. "Why does my dad do anything he does? To control the people below him."

"Including his kids?"

"*Especially* his kids." I took a sip, the bourbon barely registering over the bitterness in my mouth. "We won't step out of line if we know he can take it away with the stroke of a pen. We've seen him do it to our youngest brother. It's also why my sister called off her wedding to Jobie Walker."

"She—you're kidding."

Shaking my head, I sighed. "Dad didn't like Jobie. Didn't like the idea of some tattoo-covered rock star in his family, never mind being the father of his grandchildren. So he told Amanda that either she called off the engagement, or..." I made a *do the math* gesture.

"Holy shit. He's not fucking around."

"No, he's not." I shuddered as I brought my drink to my lips again. I would never stop being haunted by the memory of my heartbroken sister sobbing on my shoulder the day her ex-fiancé's wedding photos had been splattered all over the news and social media. Now she was on her third marriage in nine years, and I doubted this one would last any longer than the others. I put my glass down on a coaster. "And he's made it clear he won't hesitate to do that to me if I marry a man. He would have done it when I came out, but my mom stepped in and..." I gestured dismissively. "You know that story. Now it's just a matter of waiting for him to pull the trigger."

"But, what about after? If you lose your house, your car..."

"I have money saved from my job, and I've socked away a lot of the money Dad gives me every month. I'll be all right at least for a while. I have no credit because Dad signed for everything, and..." I exhaled, rubbing my forehead. "I can't believe I let him have this much control over my life."

"Did you know any better?"

"Not really. The way my dad does things is the only thing I've ever known." I could vaguely remember the arguments Dad had made in favor of putting his name instead of mine on the deeds and titles. They'd made sense at the time, I supposed—I hadn't known much about property ownership, and I still didn't. Even if I had, I'd been too focused on the idea of having my own car or my own place, both of which meant getting the fuck out of my family home. I'd been too starry-eyed at the thought of being out on my own and *free* to stop and think objectively, never mind imagine my father was merely gathering leverage to keep me in line later. "He even made it sound like it was in our best interest, and that he was doing it for our own good."

"How the fuck did he manage that?"

I released a long breath. God, my family was exhausting to think about, never mind talk about. "Remember how I told you my siblings and I got into a lot of trouble as teenagers? Plus all the shit my uncle got into?"

Hayden nodded.

"Okay, well… Dad used that as leverage. He told us that his lawyers could only do so much, and that if we fucked up bad enough, there was nothing to stop the police from seizing our assets. That was what happened a couple of times with my uncle—when he was arrested for this or that, his shit would get seized. I don't even know if that's what really happened, but it's what Dad told us. And he told us that as long as all our assets were in his name, we wouldn't lose anything if we fucked up like my uncle did."

Hayden's eyebrow arched. "He… did he think you were all going to jail or something?"

"I don't know if he did or not, but he put the fear of God into us, and after everything my uncle went through…" I grimaced. "I mean, I didn't know a dysfunctional family from a hole in the ground, so I trusted my dad when he said he was looking out for us. Turned out he was just making sure that if any of us crossed him, we'd be well and truly fucked."

"Holy shit," Hayden whispered. Then he straightened, inclining his head slightly. "Jesse, I need to know something."

"Okay?"

He moistened his lips. "Where is the money you're paying *me* coming from?"

I dropped my gaze and stared into my glass.

Voice soft, he prodded, "Are you tapping into reserves that you'll need once this is over?"

I still didn't answer.

Hayden slid closer and put a hand on my arm. "I need you to be honest—are you bleeding yourself dry to pay me? I mean, if you want to renegotiate how much you're paying me, we can—"

"No. I can pay you." I moistened my lips and finally met his eyes again. "All right. Okay. The truth is it's probably more than I should be paying right now. I don't have as much liquid cash as you might think." I had no idea how to tell him that what I was paying him was the majority of my cash reserves. Once he was paid and I was cut off, things would get interesting. Covering his hand with mine, I said, "But I'll have enough to survive. It'll hurt, but it's worth it if it means keeping my Dad from getting elected."

Concern creased Hayden's brow. "But I don't want you going bankrupt, especially while—"

"I'll be fine." I squeezed his hand, then let go. "Might not be the lifestyle to which I've become accustomed, but I'll be okay." *I hope.* "My job pays enough to survive in this town."

"Will you still be able to get jobs? Won't your dad blacklist you?"

I shook my head. "I'll be fine." My father *would* blacklist me, but I had connections of my own. I could work under a fake name if I had to. There were a few powerful people in the industry who were also Dad's rivals, and they hated him enough to hire me out of spite. Hopefully.

Hayden watched me for a moment, then laughed softly. "It's so weird," he mused. "You're facing the possibility of losing access to millions, but you're pretty sure you're going to land on your feet. It'll be an adjustment, but you're not going to starve or be homeless."

"Well, no. It won't be *that* bad. It shouldn't be, at least."

His lips quirked a little. "Before I met you, I was one unexpected twenty dollar expense away from having to choose between gas or groceries."

I stared at him. "Really?"

"Yeah." He laughed self-consciously. "You think we were living in that shithole because we liked the ambiance? Sweetie, I was *broke*. That's why I've been so afraid to spend any of the money you've given me. I think Ashton and Luis are hoarding what you paid them, too."

"They are?"

Hayden nodded. "They both went out and bought a couple of pairs of work shoes that will probably last forever, and I think they've had some car repairs done and thrown some money at their student loans. But if they're anything like me, they have to mentally twist their own arms to let go of any of it."

I blinked, struggling to comprehend it. "And that's... that's why you bought the used car."

Cheeks coloring, he nodded again. "I've never had money like this. Neither have they. It's actually harder to spend it now than when I was poor, even spending it on necessities, because I'm afraid of that financial security slipping away. I don't want to go back, you know?"

"Wow. I never thought about that."

"You've never had to."

"Not until recently, no."

Hayden stiffened. "Oh. Right. I guess... I guess that's..." He chewed his lip, searching my eyes. "Can I ask you something?"

"Sure."

"What we're doing..." He fidgeted on the couch. "I know it's going to hit you in the balls financially, but what's going to happen with your family?"

"What do you mean?"

"If your dad cuts you off, what happens with your mom and your siblings?"

I laughed humorlessly. "You really think they'd choose me over multimillion dollar bank accounts?"

Hayden stared at me, stunned. "Would he make them choose?"

"*Oh* yeah. Without a doubt. Anyone sides with me or even tries to stay neutral—anyone who doesn't openly and loudly shun me—is getting cut off too. There's a reason my younger sister and I don't advertise to our parents that we're still in contact with our youngest brother."

"Does that bother you? That you'll lose your family after all of this?"

I considered it for a long moment. Finally, I drained my drink and put the glass down. "If my family was like yours, I'd be crushed just thinking about losing them. But mine?" I shook my head and stared out the window at the darkening sunset. "It hurts, but honestly it doesn't seem like that much of a loss."

"Really?" Hayden's brow pinched. "That's…. God, that's really sad."

"I know it is. And it's…" Ugh, I did not have the energy to go into the story of my younger brother's disownment. Probably because it hit a little too close to home right now. "Don't get me wrong—my siblings aren't bad people. It's heartbreaking to imagine being cut off from them permanently." I absently played with the Velcro on my brace. "But we're barely involved with each other's lives. We're pretty much strangers. I honestly don't hate them—they just came out of the same cesspool I did, and we were all raised to see each other as competition."

Hayden eyed me. "So you don't think it's fucked up for your sister to waltz in here and try to dig up dirt?"

"Oh, no, I do think it's fucked up." I shrugged. "But I think Dad put her up to it, and we've all been brought up to do whatever Dad says unless we want to be the one in his crosshairs. He probably convinced her that I was going to upset the status quo somehow." I sighed. "That, or she's doing it on her own as a way to stay in his good graces."

"So, what? Like storing up credit in case she fucks up in the future?"

"Pretty much, yeah. Now if she steps out of line, she can remind Dad that she tried to throw a monkey wrench into what I'm doing."

"Does that actually work with him?"

"Sometimes."

"Wow."

"Welcome to my world." I rubbed my eyes, exhausted just from talking about my family. Lowering my hand, I said, "My brother and sister really aren't bad people. We just never had any good people as role models, you know?"

"How the hell did you come out of it without turning out like them?"

I swallowed, my throat suddenly tight. "I guess being something my father hates isn't entirely a bad thing."

Hayden's eyebrows jumped.

"Gave me perspective," I said. "Carson and Amanda never had a reason to gain that perspective. At least not as kids."

"What about your younger siblings?"

"Reanna did. Long story short, she has a pretty serious eating disorder."

Hayden sat straighter. "Oh no."

"Yeah. It didn't help that my mom and Amanda both have crazy lightning fast metabolism, and Reanna had a much easier time gaining weight than losing it." I shook my head. "Turned out years later she has a hormonal thing that screws with her weight."

"Ugh. Jesus. My sister-in-law has something like that. And she wound up with an eating disorder too." He paused, then quietly added, "She and my brother actually met at a support group for it."

"Your brother has one too?"

Nodding, Hayden scowled. "Figure skater."

"Oh, right. I guess that comes with the territory."

"It can." He tilted his head. "How is your sister doing with it now?"

"I think she's got it under control. We, um, don't talk much, but I see her on Facebook and she seems happy and healthy these days." I drummed my fingers on my knee. "Thing is, when she was about sixteen, she starved herself so badly she wound up in the hospital. And my mom just kept asking the doctors what they could do to treat her without causing Reanna to get fat again."

Hayden blinked. "Sorry. *What?*"

"Yeah. She thought Reanna looked better than she had in ages, and she wanted to help her get healthy... but stay thin."

"Jesus H. Christ." Hayden rolled his eyes. "That must have done terrible things to your sister's head."

"It did. And I think that was when she had the same epiphany our younger brother and I did—that our family was something to get as far away from as possible and try really hard not to emulate."

"Good for her. Shame your older siblings didn't figure it out."

"It really is." I sighed. "But they're adults. I've tried. I really have. At this point, if they can't see our family for what it is, then there isn't much I can do."

Hayden studied me. "I guess now I get why you're not mad that I was kind of a dick to Amanda tonight."

"No. In fact, you were smart. She probably won't like you after this, but she'll know she can't walk all over you."

"Well then." He grinned triumphantly. "Mission accomplished."

L.A. WITT

Chapter 13
Hayden

All things considered, Jesse and I had this whole domestic thing down. We never really hammered out things like chores and whatever, but within days of me moving in, we'd fallen into a groove without even realizing it. He liked his kitchen immaculate, and I'd lived in a couple of places with roaches, so I'd long ago gotten into the habit of cleaning up every single crumb before they'd landed on the counter. Neither of us let dishes pile up.

We each did our own laundry, though sometimes if he was doing a load, I'd ask if I could toss in a few shirts or socks, and he did the same. Jesse's hands bothered him sometimes, so I'd gotten in the habit of taking out the trash and recycling so he wouldn't have to. At some point, it had become a thing that I cleaned the bathroom on Mondays and he did it again on Thursdays.

Between the two of us, the condo stayed pristine, and we didn't butt heads over it. We'd also started grocery shopping together. Sometimes I'd run to the store while he was at work, but the big weekly shopping trip was always both of us. It was another one of those things that just sort of happened. There was no conversation about it. One day he'd asked if I wanted to come with him, and it had been our routine ever since.

I loved it. We operated as smoothly as I had with Ashton and Luis, and considering some of the horror stories I'd heard about awful roommates, I counted myself ridiculously lucky. I'd wondered sometimes if I was using up all my roomie luck on those two, but apparently not. Though now that I'd lived peacefully with Ashton, Luis, and Jesse, I was probably due for a drummer who moonlighted as a serial killer and had never heard of a sponge. Or maybe that Nigerian prince of clown porn I'd imagined when I'd gone to meet Jesse the first time.

For now, though, I was in cohabitation heaven, and I was going to enjoy it for as long as I could.

Today was grocery day, and my reliable little Focus crawled through early evening traffic. Jesse lounged in the passenger seat and I absently tapped my thumb on the wheel while I waited for the light to turn green. We'd been chatting idly ever since he'd gotten home from work, and that continued on our slow drive to the supermarket.

"Hey, so." I glanced at him. "I think I found a dentist so I can finally get my teeth unfucked."

"Did you?"

"Yeah. Did you know there are dentists who will knock you out for anything?" I shook my head. "Why the hell did I never get the memo that I could skip right past being kinda numb and go straight to having my ass knocked out for the whole thing?"

Jesse laughed. "Yeah, that's been around for a while now. It's amazing. Is that what you're going to do?"

"Might as well." I shrugged. "I mostly just need some old fillings replaced, and then a deep cleaning, and he said he wants to put in a couple of crowns. Not like a root canal or anything, but if I don't have to be awake to listen to the drill?" I shuddered, and so did Jesse. "Hell yeah. Take my money."

"I'm with you. The first time I heard about sedation dentistry, I was on it like white on rice. Best invention ever."

"Right? I'm actually looking forward to getting all this crap done. Can you believe that? Looking forward to going to the *dentist*?"

"I can, yeah." He nodded. "Especially if you'll feel better after the work is done."

"I definitely will. I mean it's not bad, but this one filling has been loose since forever and I'm always worried it's going to pop off. Plus my mom had to get a ton of really painful shit done to her mouth a few years ago, and I'd like to, you know, not."

"Totally understand."

I slowed to a stop at a red light. "He, um, says he can get me in next Thursday. Is there…" I chewed my lip.

"Hmm?"

I kept my gaze fixed on the traffic light. "Luis and Ashton both have to work, so I… Is there any way you could drive me to and from? I can't drive after the sedation."

"Yeah, sure. I might be scheduled on set that day, but I've got a friend who owes me a favor after I filled in for her, so as long as she's available—yeah, no problem."

"Really?" I stole a glance at him. "You don't mind?"

"Nah, of course not. Just let me know what time you need to be there."

"Thanks." I smiled. "I really appreciate it."

I woke up to darkness, but as I blinked my eyes into focus, warm light was peeking in around the edges of the blinds. What the hell time was it? And why did my mouth taste weird?

According to my phone, it was almost 4:00.

As my mind cleared, the taste made sense too—I'd been at the dentist earlier. In my sleepy haze, I wondered if I'd overslept and missed my appointment because I didn't remember anything, but then I realized my mouth wouldn't taste like this if I'd missed the appointment. Whatever drugs they'd given me had been some *good* shit.

Cautiously, I tongued my teeth. My mouth wasn't numb anymore, and my jaw ached, but nothing really hurt. There were definitely some new fillings and the promised crowns. The filling that had been loose was gone, replaced by something much more solid that didn't wiggle precariously when I touched it.

I didn't remember a thing. Well, I vaguely recalled getting to the office with Jesse and settling into the chair, but after that? Nada. I didn't even remember coming home.

Slowly and carefully, I sat up. My head was a bit light, but I didn't think I was in any danger of passing out, so I stood. I was still in the sweats and T-shirt I'd worn to the dentist, and now that I'd slept for a few hours, everything was rumpled. Hell, I felt rumpled.

Shower. A shower sounded amazing.

After a shower—and pausing in front of the mirror to inspect the renovation of my mouth—I got dressed again and shuffled out to the kitchen.

Jesse was in the living room, resting his Kindle against his braced arm on top of a pillow, and he looked up when I came in. "Hey. How are you feeling?"

"Not bad. Kind of hungry." I tongued my teeth again. "Thinking I should stick with something soft for a while."

He put his Kindle aside and stood. "We still have soup. That sound good?"

"Yeah, it does." I motioned him back to the couch. "I can make it. Don't worry."

"You're supposed to be resting until the drugs are out of your system. Sit."

On any other day, I would have argued because I'm stubborn like that, but the truth was, just getting up, taking a shower, and coming out here had left me feeling more tired than I'd expected. So I huffed like a diva and flopped onto the couch. "Fine."

Jesse chuckled. "That's what I thought."

He heated up a couple of bowls of canned minestrone. I pretty much inhaled mine because, oh yeah, I hadn't eaten anything since before midnight last night. Then I sat back against the couch and sighed happily. "Much better."

"I figured you'd be getting hungry. You haven't eaten in about four hours."

"Dude, I haven't eaten since last night."

"No, we stopped at McDonald's on the way home. You had a cheeseburger."

I blinked. "I did?"

"Mmhmm." He ate some more of his soup. "You were starving and said it sounded good. I think you fell asleep as soon as you finished it."

"Whoa. I don't remember any of that."

"The nurses said you probably wouldn't. The dentist gave you another dose of something and numbed the hell out you again after he was done."

"Explains why I slept so hard. I don't even remember coming home."

He laughed softly and set his empty bowl on the coffee table. "Yeah, you were seriously weaving when we got back."

"I was?"

Jesse nodded. "And no, I didn't video any of it to put on YouTube."

"You better not have." I shot him a playful glare, but a weird feeling hit me. I really *didn't* remember anything. Nothing I'd done. Nothing he'd done. Somehow, he'd gotten me out to the car, up to the condo, and into my bedroom—and he'd been sweet enough to close the blinds—and I remembered nothing. With anyone else besides my family or my former roommates, I wouldn't have been comfortable with that. I could even think of a few recent exes who I would not have trusted with me being that far out of my head.

But with Jesse, it didn't bother me, and the fact that I *was* so comfortable with him kind of made me uncomfortable. We hadn't known each other long. We were supposed to be a happily engaged couple on the surface, but basically roommates in reality. I wouldn't have asked anyone else to take a day off and haul my drugged ass home from the dentist after he'd only known me a few weeks. With Jesse, it had made about as much sense as asking Ashton or Luis or one of those exes I *would* have trusted. Of course I'd trust him. Why wouldn't I?

Because I barely know you.

But it felt like I did know him. Like we were putting on an act when other people were around, but alone, we effortlessly slid into this comfortable, relaxed coexistence. Being with him was so much easier than it should have been.

I surreptitiously watched him collect our bowls and take them into the kitchen.

Why can't it be this easy with someone who actually wants me?

Knowing what I did about the Ambrose family, I was seriously not thrilled when Jesse told me we'd been invited to one of his dad's famous parties. A night of rubbing elbows with all the people who dutifully showed up to wedge their noses into Isaac's wrinkly buttcrack? Ugh. No, thanks. Especially now that I'd made peace with bowing out of acting and didn't need to partake in the communal ass-kissing.

But if Jesse and I were going to convince the Ambrose social circles that we were a happily engaged same-sex couple—not to mention be a thorn in the Ambrose patriarch's side by showing up to his party as a happily engaged same-sex couple—then we needed to go. I floated the idea of bowing out due to a horrifically contagious mutant version of a flu-measles-leprosy hybrid, or even something simple like rabies or the plague, but Jesse helpfully pointed out that he had to be back on-set on Monday. Unless I could come up with an explanation for his miraculous recovery, it wasn't going to fly.

"What about food poisoning?" I asked in the car. "Or the norovirus? Those clear up fast, and nobody would blame us for not wanting to socialize."

"Sorry." Jesse chuckled as he pulled out of the condo's parking garage. "We have to go. Showing our faces at these parties is all part of my evil plan."

"You're no fun." I pouted playfully, but he just laughed.

"You'll have a better time than you think. I promise. Just think of it as a performance." He paused long enough to make a left turn. "This won't be like when you met my parents the first time. You'll probably spend about thirty seconds in my dad's company, and spend the rest of the party chatting with anyone who's anyone in the industry."

"Oh. Well, when you put it like that it doesn't sound quite so terrible." Especially since I had nothing to lose now, so if I said something stupid? Oh well.

At least this time we didn't have to go all the way the fuck out to Joshua Tree. Tonight's shindig was happening at Isaac's crash pad in Beverly Hills.

Crash pad. In Beverly Hills. What the hell kind of parallel universe privileged-ass white people nonsense was that?

Turned out it wasn't that impressive, all things considered. Yeah, yeah, yeah—eighty million square feet, huge driveway, servants in tuxes, big water-wasting fountain, a crystal chandelier that some underpaid staff member probably had to hand-dust every other Tuesday. Yawn. After the place in Joshua Tree, it was just another gaudy mansion that wasn't quite ambitious enough to include a giant door and a swimming pool that could accommodate an aircraft carrier making a U-turn. How exciting—a three-dimensional representation of what people did when they had waaaay too much money.

Inside, we handed off our coats to the coat check. Seriously, he had fucking coat check in his house. Apparently piling everyone's coats on the bed wasn't good enough for these people. Christ.

I'd snapped a photo of the house before we'd come in, and I quickly sent it to Ashton and Luis with, *This is my FIL's crash pad. WTF.*

Then I pocketed my phone, made a conscious effort not to have *you've got to be shitting me* written all over my face, and walked with Jesse into the ballroom.

It wasn't hard to pick out couples in a crowd. You could always tell by how close people stood to each other. The casual contact. The occasional shared glances that were filled with either lusty secrets or barely-contained contempt, depending on how solid the relationship was.

In this ballroom alone—who the fuck has a *crash pad* with a *ballroom?*—I counted at least nine same-sex couples. I recognized three A-list actors who were here alone, but were very publicly out as queer.

The observation nauseated me. There should have been a feeling of solidarity. Some hope for the future because we could all be conspicuously here with our partners.

But it just turned my stomach.

Do any of you know that tonight's host is going to disown his son for marrying me?

I gritted my teeth. Well, if I'd been having any second thoughts about going through with this, they turned to dust as I counted the queer people at the party. They probably didn't know. They probably bought Isaac's bullshit about supporting equality, and God knew how much they would contribute to his campaign when the that time came. Hell, maybe they already had. There'd been some noise recently about the old bastard starting some fundraisers.

Ugh. Jesse and I needed to go elope, announce on a goddamned billboard that we're married, and light a fire under that man's homophobic ass.

Do it, you son of a bitch. Disown him and be fucking done with it so all these people see who you are.

And with that I decided I needed to go find a bar and throw back a couple of shots of something strong.

I turned to Jesse. "Hey, do you want something to drink?"

"Now that you mention it, yes." He gestured at the opposite end of the ballroom. "Bar's over there."

I followed him, and my mouth watered as I watched the tuxedoed bartenders pouring drinks. Would it be gauche to ask then to turn the bottle over above my open mouth? Maybe I could just double-fist. That was more or less polite, wasn't it? If anyone got judgy about it I guess I could say I was holding someone else's drink and hope nobody noticed me gulp—*sipping* from both.

By the time we made it to the front of the line, I'd settled on a beer. At least then I wouldn't drink it too fast—I could not drink beer quickly—and I'd be full long before I got drunk enough to say or do anything stupid. Jesse went with a martini. As we stepped away from the bar, I stole a glance at him, and literally tripped over my own feet. Christ. In a suit with his hair flawlessly styled, casually sipping a martini, he looked like James Bond or

214

something. Damn, he was sexy.

He eyed me. "You been pre-gaming?"

"Hmm? What?"

"You stumbled. You been sneaking sips from a flask I don't know about?"

"No, but I'm thinking a hip flask would be awesome at these parties."

"Yeah, you're probably right." He scanned the room. "Definitely something to invest in before the next one."

The next one. Oh God. Being an Ambrose *sucked.*

Being here with a hot Ambrose dressed like James Bond wasn't so bad though, I supposed.

So about that part of the contract that says sex isn't required—

"Jesse. Hayden." Isaac's voice made my hackles go up, but I forced my expression to stay neutral as I faced him. As Isaac shook hands with each of us, he smiled that phony smile that made me want to slap those gold crowns right out of his facehole. "I'm glad you boys could make it."

"Thanks, Dad," Jesse said dryly.

"This is a gorgeous house, Mr. Ambrose." I gestured over my shoulder. "I didn't know they made doors like that."

Isaac cocked his head. "Like what?"

"You know." I motioned toward the front of the house again. "Small."

Beside me, Jesse almost spat out his drink, and I should have been given an honorary goddamned Oscar for being able to keep a straight face right then.

Isaac's eyes narrowed slightly, but he quickly recovered and schooled his expression. "Well." He cleared his throat. "Actually, I wanted to chat with you, Hayden."

Jesse tensed. My blood turned cold.

"Um." I took a quick sip of beer. "Sure. What about?"

He snaked an arm around my shoulders, making my skin crawl beneath my suit. "Come with me. I want to introduce you to a few people."

I shot a *help me?* look at Jesse, but he just nodded and made a *go ahead* gesture.

So, I let Isaac herd me into the sea of suits and ties and faces I recognized from TV, movies, and goddamned billboards. I glanced over my shoulder, and to my relief, Jesse was nearby. He wasn't hot on our heels, but he was clearly staying close.

Just don't leave, okay? Please?

As if he could hear my thoughts, he smiled and gave me another nod.

Reassured that I wasn't on my own in this pool of piranhas, I pushed my shoulders back, took a deep breath, and let the introductions begin.

Chapter 14
Jesse

I hung back and kept an eye on Dad and Hayden. Everyone who mattered in Hollywood was here tonight, and Dad was in the process of introducing Hayden to *all of them*. After all, there was one undeniable truth in Hollywood—success depended not on what you knew, but on who you knew, and Dad still thought Hayden wanted to act.

I stayed close because I wasn't quite comfortable letting Hayden out of my sight. He seemed to be doing okay, though. If he was nervous, he wasn't showing it. He smiled broadly with every introduction. Shook hands firmly and confidently. Looked people in the eye. Didn't seem to shy away from conversation with anyone, not even when he was suddenly facing down three powerful producers and a couple of directors. Hell, he wasn't just handling it well—he was charming the shit out of them.

I smiled to myself. Trust Hayden to mesmerize the

Hollywood elite. Even my dad seemed genuinely interested in whatever Hayden was saying right then. Maybe it was because Hayden had decided to let acting go. He really didn't have anything to lose, so he had no reason to be nervous, and he was effortlessly chill and charming. God knew he charmed me at every turn, but I supposed I was biased. He didn't even have to speak to have me hypnotized. Laying on the charm in a tailored suit? Lord help me.

I watched my father as I sipped my martini, and I suddenly wished I'd gotten a glass of something stronger. As pleasant as he was being right then, I kept my guard up. He was much too business savvy to make a scene at something like this, but I was much too jaded to trust him to be doing this out of altruism.

"Your fiancé seems to be enjoying himself." My mother appeared beside me. "You'd never know he wasn't born into this world."

The snobbishness in her tone set my teeth on edge. I turned to her, but paused. She was watching Hayden, and I took a moment to watch her. She was a wizard at using makeup to make herself look thirty years younger—her artistry was part of what had inspired me to go into makeup to begin with—but there were things that couldn't be brushed over. Frown lines could be concealed. The frown itself? Not so much. She could make her eyes look bigger and brighter, but there was only so much she could do to hide the sadness and fatigue.

My heart sank. As much as she tried to convince the world that she was blissfully happy as Mrs. Isaac Ambrose, she'd always struck me as lonely and depressed. Maybe she could fool the cameras, but not her kids. At least not me.

I pulled my gaze away from her, and we stood in silence for a moment, watching Hayden chat with Dad and some of his Hollywood elite friends. Without turning to me, without raising her voice so that anyone but me would hear, she said, "Your father isn't going to stand for this."

I know. That's the idea.

As I brought my martini to my lips, I said, "He's letting us get married at the big house."

"Because he knows I wouldn't have allowed any less."

"Uh-huh." We exchanged glances. My mother tsked, and when she opened her mouth to speak, I put up a hand. "Not here. Let's do this outside."

Outside, where there's less interference for my phone to record.

She set her jaw. "Fine."

"Just give me a second." I didn't wait for a response and stepped up beside Hayden. I touched his shoulder and quietly said, "Hey."

He turned, smile still in place. "Hey. What's up?"

"I was just going to step outside for a few minutes with my mom. You good on your own?"

"Yep, I'm good. Take your time." Nothing about his tone suggested he was trying to convey that he really *wasn't* good and I'd better *not* leave, and his expression still seemed genuine.

"Okay. Shoot me a text if you need to find me."

"Will do." And with that he turned back to the directors he'd been chatting with, and picked up the conversation without missing a beat. "I don't know what they were thinking, suspending a light that heavy right over our heads, but…"

So much for needing to keep an eye on him.

With Hayden happily schmoozing, my mom and I

walked together out to one of the balconies overlooking the sprawling lawn and glittering lights of the other immense mansions. It was a different time and place from the private conversation we'd had outside the house in Joshua Tree, but there was definitely some déjà vu. I was pretty sure I wouldn't feel any better after this one than I had after the last one. Or any less guilty about surreptitiously recording it.

Her glass made a delicate clink when she set it on the stone railing. "Have you thought any more about what we discussed? About how your father is going to respond once the two of you get married?"

"Yes, I have."

We held each other's gazes. I was sure she was waiting for me to elaborate with the conclusions I'd come to. I figured she could read between the silent lines, though—yes, I'd thought about it. No, it hadn't changed a thing.

"Jesse." She sounded more exhausted now than she looked. "Your father doesn't bluff. All those years he said he'd disown you for marrying a man…" She turned to me, the warm light from inside illuminating one side of her face. "Do you *really* think he won't go through with it?"

"I'm sure he will."

"But you're going through with it anyway."

I swallowed. "What am I supposed to do, then? Wait until Dad's dead before I get married?"

She sighed heavily and looked out at the darkened landscape again. "I didn't raise you to be a stupid romantic."

I was used to Mom's bluntness, but admittedly, that one made me flinch.

"I may not see eye to eye with your father on a lot of

things," she went on, "but he controls the money, Jesse. If he disinherits you, there is nothing I can do to stop him."

"He's had ample opportunity to. Is he going to wait until after the wedding? Just to be sure?"

Mom scowled. "This isn't funny."

"No, it isn't. And I don't get what you want. Do you think I should call off the wedding so Dad doesn't cut me off, or what?"

She pursed her lips and pushed a sharp breath out her nose. "I think you need to think about what you're getting yourself into. How long have you even known this man?"

I took another drink because my mouth had suddenly gone dry, and anyway I was way too sober for this conversation. "I haven't known him very long, but sometimes you just know."

Another heavy sigh. "Jesse. For God's sake. Even after we talked about this… knowing he'll… You're really going to gamble with your place in this family and your financial future over someone you just met?" She tsked again, shaking her head. "What do you think will happen when things don't work out? Once you and Hayden divorce—because God *knows* this won't last—do you honestly believe your father will let you come crawling back just because you have nothing and no one?"

I gritted my teeth, still struggling to comprehend that my mother had accepted—and was even defending—that my father would disown me. Going into this arrangement with Hayden, I'd banked on getting disowned, but it took my breath away to hear my mom once again talking about it like a foregone conclusion. In her mind, it was inevitable that I'd be disowned, my marriage to Hayden would fail, and I'd eventually come crawling back. Somehow it never seemed to occur to her that it would be my dad who should be groveling for forgiveness.

"You need to think long and hard about what you're doing," she went on, her tone flat. "I'll plan your wedding and send you on a honeymoon, but don't expect me to get in your father's way. You knew the consequences if you went through with this. I've—" She paused, and seemed to be steeling herself. Setting her jaw, she glared up at me. "I've already lost one son who challenged your father. Don't expect me to forgive you any more than I'll forgive your brother."

"You didn't lose Alex because he challenged Dad," I snapped. "You lost him because Dad's a racist and you stood by him."

Her features hardened. "Alex made his choices. You're making yours." Her shoulder rose in the stiffest half-shrug I'd ever witnessed. "You're grown adults."

"And we're—"

"Jesse, I'm not going to argue about this." She put up a hand. "I'll make sure you have a wedding and a honeymoon because you're my son. I won't be pulled into the middle of you challenging your father." She brought her wineglass up to her lips, and her eyes narrowed slightly. "You know how this will end, don't you? You might win a battle or two, or at least think you have, but you will lose the war. You *know* that."

"Yeah. I do."

Taut silence hovered between us. My mother wasn't telling me anything I didn't already know, but it hurt to hear it. Battle lines were just abstract things until it was time for people to pick a side. We'd picked our sides, and now one of those years-old battle lines was carved on the ground between my mom and me. That… turned out to be a lot more painful than I'd anticipated.

I cleared my throat. "I need to know something."

She set her shoulders back. "All right."

And suddenly I wasn't sure I wanted to know, but I took a deep breath and spoke anyway. "You said you and Dad don't see eye to eye on a lot of things." I searched her expression as much as I could when she was mostly hidden by shadows. "Is this one of those things?"

"You mean your marriage to Hayden?"

"Marrying a man at all. Not because it goes against Dad's ultimatum." I shifted nervously. "I mean do you agree with him? About rejecting me for marrying the man I love?"

Mom held my gaze for a long, tense moment. Then, abruptly, she broke eye contact, picked up her glass with a faint scrape, and turned to go back inside. "We're missing the party. Let's not be rude to our guests."

And just like she'd done when I'd asked if she'd try to stop Dad from disowning me, she went back inside without answering my question.

I released a breath and gazed up at the night sky, flattening my palms on the cool railing as I stared out into the night. Prior to posting my ad, I hadn't given much thought to how my mom would feel about me getting married. She'd kept me from getting booted out for being gay when I was fifteen, and she'd negotiated with Dad to keep me from getting disowned as long as I didn't get married. But how would she feel when I actually did get married? Guess now I knew.

Closing my eyes, I rubbed my throbbing forehead. Maybe all those years ago, Mom hadn't wanted me thrown out because it would have made her look bad. Image was everything, after all. Or maybe she'd been afraid that if he disowned me and she tried to continue supporting me, her finances would be cut off too. She still had money of her own, but nothing like what my father provided, and the prenup made it clear she wouldn't see another cent of Ambrose money if they divorced.

So I'd had no idea if she'd been trying to protect her son or herself. More and more…

"I didn't raise you to be a stupid romantic."

I let my head fall back, and I stared up at the clear, star-sprinkled sky. I knew what she meant. Though she'd never said it out loud, she'd expected me to either remain a bachelor or marry a woman. Ideally an attractive and connected scandal-free slim white woman who'd never been married before. Anything else would jeopardize my—and her—place on my father's bankroll.

Or maybe that was all in my head, but what I did know was that my father hated what I was doing with Hayden, and my mother wouldn't come out and say he was wrong. All that mattered was maintaining the status quo. She'd never forgive my brother for upsetting that status quo, and she'd never forgive me for doing the same.

Thanks, Mom. Love you too.

I turned off the recorder on my phone. How ironic. I was at a party with my family, in a house jam-packed with people, many of whom I'd known since I was a child.

And I had never felt more profoundly alone in my life.

Chapter 15
Hayden

Today was the day.

Weeks of preparation—done. Obscene amounts of money—spent. Hordes of people I'd never met—arriving.

Standing alone in one of the eighty-seven million guest rooms of the Ambrose estate, I tried not to think about anything except putting myself together. My about-to-be mother-in-law had given us each a pair of diamond cufflinks last night—seriously, solid gold cufflinks covered in fucking *diamonds*—and I was extra grateful for them today. They gave me something to obsess over. Every time I moved my hand, I was absolutely certain one of the cufflinks was going to fly off and disappear down a vent or something. The Ambroses probably had their own personal HVAC staff who'd swoop in and fish it out, but still, I was worried sick I might lose one. These fuckers were probably worth more than my car or a black market kidney, for God's sake.

Sweating bullets over a lost cufflink was a lot easier

than overthinking everything that was about to go down. As it turned out, though, I could multitask like a boss. I could seriously consider jury-rigging a paperclip or something to keep my cufflinks in place, and at the same time, work myself into a panic over the fact that *I was getting married.* Today. In like half an hour. Crap. And it didn't matter that the marriage was fake. Ish.

I checked my cufflinks for the millionth time, then turned to face the full-length mirror. I loved how this tux looked, though the trousers were slightly more snug than they'd been at the tailor shop. Not surprising—I had definitely gained a little bit of weight since I'd moved in with Jesse. I supposed that was to be expected now that I was consuming more than one meal a day, and I'd been so underweight for a while that gaining even a handful of pounds was noticeable. My mom was happy, and I was good with it too, but I didn't want to suddenly wake up and realized I'd put on fifty pounds, so I'd started making religious use of the gym on the complex's second floor. I mean, how cool was that? Free access to a gym. Well, okay, so everyone else in the building had to pay arms and legs to live there, so I supposed it wasn't technically a free gym for them, but it sure was for this unapologetic husband-for-hire.

I held my own gaze in the mirror, took a deep breath, and slowly released it. This was it. Once we were married, it was only a matter of time before Isaac made his move. Jesse figured it could be six months from now, or it could go down today, and that was a degree of uncertainty I did not like. I wanted a schedule, goddammit, but apparently shit like this didn't happen on a schedule, and I was going to break out in hives before it was all over. Would he wait until our first anniversary? Or maybe drop the hammer today? Wasn't he giving a toast at the reception? Oh, Lord, that could get awkward. But at least it would be done.

Were real weddings this stressful? Because this fake one was seriously making me queasy.

It was probably not so much the wedding making me want to hurl, but the upcoming aftermath. Once we made it through today, we'd be married, and it would be up to Isaac to make good on that threat he'd issued since Jesse was a teenager. Jesse and I were both sure it would happen. It was just a question of when, and how, and how nasty the fallout would be.

Yep. Adios acting career. You either had your name in lights or your name on Isaac Ambrose's shit list. Not both.

I closed my eyes and pushed out a breath.

Please, God, let this be worth it.

Someone knocked at the door.

"Come in."

I turned, and my heart jumped into my throat.

Sliding his hands into his pockets, my brother came across the room. His tux was identical to mine, and it was like shifting my attention from one mirror to another. Except... not. Brian had lost some of the gauntness he'd had during his competitive days. Back when we'd joked his cheekbones were sharper than his skates. He still had some circles under his eyes—keeping up with toddlers would do that to a man—but he looked well-rested and well-fed for once in his life. Relaxed, even. As much as he could be when we were in the same room.

In that respect, he wasn't a mirror image of me at all. I was tense and nervous. Queasy. Wondering if I could get through the ceremony without throwing up on Jesse's shoes because… I mean holy shit, we were doing this.

Back in the day, Brian had been the wound up and too-thin one, and I'd been the bright-eyed twin who hadn't sacrificed any meals in the name of staying svelte. Now the roles were reversed, and I didn't know how to feel about that. It wasn't like I was going out onto the ice with millions of people watching me try for one of three medals on a world stage, but I felt the world on my shoulders anyway, and I wondered if this was how he'd felt before his competitions.

Except he wasn't pretending to skate in order to screw over some—

"So, you're finally getting hitched," he said, breaking the silence and startling me. An odd smile formed on his lips. "Congrats."

"Thanks."

We stood there awkwardly for the better part of a minute. I had no idea what to say. He didn't seem to either. I mean, it was great that we weren't fighting like we'd done as kids, but in its own way, this was worse. Screaming at each other and saying shit we regretted seemed more appealing somehow than the uncomfortable distance between strangers. This was how I should have felt if I were stuck in an elevator with an ex and his new boyfriend, not with my *twin*.

But here we were.

"Well. Um." Brian cleared his throat. "I just, um, wanted to come up and say congrats. I should let you finish getting ready."

"Yeah. Thanks." I tugged at my jacket sleeve just for something to do. Checked the cufflinks just to make sure they hadn't jumped ship. "Have you seen Mom and Dad?"

Brian nodded, gesturing over his shoulder. "They're downstairs with the kids. I should, um, probably go help them."

"Okay. Sure. Thanks for coming up."

He flashed me an awkward smile.

Then he turned to go, and as he walked away, the preemptive relief turned my conscience to acid. I wasn't supposed to want my brother—my twin—to be someplace else. As he reached for the doorknob, I had a flash of us as kindergarteners. Switching our names to screw with people. Refusing to dress alike on some days and demanding to on others. Playing together without so much as an inkling of what was going to happen after that coach came up during our birthday party at a local ice rink when we turned eight.

"Brian." I spoke around the lump in my throat, and almost choked when he turned around again.

"Yeah?"

I swallowed hard. "Listen, um… after I get back…" I coughed to get my breath moving. "We don't see much of each other anymore."

I half expected a scowl or a bitter comment about things being a two-way street. To my surprise, his expression softened, and he took his hand off the door. "No. We don't."

Silence hung for a couple of seconds before I managed to choke out, "We should… you know, do something about that."

His eyebrows rose, and he searched my eyes as if he wasn't sure he'd heard me right.

I moistened my lips. "We're adults. The past is…" I waved a hand, and for a moment, I struggled to find the words, but then they tumbled out on their own: "I miss you."

Brian dropped his gaze. "Yeah. Me too." He came closer again, and with some effort, met my eyes. "Look, about everything before... We were kids."

"I know. And I'm not mad about anything anymore."

"You're not?"

"No. Are you?"

He shook his head.

"So maybe when I get back, and things quiet down a bit…" I shrugged. "I can finally afford to come visit Mom and Dad again, so I can come to town. See you. Get to know the kids."

"That'd be great." Brian laughed softly. "And, yeah, you're kinda loaded now, aren't you?"

"Kinda, yeah." I felt myself blushing. "It's a weird feeling."

"It is. Just don't assume the cash will always keep coming. Trust me."

I nodded. "Duly noted."

The silence set in again, and he shifted his weight. "Listen, I'll let you finish getting ready. But we'll talk more, all right?"

"Okay. Yeah." I smiled, and this time the relief coursing through me didn't make me feel guilty. "We'll talk soon."

"Good." And with that, my twin stepped closer, hugged me fiercely. As he let me go, he said, "Now get your shit together. You've got a smoking hot dude to marry."

"Hey, quit ogling my groom." I laughed despite the sudden rush of panic. For a moment, I'd actually forgotten why we were both standing in this lavish house in expensive tuxes. And now the guilt came crashing in. Brian didn't know the truth. I couldn't tell him the truth. Maybe in the future, but not now.

Yep, my conscience is going to eat me alive. Fuck.

Brian left, and I didn't stop him this time. A few minutes later, there was another knock. This time it was my parents. As Dad closed the door behind them, the mix of relief and guilt had turned into some serious queasiness. They were about the only people I wanted to see right now, but I still felt shitty dragging them through this. At least I wasn't lying to them, though I was making them lie to my brother. *Christ.*

"You about ready?" Mom asked. "They're making some noise about getting started."

Oh, God…

I took another deep breath. "Yeah. Yeah, I'm…" I glanced down at my tux. "Do I look all right?"

"You look fine, sweetheart." Mom hugged me gently. "Like a real groom."

I laughed dryly. "Mission accomplished, I guess."

"And you're really sure about this?" Dad asked.

I nodded. "Yeah. I am. And, um, thanks. For going along with it."

My parents shared bemused looks, but smiled.

"How are you doing?" Mom asked. "Nervous?"

"Uh, you could say that." I laughed uneasily. "If I'm this nervous today, I'll probably pass out the day I get married for real."

Mom smiled and patted my hand. "You'll be nervous, but you'll be there because you want to be. Not because you're… well…"

"Putting on a show?"

She nodded. "Maybe a bit less performance anxiety."

"Huh. Who would have thought the real thing would mean *less* performance anxiety?"

Her lips quirked, but neither of my parents had an answer for that.

And there wasn't time to discuss it because there was yet another knock at the door, and suddenly we were all getting herded downstairs and out into the sprawling backyard for the ceremony. For my wedding. Oh shit. Here we go.

The painstakingly landscaped backyard was like the Ambrose family's own gigantic oasis in the desert. Trees and flowers grew out here that had no business in the desert, and I could only imagine how much water was wasted keeping them alive.

In the middle of it all, a white archway had been set up, and a long white carpet had been rolled out between rows of folding chairs. Guests were already sitting down. A string quartet was playing unobtrusively off to the side.

This was it. It was time. All I needed now was my groom.

My mother-in-law had insisted on keeping Jesse and me apart before the ceremony. Apparently seeing each other beforehand was bad luck. It seemed kind of ridiculous under the circumstances, but Carolyn didn't need to know that, so we'd gone along with it.

Now it was go time, and as I took my place at the beginning of the aisle...

Oh God.

There he was.

Jesse appeared beside me, suited and booted just like

me and looking good enough to eat. His light brown hair was meticulously arranged as always, and something about the black tux or the warm California sun or maybe both made his blue eyes extra vivid. Hypnotic, even. He really was like James Bond with a softer edge, and was it time for the honeymoon yet? Could we maybe pretend it was a real honeymoon and—

Music started playing. Everyone rose and faced us.

My pulse was racing, and when Jesse smiled and offered me his elbow, my heart pounded even harder. Tamping down my nerves—well, trying to—I curved my hand over his arm, and we started walking.

The faces on either side of us all kind of blurred together. I managed to pick out my family and my former roommates, but mostly I was a tornado of nerves, focusing on not tripping or passing out or throwing up. Though as I met Isaac's scowl a second before he put on a fake smile, I decided I could live with throwing up on him.

For the most part, I just concentrated on keeping my feet under me as I walked down the aisle with Jesse. And I also compulsively checked to make sure I hadn't lost one of those bazillion dollar cufflinks because God knows that would be my luck.

I chalked it up to years of training as an actor—and maybe a pinch of divine intervention—that I made it to the altar without vomiting, tripping, crashing into Jesse, or losing one of the stupid cufflinks. Joining hands, we faced each other.

As soon as I met Jesse's eyes, all I could do was stare. He was just so... fuck, he was hot. When he was lounging on the sofa in gym shorts and a threadbare tank top, he was hot. When he was shuffling around in slippers and sweats with a laundry basket on his hip, he was hot. When he was laughing at something and his eyes sparkled, he was hot.

And standing in front of me in a custom made tuxedo, his own pair of diamond and gold cufflinks, and a warm, sweet smile? Jesus Christ, he was *smoking* hot.

Do I take this man…? Hell yeah, I do. Where do I sign?

Of course I knew we weren't really a couple and we weren't really getting married, but his gorgeous face definitely made it easier to go through the motions.

The ceremony was pretty straightforward. The minister went on about love and romance and commitment, and he quoted some Bible passages, and then there were the customary vows. I'd been to enough weddings and seen enough on TV that I could pretty much recite the vows in my sleep, so it was just a matter of keeping that smile in place and selling it that I really meant what I was saying. It helped to imagine that everyone here believed I was going to spend tonight getting naked with Jesse. Hey, sometimes when you bat out of your league, you still get a home run.

Those thoughts kept me smiling, and they *almost* made me forget about the not-very-traditional nervousness in the pit of my stomach. Isaac was still sitting quietly, but I'd seen that fleeting look on his face. He was not happy, and at any moment, he was going to say or do something.

If they ask for objections, is he going to stand up?

Except I'd never actually been to a wedding where they asked for objections, and I was pretty sure people didn't do that anymore, and the minister hadn't said anything about it while we'd been finalizing the ceremony. So why the hell was I surprised when he *didn't* ask? I mean besides the fact that I was convinced Isaac Ambrose was going to jump out of his chair and make a scene at any moment.

The minister didn't ask. Isaac didn't object.

Before I knew it, we'd been through the whole ceremony. We'd said "I do." Shit, we'd actually done it.

Then the minister closed the book and smiled. "You may kiss your husband."

And I froze.

In all the upheaval and chaos, it hadn't even crossed my mind that when we got up here to the altar, we'd be doing more than saying vows. Oh shit. Okay, a stage kiss. I could do that. Especially with a costar this hot. Just... had to remember... how to move. What do I do with my hands? Am I supposed to... do we...

Thank God, Jesse wasn't quite so paralyzed. He stepped closer, smiling down at me, and the warmth of his hands on my face made my heart flutter.

And then he pressed his lips to mine, and the whole world... was just... still.

This wasn't a stiff *let's get this over with* kiss. No quick peck to seal the deal without getting too carried away. No, Jesse seemed perfectly happy to get carried away, and right then, I didn't give two shits if it was for the cameras or if he meant it. I'd never been kissed like this—long and gentle and sweet, with a soft brush of his thumb over my cheekbone and the subtlest motion of his lips to encourage mine to move too. For a kiss this fake, it sure *felt* real.

I might have forgotten where we were and about all the people watching if they hadn't erupted into applause.

As we pulled apart, our eyes met, and we both smiled, and we were both out of breath, and wasn't this supposed to be an act? Because seriously the way my head was spinning and my heart was thumping and I just couldn't stop smiling—none of that was fake.

"Ladies and gentlemen," the minister said with a big grin. "Mr. Jesse Ambrose and Mr. Hayden Somerset."

More applause, and we exchanged smiles before, hand in hand, we walked up the aisle.

And… that was it. The ceremony was over. We were married.

"I don't know about you…" Jesse still sounded breathless. "But I could use a drink."

I laughed, squeezing his hand. "Make that two."

We hurried toward a table covered in champagne flutes that had already been filled. While the staff and wedding planner started herding everyone toward the reception area, we had a much-needed lull. We were away from everyone else, no one was pulling us in any direction, and we could decompress for a minute or two, ideally with some of that champagne.

"I'm actually surprised," Jesse said as we walked. "That was pretty painless."

"What?" I eyed him with mock offense. "Did you really think marrying someone this fabulous *wouldn't* be painless?"

Jesse laughed. "That's not what I meant."

"Mmhmm. Sure it wasn't."

Chuckling, he pushed a champagne flute into my hand. "Shut up and drink."

"Oh, I can do that." I swallowed a good half of the contents of my glass because holy crap, the ceremony was over and so far no one had figured out what we were doing.

And *holy crap*, I was *married*. Legally married.

I mean, yeah, it was only on paper and I was totally getting paid, but still. Christ.

I put the glass down, and to hell with it, I needed another. As I reached for the glasses, something tugged at my cuff, and I caught a glimpse of something small and shiny careening away from my hand. There was a clink, another, and then something rattled, and I realized to my horror that one of those diamond and gold cufflinks had—just as I'd been terrified it would—gone flying off and made its escape.

I lunged after it, but Jesse was faster. We both straightened, and he held up the cufflink between us.

"I think you dropped something," he said softly.

My face burned. God, was I really so bad at all this that I couldn't even put on a cufflink right? "Yeah, I... guess I did." I gently took it from him and gazed down at it. This thing was way too expensive and fancy. It was heavy, for fuck's sake. Because it was solid *gold*.

"Need a hand putting it back on?" Jesse asked.

I hesitated. I so wanted to suggest taking the other one off and leaving them that way, but then my sleeves would flail around and look awful. Wouldn't our wedding portraits look fabulous like that? Ugh.

Like it or not, I had to wear the damn things, so I handed the escapee to Jesse. "Thanks."

"Don't mention it." He held up his champagne flute. "Hold this?"

I took the glass, and now that his hands were free, he carefully slid the cufflink back into place.

I cleared my throat. "Do they usually come off that easily?"

"They shouldn't. And nothing is loose. Let me see the other one."

I held up my other hand. He inspected the cufflink, then smiled. "This one's fine. It must not have been seated quite right, but you're good now."

"Okay." I exhaled. "I've been paranoid all day about losing one. I must have loosened it while I was fussing with it or something."

Jesse nodded. "Maybe. It happens."

"Yeah, well, I'm not used to wearing anything quite this expensive, so…"

He frowned. "It's really bothering you, isn't it?"

"Are you kidding? I flailed a little too hard and something with gold and diamonds almost ended up lost in the grass." I rubbed the bridge of my nose. "Because I don't have enough to fucking stress over today."

Jesse studied me. Then a smile slowly appeared. He looked around. Guests were still slowly making their way from the ceremony seating to the area cordoned off for the reception. The photographer was waiting nearby, probably wanting some photos of the two of us.

Jesse beckoned her over. "Hey, do you mind if we step out for about five minutes, and then we'll meet you by the fountain in front of the house?"

The photographer shrugged. "Sure."

As she left, I turned to him. "What are we doing?"

He took my hand and nodded toward the house. "I'll show you."

Chapter 16
Jesse

While our guests were transitioning from ceremony to reception, I took Hayden to the bedroom where I'd been getting ready earlier.

"Um, what are we doing?" he asked.

I pulled a small box out of my suitcase. "I don't want you spending the whole day worrying about losing one of those cufflinks. So…" I took out a pair of silver and amber cufflinks and offered them to him. "Why don't you wear these instead?"

"So, something cheap?"

"They're not *cheap*. But if one gets away…" I shrugged. "It isn't the end of the world."

He glanced back and forth from me to the cufflinks.

"I just don't want you worrying about jewelry," I said softly. "Today is stressful enough for both of us. No point in wasting energy on something like this."

Cautiously, maybe a little reluctantly, he took the cufflinks. "Your mom won't mind?"

Oh, she would, and she'd have words with me about it, but she wouldn't say anything to Hayden. She didn't know him well enough yet. "Eh, she'll be fine. I can just tell her they didn't fit quite right and kept coming loose." I started to take off my own pair. "I'm not a big fan of them myself."

"Really?"

"Nah. A bit too flashy for my taste." I carefully put them into the box, then selected a pair similar to the one I'd given Hayden. "To tell you the truth, I kept checking to make sure I hadn't lost one too. I don't mind an expensive watch or a ring or something because they're not going anywhere, but I lost a cufflink at an event a few years ago, and now I get paranoid."

What seemed like years worth of tension melted out of Hayden's expression and posture. "So, it's not stupid?" He started putting on the amber cufflinks. "Being worried like that?"

"Nah. I mean, most of the time, they stay in place. That's what they're supposed to do." I paused to secure one of mine. "But all it takes is losing one *once*."

He laughed dryly. "No kidding. I, um… I feel a lot better, then. I thought I was just being ridiculous because I'm not used to all this fancy shit."

"You're not. I promise. And if one of these falls off?" I gestured at my own. "I know where to replace them. So don't sweat it."

Hayden's sweet smile made my knees weak. "Thank you."

"Don't mention it."

He held my gaze, and for a moment, I thought he'd say something. Then, to my surprise, he stepped closer, pushed himself up on his toes, and pressed a kiss to my lips.

It was as brief as it was mind-blowing, and as he drew back, I was suddenly as out of breath as I'd been after the ceremony.

Do it again.

I kept my mouth shut, though. We locked eyes, and I thought one of us might move in for another kiss, but instead, we both looked away.

"So, um." Hayden coughed. "We shouldn't keep the photographer waiting."

"Right. Good idea." I fussed with one of the cufflinks I'd just put on. "After you."

We headed downstairs, and the whole way, I caught myself wishing we could just blow off the rest of the party and stay in that room. At least we'd be off on our "honeymoon" tomorrow, and it would be the two of us and no one else. Not a real honeymoon, but still, I couldn't wait.

Because Hayden was the only one I wanted to see.

After we'd gone through the motions with the photographer, we moved on to the reception. It was as generic as the ceremony had been. Introducing us as a couple. Dinner. Toasts. A cake that seemed way too elaborate to cut into during the also-way-too-elaborate cake-cutting… ritual? Ceremony? Whatever the hell it was called. Then there were more toasts. *So* many fucking toasts.

Finally, it was time for what people really came for—

drinking and dancing. As the music kicked on and people got up from their tables, I stole a moment to myself and checked my phone. Not surprisingly, I had a text from my youngest brother, Alex.

Congrats, man. Can't wait to meet the guy. Sorry I couldn't be there.

I smiled and wrote back, *Thanks. Let me know when you're in LA again.*

Will do. Probably soon. Go enjoy your party, dumbass.

I chuckled, pocketing my phone. Alex was the only one of my four siblings who I'd ever been close to, and I would have loved to have him as my best man for my wedding, but it was just as well he wasn't here. I didn't want to lie to him about my marriage. And anyway, he couldn't be in the same room as our parents without it turning into Battle Royale. I'd always known that whenever the time came for me to get married, he wouldn't be at my wedding, and I understood. I resented the shit out of my parents for alienating him like that, but I understood why he stayed away.

In case anyone ever wondered who the smartest of the five Ambrose kids really is…

And speaking of my siblings, the other three were present and accounted for. I had the briefest conversations I could manage with Amanda and Carson, and finally managed to catch up with Reanna.

My first thought when I saw her was that she looked great. She seemed healthy and happy, and I was thrilled to see that she was still with the boyfriend she'd had when I saw her last. Jay, I thought his name was? Nice guy. Always smiling and joking. He was a computer programmer, I thought, and he adored her. The family sneered at him because he was bald with a beard, glasses, and a potbelly, and he clearly wasn't rolling in money. I had to admit, the fact that he didn't fit into my family made me like him even more.

I shook hands with Jay, and Reanna and I exchanged a stiff hug and uncomfortable smiles. We didn't have the sour relationship like I had with Carson and Amanda, but we'd never been close either. The day I'd moved out of our parents' house, we'd stopped having much contact beyond social media and showing up to the same family functions. I checked on her now and then to make sure her health was still on the rails, and she pinged me once in a while to see if I was doing all right. Other than that, I couldn't remember the last actual conversation we'd had.

It usually didn't bother me, but it made me sad today. My two older siblings and I could barely stand each other, my younger sister and I didn't know each other, and the one sibling I was close to couldn't be here because he was estranged from the rest of the family.

How the hell had we all been this fucked up for this long without even realizing it?

For that matter, did my older siblings realize how fucked up our family was the way Reanna, Alex, and I did? Maybe they did. Maybe they didn't. I doubted they'd ever stop toeing the line, though. Not if it meant cutting off Dad's money, not to mention seriously damaging both of their careers. As high-profile actors, they were tangled up in the spider web whether they liked it or not. Like I needed any more reason to be glad I hadn't gone into acting like our parents had wanted all of us to do.

The reception went on. I kept a comfortable distance from my family, though to my surprise, the comfort zone between Hayden and me had shrunk considerably. Ever since the ceremony, we'd stayed close, and although I knew we were doing it to sell the charade of a happy pair of newlyweds, it was easy. So easy it was jarring. It felt natural to have an arm around his waist, or slow dance with him, or casually hold hands during the toasts. When the photographer asked us to kiss for a photo, I didn't even hesitate. And that was to say nothing about that kiss he'd stolen earlier in the guest room.

This was all supposed to be an act, but it wasn't like I had to psych myself up for any of the physical contact. In fact, as we took a breather at the head table, our fingers laced together while we watched people getting shit-faced and dancing, the contact centered me. Soothed my anxiety in a way it had no right to. I didn't want to keep my hands off him. Or my eyes off him. He was gorgeous in his tux, and that beautiful smile… my God.

I shouldn't have needed to keep reminding myself that this was a charade. Just because Hayden was really, really good at making his vows sound convincing, not to mention pulling off those sweet smiles and longing looks, didn't mean what we were doing was real. He was an actor, and a better one than I'd expected.

But does it mean it can't ever become real?

"Holy shit." Hayden gaped at the car parked at the bottom of the marble stairs in front of the house. "Is that… for *us?*"

"No, sweetheart." I patted his shoulder. "That's the caterer's car."

"Shut up." Chuckling, he elbowed me. "I've just, uh, never seen a stretched Rolls before."

"And now you get to ride in it."

He grinned. "Lucky me."

Lucky me, *because after tomorrow it's just you and me for two weeks. Are we there yet?*

I shivered, and no I was absolutely not counting down the hours until we left for the airport in the morning.

We couldn't leave quite yet, though. Our immediate families had come down to see us off, and after I'd shaken hands with Hayden's parents and brother, I turned to my own. My cell was in my breast pocket, recording every sound just in case things went down right here and now. I steeled myself for the... best? Worst? Hard to say.

My mom hugged me stiffly and kissed my cheek. "I hope you two have a wonderful time on your honeymoon."

"Thanks, Mom. And thanks for setting up the cruise."

"Of course." She pulled back and smiled, though her eyes were filled with feelings no mother should have at her son's wedding. "Nothing but the best for my baby and his husband." Her expression added, *"It's the least I can do while you're still part of the family."*

My mouth had gone dry, but I managed to croak, "Thanks."

Dad shook my hand, then pulled me in for a half-hug. For a split second, I was stunned by this unusually affectionate gesture from my father.

Then he clapped me on the back and whispered just loud enough for me to hear and no one else, including the phone dutifully recording from my pocket:

"You're an embarrassment to your family, Jesse."

My teeth snapped together. The sentiment was hardly unexpected, but the words still cut deep. "I love him," I growled back as if it would change anything.

I didn't think I'd ever heard so much contempt packed into a single breath of laughter, but there it was. Dad clapped my back again, harder this time, and pulled away. His other hand still clasped with mine, he looked in my eyes and smiled that fake smile that had appeared on more magazine covers than I could count. "Congratulations."

Then he moved on to Hayden, and he offered the same handshake-turned-hug and said something I didn't hear. My stomach somersaulted.

Don't you dare, Dad. Don't you fucking dare.

But whatever he'd said must not have been as devastating as what he'd told me. When Dad released him, Hayden smiled the way he always did around my family—charming, sincere to the naked eye, but obviously forced to anyone who knew him.

"Enjoy your honeymoon, boys," Dad said his tone carrying an undercurrent I recognized as "*we're going to talk when you get back.*"

The sooner the better as far as I was concerned.

I swallowed hard and mumbled, "Thanks."

We climbed into the back of the Rolls, and we both released relieved sighs as the car started down my parents' long driveway.

"We did it." I put up my fist.

He bumped it. "Mission accomplished. I think I could sleep for a month."

"You and me both."

I half expected him to ask what happens now. How soon did I think my dad would make his move? How public would it be? Did he even want to know? I wondered if he'd heard what my dad had said to me.

But Hayden didn't say anything. He seemed pretty wrung out, and I didn't blame him. Though the day had been fun, all things considered, it had been stressful and crazy since the sun had come up. If I had to guess, he needed to decompress from today before he worried about tomorrow or anything beyond. I could relate.

In the silence of the limo, I stared down at the gold band on my finger, and idly thumbed it. I should have been happy. Relieved, if nothing else. There'd been no guarantee anyone would even answer my ad, never mind see it through, but Hayden had. The gambit had been a risky one, and it had taken a lot of time, cash, and energy to set up, but today it had all come together. I'd made my move. I'd married a man. Nothing left to do now except let Dad respond. If what he'd said was any indication, there *would* be a response, and I just needed to make sure I was recording when it came.

"Hey." Hayden nudged me gently with his shoulder. "You all right? You've been a little off since we left."

"Yeah. I'm good." I smiled, hoping that would make the lie sound more convincing, but from the crease of his brow, it hadn't helped. "I could use another drink, though."

Hayden didn't protest, and fortunately, the limo had a well-stocked minibar.

While we took advantage of this nice cache of booze, we didn't say much. He was probably exhausted. So was I, and I was also distracted.

And, I had to admit... devastated.

Over and over I told myself that this was what I'd set

out to do. Dad's comment meant my plan was working. The cracks were beginning to show, and it was only a matter of time before he made good on his promise.

Still, it hurt. No matter what we were doing or why, no matter how much of an act this was, there was still something emotionally crushing about hearing my dad's words, especially on what he had every reason to believe was my real wedding day.

You're an embarrassment to your family, Jesse.

I closed my eyes and released a long breath. God help me, I was going to see this through, and it damn well better be the end of my father's political ambitions.

Because I refused to believe this kind of heartache could happen for nothing.

Chapter 17
Hayden

So… honeymooning as a rich dude? Whaaat? This shit was *amazing*.

My parents and I had gone to some of my brother's competitions, including both trips to the Olympics, so it wasn't like I'd never flown before. And once or twice, we'd scored a cheap upgrade and gone first class on a short trip somewhere.

International business class to Barcelona, though? Holy crap. My seat had a massager in it. A *massager*. That alone blew my fucking mind, but there was also real food—like, food you could actually identify and had actual flavors and real honest to God silverware. I decided to splurge on a glass of wine, but the flight attendant forgot to charge me for it, and then Jesse told me they *didn't charge for it*. Whaaat.

And all of that was before we got onboard the cruise ship. And opened the door marked Honeymoon Suite.

And...

Holy crap. I mean, weren't cruise ships accommodations kind of notorious for being hilariously small? Because this cabin or stateroom or whatever was literally bigger than the apartment I'd shared with Ashton and Luis. I was pretty sure the *bed* was bigger than that apartment. I'm not even ashamed to admit I spent the first hour exploring the suite like a kid in a theme park. Gilded bathroom with the square footage of a small parking lot? Check. Liquor cabinet stocked with basically everything, plus a number to call in case we wanted more? Check. Closet the size of that warehouse at the end of Raiders of the Lost Ark? Check.

Jesse didn't seem too enthusiastic about the place, though. At first I thought he might be jetlagged. Or maybe he wasn't impressed with our digs, which wouldn't really surprise me considering his dad's house.

But something didn't seem right.

It wasn't just a lack of enthusiasm over our accommodations, and it had started before the jetlag became an issue. He'd been in a good mood throughout the wedding and reception, but in the Rolls on the way out, he'd been... somewhere else. I'd chalked it up to a lot of things—relief that he'd made his big move, a need to decompress, worry over what his dad would do now—but none of that seemed to fit either.

I gave him some space while we both settled into the suite. I was gross from traveling for the thirty-nine years it had taken to get from Los Angeles to Barcelona, so I quietly went in to take a much-needed shower. When I came back out, he was on the balcony, shirtless and leaning on the railing. Staring out at the sea, he looked like his mind was a million miles away.

I paused to take in the sight of him. Though I was concerned about him, it was hard not to steal a moment to shamelessly ogle him. Broad shoulders. Sun-kissed skin. Arms for days. An ass that looked so good it should have been criminal. And I was totally married to this guy. Shame I couldn't touch him.

I could, however, stop perving on him and go see what was wrong, because he really did seem unhappy, and I mean, I liked the guy. A lot. I was worried about him. Checking him out could wait. Checking *on* him couldn't.

I figured since he hadn't bothered with a shirt, I didn't need to either. In a pair of gym shorts and nothing else, I opened the sliding glass door. He didn't respond. As I stepped out, I cautiously asked, "You okay?"

Jesse sighed, staring out at nothing. "Yeah. I'm good."

"You don't seem good." I joined him, forearms on the railing, and looked at him while he continued staring at the water. When he didn't respond, I gently nudged his shoulder with mine. "Look, I know this isn't a real honeymoon, but it *is* a real vacation. There's nothing wrong with letting ourselves have a good time."

That got a halfhearted little smile out of him. He laughed and turned to me. "You're right. I'm sorry. I didn't mean to be a downer."

"You don't have to apologize. I'm just worried." I raised my eyebrows. "Seriously. What's wrong?"

Jesse swallowed, dropping his gaze again. "You know when we were getting ready to leave the reception? When my dad hugged me?"

I nodded slowly. Now that he mentioned it, that had been the moment his demeanor had changed. Something in Jesse had shifted, and he'd been distant for the rest of the night. Not cold or prickly, just folded in on himself.

Jesse whispered, "He told me I was an embarrassment to the family."

My heart dropped. "He actually said that?"

"Yep. And it's not like I didn't know. If anything, I should've been surprised he didn't say it into a microphone or something." He thumped his knuckle on the metal railing. "I knew he felt that way, but God, hearing it? Hearing him actually say the words out loud at my wedding?" He pressed his lips together and shook his head, but didn't finish the thought. I supposed he didn't have to.

"I'm sorry." Ugh, that sounded so stupid, but I had no idea what else to say.

Jesse sighed, lowering his gaze. He rested his forearms on the railing again, hands loosely clasped together, and returned his stare to the water. "I knew it was coming. I knew." He sniffed and made a gesture like he was scratching his face and not wiping his eye. "I fucking knew it, but I had no idea how much it would hurt to hear him say it."

"It's not the first time he's said it, is it?"

He shook his head. "Not even close. But as far as he knew, that was my real wedding, and you and I are in it for the long haul." He swallowed, and his voice was thick as he went on. "I guess I didn't realize until that moment how much I was hoping my dad *would* have a change of heart. Like… maybe when he had to put his money where his mouth was and decide if he wanted to keep that promise to disown me, he might…"

"Realize he didn't want to do that?"

Jesse nodded without looking at me. "I thought he might realize at the last minute that at the end of the day…" His voice wavered. "At the end of the day, I'm his *son*."

"And he should be happy for you on your wedding day."

He nodded again, lips pressed tightly together. "I didn't really think he would." Jesse laughed bitterly. "In fact I might've had a heart attack if he had. But on some level… I just held out this *tiny* little inkling of hope that my dad could love me unconditionally. Or just love me at all."

The sudden ache in my chest pushed the breath right out of me. "Jesus. I… I can't even imagine." I had no idea what else to do, so without another thought, I wrapped my arms around him, and he sighed as he leaned into my embrace. His skin was hot from the Mediterranean sun, and the warmth should have felt good, but I was too busy being sick for him. "Your dad doesn't deserve you. And you deserve better than him."

"Too bad there's no returns or exchanges."

"No kidding." I stroked his hair, fighting the urge to press a kiss to his temple. I never understood why anyone was cruel to anyone, but Jesse was just so… he was such a sweet guy. And to have his own family shitting on him? I didn't even know what to say to that. All I could think was he needed to get his mind off things, so I went with, "You want go get shit-faced and then find a dancefloor to make asses of ourselves on until we forget about him?"

He laughed, the first truly genuine laugh I'd heard from him all day. As he drew back, he smiled faintly. "You go ahead. I think I might just hang out in here and…" He ran a hand through his hair. "I don't know. I just don't think I can people tonight."

"I don't blame you."

He stared at the water again, eyes distant and jaw working. My heart ached for him. His whole plan to upend his dad's political career had been so calculated, I hadn't realized how much he was putting on the line emotionally. It was hard to imagine how someone could know his father was such a trash fire of a human being who needed to be kept out of power by any means necessary, and still cling to a threadbare scrap of hope that the person might change. That somewhere under all that flaming debris was the unconditional love I'd always taken for granted from my own dad. It was physically painful to watch Jesse grappling with the reality that, no, his father didn't and wouldn't love him unconditionally, and that he'd meant it when he'd said marrying a man would get Jesse evicted from the family. How did someone process that? I'd had disagreements with my parents, especially when I was younger, but I couldn't imagine them turning their backs on me like that.

The one time in my life when I'd thought they would was when I was twelve. I'd been terrified to come out to them, and I hadn't been able to stop crying as I'd said the words because I was convinced they wouldn't love me anymore. But then my dad had hugged me tight and said he'd pretty much known I was gay since I was five, that it didn't change a damn thing, and that of course he and my mom still loved me. I'd instantly felt stupid for ever thinking any differently. Because really, what parent would do that to their own child?

Isaac Ambrose, apparently.

Fifteen-plus years after coming out to my parents, I

was standing on the balcony of a luxury cruise ship with the man I'd married in the name of taking down a homophobe, and it was like watching everything I'd been afraid of back then come to life. I'd had a mental horror movie playing over and over in my head back then, one where my parents walked out of the room and I just sat there, devastated beyond words and so, so alone.

The lump in my throat was almost too big to swallow past as I watched Jesse stare at the ocean. I wanted to tell him he wasn't alone, but the company of a guy he'd known a handful of weeks probably didn't stack up to much next to the void his parents would be leaving.

There was no one else around, though, and I wasn't about to leave him twisting in the wind. I had no idea what to say, but it was a safe bet he could use another hug, so without a word, I pulled him close again. Like he had the first time, Jesse sighed and leaned into me as he wrapped me up in a tight embrace. He felt so brittle and unsteady, like even though he was bigger and broader than I was, a strong wind off the water might have toppled him right here on the balcony.

"I'm sorry," I said. "Your family sucks."

"Yeah, they do," he murmured into my hair. "Thanks, though. And it's nice to not be alone right now."

Okay so apparently an almost-stranger's company was better than the alternative. Christ, how lonely did a man have to be for someone he barely knew to be the nearest source of support after something like this? And not just the "*let's fall into bed and forget the world exists*" kind of support, either. I could see getting that from a stranger. But this?

I held him tighter. Every time he peeled back a veil

and showed me more of the wounds his family had given him, my heart broke for him all over again.

"You deserve so much better," I whispered.

Jesse just sighed again.

After a while, we drew apart enough to look at each other. When our eyes met, something rippled through me, but I quickly tamped it down before I could give it a name. Standing this close to an attractive, shirtless man who had his arms around my own shirtless torso—yeah, certain reactions were inevitable, but that wasn't what he needed right now. Or, well, if it was, he had to be the one to initiate it. I wasn't going to take advantage of him when he was this raw.

I rested a hand on his back, pretending not to notice the way his muscles quivered beneath my touch. "You sure you want to stay in tonight? We really could go out and distract you."

Moistening his lips, Jesse nodded. "Yeah. I, um, I think I just need a night to relax. But… go ahead. Don't let me keep you cooped up."

I had a funny feeling that the message between the lines was that he wanted to be alone. After being bombarded with people for the last couple of days—it had been nonstop human interaction from the rehearsal dinner to finally arriving at our suite—he probably needed some time to himself.

"Okay." I broke the embrace, suppressing a shiver as the wind brushed skin that was no longer pressed against Jesse's, and I stepped toward the sliding glass door. "Take it easy. I'll see you later tonight."

"Okay. Have fun."

We locked eyes and both smiled weakly.

Then I turned to go, but I didn't get far.

"Hayden."

Hand on the sliding glass door's handle, I faced him. "Yeah?"

Our eyes met again, and something about the way he looked at me right then made my pulse go up. The heartache was still there in his expression, but there was something else now. He pushed himself off the railing and cautiously came closer. "I, um…"

I let go of the door, facing him fully. "Hmm?"

Another step across the tiny balcony, and we were so close we could touch. My heart started racing. The way he was looking at me just then… fuck, how was I supposed to breathe?

Somehow I found enough breath to ask, "What's on your mind?"

"You." He swallowed. "That's… that's really it. Just you."

"Just me?"

"Yeah. I…" He narrowed some more of that space. I fought the urge to draw back from the sheer intensity of his presence. I was afraid if I pulled away at all, he'd lose his courage.

Jesse swallowed hard. He leaned in tentatively, sending my pulse skyward, but he hesitated. He started to speak. Then his eyes flicked to my lips, and he seemed to lose his train of thought. And then his nerve. Cursing softly, he pulled back an inch or two.

"Jesse," I whispered.

He looked in my eyes.

"Whatever you're thinking," I said, my voice shaking, "it doesn't have to happen right now."

He swallowed. "*Can* it happen right now?"

It was my turn for a nervous swallow. "I just don't... if you're feeling... with everything that's..."

"I don't want to think about any of that tonight."

"Neither do I, but I don't just want to be your distraction either."

That startled him, but after a second, he smiled and closed some more of the distance between us. "I don't think you understand how much you've been distracting me from everything. Since day one."

I drew back a little from the smoldering want in his eyes, and my shoulder blades met the cold sliding glass door. "Have I?"

Jesse nodded. "I don't want you because you're distracting." He moved in closer, close enough to touch. "You're distracting because I want you."

Oh be still my beating heart and hardening dick.

I slid a hand over his waist, and apparently that was all the encouragement he needed, because he closed the remaining distance, and he kissed me.

The soft warmth of his lips took me right back to that moment at the altar, when what was supposed to be a stage kiss had made me forget all my lines and where we were and why. The whole world had concentrated itself between us, and that was exactly what happened this time. It also took me back to that brief kiss after he'd given me the amber cufflinks, and now I suddenly had the chance to kiss him the way I'd wanted to in that room.

Slowly, I draped my arms around his neck, and as I deepened the kiss, his breath rushed past my cheek and he pulled me in closer. The heat of his bare chest against mine and his arms against my shirtless back made my knees shake.

We'd kept it chaste at the altar, kept it quick in the guest room, but now there was no one around to see us, and no one around to care, and I was pretty sure Jesse needed this more than air right now, so I deepened the kiss, and we lazily explored each other's mouths.

I slid a hand up into his hair, and he growled into my kiss as he tightened his arms around me. I decided then and there that I *loved* how our bodies fit together.

"You know, if your heart… isn't too set on going out tonight," he panted, "I think I've got a better idea… than getting drunk and dancing."

"Yeah?" I was breathless too. "What've you got in mind?"

"I'm thinking we go inside." He nodded past me at our suite. "And see how much that bed can handle."

I blinked, startled by the comment.

He tensed. "I mean, or we could—"

I kissed him, and as I fumbled with the door behind me, I murmured against his lips, "You, my dear husband, have a dirty mind."

"Mmm, yeah, I do." He curved his hands down over my ass. "That a good thing or a bad thing?"

The door finally opened. "Shut up and take off your pants."

L.A. WITT

Chapter 18
Jesse

Making out with Hayden and stripping off what little clothing we had on—hell, if I'd known this would break me out of my funk, we'd have fucked right there in the limo last night. It was like this dark cloud had been hanging over my head ever since that moment with my father, and now that Hayden and I had finally crossed this line, the clouds scattered. No, it wouldn't fix anything, and yes, the bullshit with my father still existed, but right now, I finally had my hands and mouth and body against Hayden, and everything was perfect. He dragged me down onto the bed, arms wrapped tightly around me as his lips and tongue explored mine, and I was in heaven.

Finally. I get to touch you the way I've been fantasizing about. God, finally.

He was everything I'd imagined too. He kissed aggressively, and his hands roamed my skin without a hint of tentativeness. Even his thighs—parted around my hips—weren't passive or still. He squeezed my hips, lifted his own to rub our cocks together, hooked a leg around mine to keep me against him. This was not a guy who lazily laid back and let his partner do all the work, and if his lips turned out to be *half* this enthusiastic on my dick... oh, Jesus.

I broke the kiss and started on his neck, and he arched under me, digging his nails into my shoulders.

"Fuck, Jesse..."

I nipped his collarbone, then let my lips skate along his throat. "Do you have any idea..." I panted, "how hard it's been to keep my hands off you all this time?"

He moaned, lifting his hips to rub our cocks together again. "Think... think I have some idea, yeah."

The thought of him fantasizing about this as much as I had? Oh fuck.

As I explored his neck, he said, "So, um, I guess a day or two into being married is a bit late to ask, but... what's your status?"

"Negative," I murmured against his throat. "You?"

"Same." He dragged his fingers up my sides. "Still should... should be safe and..."

"Mmhmm. I think they have condoms at some of the gift shops. Probably lube too. I could run down and—"

"Nah, I have some."

I lifted my head. "You brought condoms and lube?"

"Well, yeah." He grinned, somehow combining innocence and wickedness into the same expression. "I was going on a cruise. Had to be prepared in case I got lucky." He bit his lip as he combed his fingers through my hair. "Who knew I'd be getting lucky with my own husband?"

I groaned and came down to kiss him again. There was nothing in our agreement that said we had to be monogamous, especially since sex hadn't been part of the equation, but the thought of him with other men made me feverishly possessive. Not angry or like I'd stop him from hooking up with someone else, but like I wanted him, and the thought of him in bed with another man made me want him even more. I wanted him so blissed out and satisfied that he didn't want to be anywhere but here with me. Maybe that meant I was insane, but I didn't care because I had my arms around the most beautiful man I'd ever seen, and he was naked and panting and rubbing his thick cock against me, so I was cool with being insane as long as we didn't stop.

I explored him with my hands and mouth as if I'd never touched anyone in my life. I needed to touch and memorize every inch of him, and I was hooked on the sounds he made and the way his fingers twitched against my skin whenever I made him gasp.

"Oh my God, Jesse," he whimpered. "Let... let me get those condoms."

As much as I didn't want to break contact with him, I couldn't argue. The sooner we had the rubbers and lube, the sooner things could get *really* wild.

So I lifted myself off him, and he rolled to his feet. It only took him a second of rifling through his toiletry kit before he pulled out a strip of condoms and small bottle of lube, and as he sauntered back to the bed, he winked at me.

As soon as he was within reach, I pulled him back down onto the bed with me. The condom and lube tumbled somewhere onto the mattress. More or less within reach, so good enough for me. They could wait a minute while Hayden and I kissed and groped and wound each other up. I could not get over how much I loved touching and tasting him. It was cathartic after I'd been feeling like crap, but it was also amazing in its own right. I had my hands on *Hayden*. I was in bed with *Hayden*. Somehow the planets had aligned and now I was turning on a very naked, very hard, very sexy *Hayden*.

"I've been wanting you like crazy," I murmured between kisses. "Jesus, Hayden…"

"Mmph. Me too." He nipped my lower lip. "How many times do you think we can fuck on a two-week cruise?"

I shivered hard. "Only one way to find out, right?"

"Mmhmm."

I kissed him again, then growled, "Turn over."

He bit his lip and met my gaze, his eyes full of lust so intense it bordered on predatory. "You assuming I bottom?"

"Do you?"

"Sometimes."

"Good to know." I kissed him lightly and murmured, "But I wasn't planning on *fucking* your ass quite yet."

He shivered. "Ooh. Well in that case…" He turned onto his stomach.

I didn't go right for his ass. Instead, I sank down on top of him, pressing my cock against him as I started kissing the back of his neck. The pillow muffled some swearing, especially when I paused to nip just above his shoulder.

"Jesse…" His helpless moan made me shiver. "Ungh. Your mouth…"

I grinned against his skin. Then I started kissing my way down his spine. I took my sweet time, and I lingered on his lower back for a moment just to tease a few more delicious moans out of him before I continued downward. I spread his cheeks and ran my tongue along his crack, and a shiver ran through his entire body.

"Oh *Jesus*."

I laughed, and he gasped, probably at my breath rushing across his skin. I didn't give him a chance to recover before I ran my tongue his hole. He swore and groaned, and I went to town on him just to drive him crazy. I'd always enjoyed rimming, especially when my partner got into it. With someone as vocal as Hayden? Oh Christ, yeah, I could do this all day and all night. I was painfully hard, and the need to fuck him was almost unbearable, especially as I kept teasing him, but the way he gasped and writhed while I ate his ass was too good to pass up.

"Fuck," he groaned. "I usually top, but god*damn*, if you don't put that thing in me…" He trailed off into a whimper.

As if I needed any encouragement to lick and taunt him until I lost feeling in my tongue. I hadn't thought I'd ever actually have Hayden like this, and I intended to savor every second of it.

"Jesse. C'*mon*." He felt around clumsily, then snatched the strip of condoms off the comforter. Something tore, and he tossed one of the condoms back at me. "Put it on, dammit."

Well, hell. Who was I to turn down a chance to fuck him?

I sat up and tore open the wrapper, then rolled onto

my back. As I put on the condom, I said, "Why don't you get on top?"

"Ooh, I like the sound of that." He grinned, and as I slicked myself up, he straddled me. Holding my breath, I guided him down onto the head of my cock and let him take over.

Hayden groaned softly as he eased himself down. I gasped as my cock started to slide into him, and the room spun as he fucked himself a few times on only the head like he just wanted to enjoy that initial penetration. I didn't rush him—I loved that part too whenever I bottomed, and no matter how much I wanted to be buried in him, I wasn't about to rush him through something he so obviously liked. Especially not after I'd teased him for so long.

Slowly, though, he came down farther, and I sank deeper inside him. It was a struggle to stay still—always was in this position—but I did. I held his thighs just so I could touch him, but not enough to hinder his movements, especially as he found an amazing, fluid rhythm. Just as well he was in control because I didn't think I could have been. I was too caught up in how incredible he felt and how gorgeous he was, and lying back and being ridden was about all I was good for right then.

Hayden shivered, letting his head fall back. "Fuck, why didn't we do this sooner?"

"Don't know. But... Oh God..." I panted. "Ungh... Hayden. I'm gonna come if you keep that up."

Oh, he didn't just keep it up—he doubled down. He rocked his hips and rode me harder, faster, and a cry escaped my lips as I grabbed his waist and thrust up into him as hard as I could. In seconds, I was coming, moaning his name and God knew what else as he kept on writhing until I couldn't take it anymore.

As I sank back to the bed, Hayden braced one hand on my shoulder, and with the other, he started furiously pumping his cock. Eyes squeezed shut, lips parted, my dick still in him, he jerked himself off, and I was utterly mesmerized by the sight of him unraveling on top of me.

I reached for his cock. "Here," I whispered, my voice as shaky as my hand. "Let me."

He let me nudge his hand out of the way, and he bit back a moan as I took over pumping him. "Fuck. Oh yeah. Like… like that."

This was easily the sexiest, most pornographic thing I'd ever seen. Hayden. Hot. Naked. Sweating. My dick still hard and buried inside him. His breath coming in shorter, sharper gasps. His muscles tensing with every stroke I took.

And then, all at once, he jerked, threw his head back, and unloaded all over my stomach with a low, strangled groan. I kept stroking him until he stopped me, and as soon as I did, he slumped forward onto shaking arms. "Oh God…"

I wrapped my arms around him, letting him sink all the way down onto me, and for a moment, we just breathed and trembled. Closing my eyes, savoring the warmth of his body and the aftershocks of my orgasm, I was aware that my world wasn't right. I just… didn't… care. I was naked and satisfied with the hottest man I'd ever touched. Everything else could go fuck itself.

Eventually, we pried ourselves apart, cleaned ourselves up, then collapsed in the rumpled bed again. Hayden cuddled up next to me, head on my shoulder, and I wrapped an arm around him.

"For the record," he slurred, "you've definitely talked me out of going anywhere tonight."

"Oh yeah?" I trailed a fingertip up the middle of his sweaty back. "What are you going to do instead?"

"You. As many times as I can." He glanced to the side, then rested his head on my shoulder again. "Might have to get dressed long enough to go get more condoms."

"Eh. We have enough for a few rounds."

"True. Can't hurt to stock up, though."

"Mmm, yeah. Good idea. Just... in a minute."

We lay like that for a while, basking in the afterglow and absently touching each other. Neither of us said anything. I supposed we didn't need to.

Out of nowhere, though, Hayden stifled a laugh. He covered his mouth, but with his body pressed up against mine like this, there was no hiding how much he was vibrating with barely contained laughed.

"What?" I asked.

He shook his head. "Nothing. Nothing."

"Bullshit. C'mon."

"I just..." Hayden snorted, then met my eyes with a wicked grin. "Never saw myself having sex with my husband for the first time on our honeymoon."

I laughed too. "Goddamn. Did we accidentally do things the 'right' way?"

"Right way, hell." He huffed. "No way am I signing on the dotted line with a man until we've screwed enough times for me to know he can actually get me off."

I chuckled, but cocked my head. "You're not exactly difficult to get off."

"I know, right? But there are some dudes out there..."

He made a disgusted sound and rolled his eyes. "I am not getting married and then finding out my husband has all the sexual prowess of a garden gnome."

"A garden gnome? Exactly how much sexual prowess does a garden gnome have?"

"Not much. They're stiff and pointy, but then they don't move, don't blink, and sure as hell don't eat ass."

A laugh burst out of me and I shook my head. "I really shouldn't be surprised that you've thought this through." Before he could respond, I kissed him. We were both still grinning, but our lips softened as the kiss went on. The playful kiss turned into a longer one, and that longer one turned into a deeper one, and before I knew it, we were tangling up again as our dicks hardened between us.

"Good thing I brought lots of condoms," he whispered. "Think... think we're gonna need 'em."

"Mmhmm." I kissed my way down his jaw and onto his neck, and in between kisses, I purred against his throat, "You sure you don't want to go out tonight?"

"No way. Because if we're going out, that means you can walk." He arched under me. "And if you can walk, then I am definitely not done with you."

L.A. WITT

Chapter 19
Hayden

This was the life.

A pair of deck chairs. The Mediterranean sun. A bottle of wine we weren't even bothering to pour into glasses because we were classy like that. A gorgeous view of both the ocean and the shirtless man who'd spent half the morning happily moaning around my dick.

"Man, I could get used to this." I took a swig from the bottle, then handed it over to Jesse. "We might need some more wine, though."

"Already?" He peered into the mouth of the bottle like he was looking into a telescope, almost touching it against his sunglasses, then shrugged and took a deep swallow. "Good thing I brought more out here with us."

"Smart man."

He drained the bottle, put it in the champagne bucket we'd commandeered to keep the empties from rolling around on the balcony, and pulled the unopened one free.

Scowling, he looked around. "Son of a bitch. I brought an extra bottle, but a corkscrew?" He pushed himself up with a long-suffering sigh. "Be right back."

I watched him go into the suite. There were a couple of faint marks on his back, and a distinct bite on his shoulder. I probably had a few myself, though Jesse wasn't quite as prone to using teeth as I was.

Grinning, I sat back in my deck chair and gazed out at the ocean. I could definitely get used to this. Wine, sex, and laziness. Life just didn't get more deliciously decadent.

He came back a moment later, and he gave my bare shoulder a gentle squeeze before he sat down again. He picked up the wine bottle and started to twist the corkscrew, but winced, and I jumped.

"Whoa, dude." I reached for the bottle and corkscrew. "I forgot your wrists are jacked up. Let me do this."

"I can—"

"Jesse." I wagged a finger at him. "I need your hands in working order. Gimme."

He huffed dramatically and surrendered the bottle and corkscrew. "Fine. So does this mean you're going to want me using my hands later?"

"Um, yeah?" I shot him an *are you kidding?* look as I opened the bottle. "Hands, mouth, dick—you're going to be using everything tonight, baby."

"Tonight?" He tsked. "But that's hours away."

"I didn't say you wouldn't be using them before that."

He laughed, sliding a hand up my thigh. "Have I mentioned that I really like your dirty mind?"

"Pretty sure you said something to that effect while I was balls deep in you last night."

He shivered.

The cork was stubborn—shut up, I wasn't that drunk—but it finally came loose. I put the cork and corkscrew on the table, took a swig straight from the bottle, and handed it to Jesse. He took a drink too, and I absolutely one hundred percent did not watch his throat as he swallowed. Hand to God, I didn't!

Okay I did.

Because fuuuck who wouldn't?

Fortunately, he didn't seem to notice. He handed the bottle back, and as I took another swig, he gestured at the tall white wall next to his chair. "I love how they have dividers up between all the balconies. You could do pretty much anything out here, and no one would see."

"Not unless they're out there." I motioned toward the water. "Wouldn't that be weird? Banging over the railing, and then—hi!" I waved at an imaginary boater.

Jesse laughed. God, I loved the way he laughed. I especially loved how it made his eyes sparkle, but he had on dark sunglasses at the moment. Still, he was adorable and sexy even when I couldn't see his eyes.

We sat back in our chairs, passing the wine bottle back and forth. I'm so not joking—this was the life. Good wine, good company, gorgeous view both on and off the balcony. And to think, it hadn't been all that long since I was delivering pizzas and hoping my car didn't crumble. Now I was somewhere in the Med on a cruise ship with a seemingly endless supply of wine, condoms, and lube. Fuck yeah.

"So what's the story behind that?" Jesse gestured at me. "You a Garfield fan?"

I glanced down at the fading tattoo on my chest. I'd had it for so long, sometimes I forgot it was there at all.

"Oh. That." I chuckled and took a pull of wine before passing the bottle back. "That was what happened the last time my dumb ass was flush with cash."

Jesse drank some wine. "What do you mean?"

"It was a few months before my brother got hurt. Some endorsements and sponsorships were on the table, and a lot of people were saying that all the money my parents had dumped into his career was about to pay off. Which—about fucking time. They'd taken out like three mortgages to keep him in training."

"It's that expensive?"

"*Oh* yeah. Lot of people pretty much bankrupt their families getting to the Olympics, and you stay that way unless you medal and score a bunch of top dollar sponsorships."

He offered the bottle again, and I took a deep swallow.

"So anyway, things were looking good, and my dad got a bonus at work. He figured since they'd been doing so much to finance Brian, it would be nice to give me some cash." I smiled sadly. "Which was a nice change. And with the sponsorships and all right around the corner, I figured this was just the start. Got myself a tattoo"—I gestured at Garfield—"and spent the rest of the money on stupid shit because for once in my life, I could. And before I knew it, it was gone."

Jesse watched me for a moment. "That explains why you're so cautious with money now."

I nodded slowly. "Yep. Sometimes it's tempting to go wild, but I have this little orange and black striped reminder"—I tapped Garfield with a finger—"that I should be careful."

"Smart."

"Eh. Once bitten, I guess." I tilted the bottle back, but only half a sip's worth of wine slid out. "What the hell? Are they even filling these bottles? Or are we really drinking them that fast?"

"I think we're drinking them that fast." He had a hint of a slur in his voice, and now that I thought about it, so did I.

"Hmm. You're probably right." I put the bottle in the bucket. "Does it still count as day-drinking when we're on vacation?"

Jesse shrugged. "Don't know. But I won't tell if you won't."

I put a finger to my lips. He chuckled.

"Think we should slow down?" he asked.

"Pfft. I think we need another bottle." I stood, wobbling because, okay, maybe we didn't actually *need* another bottle. "There's more in there, right?"

"Yep. At least two more, and we can always call if we run out."

"I fucking love cruise ships." I started past him, but he slung his arm around my waist and pulled me back. I laughed and stumbled, and the next thing I knew, I was sitting across Jesse's lap in the deck chair. "I thought you wanted some more wine."

"I do." He kissed the side of my neck as he slid his hand across my bare stomach. "But it can wait."

I bit my lip and closed my eyes as he kissed up and down my neck and along my jaw. Between the wine and the motion of the ocean, I was dizzy already. Add Jesse's hot skin and soft lips and his hands all over me? Good thing I was sitting down.

"Get up here," I murmured, and when he lifted his chin, I found his mouth with mine, and he slid his fingers up into my hair as we made out like a couple of teenagers. A year ago I hadn't even had time to think about dating, and my hookups had consisted of whatever sex I'd had the time and energy for. This? Lounging around, kissing lazily with no need to steal glances at the clock or throw back a Red Bull? This was a level of luxury that I could absolutely get used to. Forget fancy cars and overpriced rocks—just give me the delicious decadence of taking my sweet time with a man who was as unhurried as I was.

My back was starting to cramp up from twisting like this, though, so I tried to shift as gracefully as I could in the confines of the deck chair… which was about the time I remembered that Jesse and I had killed two bottles of wine in rapid succession, and graceful wasn't happening.

"Shit!" I flailed as I lost my balance, but Jesse wrapped an arm around me and kept me from falling.

"You okay?" He was laughing, so I was pretty sure he knew the answer.

"I'm good. Just… maybe a little too much wine to be sitting like this."

"Might be a bit steadier if you face me."

"Yeah?"

"Worth a try."

With him steadying me, I straddled him, and—oh yeah, much better. Now I was balanced, I wasn't contorting painfully, and instead of his erection pressing against my ass, it rubbed my own cock through our shorts.

"Why didn't we think of this earlier?" I asked between kisses.

"Dunno. I say we blame the wine."

"Yes. Definitely. Fucking bastard wine."

He laughed, which made it impossible to kiss, so I leaned down and kissed his neck. The second my lips met his warm skin, he gasped, and he held me tighter and tilted his head to give me more access. "Fuck, Hayden…"

"You like?"

"Ya think?"

I nipped his shoulder, which earned me a low groan.

"You know, at the rate we're going," he murmured, "we'll end up spending this entire cruise naked in our suite." He slid his hands down over my ass. "We're going to miss all the excursions."

I rocked my hips just right to rub our dicks together. "You make that sound like a bad thing."

"Mmm, not at all." He kneaded my ass, pulling me against him. "Just saying."

"Well, duly noted." I lifted my head so I could look in his eyes. "For the record, I have no problem with crossing out the itinerary and replacing it with 'annoy the neighbors with loud sex.'"

Jesse laughed. "I did hear the neighbors coming back to their suite when I went to get the corkscrew." He slid his hands up my back. "Think we should go annoy them?"

"Fuck yes we should."

L.A. WITT

Chapter 20
Jesse

"You mean we actually have to put clothes on?" Hayden sighed theatrically as he dried off after the shower we'd shared. "But I was enjoying being naked."

I chuckled. "If we want to go to dinner, yes, we need to get dressed." I hung my towel on the rack. "Or we could stay in if you're really averse to putting on pants."

He lifted his gaze, wet hair tousled and eyes wide with hope. "That's an option"

I tsked, hooked a finger under his chin, and kissed him. "Get dressed."

Another dramatic sigh, followed by a playful wink.

He was adorable. Not to mention hot, especially naked. For a moment, I entertained the idea of skipping dinner and dragging him back to bed, but to be honest, I needed a break and I was pretty sure he did too. Spending an evening doing something other than fucking each other senseless wouldn't kill us. In fact, at this rate, another evening in probably *would* kill us.

Tonight we were eating at the high-end steak and seafood restaurant. This place required formal attire, so it was back into the tuxes we'd worn for our wedding. That alone was enough to motivate me to make sure we actually went out tonight. Hayden was stunning in his tux, and I was the lucky bastard who'd be on his arm this evening. Hell yes.

Hayden sat on the foot of the bed, one knee bent as he tied his shoe. "So I guess we don't have to worry about a DD tonight, right?"

I laughed, adjusting one of my cufflinks. "Well, it probably wouldn't hurt if one of us stayed sober enough to find the way back to the room."

"Pfft." He put his foot down and brought the other one up. "That's half the adventure."

"What? Finding our room while we're too shit-faced to stand up?"

"Exactly."

"Uh-huh. It's all fun and games until someone falls overboard."

"Well yeah. Because then it's a game—find the drunk guy in the water."

Chuckling, I shook my head. "If you go overboard, you're swimming home."

"What?" He tugged the laces into place, put his foot down, and looked at me with mock hurt. "You'd just leave me out there?"

"If I'm drunk enough to let your hammered ass go overboard? Probably."

He huffed as he rose. "You're no fun."

"You say that now." I hooked my fingers in his

waistband and pulled him closer. "But when you're hung over in bed and not out floating in the Med somewhere, you might be singing a different tune."

"Ugh. You and your *logic*."

"I know. I'm such a dick."

"You are." He slid his hands up my chest and around the back of my neck. "I'd say you suck, but we both know that already."

I laughed, reeling him in closer, and we were both still grinning when our lips met. I fucking adored this playful banter and our ridiculous, silly conversations. He was sweet, sassy, and sexy—the trifecta of a perfect partner.

"You know, if we keep doing this," he murmured between kisses, "we're never going to get to dinner."

"Uh-huh." I kissed him once more, then pried myself away and took his hand. "Let's go, because if we start fooling around again, you'll probably kill me."

"Well… I mean… not on *purpose*."

"Oh, well, that changes everything, doesn't it?" I tugged him toward the door.

"I think it does." He let himself be led out of our stateroom. "And besides, what a way to go, right? Death by fucking?"

Of course a straight middle-aged couple picked just that moment to come around the corner. The woman gasped, the man glared, and Hayden had the decency to smile apologetically. He actually pulled off sheepish— blush and all—as they walked past us, but just before they stepped into their own room across the hall, he added a slightly-louder-than-necessary, "If you really need a break, I guess I can bottom this time."

That earned another horrified gasp followed by a door

closing very abruptly, and Hayden smothered a wicked giggle.

I just laughed as I pocketed my key card and took his hand again. "Can't take you anywhere, can I?"

"You can," he said as we started down the passageway. "But I can't promise I'm appropriate for mixed company."

"So I'm noticing." I glanced at him, and his grin made me laugh again. "I'll take my chances."

"Ooh, a risk taker. Next thing I know you'll be bungee jumping off a bridge or jumping out of a plane."

"Um, no. I don't think so."

"Stepping out in public with your filter-less husband is as reckless as you get?"

"That's pretty reckless, don't you think?"

"Hmm. Now that you mention it…"

We exchanged playful looks and continued toward the restaurant.

When we arrived, they stuck us at a table with eight other passengers. Eight strangers. Oh, fuck my life. Hopefully they weren't expecting much in the way of conversation from me.

As it turned out, I didn't need to worry about providing conversation. Hayden was instantly everyone's best friend, and before the appetizers had even come out, he had the whole table hanging on his every word. And he wasn't quite so crass in this setting, which I appreciated. Not surprising—I'd learned early on that he was generally pretty good at knowing when to censor himself and when he could be less restrained.

I couldn't help smiling as I watched. It was easy to see how he'd pulled off the class clown thing as a kid—he had the kind of charm and charisma that commanded attention. It wasn't obnoxious or off-putting. Quite the opposite—he was mesmerizing. Like the class clown who'd grown up into someone who could keep a group of strangers entertained. I wondered a few times if it was just me, but then I'd glance around the table and notice how many other people had all but abandoned their food and were enthralled by him instead. Especially when he and two of the women started howling with laughter in between comparing notes about some long-ago season of RuPaul's Drag Race. Their husbands exchanged bemused looks with each other and with me, and we all chuckled.

Judy, a woman who I thought was in her seventies or so and was seated right beside me, leaned closer. "Your husband is delightful."

I smiled. "Yeah, he really is."

"You boys are on your honeymoon, aren't you?"

"How'd you guess?"

She shot me a knowing look, then patted my arm. "You lovebirds aren't really subtle, you know."

"We—" I coughed to get some air moving. "We aren't?"

"Oh Lord, no. It just tickles me to see two boys in love like you are. Reminds me of my son and his husband."

"Is that right?"

She nodded and gave my arm a gentle squeeze. "My son-in-law isn't quite as pretty as your husband, though."

For reasons I couldn't begin to explain, I felt myself blushing. "Hayden definitely turns heads."

In fact, he'd turned a few heads on our way to the restaurant and to our table, and I indulged in a little smugness over it. He was the most gorgeous man on the ship, and while they'd all been shamelessly ogling him, he'd had his hand firmly in mine. At the end of the night, I'd be in his bed.

Another lady at the table gestured at Hayden and me. "So how did you two meet?"

At the same time I said "At work," Hayden deadpanned "On Grindr."

We looked at each other.

He shrugged, feigning innocence even as mischief sparkled in his eyes. "Eh, close enough. It counted as 'at work' for me."

I snorted. "Really?"

"Grindr?" the lady asked. "What's that?"

Hayden opened his mouth to speak, but a firm nudge with my knee under the table shut him up.

"It's a dating app for gay men," I said.

"Right." He eyed me innocently. "That's what I was going to say."

"Sure it was, dear."

We exchanged good-natured glares, then laughed.

One of the women at the table started telling the story about how she and her husband had met a few years ago, and as we listened, I put a hand on Hayden's thigh. A second later, he put his hand over mine, and we glanced at each other, smiled, and continued listening to the passenger's story.

Dozens of stories, a few glasses of wine, and an amazing meal later, we said goodbye to the other passengers and headed out of the restaurant. I slipped an arm around Hayden's waist as we strolled back in the general direction of our suite.

About halfway back, as we were walking along one of

the outer decks, Hayden stopped. "Wow, it's gorgeous out here." He rested his hands on the railing and gazed out at the moon glittering on the calm water.

I leaned my hip against the railing beside him. "Nice break from the city, isn't it?"

"God, yeah." He turned toward me, the lights from the ship catching in his eyes. "I'm starting to see why people enjoy cruises so much."

"Are you?"

He nodded. "I always thought they'd be kind of boring, but what's not to love about the sun, mountains of food, and an endless supply of condoms and lube?"

I laughed, sliding a hand onto his back. "You should get a job marketing cruises. Put that on a website, and you'll sell out in a heartbeat."

He chuckled and leaned in close to me. I swear I was enjoying this part almost as much as the sex. He was a little shorter and narrower than me, and when I wrapped my arms around him, we fit together perfectly. My body was exhausted from all the sex, but this? Oh, we could keep doing this.

After a moment, Hayden looked up at me apologetically. "So fair warning—I absolutely stuffed myself at dinner. Probably going to need a raincheck on everything in bed."

"Ugh, that's fine by me."

"You sure?"

"Definitely. I can barely move." I ran my hand up his back. "In fact, we could always go back to the room, climb into bed, and watch a movie."

Hayden met my gaze. "You won't be offended if I fall asleep, will you?"

You? Falling asleep with your head on my shoulder? Baby, 'offended' isn't the word I'd use.

But I just said, "No, definitely not."

His soft smile made my heart flutter. All the feistiness from earlier was gone, and his expression melted my heart.

Without a word, he curved a hand behind my head, drew me down, and kissed me. "In case it's not obvious," he whispered, "I'm having an amazing time on this cruise."

"Me too." Talk about an understatement.

He drew back again. "So, back to the room for that movie?"

"Sounds like a plan."

One more kiss, and we started walking. I kept my arm around his shoulders and he kept his around my waist, and I didn't think it was the wine or the big meal that had us strolling so slowly back to our cabin. There was just no rush. We were out on the deck of a cruise ship, lightly buzzed after an amazing meal, and we were touching with no pressure to perform.

As we walked, I kissed his temple, and he glanced up at me with a smile.

It just didn't get any better than this.

Ever since I'd first thought of this scheme to reveal my dad as a homophobe, I'd questioned many times if I should go through with it. Was it ethical? Was it worth it? Would it even work? Dropping the hammer on this plan had scared the shit out of me from day one for a lot of reasons, especially since I knew the endgame was going to be hell to live with. How many hours of sleep had I lost in the last year or so because of this? A lot. I had literally written the ad a dozen times, then posted and deleted it seven times before I'd finally put it up and left it up.

I didn't go into this lightly, and I knew there were plenty of ways it could catastrophically blow up in my face.

But I hadn't obsessed over *every* possible outcome. There was at least one that didn't cross my mind until it was way too late.

The moment I realized I was in over my head was when I woke up beside Hayden in the middle of our honeymoon suite's bed the tenth morning of our cruise.

We'd barely done anything on this ship except each other. Once we'd started making out that first day, it had been game on. We'd left the suite for food and had made a couple of trips to the gift shops to top up our lube and condom supply, but otherwise... we were here, and we were usually naked, even if we were watching a movie or lounging out on the balcony. On two separate occasions, we'd been dressed and ready to go join some other passengers for an excursion on shore, but then the next thing I knew, shorts and T-shirts were landing on the floor and the excursion was forgotten. This may not have been a real honeymoon, but we were sure fucking like it was.

Usually, he woke up before I did, but this morning, I was awake at some ungodly hour. The sun was barely up, so no way in hell was I getting out of bed yet. Lying there in the pale light, I turned to him, and... whoa.

He was still snoozing away beside me, and I couldn't stop staring at him. God, he was gorgeous. The curtain-filtered early morning sun cast soft shadows on his face and added some warmth to his complexion. He was disheveled, unshaven, and probably had morning breath as bad as I did, and I didn't think any man had ever been more beautiful.

My spine prickled as reality set in.

Ah, shit. I'm in way over my head, aren't I?

Yep. I totally was. This was supposed to be a business arrangement with a political goal. Sex wasn't even supposed to be part of the deal, but now we were sleeping together, and now he was snoozing adorably on the pillow beside mine, and oh my God, this wasn't fake anymore, was it? In fact, now that I thought about it, it hadn't been fake for a while. I couldn't say when things had changed. Maybe they'd evolved over time. Maybe there'd been a sudden shift I'd been too oblivious to notice.

I couldn't put my finger on the process, but I could definitely nail down the end result:

I was in love with Hayden.

Ridiculously, stupidly, giddily, undeniably in love with the man I'd paid to be my fake husband.

Hashtag *not* part of the plan.

And now that I knew it, it made perfect sense. Why *wouldn't* I fall for him? Living with him, hanging out with him, talking with him—it was all so… *easy*. We bantered effortlessly. We could talk about anything, whether it was a TV show we'd just watched or my family's deep, dark toxicity. He didn't give me grief for long hours or get impatient when I needed to ice my wrists and couldn't cook or clean. Once sex had entered the equation, that had been easy too. No self-consciousness. No performance anxiety.

I sighed and rubbed my eyes. Trust me to find some way to make this whole thing way more complicated than it needed to be. Than it was allowed to be if we were going to see it through.

So what the fuck do I do now?

Beside me, Hayden stirred. He murmured in his sleep, then felt around, and when he found me, he slid closer. I shut my eyes as his skin warmed mine. Damn. Now I couldn't think. Not when I was warm and comfortable and wrapped up with him. It was early anyway. Maybe I should just sleep on it some more. Wasn't like I needed to shake him awake and tell him everything. I could think. I could figure out what I really felt and how to feel all those things while we were pretending to be married.

Stroking his hair, I kissed his forehead, and he mumbled something I didn't understand before he went still again. I could always just enjoy it, right? Enjoy the closeness and the sex and the affection, and then think about putting names on things later? What was the rush aside from my own near-panicked need to say the words out loud and make sure he knew?

Later. Sleep now. Talk later. I could do that.

Eventually, despite my mind going a million miles an hour and no idea how to tell Hayden—or if I *should* tell Hayden—that I loved him, I drifted back to sleep with him in my arms.

L.A. WITT

Chapter 21
Hayden

I was seriously never leaving this bed. Like ever. It was amazingly comfortable, and anyway, my hips and legs weren't quite connected right anymore. Ten solid days of sexy times with Jesse had taken their toll. Not that I was complaining.

I gingerly turned on my side, propped myself up on my elbow, and watched him sleeping beside me. His hair was ruffled, and I was pretty sure he hadn't bothered shaving yesterday, so the five o'clock shadow was heavy on his sharp jaw. Good Lord. I'd thought he was pretty the day I met him, but something about having carnal knowledge of him made him a million times sexier. I knew what those lips were capable of and how that stubble felt against my collarbone or my thigh or my ass cheek. His features were totally relaxed now, but I knew what they looked like in that tense instant right before he came.

Suppressing a shiver, I stared at him because why the

hell not? He was gorgeous. I'd been with some hot men in the past, but somehow the universe had seen fit to drop this man into my world and let me see his oh-face.

Jesse shifted a little. He rubbed his eyes and grumbled something, then lowered his hand and looked at me. The instant he met my gaze, his face broke into a sleepy smile. "Morning."

"Morning." I trailed my fingers over his shoulder. "Sleep well?"

"Are you kidding?" He winked. "Like any man wouldn't sleep like the dead after getting fucked like that. Especially twice."

I chuckled. "Good thing we're bailing on the excursion today, yeah?"

Jesse groaned. "They'd have to carry me down the ramp. Walking through town? I don't think so."

"Mission accomplished."

"Oh yeah?"

"Well, yeah." I grinned. "Just means you'll be stuck on the ship with me, and if I'm lucky, you'll get bored and want to fuck again."

"Bored." Jesse snorted. "I'll want to fuck again long before I start getting bored." He sat up with a groan. "Assuming I can move."

"Eh, moving's overrated."

"Uh-huh." He laughed and patted my sheet-covered hip. "If I can't move, I can't fuck you."

"No, but you can lie there and enjoy it while I fuck you."

His eyes widened. I just grinned.

He shook his head. "You're insatiable."

"You're welcome."

"Yeah, yeah." He gave my hip a squeeze. "I'm going to get a shower. Buffet afterward?"

Now that he mentioned it, I was starving, so I nodded. "Definitely."

"Okay. Give me a few."

"Take your time."

He leaned down to kiss my cheek, then got up, and I watched his fine, naked ass until he'd disappeared into the bathroom. Alone in the suite that had become our own personal porno set, I grinned to myself.

Dear Penthouse Forum...

The thought made me snicker. Did Penthouse Forum even exist anymore? Huh. Now I was curious. Maybe I'd have to check. And maybe I'd have to write them a letter, assuming they were game for publishing a story about two gay dudes banging each other senseless on a cruise ship. *I'd* publish it.

While Jesse showered, I fumbled around and found my phone. Now that we were in port, we had some decent cell signal, so I took advantage of the connection to log into my bank account. It had been a few days since I'd been able to compulsively check it and make sure some phantom bill hadn't bled me dry.

The login was slow because of course it was, giving the usual financial apprehension time to twist my stomach into knots, but it finally connected.

The balance made me do a double take. How the hell was it that high?

Oh. Right. First of the month. The automatic transfer Jesse had set up must have gone through. I was $100,000 richer than I'd been when I'd checked the other day. It should have made me giddy, but the fluttering in my stomach wasn't giddiness. I suddenly felt disgusting.

I pulled the covers up over me and hugged myself as I eyed the screen. It wasn't like I'd forgotten that this marriage was a paid gig. I just... hadn't really thought about it recently. In part because Jesse and I had been too busy testing the structural integrity of our honeymoon suite's furniture, and I hadn't thought about much of anything except when and how we'd be screwing again.

Yeah, I seriously felt dirty now. Like I was... I don't know. Jesse's whore? His sex toy? A convenient hole for his dick?

A convenient bought-and-paid-for hole?

I shuddered, bile burning the back of my throat. The thought of having sex with Jesse again made me feel literally ill. Acting as his husband was something I could do for money. Sex? No. I had some friends who were sex workers and were totally happy with it, and I fully respected that, but it was a hard limit for me.

Even if I *was* going to have sex for money—and it had crossed my mind a time or two during some really desperate periods—it wouldn't be like this. Not an arrangement where we agreed on a set of rules, agreed on a price, and then sex happened and suddenly the lines were blurry.

Ugh. Gross. Right now I couldn't see myself in bed with Jesse again without wondering if this was expected of me, or if it was like "*you're here, I'm here, we're good in bed, so let's fuck around.*" What if he wanted to fool around and I didn't feel like it? Could I say no? Or was this like when I took on some new task at the pizza joint, and my boss expected me to keep doing it even though my job description hadn't changed on paper?

I swallowed hard, eyeing the closed bathroom door. Figures we only had one bathroom, and I really didn't want to crash his shower by strolling in to heave my guts out. He'd want to know what was wrong, and while I considered myself a halfway decent actor, I didn't think I could sell "*probably just food poisoning*" right now.

I tossed my phone aside and rubbed my eyes with the heels of my hands. This was not how things were supposed to go. I couldn't even find the headspace to be disappointed that all that awesome sex was over, because every touch we'd shared was suddenly soured by the realization that I'd obliviously volunteered to be Jesse's personal prostitute.

Yeah. Definitely not happening again.

And I needed to get dressed before he came out of the bathroom, or else things would get even weirder. I wasn't sure if that was possible at this point, but I wasn't going to lounge around naked and wait to find out.

So I got up and got dressed as quickly as I could.

Chapter 22
Jesse

As I showered, I couldn't stop thinking about everything that had been on my mind since the wee hours of the morning. I'd wondered for a while if I'd just been half-dreaming or something, but now that I was actually awake? Nope. Those feelings were really there. I really was in love with him, wasn't I? I so fucking was. This thing had rocketed right past infatuation and turned into something that made my chest ache every time I looked at him.

We'd been getting steadily closer ever since he'd moved in, but once the physical barriers had gone down— the kiss during the ceremony, that stolen kiss in the guest room, the easy touching throughout the reception— everything had gone full throttle. The sex had been like the last wall still standing between us. Now that we'd knocked it down... God, it was like we'd been keeping a safe distance, and now I wondered why the hell I hadn't crossed it sooner.

I grinned to myself as the shower spray kneaded the

back of my neck. This definitely wasn't what I'd bargained for when I'd put up that ad. A partner in crime to take down my dad? Yes. A hot, sexy man I couldn't help but fall for and couldn't get enough of in bed? Not quite what I'd expected.

And I'm definitely not complaining.

Now I just needed to figure out how to tell him. And when. And if. Should I bring this up sooner than later? Maybe feel him out first. See if I could get a bead on how he felt. Might not hurt to wait until after the cruise, just in case things got weird. This stateroom was huge, but awkwardness could make walls close in fast. The same could be said for the condo, I supposed.

Eh, there probably wasn't much to be done except feel him out and wait for the right time. There would always be the potential for awkwardness and rejection, but nothing ventured, nothing gained, right?

Hayden was already dressed when I came out of the bathroom, which was unusual. We'd spent most mornings lounging around in, at most, our boxers. Now he was in shorts and a T-shirt, and he was quickly—and a little shakily—tying his shoes.

He also wasn't looking at me.

The nervous feeling in my stomach shifted gears from *how do I say I love you?* to *oh shit, what's wrong?* Alarm bells went off in my head, and I tried to tell myself I was overreacting. Maybe he was hung over. He'd had more to drink than I had last night, so it was possible.

Or maybe there really was something wrong.

As I pulled on a pair of sweats, I casually asked, "Getting an early start?"

Hayden glanced at me, but he still didn't say anything.

So I tried, "You want to go get breakfast?"

Still nothing.

He got up and was rifling around in his bag, back to me.

"Hayden?"

He tensed, but didn't turn around.

"What's up?"

He blew out a breath, and as he rubbed the back of his neck, the tightness of his muscles was visible from here. Half an hour ago, I wouldn't have hesitated to gently nudge his hand aside and rub out that tension for him. Now I suddenly didn't think that touch would be welcome.

Cautiously, I stepped closer, and I kept my voice soft. "Talk to me. What's wrong?"

Hayden finally turned around, but he kept staring down at his wringing hands.

"Didn't we agree in the beginning that we'd talk if there was a problem?" I asked.

His shoulders dropped and he sighed. "Yeah. We did. And… I'm sorry. I wasn't trying to keep anything from you. I just didn't know how to say it."

My stomach flipped. Something told me we hadn't been struggling to articulate the same thing. "You didn't know how to say what?"

The silence that followed was so heavy it was almost unbearable, but I waited for him to gather his thoughts. If it was this hard for him to say it, maybe I didn't want to hear it? Not that I had much choice.

After a long moment, he took a breath. "Look, I was fine with everything, and the sex has been…" He flashed a smile so faint and quick I may have imagined it. "It's been amazing. But then I looked at my bank this morning, and the next payment came through. From you."

"Right? It's the first of the month, so I—" I studied him. "Wait, what? Is that... is that a bad thing?"

"No. It's not bad. It just made me..." He swallowed. "I think it kind of put things in perspective, I guess?"

"How so?"

"The lines are getting blurry, you know?" He ran a hand through his hair. "You're paying me to be your husband. So does that mean you're paying me for sex?"

My jaw went slack. "What? Oh my God, no. I... Jesus, no. We started sleeping together because we wanted to. Right?"

"I thought so, but now... I mean... you're paying me, and we're having sex, and I'm..."

"Hayden, you're not a whore."

He looked right in my eyes. "Then why do I feel like one?"

He may as well have hit me in the gut. "You do?"

Dropping his gaze again, he nodded. "Yeah. And I don't know why it's bothering me this much. With everything else we're doing, and..." Sighing, he shook his head. "I don't know. It just bothers me, and I need to stop."

"Okay. Then we will."

He met my eyes again. "Are you sure?"

"Well, yeah. If you don't want to, then we won't. It's that simple."

Hayden swallowed. "Okay. Okay, good." He paused. "And for the record, I *will* see this through. I'm in for as long as it takes for your dad to show his homophobic flag, and I'm not taking what we're doing lightly." He folded his arms loosely across his chest, more like he was warding off a chill than being defensive, and he shrank back a little. "I just need to take sex off the table."

"Then we will. Absolutely. For what it's worth, I never thought what we were doing was because of the agreement. Or because you owed me. I just wanted you. So, I'm sorry I let the lines blur."

"It's okay. It took two." He avoided my gaze. "And I'm not saying I didn't enjoy it. Because I did. A lot. But I just…"

"You don't want to get paid for sex. I get it." I paused. "Hayden, look at me."

He hesitated, but finally lifted his chin and met my eyes.

"It's okay," I said. "I promise. The last thing in the world I want is for you to feel obligated to sleep with me."

Little by little, he relaxed. "So, you're okay with this?"

"Okay with—of course I am. The sex is fun, but not if it's making you feel like…" I grimaced. "Like I'm using you or that you're a whore."

He searched my eyes. As he did, my heart ached. I desperately wanted the man I'd been bantering and cuddling with to come back. I missed the playfulness and how effortless things had been between us. Even if we never touched again, was it too much to ask to have that back? Maybe it was. If I'd made him feel like a whore…

I cringed at the thought.

Hayden broke eye contact, and he cleared his throat. "Listen, I think… I think I'm going to go take a run. I'll be back in a bit."

"Okay. If I'm not here, I'm probably out… I don't know. Checking out the ship, I guess."

He nodded without looking at me. "All right. I'll see you, um, when I see you."

"Right. Have a good run."

Another nod, and without a word, he left.

As soon as the suite's door shut behind him, I released a long breath and sank onto the foot of the bed.

Well, good thing I hadn't put all my cards on the table and told him I loved him. We still had four more days on this cruise, not to mention all the hours it would take to fly home.

And I knew without a doubt they were going to be awkward as hell.

L.A. WITT

Chapter 23
Hayden

Not a moment too soon, we were back at Jesse's West Hollywood condo. The huge place was instantly suffocating, though—however many hundred square feet was just not enough room for all this silence.

Thank God, I'd barely stepped inside before Ashton texted to let me know he was in the garage downstairs. We'd been texting since I got off the plane, and I'd been so relieved when he'd said he had some time this afternoon because, holy shit, I could *not* get away from Jesse fast enough. I felt like a total dick, bailing the second we set our suitcases down in the condo, but Jesus fucking Christ—after four days and four nights, plus the long-ass flights home, I was just done. I needed a break from the perma-awkwardness.

After I'd left my suitcase in my bedroom, I quickly changed into something I hadn't been wearing for eighteen-plus hours. I could have used a shower, but I didn't want to keep Ashton waiting. That and I didn't want to stay here any longer than I had to.

Jesse's bedroom door was open, and he had his back to me as he unpacked his suitcase.

In the doorway, I cleared my throat. "Hey, um, I'm going to take off for a bit."

He turned around. "Oh. Already?"

"Yeah. Ashton's downstairs. We're going to…" Why was I explaining myself? "Anyway, I'll be back later."

"Okay." He gestured at a laundry basket by his feet. "You want me to wash anything while you're out?"

Guilt needled at me. "No, I'm good. I'll take care of it tomorrow." I motioned down the hall. "I'll see you later."

Jesse nodded and turned back to finish emptying his suitcase. I hesitated in the doorway, staring at his back while my emotions went haywire. Truth was, I didn't want to be away from him. I wanted us to go back to the way things had been before I'd checked my stupid bank balance on the cruise. But we couldn't because we'd fucked and I wanted to fuck again without feeling like a whore.

I pulled my gaze away from him and got the hell out of the condo.

Ashton's immortal car was idling just inside the parking garage, and I sighed with relief as I slid into the passenger side.

"Hey." He eased the car into motion as I put on my seat belt. "You sure you want to go somewhere? I figured you'd be jetlagged as fuck."

"I am. But I need to get away from Jesse for a while."

"What? Why?" He glanced at me, alarm written all over his face. "What happened?"

As he drove us away from the condo, I told him the story. I spared him the details about exactly what Jesse and I had done together during those blissful pre-bank check days, but I was pretty sure he got the idea.

"Then one morning I looked at my bank balance, and his payment had just come through. And… I don't know. It just felt weird." I squirmed in the passenger seat, rubbing at my arms. "Like I swear it felt like I'd been screwing him for money."

Ashton whistled. "Wow. That's heavy."

"So you don't think I'm overreacting?"

"Nah. I think it would be weird. Like if I was with a girl and it felt like I had to put out whenever she wanted me to?" He wrinkled his nose. "I don't think I could do that."

"I definitely can't. And now things are all weird with Jesse, and—" My phone vibrated, and I cringed. It was probably Jesse. The air between us was weird, and he probably wanted to *talk* about things. "Speak of the Devil."

Except when I looked at the screen, the caller wasn't Jesse.

It was Carmen.

My agent.

I winced. I hadn't gotten around to letting her go, because hello, coward, and now she was calling. Crap.

"I have to take this." I snatched up the phone. "Hey Carmen."

Ashton's eyes widened. He and Luis always got as hopeful as I did whenever she called, and I also hadn't explained to them that I was giving up the dream.

"Hey, hon. You're back in town, right? I didn't wake

you up from a jetlag nap or—"

"No, I'm awake. I'm just out with a friend." *When can we meet so I can tell you I'm quitting?* I made myself sound casual as I asked, "So, what's up?"

"Well, let's just say I've been extra busy since you've been gone."

My stomach flipped. "Uh, what?"

"Mmhmm. So. Now that you're home from your honeymoon, Mr. *Ambrose...*" She said Jesse's last name with a grin in her voice. "Your name is all over Hollywood right now, sweetheart. Everyone and their stepfather wants to be the first to put Isaac Ambrose's gay son-in-law's name in lights."

I did not have the mental or emotional capacity to unpack all that. Of course everyone who came to this town knew that who you knew—or more importantly, who knew you—mattered more than anything else. I got that. I really did. And despite making peace with quitting, these opportunities were a siren's call if I'd ever heard one. What was the harm in an audition or two? Couldn't I have just a little bit of peril?

But when doors were swinging open because I'd fake-married the son of the closeted homophobe who happened to be the most influential director and producer in Hollywood right now? And I was actually considering stepping *through* those doors? I mean, how much further into this did I have to get before Satan himself walked in to sign the final paperwork on my soul transfer? Because seriously if I wasn't going to hell at this point...

"Hayden? Honey?"

I shook myself and cleared my throat. "Sorry. I, um. So... really?"

"Oh hell yes. We should have hooked you up with that man ages ago. You'd be on the Walk of Fame by now."

I fought back a surge of bile. "Awesome. Then people could walk all over my name and occasionally piss on it."

"Such a pessimist." She tsked. "Anyway. I've got a lot of auditions in the works for you. The kind where they're specifically asking for *you*. I just need to know when you're available."

"Oh. Um." I coughed again because holy fuck it was getting hard to breathe. "Any time, really." Was I doing this? *I am so going to hell.*

"Are you sure? How jetlagged are you? You're going to want to be sharp for these auditions."

Well, Christ, I was wide awake now.

"Um." I cleared my throat. "Okay, maybe give me a day or two. Then I should be running on all eight cylinders." Aside from being distracted as fuck by the man whose asshole dad was opening all these doors for me, and the man I couldn't figure out how to feel about. *Fuuuck.*

"Good enough," she chirped. "I'm going to start scheduling them, and I'll text you with the info."

"Sounds great. Thanks, Carmen."

As soon as I'd ended the call, Ashton glanced at me. "Well?"

I swallowed. "Apparently she's been getting a lot of calls. People who want me to audition."

"Holy shit—seriously? That's awesome, dude!"

"Yeah, it is." I couldn't hide my own lack of enthusiasm. This was something I'd been waiting for and praying for ever since I'd first come to Hollywood, and now that it was coming together, I kinda felt sick.

Especially since I'd assumed my career prospects were toast. I just couldn't resist even though I wished I could. It was easy to walk away when I couldn't get a callback to save my life. When people were asking for me? When I had auditions for *real* roles?

Lead me not into temptation for I already know the way.

Ashton slowed to a stop at a red light, and he furrowed his brow. "You don't sound happy about all this. What's up?"

I pressed my elbow against the window and kneaded my forehead. The jetlag was catching up with me now that I wanted to get my thoughts into some semblance of order. God, I was tired all of a sudden. "They all want me because I'm Isaac Ambrose's son-in-law."

"Okay. And?"

"That doesn't seem fucked up to you?"

He shot me an inquisitive look. "You having second thoughts about all this or something?"

"I… well…." I sighed. "Now that you mention it? Yeah, I kind of am. It's… I mean, the money has been awesome. But it kind of feels like the Devil's coming to collect, you know? Like suddenly Jesse and I are married—for real legally married—but I can't handle sleeping with him because it makes me feel like a whore. Doors are opening up for me all over the place, but they're because of the man whose political career I'm trying to help Jesse screw, and God knows how that's going to come bite me in the ass. Even if it doesn't, I feel guilty for—"

"Hayden. Dude." Ashton made a *calm your tits* gesture. "Settle down, man."

"How?" I sounded so pathetic. "I feel like I've made a mess of my entire life, my career, any shot I have at an actual relationship with Jesse…" I scrubbed a hand over my face, then dropped it into my lap. "What the fuck do I do now?"

"Look." He glanced at me again as he followed the steady crawl of traffic. "Things are complicated between you and Jesse, but it's nothing you can't come back from, you know? Even if it just means ironing things out enough to live with each other. Maybe when this is all over"—he shrugged—"you can see if dating him works or something. But it's not like one of you did some horrible thing, you know? And I mean, you said he backed off when you asked him to, right?"

Now I felt even guiltier. Jesse hadn't been an ass about it at all. If anything, he'd seemed worried about me, and horrified that he'd made me feel used. He'd *instantly* agreed to shelve the sex. No hesitation at all in that department. There were any number of ways he could have been a complete and utter jackhole about it, but he hadn't. "Yeah." I sighed. "He was awesome about it."

"Okay, so, it's not like anybody's pissed at each other. Talk it through, you know?"

I nodded, staring out the windshield at the line of taillights in front of us. "Yeah. Good point. But what about all the stuff with my career? I'm totally taking advantage of doors being opened by a guy who I'm trying to fuck over."

Ashton was quiet for a moment, tapping his thumbs on the wheel as he inched through traffic. "He's opening all those doors because you're married to Jesse, right?"

"Yeah."

"And he doesn't approve of Jesse being married to you, right?"

309

"Right. He actually told Jesse at the wedding that he was an embarrassment to the family."

Ashton rolled his eyes. "So he's getting you a foot in the door with acting, but he's also treating your husband—who he doesn't *know* is your fake husband—like garbage just for marrying you." He shrugged. "If I were you, I'd take whatever he gave me and not feel bad about it. The guy's a douche. You might as well take anything good you can get out of this."

I drummed my nails on the console. "Okay, I see your point, but I still feel… I don't know. I feel weird about it."

"That's because you're good people. Always have been. This guy?" Ashton shook his head. "Think of it this way—he's got a reputation for fucking over anyone in the industry who doesn't kiss his ass the right way. If he gets you into the business, and then he gets screwed because of you being married to Jesse? That sounds like karma to me." He paused. "And it's not like anyone is making him disown Jesse over you. Literally all you're doing is pretending to be married to Jesse, and letting Isaac react however he's going to react."

"So, I'm the bear trap, but nobody's making him step on me."

"Basically."

"Hmm." I still wasn't quite comfortable with the whole thing, but he'd settled some of my worries. "Guess we'll see how the auditions go." Might as well enjoy it all before I was blacklisted.

Ashton smiled. "Awesome. Fingers crossed for you, man."

"Thanks. And by the way, how are you and Luis doing? With two people paying all the bills instead of one?"

"Are you kidding?" He laughed. "You paid the rent for all three of us for the next six months. We're sitting prettier than we have in ages. Hell, I even got this old girl fixed." He patted the dashboard. "You hear that? No rattling or squeaking."

I listened, and he was right—the car's usual mystery noises were gone. "Wow. Still has some life in her after all."

"Yep. Good thing I got her into the shop, too." He grimaced. "Mechanic said she might've made it another five hundred or a thousand miles before the timing belt broke."

"Oh shit. That would have been…"

"Ugly and expensive," he said with a nod. "But I got the timing belt replaced along with a bunch of other shit, and I'm saving money now to buy something new in a few months." He glanced at me and smiled. "This thing you did with Jesse? It's been a lifesaver, man. Between not having to worry about rent for a while and the cash Jesse gave us—things are going pretty fucking good."

"Glad to hear it." Knowing my former roommates were on solid ground did a lot to ease my conscience. I still wasn't so sure about taking advantage of my father-in-law's connections—or about how long any of that would even last before Isaac had me summarily shunned—but I felt better about being involved in Jesse's plan in the first place.

The Devil would come to collect sooner or later, but at least my two best friends wouldn't be out on the street.

L.A. WITT

Chapter 24
Jesse

I was lying back on my bed, wrists in their usual braces and my Kindle propped on my knee, when a knock at the door startled me. Hayden had been out with his old roommate, and I had no idea when he'd gotten back.

"Uh. Yeah? Come in."

It opened, and Hayden peeked in. "Hey, um." He muffled a cough, then held out his hand. "I just wanted to give these back to you."

The overhead light glinted off the amber and silver of the cufflinks I'd loaned him for the wedding.

"Oh. Great. Um." I started to get up, but paused. "You know what? Why don't you hang onto them?"

"Are you sure?"

"Yeah." I smiled nervously. "You've got the tux now, and you'll need cufflinks to go with it."

"Oh." He stared down at the pair in his hand, and swallowed. "I can probably buy a couple sets. I don't need… you don't have to…"

"It's fine. Honestly I have so many…" I didn't know how to finish the thought.

"Okay. Well." He smiled, though his eyes didn't seem to echo it. "Thanks."

"You're welcome." And if this awkwardness lasted for another minute, I was going to lose my mind. "Listen. While you're here." I put my Kindle aside and sat up, swinging my legs over the side of the mattress. "I wanted to apologize. For things getting weird on the cruise."

"It wasn't your fault. Like I said, it took two."

"I know, but with what we're doing and why we were even there, I should've thought about it before I moved in on you."

"I probably should have too. But we didn't, and we can't do anything about it." He looked in my eyes. "I really don't want things to get weird, though. Or, well, stay weird."

"Yeah. Same. Guess it'll just take some time?"

"Guess so, yeah."

He nodded. For a moment, I thought he was going to go, and I wasn't sure if I wanted to shoo him out or beg him to stay. Then he cleared his throat. "So, um, my agent called. I, um, never got around to letting her go when I decided to give up acting, and… anyway." He gestured sharply. "Apparently her phone has been ringing off the hook since before the wedding, and she's got a ton of auditions lined up for me."

"Oh really? That's great!"

"Yeah, it is."

I studied him. "You don't sound happy."

Hayden lowered his gaze and pressed his shoulder into

the doorframe. "I am, but I'm... I feel weird about it."

"How so?"

Staring at the floor, he folded his arms loosely across his chest. "My roommate says I shouldn't feel bad about benefitting from your dad opening doors. Because I mean, it isn't like anyone's forcing him to disown you for marrying me."

I winced, thankful he wasn't looking at me right then.

"So you would think it's karma, right?" Hayden said. "Whatever happens to him and his career because of us, it's on him. And part of me just can't resist one last shot at acting. Or maybe I wasn't as ready as I thought I was to give it all up." He met my gaze through his lashes. "But I still feel guilty just like I feel guilty accepting a pair of diamond cufflinks from your mom."

Sighing, I nodded. "Yeah, I get it. I do. This whole thing has done a number on my conscience too."

"Really?"

"Oh yeah. I'm lying to my mom. I'm setting my entire family up for some serious upheaval. Hell, for all I know, whoever gets elected instead of my dad will be ten times worse." I slouched, suddenly dragging as if the jetlag had kicked in all at once. "Believe me when I say I've lost my share of sleep over everything. I'm sorry it's affecting you that way too."

"It is what it is, I guess. But I mean, what do I do?"

"About what? The auditions?"

Hayden nodded.

I shrugged. "Go to them. Knock them out of the park. Be the movie star you always wanted to be."

He blinked. "Really?"

"Why not? Look, Dad's connections got you in the

door, but you still have to sell it. If you get the part, it's because you earned it."

Hayden smirked. "You mean like your sister earns hers?"

Laughing, I rolled my eyes. "Ugh. God. Okay, point taken. But still—you know you're good at what you do, and you know politics are part of this industry."

"This cutthroat bloodbath of an industry," he muttered.

"You are not kidding."

He shifted his weight. "So you really think I should just do it?"

"Definitely. Those doors aren't going to stay open for long. I say go for it while you can. Just, um, don't be surprised when they all slam shut."

"I know. I'd kind of accepted they were shut already." Hayden gnawed his bottom lip. "I guess it would raise some eyebrows if I said no, too."

"Hmm?"

"If I turned down the auditions. Someone might figure out something's hinky."

"Oh." I blinked. "I hadn't even thought about that."

"Can you tell I've been obsessing over it?"

"Eh, I don't blame you."

"Right? You know, when this is all over, I feel like we should go find a beach somewhere and smoke a bowl to celebrate."

I laughed. "Would be a nice switch from all the stress."

"So much." Hayden straightened up and smiled. "Anyway, I won't keep bugging you. Thanks for the advice." He paused. "And the cufflinks."

"Don't mention it."

He started to go, but hesitated and faced me again. "So are we…" He gestured at each of us. "Are we okay?"

"Of course."

"Are you sure? Things have been so weird."

"Yeah, they have. I guess we both needed to adjust to everything. But yeah, we're okay."

He exhaled, shoulders drooping. "Okay. Good. It's been driving me crazy."

"Me too." *For reasons I wish I could tell you.*

We exchanged smiles, and he left the room, shutting the door behind him. A moment later, his bedroom door clicked shut across the hall.

I stared at my door for a long moment. Yeah, we were okay, but why didn't everything *feel* okay? And why did it feel so weird to stay in my own bedroom while Hayden went back to his?

Oh.

Right.

Because we'd been sharing the suite on the ship, and even though we'd stopped sharing the bed a few nights ago, we'd at least been in the same room. Which of course had driven me crazy because I'd wanted him, but didn't want to make things weird with him.

Now we were home, and we had two closed doors between us, and everything felt all kinds of wrong. My bed felt empty without him even though I'd never shared this bed with him, and I hadn't shared it with anyone in the better part of a year.

But what the hell could I do? Hayden had already put a stop to us having sex because it made things weird, and I understood where he was coming from. If I was paying him to be my husband, and then we were sleeping together, was I paying him to sleep with me? Yeah, I could see why he wasn't thrilled about that. In his shoes, I probably wouldn't have been down with it either. There needed to be lines, and we needed to toe those lines, and no matter how good the sex was—holy fuck, it was so good—we couldn't sleep together without *crossing* those lines. End of story.

So now we were back where we belonged. Married on paper for reasons that had nothing to do with sex or love. Sleeping in separate bedrooms while I dropped monthly payments into his bank account. All was as it needed to be.

Except for the part where I had fallen so hard for Hayden it wasn't funny.

Well, Hayden, if you thought sex made things weird, you won't believe how much weirder I can make it!

I closed my eyes and wiped a hand over my face.

I could live with us not sleeping together. It was frustrating, but I could live with it. The emotions, though? Shit. What was I supposed to do with all that? Tell him? Keep it to myself?

Hayden had agreed to a full year of this. If I told him how I felt about him, was that a line we could uncross like the one in the bedroom? We could stop getting physical, and we had. I couldn't stop having feelings. Especially not the feelings that had been on the tip of my tongue when he'd said we had to rein things in.

I didn't blame him. I wasn't angry. If I were in his shoes, and my employer-slash-husband brought emotions into it, I didn't imagine I'd be comfortable with it. Would I feel obligated to at least pretend those feelings were mutual? Oh God, that thought made my skin crawl. Okay, yeah, I definitely wasn't saying anything to Hayden.

I sighed into the stillness of my empty bedroom. I'd imagined a lot of ways this arrangement could get complicated.

Falling in love with my husband had *not* been one of them.

L.A. WITT

Chapter 25
Hayden

It was grocery night again. Me and Jesse, in the Focus, on the way to the supermarket with a list we'd actually remembered this time. It felt normal, and I could almost believe things hadn't turned weird on the cruise. It'd been getting easier between us. It didn't happen overnight, but the post-cruise awkwardness had lightened a little, and day by day it was getting better. I had hope it would eventually go away, or at least fade to a dull roar.

Instead of stilted conversations and broken eye contact, we were back to talking on the couch until we realized we'd stayed up way too late and he needed to go to bed. If we brushed against each other while we were navigating the narrow confines of the kitchen, we'd exchange smiles and murmurs of "sorry," and go back to what we were doing.

We were back to being platonic roommates just like I'd been with Ashton and Luis. Everything was perfect.

And any goddamned day now, I might stop pining after him and wondering if I'd made a huge mistake by shelving that amazing sex we'd been having on the cruise. Did I really *have* to take it off the table? Was it really so bad if he was paying me and we were fooling around? Because it wasn't like he'd started paying me more after we'd gone to bed together. He'd been emphatic that sex wasn't expected, and he'd been fine with putting a stop to it.

And damn it, the sex had been *so good*. Not just the sex—the intimacy. The affection. Those moments when it seemed like nothing existed in his world except for me. For a few short days, we'd been a real couple, and that taste of being Jesse's real partner and not a paid actor had left me hungry for more. Problem was, I couldn't figure out how to separate the money from the rest of it. Fuck.

Jesse's phone beeped with a generic text tone, startling me out of my thoughts. He quickly sent a reply, then put his phone facedown on his leg. "So, my little brother is coming to town next week. I'd love to have you meet him."

"Your little—" I glanced at him. "Is this the one who couldn't come to the wedding?"

"Uh, more like *wouldn't* come."

I arched an eyebrow. "But you want to see him?"

Jesse nodded. "Definitely. He and I are close. I wasn't the one he was avoiding by skipping the wedding."

"Your dad?"

"Yep. My brother's been proudly disowned by our father for almost five years."

"Oh my God." I shot him a horrified look before facing the road again. "Is disowning his kids like your dad's hobby or something?"

Jesse laughed humorlessly. "You have to admit—when it comes to keeping his kids in line, it's got an eighty percent success rate."

"That's…" I blinked. "I don't know if anyone has pointed this out to you recently, but dude? Your family is messed up."

"You don't say."

"I just… wow. I mean, do I even want to know what sin got him excommunicated from the family?"

"On paper, knocking up a girl and refusing to do the right thing and marry her."

I cocked my head, gaze still fixed on the road. "And the part that wasn't on paper?"

Beside me, Jesse sighed. "That my nephew is biracial, and my dad would have lost his shit if Alex and Piper had gotten married."

"Oh for fuck's sake. Are you telling me your family is racist too?"

"Have you *seen* my dad's movies?"

In my mind's eye, I saw Luis going off on one of his rants about Isaac's "stupid racist ass excuse for movies," and I nodded. "Oh. Right. Good point." Funny how even knowing what kind of crap Isaac put on the screen, not to mention what he was going to do to Jesse, it was *still* hard to grasp him rejecting his own grandchild. "Man. Your dad's an asshole."

"Are you really surprised he's a racist? This is Hollywood, sweetheart." Jesse patted my leg. "The award shows didn't just randomly turn blinding white on their own."

I scoffed. "Wouldn't his voting public love to hear about that?"

"Alex and I talked about it, actually. But…" Jesse shook his head. "He didn't want to put his family on the radar like that. It was easier to just let Dad paint him as an irresponsible deadbeat."

"Okay, that makes sense."

"At least with our arrangement"—he gestured at me—"you know what you're getting into from the get-go."

"And there aren't any kids involved."

"Exactly. Alex has always had to tread a lot more carefully than I do because he has to protect his wife and son."

"Wait, his wife? So they *are* married?"

"They are now, yeah. But they waited until everything had quieted down. He didn't want to draw any more attention to her than he had to."

"Knowing what I do about your family now?" I whistled. "Can't imagine why."

Jesse grimaced. "I know. I'm sorry. Even though you knew what you were getting into, it can't be fun."

"No, it's not. But it's worth it."

"It is. I can't fucking wait until it's over, though."

I blinked. "Oh."

Jesse jumped like I'd smacked him. "No! No, I didn't mean… I meant all the shit with my family. Not…" He gestured at us. "You know what I meant, right?"

"Yeah, I do. I get it." I forced a smile as I pulled into the grocery store's parking lot. "No worries."

It wasn't like I could explain to him why I didn't *want* it to be over any time soon.

As we walked inside, we moved on to lighter topics, thank God, but my mind kept circling back to that one. The idea of this coming to an end wasn't unexpected, but deep down, it was hard to imagine it being over. I was itching for everything to go down with the Ambrose family so we could be done with that part, but what about this part?

What happens to us *when it's all over?*

Somehow, having this train of thought while we were on our weekly grocery shopping trip didn't help. It seemed kind of ridiculous, but the domestic stuff like this made it exponentially harder to tell myself we weren't and wouldn't be a real couple. Strolling through the grocery store, talking about the most inconsequential things, made me want to do this with him all the time. It was one of those parts of a relationship I'd always secretly loved—when the honeymoon period was over and we were happily bored together. When a relationship became comfortable and reliable. Which was exactly how this relationship felt when I could ignore the money changing hands and the sex being off the table.

Awesome. Most effortless relationship I'd ever had, and it wasn't even real.

"Did we need more laundry soap?" Jesse skimmed over the list. "I thought we were getting low."

"Hmm, I think there's enough for a few more loads, but it probably wouldn't hurt. We definitely need dish detergent though."

Two aisles later, I said, "Oh, I forgot to get mustard."

"I'll get it." He gestured over his shoulder. "I meant to get some barbecue sauce too."

"Okay. I'll either be here or in the next aisle."

A quick smile, and he headed off in search of the forgotten condiments.

I watched him go, a ball of lead sinking in my

stomach.

Comfortable. Reliable. Happily bored.

If what we're doing is fake, then why is this part so perfect?

More and more, I wanted to know what it would be like to be in a real relationship with Jesse. No contracts. No fake marriage. No strings. Just sex and grocery shopping and talking all night and everything normal people did in normal relationships. I wanted us to fight over stupid things and deal with big things and drink cheap wine in our sweatpants. *Normal* shit.

Unaware of everything going on in my mind, Jesse reappeared at the end of the aisle, mustard and barbecue sauce in hand. The instant I saw him, a lump materialized in my throat.

It's not fair to be married to you and not be able to tell you how much I love you.

Because that was what it came down to, wasn't it? I loved him. I was in love with the man I'd married for money, the man I couldn't screw without feeling like a whore, and I had no idea what to do with that.

You need to get it out of your head is what you need to do with it.

Wasn't that the truth? If this arrangement wasn't compatible with sex, it sure as shit wasn't going to work with love. As long as that contract was in place and the money kept coming, there was no separating our marriage from our deal. Even if I had him modify the contract and kill the payments so money didn't muddy the waters, this was still a business arrangement. This wasn't romance, it was sabotage.

I was here to do a job. Between now and when that job was done, I'd enjoy as much time as I could with Jesse because… well, because apparently I was a masochist. The fact was, though, I wanted to be with him, and I wanted to enjoy this comfortably boring "relationship" we had going. I wanted to enjoy what time we had left before my obligation was up.

When it was over, it would be over. All of it.

And one way or another, I would move on.

~*~

Jesse's little brother flew in a week later. We waited in the cell phone lot at LAX until he texted that he was in baggage claim, and then Jesse drove up to the terminal.

"I seriously need to trade my car in for something like this," he muttered as he parked my Focus on the curb. "I'm getting spoiled by all this trunk space."

I laughed. "What did you do before when you needed to pick someone up?"

"Rented something if I had to."

"Really?"

"Well, yeah. What else would I do?"

I held his gaze, then chuckled and shook my head. "Rich people, man…"

"What? How are—oh there he is." Jesse got out, and I joined him.

Given Alex Ambrose's status as black sheep of the family, I'd envisioned him as some kind of rock star type. Leather jacket even though it was hot as balls in LA right now. Half-laced combat boots flopping with every step. Long hair that may or may not have been his natural color. He was the rebellious youngest child of the Ambrose clan, so clearly he'd wear his rebelliousness on his sleeve.

Yeah, remember how I thought Jesse would look and I was totally wrong? Turned out I was batting 0-for-2 when it came to predicting Ambrose men's styles.

I knew in an instant that the man striding out of baggage claim was Jesse's brother. They had the same eyes and sharp features, though Alex wore glasses and kept his hair long enough to let the ends start to curl.

Jesse and Alex shared a quick hug, and Jesse introduced me.

Alex extended his hand. "Ah, so you're the gullible idiot who married this jackass?" He had an accent from living in New York.

"Oh honey." I shook his hand. "Give it a day and you'll figure out who's the real gullible idiot in this equation." I cupped my mouth and added in a stage whisper, "But don't tell Jesse."

Alex laughed, clapping my shoulder as he said to his brother, "I like this guy already."

"Great." Jesse groaned and rolled his eyes. "Would you two get in the damn car?"

Alex and I both snickered. They hoisted Alex's bags into the trunk, and we all climbed in so we could move and let someone else pull up to the curb.

As Jesse took us out of LAX, he glanced at Alex in the passenger seat. "So what's your plan while you're in town?"

"I've got meetings all day tomorrow," Alex said, "but I'm all yours for the weekend. I mean, if you two don't already have plans."

"Nah, we're free," Jesse said. "We were planning on hanging out with you." He looked at me in the rearview, eyebrows up as if to ask, "*We were, weren't we?*"

I nodded. "Nothing else on my calendar."

And it means spending time with you, so hell yeah. God, I really am a masochist.

"Cool," Alex said. "I'll keep the weekend open too. And by the way, Piper says hello. She wanted to come, especially to meet the new ball and chain, but her gallery's got a big event this weekend that she can't miss."

"Her gallery?" I asked.

Alex beamed proudly. "Yep. She's an artist, and she co-owns a couple of galleries in New York and one in London. If you guys make it to the city one of these days, you should stop in. She's got some really incredible art on display right now."

"That sounds awesome," I said.

"He's not kidding," Jesse said. "Her work is amazing, and the stuff she usually has in her gallery is..." He whistled.

Alex beamed. "Just wait till you see the exhibit she's working on right now. I swear it's some of her best paintings *ever*."

"Definitely looking forward to seeing it."

"Me too," I said, but my heart wasn't in it. Jaunting off to New York to meet Alex's wife and see the art in her gallery sounded incredible. If I suggested it with any seriousness, Jesse might even go for it.

But it was a bad idea. It was a *terrible* idea. It would just make me feel more like we were a real couple, that I was really part of this family, and that I was really meeting my new sister-in-law and nephew, and...

I couldn't do it. In fact, if Jesse suggested it for real, I might be the one to veto it. This thing between us had a shelf life, and though I kept finding reasons to spend time

329

with him, I needed to start thinking about my own sanity. I needed to start making peace with the idea of all this being over in the foreseeable future.

It didn't matter how much I absolutely felt like I was hanging out with my husband and my brother-in-law right now.

At the end of the day, this was an act.

It was a lie.

And soon, it would be over.

Chapter 26
Jesse

We spent most of Alex's visit lounging around the condo. He was in town on business, and after running around to meetings, he was perfectly happy with some downtime. Wasn't like Los Angeles was exactly a novel place for him, either.

On his last night in town, though, we made reservations at a beachfront restaurant we'd both loved since we were kids. It was fairly casual, had some of the most amazing seafood in Southern California, was *the* most gorgeous place to watch the sun go down, and Hayden had never been there. Perfect.

It was also up in Santa Barbara, so we left early to make the long but scenic drive up the 101. With traffic, it would be a solid two hours, but none of us were in a big hurry. We left plenty of time to still make our reservation even if there was a wreck or something.

Since no one could fit comfortably into my Porsche's

sad excuse for a backseat, we took Hayden's car.

Traffic was backed up in every direction because it was Los Angeles and of course it was backed up. It didn't seem to bother Hayden, though. He crawled up the on-ramp, merged into the gridlock, and wasn't the least bit tense as we followed a mile-long line of bumpers up the I-5.

Alex took out an e-cig and gestured with it. "Either of you mind if I vape?"

Hayden shrugged and I shook my head.

"Just open the window if you don't mind," Hayden said. "I just bought this thing."

"Can do." Alex rolled down the window, took a long drag from the e-cig, and turned his head to blow out the cloud of sweet-smelling vapor out the window. Some of it stayed in the car, though.

"Ugh." I wrinkled my nose. "What the hell flavor is that? Garbage fire bubblegum?"

"It's strawberry, numbnuts. Now shut up or I'll blow the next one at you."

"That's what she said," Hayden muttered.

My brother barked a laugh. "I'm serious, Jesse—I like this one. Just the kind of smartass to keep you in line."

"Just don't ever put him in the same room as Piper. They start comparing notes, we're both fucked."

Alex sobered, and he said around the e-cig, "Good point."

"Oh yeah?" Hayden said. "She a spitfire too?"

I snorted.

Alex blew another vape cloud out the window. "Nobody thinks as fast as she does. I try to get her with a witty comeback?" He shook his head. "She'll always have a better one. Always."

"As if that takes much," I said.

"Zip it."

"See?"

Hayden laughed. "Sounds like my brother's skating coach. Brian tried to mouth off at her a few times, and…" He shook his head, grimacing. "Not smart. Not smart at all."

"Skating?" Alex asked.

"Yeah, my brother was a figure skater for a long time."

While Hayden told Alex the story of his brother's career, I slung my arm across the backseat and just watched the two of them. It didn't surprise me that they'd instantly gotten along. Alex was about as laidback as they came, and Hayden hadn't met a stranger he couldn't befriend in two seconds flat.

I had a lot of weird feelings as I watched them, though. It was good to see Alex—we didn't spend nearly enough time together thanks to work schedules and that enormous landmass someone had inconveniently put between New York and LA. When he'd been cut off from the family, I'd been terrified he'd sever contact with all of us. To this day, I could still feel the profound sense of relief I'd had when I'd realized he wanted us to stay close.

And then there was Hayden. The man I'd fallen stupidly in love with, but couldn't tell him because I was paying him to pose as the man I loved.

I squirmed in the Focus's backseat. I felt guilty for not telling Alex the truth about Hayden. I felt guilty for not telling Hayden the truth about my feelings for him. Before this whole thing was over, I was pretty sure my conscience was going to eat me alive, assuming all these unspoken emotions didn't get to me first.

If Hayden or Alex noticed, they sure as hell didn't let on. Hayden kept driving, the two of them kept talking, and I kept watching, and my God, it was surreal to watch Hayden chatting easily with the brother I'd once been scared of losing forever. They fit. My brother and my husband. Brothers-in-law. This seemed real and right, like Hayden was as much a part of this family as Alex was. Which was kind of ironic, given that Alex had been exiled from the family. Just like I would be soon.

I flicked my gaze back and forth between them. Imagining a future where this was my family—Hayden and Alex, plus Piper and their son—made sense. I could absolutely envision it.

But Hayden had signed a contract. All he had to do was hold up his end of the deal, and when we reached the end of that year, he'd be gone.

Jesus. There was really going to come a time when Hayden was out of the picture.

And when that time came… where the hell did I go from there?

After a long, leisurely, and utterly fantastic dinner, we wandered out onto the beach to walk off some of the food—bantering the entire way, of course.

"Don't let this guy bullshit you," Alex said to Hayden as he wagged a finger at me. "He talks a good game, but no one has been defeated by more theme park rides than him."

"What?" Hayden eyed me. "Tell me he's lying."

"Yes, he is." I elbowed Alex. "Or do we need to talk

about the guy who had nightmares after riding the Matterhorn?"

Alex huffed. "Whatever, dude. Hayden, I'm not joking—first time we went to Knott's Berry Farm, this guy puked all over us and the two girls sitting in front of us."

I rolled my eyes. "At least that was on a roller coaster. First time we took you to Disney, you puked on everyone and everything."

"I was six months old!"

"Still! That's fucking rude, man!"

Hayden laughed. "Jesus, you two are worse than me and my brother when we were kids."

"Yeah?" Alex said. "Your brother older or younger?"

"About ten minutes younger." Hayden smirked. "And you're damn right I don't let him forget it."

"Twins. Wow." Alex laughed and elbowed me. "Mom's worst nightmare, am I right?"

"She didn't want twins?" Hayden asked.

"She could barely handle us one at a time," I said.

Alex sniffed with amusement. "And she had staff. Me and Piper? It was just us and the baby. Mom had like fourteen nannies for each of us. You'd think if we were such a hassle, she'd have stopped at one or two."

Hayden's eyebrows rose with a hint of alarm.

"What?" I chuckled at Alex. "You're not going to have four more?"

Alex groaned. "Dude. No. Piper sometimes makes noise about wanting one more, but every time she suggests it, I remind her of everything we went through with Gavin, and she drops it."

"I don't blame you," Hayden said. "My brother has two that are less than two years apart, and I don't know how he and my sister-in-law haven't torn their hair out yet."

"Two in less than two years?" Alex shook his head vigorously. "*No*, thank you. I love my kid more than life itself and wouldn't trade him for the world, but sign up for more diapers and sleepless nights? Nuh-uh."

Hayden and I both laughed.

"I think it's karma," I said.

"Karma?" Alex scoffed. "For what?"

"For you waking up everyone in a twenty-mile radius when you were a baby. Dude, I was eight when you came along, and by the time you were like two weeks old, I'd decided I was never having kids."

"Well, good. God knows the world doesn't need two of *you*."

"Shut up." I playfully smacked his arm, and he returned it.

"Oh my God." Hayden laughed. "I swear even if you two didn't look alike, I'd know you're brothers."

"What?" Alex looked me up and down, his expression full of exaggerated indignance. "I do not look like him."

I made an equally indignant face. "Yeah. No. Not at all."

"Pfft. Whatever helps you boys sleep at night, because…" Hayden wiggled a finger at both of us and singsonged, "Twinsies. And I'm an identical twin so I'm an authority on the subject."

"Ugh. Whatever." Alex tried to look annoyed, but he couldn't hide the laugh. Neither could I.

Hayden grinned at me, and his snarky little wink screwed with my equilibrium. Not that I was surprised. Every time I looked at that man, my heart went crazy. I was so stupidly head over heels for him, and just a glance was enough to make me trip over my own feet.

Sometimes I wondered if this was all because we'd slept together on the cruise.

Except, no. For one thing, I'd slept with guys before and not felt particularly sentimental about them.

For another, these feelings had started sneaking in long before I'd ever so much as kissed Hayden. Falling into bed with him? That hadn't been a turning point in my feelings for him—it had been the end of me *restraining* those feelings, and I'd stopped restraining them right up until I'd had to rein them back in.

Holy hell, I am such a wreck for you.

The three of us continued down the beach, bantering and laughing, when Hayden suddenly jumped like someone had smacked him. He took out his phone, and sucked in a breath. "Oh! This is my agent. I need to take it."

"Of course," I said. "Go!"

He flashed us both a quick smile, took the call, and wandered back up the beach, probably for a little privacy.

Alex watched him for a moment. Then, out of the blue, he said, "I can see why you married this one."

I almost choked on nothing. "Oh yeah?" I sputtered. "Why's… why's that?"

Alex shot me one of those *you're such an idiot* looks. "Come on, man. I've seen you with boyfriends before." He gestured at Hayden. "I have never seen you as happy as you are around him."

Well if that wasn't an emotional kick in the balls. Partly because of the arrangement I had with Hayden. Partly because… fuck, it was true, wasn't it?

Oh, but Alex wasn't done yet. "I'm surprised Dad is putting up with this."

"Hmm?"

"You know." He nodded in the direction Hayden had gone. "You being married to a dude. After all the shit he talked about that when we were younger—did he get visited by the Ghost of Pride Parades Past or something?"

I laughed dryly. "I wish. No, he's not thrilled."

Alex inclined his head. "But what about everything he's said about disowning you? Because, hello"—he gestured at himself—"Dad is not below disowning his kids."

I swallowed, avoiding my brother's gaze. "Yeah. I know. I think…" God, I felt so guilty keeping this from Alex. And why was I keeping it from him of all people? If there was anyone on the planet I could trust—non-disclosure agreement or not—it was my younger brother.

I glanced around, making sure we were absolutely alone. "Listen, there's something you should know. And this has to stay between us."

Alex turned to me, eyes wide. "What's up?"

"The thing is…" I chewed my lip, struggling to hold his gaze. "Hayden and I… we're not really…" *Why do I feel like I'm lying?* "We're not really a couple."

Alex's lips parted.

I took a deep breath. "We're married. Legally. But this…" I rubbed the back of my neck. "I hired him."

"You *hired* him?" Alex stared at me. "What the hell?"

I slid my hands into the pockets of my shorts and shifted my weight on the sand. "Here's the thing—Dad hasn't changed. At all. If anything, he's gotten worse. And he's planning on going into politics next year."

Alex squeezed his eyes shut and groaned. "Are you fucking kidding me? He's actually doing it?"

"He hasn't made a public declaration yet, but trust me, it's in the works. They're planning campaign fundraisers as we speak."

My brother made an unhappy noise and shook his head. "Do I even want to know what office he's planning to run for?"

"He's aiming for governor right now, but I have no idea how high up the food chain he'll try to get."

"Jesus."

"Right? The thing is, he's been gaining a ton of support from the liberals and progressives in LA, and people fucking love him." I exhaled. "Alex, I'm scared shitless that if he runs, he'll win."

My brother nodded. "Yeah. I don't see how anyone could beat him, to be honest."

"Exactly. So I…" I closed my eyes, took a deep breath, and squared my shoulders. "So I'm forcing his hand. I know he hates what I'm doing with Hayden, and it's only a matter of time before he makes good on that promise to disown me if I marry a man."

"Holy shit," Alex whispered. "But… he hasn't. Has he?"

"Not yet. I suspect he's holding out to see if Hayden and I are really in it for the long haul."

"How long do you think that'll take?"

"Don't know. Hayden signed a contract for a year. Hopefully it'll happen before that's up."

"Whoa." Alex watched Hayden for a long moment, his features taut as he—I assumed—processed everything I'd said. Without turning to me, he said, "Let me ask you something, though."

"Okay?"

"What happens when this is over?"

I pursed my lips and avoided his gaze. "On paper, we get a divorce for 'irreconcilable differences', and we both move on."

"Uh-huh." Alex didn't sound convinced *at all*. "And on paper, Dad's a progressive Democrat. Meanwhile in the real world…?"

I exhaled, staring out at the ocean because I couldn't look at him. "I don't know. I really don't. I, um, think I got in over my head with this one."

"No kidding. Because, dude, if you hadn't told me, I never would have guessed. The way the two of you look at each other…"

I met his gaze. "What?"

Alex rolled his eyes. "Oh come on. Don't play stupid. Didn't I just tell you how ridiculously happy you two look?"

"Well, yeah, but… I figured you meant how *I* look at *him*."

"I did." Alex nodded sharply. "Kind of figured it went without saying that it goes both ways."

My mouth went dry. "To be fair, I'm *paying* him to—"

"Jesse. Don't." Alex shook his head. "Your bullshit doesn't work on me. And that"—he pointed sharply in Hayden's direction—"is not someone who's acting."

I had no idea what to say.

"Listen," Alex said, voice gentler, "you guys need to get on the same page about what's going on between you. There's obviously something here that goes beyond whatever you worked out on paper."

Mute, I nodded.

"Talk to him, man," he went on.

"What am I supposed to say?" I snapped. "What if he doesn't really feel the same way? He's still contractually obligated to stick around, and things already got weird after we—" I barely stopped myself before I told him more than anyone needed to know about his own brother.

Alex's eyebrow arched. "After you fucked each other's brains out?"

I stared at him incredulously.

He rolled his eyes again. "Yeah, that's what I thought. Listen, man, what you guys do and all is none of my business. But my gut tells me that if you don't grow a spine and say something to him, you're going to end up losing more than just your inheritance when all this is over."

"Yeah." I deflated, watching Hayden talk on the phone a hundred or so feet away. "I know."

Alex let the subject drop. He wasn't one to harp on things, and he'd made his point. I kind of wished he would keep harping on it this time, though. It was weirdly easier to listen to him than it was to let my own thoughts intrude on the silence. Especially since he was right. I'd gone into this arrangement with a lot to lose, and suddenly I had a lot more on the line than I'd started with.

Fuck. What do I do?

"Sorry about that." Hayden's voice jarred me back into the present, and I turned as he approached. To my surprise, he looked dazed, his phone still in his hand and his eyes wide.

Alarm made my neck prickle. "What's wrong?"

He shook his head slowly. "Nothing. Nothing's wrong. Just, um…" He swallowed, holding up his phone.

"That was my agent."

"Right?" I nudged. "And?"

He blinked a few times. "I got an offer. It's… it's not a lead role, but it's a big one, and it's…" He blinked again, then shook himself and met my gaze. "Holy shit. I got a part."

"Awesome!" Alex said. "Congrats, man."

"Yeah, that's amazing!" I grinned. "Congratulations."

"Thanks. And she thinks some of the other auditions went really well too, and I…" Hayden put a hand to his chest and laughed breathlessly. "I think I'm going to pass out."

"Don't do that." I wrapped an arm around his shoulders. "Come on. Let's go sit somewhere and have a drink to celebrate. And so you don't collapse."

He leaned into me as we walked, and I tried not to think too much about the contact. He probably needed the physical support right then because his agent's call had almost literally knocked his feet out from under him. We both knew his acting career was on borrowed time, but could I blame him for being excited about having a brief taste of success?

He was dazed, and I let him keep leaning on me as we walked. I didn't want to notice how well we fit together and how much I liked touching him like this. I didn't want to, but I did.

Over Hayden's head, Alex looked at me, and he didn't have to say a word. We could read each other like books, and everything he was thinking was written across his forehead.

Are you sure anything about this is fake?

I didn't have an answer.

As we kept walking back toward the row of bars and restaurants, I was thrilled for Hayden, but also had an uncomfortable knot in my stomach.

There were so many things I wanted to tell him, and Alex was right that I *needed* to tell him. And what if I did? While that contract was in place, neither of us could be objective about each other's emotions. Or our own. Or what to do with them.

I could wait until the end of our contract when there was no more pressure and no obligation, and then tell him. He'd be free to walk away. It would hurt like hell if he did, but I'd rather watch him leave than have him stuck with me and all this awkwardness.

God knew how I was going to keep this under my hat for months on end, but it wasn't like I could tell him now. Not tonight when he had something he deserved to be excited over. Not any time soon while we still had this arrangement in place. But what if he figured it out? My brother could see that I was in love with Hayden. What if Hayden caught on?

Great. Yet another complication I hadn't envisioned when we'd started out—how to keep my feelings off Hayden's radar until I could tell him without ruining everything.

This is going to blow up in my face, isn't it?
Oh, yes it is.
Spectacularly.

L.A. WITT

Chapter 27
Hayden & Jesse

Those huge fucking doors. I swear, they were never *not* going to make me laugh, especially now that I knew the dick-measuring story behind them.

And laughing at the dick doors was a nice distraction from my nerves over attending yet another party at the Ambrose estate in Joshua Tree. Jesse and I had been invited along with the rest of the family, and I wasn't even sure what the occasion was. An occasion didn't seem to be a requirement around here. If Isaac Ambrose wanted to have a party, he had a party, and anyone who wanted to stay relevant in Hollywood made the trek from Los Angeles with goddamned smiles on their faces.

"I have to know," I said quietly to Jesse as we walked into the grand ballroom, "where do they park all the cars? Because there's like seven billion people here, and there's only about six cars out front."

Jesse shrugged as he deadpanned, "Maybe they

carpooled." I shot him a look, and he snickered. "There's a parking lot near the edge of the property. Dad doesn't like the driveway being cluttered, so he has the valets take them all out there where no one can see them."

I rolled my eyes. "But then where will he ever stash everyone's private jets?"

"Other end of the property."

"Uh-huh."

He glanced at me. "No, really. There's an airstrip and a hangar."

"Bullshit."

He arched an eyebrow. "Want to hike out and take a look?"

I blinked. "You're… not joking?"

Jesse shook his head.

I stared at him incredulously for a moment. "Okay, maybe not tonight, but one of these days you are taking me out there because you have *got* to be yanking my chain."

He laughed, showing his palms. "I swear to God. Nothing says 'please notice how important I am' like coming to a party in a private plane."

"Especially a party that's only a three-hour drive."

"Hey, important people don't have time to waste. Well, I mean, aside from how long it takes to get to the Van Nuys Airport, but…"

I chuckled. "Every day, you remind me a little more just how different our worlds really are."

We continued into the party and made the rounds. Jesse introduced me to people I'd seen in movies and magazines, and to my utter shock, a number of people I'd met at one of the last few parties recognized me. I had well and truly found myself in a parallel dimension when Bill Wellman, a director and producer who was almost as well known as Isaac, stepped away from a crowd to say, "Hayden! Great to see you again." I mean, seriously. How was this my life? I was at a party thrown by Isaac Ambrose, and Bill Wellman went out of his way to talk to me. At this point I was pretty sure I'd accidentally taken one of Ashton's Ambien pills, and during the narcotic haze, sold my soul to Satan in an arrangement I couldn't actually remember, but was totally enjoying the hell out of (so to speak). When the Devil came to collect, well, I couldn't say it wasn't worth it.

Jesse and I were between conversations, making our way toward the bar for some more wine, when Amanda stepped in front of us.

My hackles immediately went up, but I bit back all the snide comments that were suddenly on the tip of my tongue. If you can't say anything nice… you're probably at an Ambrose family function.

"Hey, Jesse?" She glanced at me, and then faced her brother. "Could I borrow you for a few minutes?" She wasn't her usual hostile self. In fact, she was almost subdued—her expression was neutral, her eyes weren't narrow, and her tone made her sound like someone who really just wanted a word with her brother. So basically a normal sibling instead of one of the two-faced back-stabbing Ambrose kids.

"Um." Jesse looked at me. "Do you mind if—"

"No, no. I was going to go get another drink anyway." I gestured with my empty glass. "We'll catch up."

He flashed me a quick smile, then followed his sister out of the ballroom.

And suddenly I was alone in a sea of black ties and evening gowns and people who I'd spent years admiring either for their work or their… hey, look, I'm as human as the next guy, and I was currently standing twenty-two feet away from C.J. Chang, and I defy anyone to say they only admired him for his acting prowess. I wasn't the only one who became a fan after the first role where he took off his pants. Seriously, that *ass*…

I managed to tear my gaze away before anyone busted me staring. Right then, a waiter brushed past me, murmuring an apology, and in a weird way I was kind of tempted to jog after him and ask if he needed help. I'd never worked as a waiter in my life, but I was sure I'd feel more in my element running trays through this crowd than mingling as if I had any business calling myself one of them. I was not a peer of C.J. Chang or Bill Wellman.

Was I?

Did being married—well, married-ish—into the most powerful family in Hollywood mean I could speak to these people without bowing and scraping? Whoa.

Okay, definitely time for some more wine.

I hurried toward the bar, and I had just stepped into line when someone else materialized beside me, and I almost had a heart attack because *oh my fucking God it's Isaac Ambrose.*

Wait, he's my father-in-law. And kind of an asshole. Why am I getting starstruck?

Oh. Right. Isaac Ambrose.

"Hayden." He put a heavy arm around my shoulders. "I've been looking for you. I don't suppose you have a few minutes?"

I gulped. "A few… for…" *Young man, Isaac fucking*

Ambrose wants a few minutes of your time. What is there to hem and haw about? I cleared my throat. "Yeah. Sure. Yeah. What's up?"

He gestured toward the stairs. "Come up to my study with me. I want to talk to you about some of your opportunities in the industry."

Oh shit. Alarm bells clanged in my head.

Heart thumping, I swallowed. I glanced around, looking for Jesse. He was nowhere in sight, probably still with Amanda, but we both kind of wove in and out of each other's paths at functions like this. I couldn't imagine Isaac and I would be gone long enough for Jesse to actually start worrying. I'd catch up with him later. Hopefully I could hold my own alone with… gulp… Isaac.

Steeling myself, I turned to my father-in-law again. "Okay. Sure."

And Isaac Ambrose herded me out of the crowded ballroom and toward the stairs.

~*~

Jesse

"So what's going on?"

My sister leaned against one of the second floor balconies. She glanced at her phone, then put it down beside her and faced me. "Listen, I wanted to apologize. The way I acted over you and Hayden…" Sighing, she shook her head. "It wasn't okay. And I'm sorry."

I stared at her. My sister? Apologizing? That was new. Of course my immediate reaction was to get suspicious. Did she want something? Apologies were like gifts in this family—there were always strings attached.

"Um." I muffled a cough. "It's all right, I guess. I mean, I did kind of blindside everyone."

She shrugged, absently tugging on the thin strap of her red dress. "Yeah, you did, but I mean, the two of you seem really happy together."

Great. Like my conscience needed more of a reason to eat me alive. "We are. We're... he's a really great guy." I tilted my head. "Why did you try to grill him, anyway?"

Amanda sighed, lowering her gaze to the stonework at our feet. "I don't know. I guess I was just so afraid he'd be another gold digger or a ladder climber or something."

"So you were looking out for me?"

She looked at me through her lashes. "Someone had to. The whole family was worried, and we just—"

"Did they put you up to it?"

"Not... I mean, not really." She sighed, surreptitiously glancing at her phone again. "They wanted me to talk to you and make sure you were going into it with both eyes open. I guess I could have been less confrontational about it."

That was a bit of a stretch. Heart-to-hearts were not common in our household, and we sucked at them, so it would have turned into a confrontation one way or the other.

Her phone vibrated, the screen lighting up. She checked it yet again, and it was like a switch had flipped in her. Instead of this unusually pleasant side, she was back to, well, Amanda. "I guess I've kept you from the party long enough." With a smile that was anything but genuine as she tucked her phone into her purse, she added, "I'm glad we had this talk. We should do it more often."

Something cold trickled through my veins. "Amanda, what's going on?"

"What do you mean?" The smile grew bigger, but didn't gain an ounce of sincerity. "I just wanted to talk to my brother for once, and make a few things right."

Her feigned innocence turned my stomach. I glanced at the door, then back at her. "Well, as long as you're in the mood to apologize, maybe we should grab Hayden and—"

"I'm sure you can pass the message along." She started toward the door. "We should get back to the party."

Cold dread curdled the wine I'd already drunk, and I suddenly needed to find Hayden *right now*. I hurried back to the ballroom and scanned the crowd. With every face that wasn't his, my heartbeat rose steadily and panic began to set in.

My mother appeared beside me. "Jesse? Is everything all right?"

"I'm not sure." I swept another look around the room. "Where's Hayden?"

She gestured with her glass toward the hallway. "I saw him leaving with your father a few minutes ago. Why?"

"Oh no," I murmured, and without another word, darted out of the ballroom.

~*~
Hayden

Everything in the Ambrose family's house was huge, so it didn't really surprise me that Isaac's study was too. It reminded me of one of those gigantic CEO offices in the movies. The place where the terrified underlings were fired or pulled into evil business doings because The Boss said so. I wondered if that was the effect he was going for.

Isaac put his wineglass on the desk, paused to send a text, then pocketed his phone and crouched so he could reach under the desk. Something clicked and beeped, and what sounded like a safe door opened. When he stood, he had one of those metal briefcases like they use in spy movies. Okay, that was… different.

He put the briefcase on his desk beside his drink and turned to me. "So, I understand you've got the interest of quite a few directors and producers. Have any of them been in contact with you since we last spoke?"

I nodded. "Yeah. I've, uh, had more auditions since the honeymoon than I have in the entire rest of the time I've been in LA." I smiled through the sinking feeling in my stomach. I wouldn't even get to shoot that film, would I? That blacklist hammer was coming down tonight.

As Isaac held my gaze, a thin smile appeared. "Good. Good to hear. Any callbacks?"

I shifted uncomfortably, glancing at the briefcase. "A few."

"Excellent." He picked up his wine and took a sip, the whole series of motions extra slow as if he wanted me to just stand there like a dumbass and watch him take a drink.

The hair on my neck stood up. I was intimidated as fuck by this guy anyway, but something about this conversation really didn't sit right. I was expecting to be blacklisted and for my sort-of-husband to be disowned, but something about this felt wrong in a *you're about to get blindsided* kind of way. I swear I would not have been surprised if the floor opened up and Satan himself appeared to collect my soul from that Ambien-fueled deal. Not even joking. Standing there in front of my father-in-law, a random briefcase beside him that could have held anything from a still-beating disembodied heart to the cure for cancer, I would absolutely buy if this was the part where the Devil showed up, held out his hand or hoof or whatever, and said, "Soul, bitch."

And—oh shit. I'd been so nervous on the way in here, I hadn't turned on my phone's recorder. There was no way to do it now without tipping off Isaac. Damn it.

Isaac's glass didn't make a sound as he set it down on a leather coaster, but he may as well have slammed it down. I was instantly jumpy. Well, jumpier. And then he looked up at me, and I held my breath.

"I've opened a lot of doors for you, Hayden." He spoke slowly, as if to make sure I hung on every word. "You want to make it in Hollywood, don't you?"

I nodded because I didn't know what to say. It wasn't like I could out and tell him I'd already made peace with losing my shot at acting because I'd married Jesse to screw Isaac over.

"Of course you do," he went on. "But there's a lot about this industry you may not understand yet. I've been around it for decades, so it's safe to say I know my way around, wouldn't you agree?"

I swallowed, and managed to croak, "Uh. Yeah."

"Talent and drive will get you places, but they're nothing without connections. In the circles we run in, Hayden, a man's reputation is as valuable as a woman's pretty face." He paused, and once again there was an exaggeratedly slow gesture of picking up his glass, taking a sip, and setting it back down, as if he wanted to give me time to absorb everything he'd said so far. "Do you understand what I'm telling you?"

"Yes." *But* why *are you telling me? What is the point of all this? Do I smell fire and brimstone?*

"Good." He smiled a smile that made the hair on my neck stand up. "I'm telling you all of this because all those doors I've opened for you? I hope you understand how quickly and easily—and *permanently*—they can be shut again."

Oh, I knew this. Of course I did. But something about the way he said it sent an icy surge of fear through me.

Uh oh. Danger. Danger!

"Right. I know."

Isaac said nothing as he unsnapped the latches on the briefcase, opened the lid, and turned it so I could see it.

Oh God, it was like something out of a movie. No disembodied hearts or vials of chemicals. No, this was an armored case containing stacks of bills, and those were hundreds, which meant that I didn't even need to count this to know it was more money than I'd ever seen in my life.

As I gaped at the cash, Isaac said, "Do you know how much this is, Hayden?"

I shook my head slowly. My phone was vibrating in my pocket, but I ignored it. I was afraid to move.

"This, Hayden, is five million dollars." Isaac patted the open lid of the case. "Cold hard cash."

I couldn't even comprehend that much money. It still blew my mind whenever a fresh hundred grand landed in my account. I still hadn't gotten my head around commas appearing in bank balances, for God's sake.

Five million? Holy crap. That was an obscene amount

of cash. Probably change he'd found in his couch, but for me? Jesus.

I tore my gaze from the money and looked at my father-in-law. "Why are you showing this to me?"

"Showing it to you?" Isaac laughed. "I'm not showing it to you, Hayden. I want to give it to you."

I gulped, my mouth suddenly dry. My phone buzzed again. I ignored it again. "Give… what?"

"It's quite simple." Isaac looked me in the eyes. "If you want all those industry doors to stay open, and you want to take home this money, there's just one thing I need you to do for me."

My spine prickled with more *danger! danger!* but I didn't look away from Isaac. "And that is…?"

He smiled, which made his eyes seem a hundred times colder. "All you have to do is have your marriage to my son annulled, and—" He gestured at the cash. "This is all yours."

"It's…" I blinked. "Annulled? Why? Not even divorced?"

Isaac laughed dryly. "If you want the money, you'll have it annulled. I want this farce of a marriage made null and void."

My tongue stuck to the roof of my mouth. Farce? Did he know? Had he caught on somehow?

And if I admitted it, if I took the cash and ran, then everything Jesse was working for would be gone and nothing would stop Isaac from getting elected as a Democrat. Jesse could take me to court for violating the contract, but the important thing was that Isaac wouldn't lose votes.

"You're asking me to tell the world our marriage isn't

real."

"We both know it isn't." Something in the curl of his lip told me he didn't have to know our scheme to believe our marriage was a sham. We were two men and we were married. That, to Isaac Ambrose, wasn't a real, valid marriage, and legally nullifying it was worth five million dollars.

Holy shit.

Okay, I had signed up to be Jesse's legal-but-fake husband for a year, and he was paying me, and I'd even put the kibosh on us having sex because that made things just a wee bit too complicated… but it wasn't the contract that was making me balk at Isaac's offer. He wanted me to sign on a dotted line and agree the marriage had never existed. That it was invalid.

Why did that feel like a lie?

The marriage *was* a lie, but everything else…

Fuck me, but somewhere along the line, I had fallen so hard for that man that it physically hurt to imagine saying I didn't love him.

And now his dad was offering me five million dollars to tell the world my marriage was as fake as Jesse and I had agreed it was.

Apparently the Devil was coming to collect after all.

So what the fuck was I supposed to do now?

~*~

Jesse

Hand above the office doorknob, I froze.

He didn't… my father did not just…

"Are you serious?" Hayden's voice was muffled by the thick door, but I could still hear him clearly.

"Yes," Dad said. "It's really quite simple. You can continue this ridiculous marriage, or you can tell the world it was a farce, and walk away with the money and with your career prospects intact."

My throat tightened. The money? A farce? Oh God. Did he know? How had he found out?

Hayden hadn't... he hadn't told him, had he?

I fumbled with my phone, scrambling to pull up the voice recorder app with shaking hands when Hayden spoke.

"No." His voice was firm, but shaky. I'd never heard a single syllable filled with so much fear and determination at the same time. "Keep your money."

My hands froze. My head snapped up and I stared at the door.

"Think about this, son," Dad gritted out. "It's not just the money. It's all those opportunities I've created for you in the industry. Are you really going to give all of that up for—"

"Keep your money," Hayden repeated, angry but shaky. "My marriage is not for sale."

My heart dropped into my stomach and my jaw fell open.

"Don't be stupid, Hayden. *Think.* This is five million dollars in cash, and—"

"And you can keep it. I don't need to think about anything. I love Jesse. Obviously more than you do, you pathetic excuse for a sperm donor."

I stared at the door in disbelief. Did he just...

"You're an idiot," Dad snarled.

"And you're an asshole." Hayden's voice was still filled with fury, but it was wavering now, like it was on the verge of cracking. "I don't want your goddamned money. I want your son. You can close all those doors you've opened, and you can shove every single dollar of that money up your ass, because I—" His voice did crack this time, and it shook badly as he added, "I love Jesse, and whether you like it or not, I'm not going anywhere."

My heart felt like it literally broke right then.

And why the hell was I still out here, letting Hayden face off with my son of a bitch father?

Without another thought, I shoved open the door, and they both jumped, facing me. "What the hell is going on?"

"Get out of my office," Dad barked.

"No fucking way. Not until someone tells me why you're trying to pay my husband to pretend our marriage is fake."

Hayden's expression quickly went from startled to horrified, his eyes widening and face paling. "Jesse…"

I gestured past him to the briefcase, which yawned open on the desk and reveal wrapped stacks of cash, and hissed, "Are you seriously trying to pay him off and threaten his career?"

Hayden stiffened a little more. "You heard all that?"

"Yeah, I did." I reached for his hand, but he drew back.

"Oh God." Hayden covered his mouth, almost muffling the croak of, "I need to get out of here." Then he brushed past me and hurried out of the office.

I started after him, but my dad grabbed my arm. "Jesse, you knew what would happen if you married that man, and you went and did it anyway. This—" He pointed a finger at the open briefcase "—could have saved us both a world of humiliation."

"I don't care about the humiliation." I wrenched my arm away from him. "Who the fuck are you to try to interfere with my marriage and—"

He backhanded me hard across the face, his ring cracking against my cheekbone like it hadn't done since I was a teenager.

I nearly staggered back, but caught my balance, and I just stood there, stunned into silence. "What the hell?"

"I've had enough of your bullshit, Jesse." My father got right up in my face. "I have told you for years where I stand on two men getting married, and that I would not accept my son—"

"It's my life, Dad," I threw back, shaking badly. My eyes stung, and it wasn't entirely from him hitting me, but I refused to break this furious staring contest. "It isn't up to you."

"No, but it's up to me if I condone it or if I finance it, and you have been told time and again what would happen if you did this."

There it was. Dad was staying true to his word, just like he'd always said he would. This was what I'd wanted.

So why did I feel like he'd done more than just hit me?

"Dad, I'm your son," I said shakily.

"And your decisions have consequences." He set his jaw and narrowed his eyes. "What did you think would happen if you went through with this nonsense?"

I stared at him, unable to speak.

This was exactly what I'd thought would happen. I'd *banked* on it. I'd invested a million-plus that I couldn't afford just to force his hand and make it happen.

But hearing the words like this—when it was more than just a potentially empty threat over a hypothetical situation—froze me in place.

"You can still undo this, Jesse," Dad said coldly. "Annul this 'marriage' and be done with it.." He shrugged. "Then maybe we can reconsider your standing in this family."

I swallowed. What the hell was I supposed to say to that?

And son of a bitch—the phone was in my hand, but I'd never pressed Record. He'd finally said it, finally said out loud what he was going to do, and I'd been so shocked by Hayden's words and in such a hurry to run interference that *I hadn't fucking pressed Record.*

Dad broke the staring contest. He closed the briefcase, latched it, and tucked it into a safe beneath his desk. Then he paused and put a hand on my shoulder. "Think. And while you do, we have guests to entertain." He shot me a disgusted look. "I'm sure you have some makeup with you to cover that up."

My hand went to the throbbing spot on my cheekbone that would undoubtedly be a bruise. "Yeah," I said numbly. "You gave me plenty of practice covering up shit like this."

"And somehow, you still never learned." Then he brushed past me and left me in the cavernous office where I'd been berated and backhanded more times than I could count in my childhood. My knees weren't quite steady under me, but I couldn't make myself move the three feet to one of the chairs in front of the desk. I was oddly numb aside from the ache in my chest and the throbbing in my cheek.

This was what I wanted. All I had to do was tell him I wasn't backing down—and record it this time—and it would be done.

But it wasn't supposed to hurt like this.

And no one else *was supposed to get hurt.*

The memory of Hayden hurrying from the office jolted me out of my paralysis. I'd deal with my father and all these fucking emotions later.

Right now, I needed to find my husband.

Chapter 28
Hayden

Even with eleventy billion people here for a party, it should not have been this difficult to find a place to be alone. Not on a property this big. I was half-tempted to just take off outside and run until I was somewhere in the middle of the desert, because I sure as hell wasn't going to find any privacy here.

And how in the world was a house this enormous claustrophobic? The ceiling was high enough that the builders probably got nosebleeds installing light fixtures.

Whatever. It was too crowded, the walls were closing in, and I needed to be somewhere I didn't feel like I was going to suffocate. Or where I could throw up and break down—both of which were still distinct possibilities—without anyone watching me.

Outside. Outside was good. Cooler. Less stuffy. Fewer people. More bushes where I could heave my guts out if I needed to.

I found a door, hurried out, and jogged across a patio into the sprawling gardens. I found a fountain with a bench around the base, and somehow my legs stayed under me long enough to reach it. Cursing under my breath, I dropped onto the stone bench and leaned forward, rubbing my temples and willing myself not to heave. I'd been on the verge of puking when I'd left Isaac's office, and though I'd managed to hold it back, I wasn't sure that was going to last forever.

Now that I didn't have the search for a place to sit to hold my attention, all the thoughts I'd been trying to tamp down came crashing in. Had all this really happened? Or had that whole encounter in Isaac's office been some anxiety-induced hallucination?

I wish.

I was fucking sick over everything Isaac had said, but more than that, over everything Jesse had heard. How much *had* he heard? Obviously enough to know his father was trying to bribe me into annulling our marriage, which meant…

"Oh God." I struggled to keep my dinner down. Everything I'd said in that office echoed through my mind, and I was beyond mortified at the realization that Jesse had quite possibly heard all of it. That while I'd been losing my temper and lashing out at his father, I'd gone beyond tipping my hand and straight to flinging all my cards onto the table and telling Jesse I loved him.

Fuck, what had I done?

I didn't regret refusing Isaac's deal, but I kind of hated Jesse for it too. For putting me in a position to murder any shot I had left of an acting career and turn down a life-changing lump of cash. I'd just torpedoed any shot I'd ever had at the acting career I'd thought I was okay with leaving behind, passed up millions of dollars, and spilled my guts to a man who hated people like me, all in the name of refusing to say I didn't love a man who was paying me to *pretend* I loved him. I'd blurted out all my feelings for Jesse without realizing he was there to hear it. If he'd been in the room with Isaac and me, I still would have refused the money, but would I have been quite so honest?

"I don't want your goddamned money. I want your son."

"My marriage is not for sale."

"I love Jesse, and whether you like it or not, I'm not going anywhere."

I sighed into the stillness. "Oh, fuck my life." Yeah, maybe I would have said it all even with Jesse in the room because I needed to convince Isaac our marriage was real. It would have killed me to do it just like it was killing me now, but yes, I probably still would have done it. And that thought made me even sicker.

I would have done it out of obligation because Jesse was paying me. I would have even done it to keep up the charade long enough to keep Isaac out of office. And I would have done it because every goddamned word of it was true, and if someone didn't give me a fucking Oscar for convincing Jesse I was faking all of this, then I—

"Hayden?" Jesse's voice almost canceled out every effort I'd made to keep from getting sick.

I looked up just as he stepped out of the shadows and into the dim, warm light.

He had his hands in his pockets, and his expression was soft. "You all right?"

I stood, hugging myself. "I'm, um… I guess."

Jesse didn't look convinced. And he didn't look so hot

himself.

"What about you?" I asked.

He pressed his lips together and stared at the ground between us. "It's been a hell of a night, let's put it that way."

"Yeah, it has."

Jesse rubbed the back of his neck and tilted his head to one side, then the other, like the muscles were painfully stiff. I wanted to offer to knead the tension away, but I couldn't do that now, could I? God, I'd wrecked everything.

After a moment, Jesse dropped his hand to his side. "I'm sorry for all of this. I should have known he'd try to play you against me, and I…" He blew out a breath, shoulders sagging under his jacket. "I'm so sorry, Hayden."

"It's not your fault."

"Yeah, it is," he whispered. "You wouldn't be in this if it wasn't for me."

"Still doesn't make it your fault that your father is a piece of shit."

He grunted quietly and nodded.

Our eyes met again, and though neither of us spoke, the air seemed filled with millions of questions that I really, really didn't want to answer.

I swallowed. "How much did you hear?"

Jesse moistened his lips. "Pretty much everything after you said no."

My stomach lurched, and I turned away. "Oh fuck."

"Did you mean what you said?"

I folded my arms across my chest to keep my hands still. "I'm not taking his bribe."

"Not that part. The other part."

We locked eyes.

I swallowed again, this time trying to hold back tears. I quickly dropped my gaze and didn't even care that he saw me wiping my eyes. If he didn't know by now that I was an emotional guy, well, that was on him for not paying attention.

He stepped a little closer. "Hayden, it's—"

"Look, I didn't know you were there, or I would have… I don't know what I would have said." I was talking fast because I needed to get all this out before I lost my nerve, not to mention my dinner. "I know what our deal is. What we're supposed to be doing, and why, and maybe I lost sight of it, but I can't help it, okay? Everything is so easy with you, and it's so perfect, and sometimes I forget it's all fake, and so yes, I fell in love with you." Hearing myself say the words out loud was a kick to the balls I did not need tonight, but they were out there. I turned to him again, and yeah, there was no holding back the tears. I was too humiliated because Jesse knew I'd gone and fallen for him when we were just supposed to be *acting* like a married couple. Voice shaking, I said, "I know this wasn't part of the deal and I'm breaking all kinds of rules, but I can't help it. I love you, Jesse. I can't fucking help it, okay? I was stupid, and I was—"

"I love you too."

I froze. "What?"

He stepped closer, holding my gaze. "I love you, Hayden. I'd been afraid to tell you because of how weird things got on the cruise. I didn't want you to feel obligated or trapped, you know? But I mean it. I didn't go into this looking for love, but… damn. Here you are."

I stared at him, barely comprehending the words. "Really?"

"Yeah." He came closer, close enough one of us could have touched the other. "The truth is, most of the time when I'm with you, I forget all about our deal because it really does feel like a real relationship. Like…" He swallowed hard. "Like the closest thing I've ever known to a real, loving, healthy relationship. And it's been killing me that the best thing I've ever had with someone wasn't real." He touched my face. "Except maybe it was."

I pressed against his hand, struggling to keep my emotions in check. I had no idea what to say, but finally managed to whisper, "Yeah. It was. It still is."

He looked in my eyes, and the whole world came to a halt. The fountain trickling and splashing behind me drowned out the sounds of the party we'd abandoned, and for all I knew or cared, we were standing in the middle of the wilderness, completely alone except for each other.

"For what it's worth," he said, tracing his thumb along my jaw, "I was trying to find a way to tell you. If there was a way to say it without making things weird, I mean. This, um… tonight wasn't how I…"

I smiled and wrapped my arms around his neck. "We haven't done anything else the normal way. Why start now?"

Jesse laughed, and then he drew me in, and his tender kiss sent shockwaves through my whole body, from my spinning head all the way down to my curling toes. It wasn't our first kiss, but it was the first time we'd kissed with all the cards out on the table. No more act. No more pretending this was all for the purpose of keeping Isaac Ambrose out of power. I loved Jesse, and I didn't have to hide it anymore, and somehow the planets had aligned and *he loved me too.*

I touched my forehead to his. "I'm not hallucinating, am I? This is real?"

"It's real." He stroked my hair and smiled against my lips. "Unless I'm hallucinating too."

I cupped his face, ready to make a witty remark, but he flinched away from my touch. Jerking my hand away, I drew back. "What? What's wrong?" Then I saw the mark. I hadn't noticed it under the heavy shadows, but now that I looked closer, there was a thick red bar on his cheekbone. "What the hell?"

Jesse turned his head, the rest of his face coloring as he avoided my eyes and tried to keep the bruise out of my sight.

"Jesse," I whispered. "What happened?"

He licked his lips, refusing to look at me. "Let's just say my father's never been an easy man to stand up to."

My stomach lurched again. "Did he fucking hit you?"

Jesse winced, but still wouldn't look at me.

"Holy shit."

"He hasn't done it since I was a kid, but—"

"He shouldn't have done it then, either," I growled. "Fucking Christ." I glared up at the house, then met his gaze again. "He's going down."

Jesse nodded. "The sooner the better."

"Got any ideas?"

He stared at the house for a moment, jaw tight and eyes intently focused, before he said, "Yeah. I have an idea."

L.A. WITT

Chapter 29
Jesse

My father had returned to the party and was mingling as usual, making the rounds to his adoring public. He smiled and laughed, clapping shoulders and kissing women on the cheek as if everything in his world was as it should be. The back of his hand probably still stung from hitting me, but no one who could see him now would ever have a clue what he'd been doing less than an hour ago.

I couldn't lie—the man was good. He hadn't acted in front of a camera in years, but he'd had decades of practice acting in front of real people, and I doubted anyone thought there was a single thing fake about his smile or his laughter. When people talked, he acted like they were the only person on the planet, and he was hanging on their every word. I wondered how many of them knew he'd later be rolling his eyes and telling my mother about how insufferable all these idiots were with their ridiculous ideas and boring anecdotes.

Heart thumping, I approached a small group that Dad was currently regaling with a story about some charity gala he'd hosted recently. The story itself wasn't all that interesting, but I knew him—the point was to make sure everyone knew he'd been there, that he'd hosted the gala, and that he'd donated however many thousands of dollars to the charity.

He glanced at me, and he stiffened briefly, but then he smiled and put his arm around my shoulders. "You remember that party, don't you?" he asked with thickly applied fake cheer. "That was a hell of an auction, wasn't it?"

"Yeah." I forced a smile. "Hell of an auction." Then, keeping my tone as neutral as possible, I said, "Listen, um, can I borrow you for a minute?"

A scowl flickered across his face, fast enough I doubt anyone noticed but me. He looked around quickly. "Where's your husband?"

"He's gone. I just… I need a minute to talk to you about something." I flashed a well-practiced *everything's okay* smile at the people he'd been chatting with.

Dad's smile was just as practiced and just as fake. "Would you folks excuse me? We'll just be a minute."

"Of course!" the tall blond man in the group said. "Take your time."

Ugh, they sounded as fake as we did.

As soon as we'd broken away, Dad lowered his voice. "Is this really necessary right now?"

"Yes, it is," I replied just as quietly.

"Fine. Let's go up to my office and—"

"I'd rather do this outside. I need some air." I kept walking and didn't wait for him to respond.

Dad huffed at my back, but he followed me down the hall and out onto a deserted patio. As soon as we were alone, he held out his hand. "Give me your phone."

"What? Why?"

"Because I don't trust you not to record our conversation."

I scowled, took out my phone, and showed him the voice recorder app, which was not active. Then I set the phone on a wrought iron table and raised my hands in surrender. "There. Happy?"

He glared at me. Then at our surroundings. Then at me again. Evidently satisfied that we were unmonitored, he said, "All right. What's this about?"

"I just need to know." I sighed, shoulders sinking with resignation. "Did you really try to bribe my husband into getting our marriage annulled?"

Dad sniffed. "I tried to give him an incentive to spare himself and our family further humiliation."

"So you told him all his career prospects would dry up if he didn't annul our damned *marriage*?"

"I told you—incentive."

"That's cold, Dad." I laughed bitterly. "I kind of feel like I should be flattered that defending my honor is worth five million."

"Your honor?" Dad gave a similarly sarcastic laugh. "I'm defending my family's good name."

"By bribing your son-in-law to—"

"That man is *not* my son-in-law," Dad growled. "The government might recognize this farce of a marriage, but I most certainly do *not*. I won't have it. And if you value your place in the Ambrose family, not to mention your access to the family's money, I would suggest you rethink a few things."

I swallowed. He'd made this threat so many times when I was younger that it wasn't a surprise, but still, every damn time I realized he was following through, it was a fresh punch to the chest. Now that the rubber had met the road, now that there really was a husband and a marriage and the prospect of making good on that promise, the words hurt more than I'd ever imagined they would. I didn't need theatre training or eyedrops for the tears to make it into my eyes and voice.

"So you weren't bluffing." I folded my arms and forced myself to hold his gaze. "All those years you told me you would disown me if I married a man—you're really going to do it?"

Dad laughed. "Bluffing? Not a chance. Monday morning, my attorneys will draw up all the necessary paperwork. Might I suggest you start making arrangements to get the hell out of that condo by the end of the week?"

I winced. Again, not surprised, but absolutely hurt. Fucking devastated. "So that's it?" I cleared my throat, or at least tried to. "You're actually going to—"

"What is wrong with you, Jesse?" Dad threw up his hands. "This… this thing you're doing? Men don't marry men." He stabbed a finger at me. "I have let you know where I stand on this for years, so don't act surprised when there are consequences for your actions." He nearly hit my chest this time. "No son of mine would behave this way and disrespect his family's name like that, and no man who behaves this way is any son of mine."

I had to admit, no matter how much I'd expected it, hearing him say the words out loud cut me right to the bone. I was almost breathless as I said, "I'm not your son anymore. Just because I married a man."

Dad laughed humorlessly. "Did you ever think for even a moment that wouldn't be the case?"

I held his gaze with all the defiance I could muster even as a tear slipped free. "No. I didn't. Not once." Then I looked above us at the balcony over our heads. "You get all that?"

Leaning over the railing, Hayden gave me a thumbs up. In his other hand was his phone.

"What the hell?" Dad shouted. "Turn that thing off, you goddamned queer! Or I will have security confiscate that damned phone and delete—"

"Mmm, deleting it won't do you much good, Mr. Ambrose." Hayden kept right on filming. "It's live on Facebook as we speak." He gave a cheeky little wave. "Say hi to your supporters, honey!"

"What?" Dad roared. "What the hell are you two doing?"

"Just showing the world and the voting public who you really are," I said coolly as I wiped my eyes. Then I looked up at Hayden and gestured at my face. "And in case disownment wasn't enough, this is what happens to an ex-son who catches Isaac Ambrose trying to bribe his husband into claiming—"

"That little shit," Dad snarled, and stormed back inside, probably to sic security on Hayden.

I grabbed my phone off the table and hurried after him.

Dad was already barking orders at security, who started for the stairs. As soon as Dad stormed into the ballroom, though, he halted so fast I almost crashed into him. The whole place went silent. Dozens of people were staring at their phones, and I could hear the tinny sound of Dad's voice playing from every corner of the room as people watched the video. One by one, people turned their looks of disgust on my father, and the temperature in the room plummeted.

While Dad stared in shock as a chorus of his own voice repeated that he was disowning me, Hayden slipped into the ballroom and jogged to my side. Security trailed after him, but slowed when I shot them a glare.

"Isaac, what is going on?" My mother emerged from the crowd, red-faced and furious, and held up her phone. "What were you thinking? Saying all those things where someone could—" She looked at me and did a double take. Then she strode up to me, gripped my jaw and roughly turned my head to the side, no doubt so she could see the mark on my face more clearly. She inspected it, let me go, and whirled on my father. "I told you never to lay a hand on one of my children again, Isaac. I *told* you. How dare you hit my son?"

Instantly, they were shouting at each other. Over each other. I couldn't understand a word they were saying, but that may have been because everything was crashing down. The reality of what had happened. The relief that I had done what I'd set out to do, showing the world who my father really was, and the crushing hurt of realizing I'd been right all along. No amount of victory could take away from the sheer heartbreak that came from my father looking me in the eye and telling me I was no longer his son.

Hayden slipped his hand into mine. "Do you want to stay for this? Or do you want to get out of here?"

Suddenly, I couldn't leave this place fast enough.

Chapter 30
Hayden

Thanks to the Ambrose estate being the size of a small country, it took a while for the valets to retrieve Jesse's car. We waited outside, away from all the people and chaos, and neither of us spoke except to talk to the valet and to have a member of the house staff collect our things from our guest room. I felt weird, asking someone else to go get my things—I didn't even do shit like that in hotels—but I needed to stay close to Jesse, and Jesse needed to stay out here where he wouldn't risk crossing paths with his father.

When the valet brought the Porsche around to where we waited at the bottom of the stairs, I slipped him a twenty and got into the driver's seat without waiting for Jesse to say anything. Jesse didn't object. He just got into the passenger seat, and he stared out the window as the valet loaded our overnight bags into the trunk and I moved my seat forward a couple inches. Once the trunk lid was closed, I put the car in gear and followed the driveway back to the main road.

Fortunately, I knew my way back to the town of Joshua Tree, at least, and I was pretty sure the signs would take me from there to Palm Springs. So at the end of the long driveway, as the gate slowly closed behind me, I turned left.

It wasn't lost on me that I wasn't even a little excited to be driving a car this awesome. I'd admired it since the first time I'd seen it, and always thought I'd get a thrill out of driving such a fancy, expensive sports car.

It hadn't occurred to me that the first and possibly only time I'd drive it would be after a night like this. I was distantly aware of some of the car's bells and whistles and of how comfortable the seat was, but otherwise my focus was divided between the road and my silent passenger.

Jesse had won. The extent of his father's homophobia was out there for the world to see, and there was no coming back from something like that. Not for a liberal politician in California, especially one the conservatives already hated. It was up to the voters now, but I was pretty confident that with this damning video, Isaac's California political ambitions were as good as dead.

But at what cost?

I didn't regret what we'd done, but the aftermath was more than I'd bargained for, and judging by the still silence coming from the passenger seat, Jesse hadn't seen things playing out this way either. Or maybe he had. You can only prepare yourself so much for some things, and even when you know they're coming, they're hell when they actually happen.

Then again, could he really have seen how tonight would go? His dad bribing me to annul our marriage? The son of a bitch hitting him hard enough to leave that angry mark on his cheek? I had a feeling those hadn't been on Jesse's schedule.

Jesus. What the fuck was wrong with this family? I mean, when we'd left the estate the first time, I'd wondered why in the world the doors on the place were so big, and I'd laughed my head off when I'd found out it was part of an almost literal dick-measuring contest, but none of it was funny anymore. Not even the doors. Everything Isaac did was calculated to make sure his admirers kept worshipping the ground he walked on and his family—his own fucking *family*—toed impossible lines to keep from tarnishing the Ambrose name.

Right now, I would have bet every penny I'd ever had that Isaac wasn't even thinking about how his son felt right now, or how much he'd failed as a father. No, he was doing damage control. Downplaying everything he'd said on that video. Conjuring up a way to divert everyone's attention and make sure they forgot about it. Sweating bullets about his political ambitions. I didn't believe for a second that the man would spare a single thought to what this had done to his son.

If I'd ever felt the least bit guilty about joining Jesse on this plan, I didn't anymore. Fuck Isaac. Fuck his career. Fuck his reputation. I wasn't going to feel bad for taking or posting that video. You don't want the world to know what a terrible failure of a father you are? Don't disown your son for marrying a dude. Simple as that, asswipe.

At the edge of the town of Joshua Tree, I slowed to a stop at a red light. An eighteen wheeler lumbered across, and a moment later, the light changed, but... I didn't move. There was no one behind me. No one waiting to turn. The street was pretty much deserted.

Jesse didn't seem to notice that we were sitting at a green light.

I touched his knee, and he jumped, dropping his gaze to my hand before looking across the console at me. The mark on his left cheek was almost hidden by shadows, but it was there, and it would probably be a hell of a bruise tomorrow. Just what he needed—a reminder of tonight every time he looked in the mirror for the next week or so. Though even if he covered it up with some of his magician-like makeup skills, he'd know it was there. Mark or no mark, I didn't expect tonight to be far from his mind any time soon. And it was hard to tell in the dim light, but I swore he had tears in his eyes. He'd been so strong through all of this, and now that it was over, I could almost feel him cracking.

I had no idea what to say. All I could think was that I should follow his lead tonight. If he wanted conversation, he'd say something. If we rode in silence all the way back to the condo we'd be getting kicked out of soon, fine.

Whatever you need, baby. Just say the word.

The light was still green, so I started to shift gears, but then Jesse broke the silence.

"Hayden." His voice was soft, the single word sounding like it took every bit of energy he had.

Engine still idling, I turned to him. "Yeah?"

"I don't want to go back to LA tonight."

"Oh." I glanced out the windshield and in the rearview to make sure we were still alone. "Where do you want to go?"

He swept his tongue across his lips and looked in my eyes. "I just want go somewhere with you."

"Somewhere, like…?"

"I don't know. I don't care. Just… somewhere we can get out of these goddamned penguin suits"—he tugged his bowtie loose—"and not think about anything for a while."

I swallowed. "When you say get out of these penguin suits…"

Our eyes met in the darkness over the console.

"On the cruise, we agreed not to…" He dropped his gaze, staring down at his hands in his lap. "I know we said we wouldn't…"

"Things are different now." I reached over and found his hand. "I'm no man's whore, but if there's something you want from me tonight…"

Jesse swallowed hard. Then he turned to me, and even in the dim light, I could see the tears in his eyes. "I have never needed or wanted anyone like I want you right now."

My heart started pounding, and I squeezed his hand. I wondered if even he knew what he needed from me—an intense fuck to distract him for a while, or a shoulder to break down on. It didn't matter. I was ready and willing to give him either or both.

I reached for his face and leaned across the console. "I'm here."

He cupped my cheek and kissed me softly. "You're amazing. I just… I want to be somewhere with you, and not think about anyone or anything *but* you." His fingers were soft and unsteady against my face. "I swear you're the only thing right in my world."

My heart seemed to simultaneously sink and flutter and snap in two. It was every romantic fantasy come to life, knowing he felt this way about me, and at the same time, heartbreaking to realize how much was wrong in his world.

You're such an amazing man, I couldn't figure out how to say. *Why would anyone be this cruel to you?*

"It's not far from here to Palm Springs," he murmured against my lips. "Let's find a place there and stop for the night."

"Yeah?"

He ran his fingers through my hair. "Yeah."

"Okay. Then let's go find a place to—"

A car horn startled us apart.

I dropped back into the driver's seat, forgot for a second that the Porsche was a manual transmission, and promptly stalled the engine. "Son of a bitch…"

The other car screeched around us and took off, waving a middle finger out the window as they went by. I rolled my eyes, started the car again, and continued down the highway.

"Sorry about that," Jesse said with a soft laugh.

"It's okay. I'm the one who stopped in the middle of an intersection."

He chuckled again. "Oh hey, there's a motel right up there."

I craned my neck, and sure enough, there was a dumpy little two-story no-name motel with a half-burnt out sign and a greasy diner next door. "*That* place?"

"Why not? Doesn't need to be anything fancy."

It definitely wasn't fancy. In fact, the motel ironically reminded me of the apartment I'd moved out of when things had started with Jesse. It was rundown and ugly, but at least it was a roof, four walls, and running water.

And most importantly… a bed.

We dropped our bags by the door, and we littered the

ugly carpet with our tuxedos, leaving a trail of dress shoes and jackets and underwear from the door to the double bed. When I sank onto my back in the middle of the mattress, Jesse came down with me—no more penguin suits between us—and we gently collapsed together, tangled up and kissing.

Ever since the cruise, I'd fantasized nightly about the sex we'd had, and I swore none of those memories could compete with the reality of right now. The heat of his body, his weight over the top of me, the way he kissed me and touched me and how his hips fit so perfectly between my thighs—we'd stopped doing this, why?

Oh. Right. Because of the money. Because I didn't like how blurry the lines had become between who I wanted to be and who I was paid to be.

There were no blurry lines tonight. The money, the marriage, the shit no doubt hitting the fan back at chez Ambrose—it all still existed, but here in this room, we were just two men who needed each other too much for words.

Jesse lifted himself up and met my eyes. God, his face. The bruise on his cheekbone was a deepening, angry red, and his eyes were full of so many contradictory emotions—like he was hurting worse than he ever had, but at the same time, was so ridiculously in love, and he wanted to have wild, relentless sex, but he also wanted to fall apart and cry on my shoulder.

Do it all, baby. I stroked his face, carefully avoiding the side with the deepening bruise. *You can cry, you can fuck, you can cry while you fuck—I'm here for anything you need.*

"I don't want to think about anything but you tonight," he whispered between kisses. "Hayden, I—"

I cut him off with a deep kiss, gripping his hair so tight it probably hurt, and he whimpered and shivered as I forced my tongue into his mouth. Oh, I could definitely make sure he didn't think about anything else tonight. He might not be able to move tomorrow, and he might come so hard he cried, but he would absolutely think of me and only me until the sun came up, because God knew I wouldn't be thinking of anything but him.

After a moment, he broke the kiss and spoke again. "For the record…" He ran a shaky hand through my hair. "I never thought of you as a whore. On the cruise… it wasn't about the money or…" He swallowed. "I just wanted you."

I brushed my lips across his. "Me too." I kissed him again, then touched my forehead to his and panted against his lips. "Tell me what you want."

"Just you."

Grinning, I kissed the tip of his nose. "Okay, but let's be practical here. What do you want me to *do*, sweetheart?"

That got a laugh out of him, which made me even dizzier with need for him. "Fine." He smoothed my hair. "You still have that well-stocked toiletry kit?"

I winked. "You kidding? I never leave home without it."

"Hmm, maybe you should get it."

"Be right back." I kissed him lightly. "Don't go anywhere."

In under a minute, I was back in bed with the condoms and lube. Jesse opened the bottle while I put on the condom, and then he stroked on the lube, and kept stroking, and damn even with the condom he was going to make me come if he kept that up.

I grabbed his wrist. "Turn around."

He shivered hard, and a grin came to life. Oh hell, there was nothing I wouldn't do for this man if he kept looking at me like that. He'd had a terrible evening, but now he gazed at me like nothing existed in his world except sex with me.

We shared one more kiss, and then he turned onto his hands and knees. I knelt behind him and put some lube on my fingers.

And as I teased him with my fingertips, reality elbowed its way into the picture. I could distract Jesse from all the chaos outside this room, but I couldn't make it go away completely. Even if his conscious mind had shut it out, it still existed, and his body remembered. The tension was visible in his shoulders and his back, and even if I'd missed that, I couldn't miss how tight his ass was. Not *oh my God this is going to feel amazing* tight. More like the kind of tight that could put him off bottoming forever if I tried to push through.

I ran my other hand up his back, the cable-tight muscles quivering under my touch. "You sure you want me on top tonight?"

"Yes." He arched under my hand and murmured over his shoulder, "God, I want you, Hayden."

I shivered from the raw desire in his unsteady voice, and somehow managed to keep my own voice even. "I know you do. But I don't want to hurt you."

"You won't. Just… just go slow."

"You know I will." I silently debated calling this off, but he wanted it. Really wanted it. And, I mean, I'd topped a few guys who'd never bottomed before, and nothing made a man clench up tighter than nerves. With a few gallons of lube and some serious patience, they could usually relax enough to take me.

So I cautiously pressed on. I eased a fingertip into him, and his moan definitely wasn't one of protest or pain. In fact he leaned back, searching for more, and I let him impale himself on my finger. After a while, I carefully added a second finger. Then some more lube.

"Like that?" I asked.

He nodded soundlessly. He kept rocking back and forth, setting a slow, fluid rhythm. A shiver ran up his spine, and he murmured, "I want more."

I chewed my lip. Yeah, he probably wanted more. Question was, could he *take* more? As it was, he was so tight it was almost painful for me, and while I'm not exactly hung like a porn star, my dick *is* longer and thicker than two fingers. If he was this tight around my fingers—okay, he might be able to take me, but I didn't see how he'd enjoy it. Even if he could relax enough for me to get into him, it wouldn't be comfortable, and while I was absolutely ready and willing to do anything he needed for him, there were lines I wouldn't cross.

So I slid my fingers free.

"Jesse." I shook my head. "This isn't working. If I try to top you, I'm just going to hurt you."

"It's fine," he insisted over his shoulder. "Just go slow."

"No. You're too tense." I realized a second too late that in his raw, battered mental state, that probably sounded like *we can't do this and it's your fault.* "Turn around." When he did, I touched his chin and lifted it so he was looking in my eyes. "You've had a hell of a night, and anyone would be wound up after that. I just don't want to hurt you."

He pursed his lips, disappointment and shame radiating off him. "I want you tonight."

"And you've got me." I ran the pad of my thumb over his unbruised cheekbone. "I don't care if we can't fuck. We'll get there again. I'm not here for your ass, Jesse—I'm here for you. I'm not going anywhere."

That seemed to shake some tension out of his face and his shoulders. He slid his hand around the back of my neck, pulled me in close, and kissed me again, and yes, I could feel him relaxing all over. Not enough that I could safely top him, but enough that I could be sure he was taking me at my word. No, I wouldn't fuck him tonight, but I also wasn't going anywhere, and I was pretty sure that was what he needed more than anything.

"Lie on your side," I said between kisses.

He did, and after I'd taken off the condom, I faced him on my side. We came together in a kiss that started out tentative—as if he was on-edge after we'd had to give up on anal—but slowly turned into something needy and hungry. There was plenty we could do without penetration, and as far as I was concerned, as long as Jesse felt good, nothing else mattered. If he wanted to lazily sixty-nine until the sun came up, fine. If he wanted to jerk off together while we watched a porno, cool. We were in bed together. That was more than enough for me.

"God, I love you," he purred against my lips.

"I love you too." I ran an unsteady hand through his hair, and I was about to add something, but he rocked his hips just right to rub our cocks together, and my mind went blank. "Fuck…"

"Like that?"

"What do you think?"

He laughed softly. Then, arms wrapped around me, he rolled onto his back, and we both moaned as my hips settled between his thighs. Oh yeah, this was heaven. Jesse's hands roaming my naked skin. Our bodies pressed together. His thick erection right up against mine.

"Get the lube," he whispered.

Didn't have to tell me twice. I handed him the bottle, and he poured a generous amount in his hand. He wrapped his slick fingers around both our cocks, encircling them as much as he could, and I groaned as he started stroking us. Without even thinking, I started moving, rocking against him, fucking against him. We fell into a rhythm—his hand, my hips, our breathing—and the aging springs of the motel bed kept time with every emphatic thrust. Every time I moved, my cock slid against his and through his tight grip, and it was mind-blowing, and we both moaned and swore in between ragged huffs of breath.

He slung his other arm around me. We tried to kiss, but there wasn't much point when I was so caught up in how good my cock felt. How good my whole *body* felt. After the night we'd had and after we hadn't touched since the cruise, I needed him and my rapidly building orgasm and *this*.

"More," he begged. "God, Hayden... *more*."

Gritting my teeth, I dug my toes into the mattress and thrust as hard as I could, trying to drive more of those helpless moans out of him as he fell apart beneath me. When he came, he didn't make a sound, but I felt his release as if it were my own—the way he bucked beneath me and then gasped and jerked—and it was only a few more strokes before a strangled cry escaped my lips and my cum joined his between our hot, trembling bodies.

For a second, we were still, and then we sighed and melted against each other. I let my head fall beside his, and as the last shudder ran through me, I whispered, "Oh my God. I so missed this."

"Me… me too."

I kissed the side of his neck. He sniffed sharply, and I thought he might have wiped his eyes with his other hand. I didn't ask if he'd teared up, and I didn't admit that I had too. After the night we'd both had and the ground-shaking release, tears seemed kind of inevitable.

We'd shower… in a minute. We'd dry our eyes if we needed to… in a minute.

Right now, I had a feeling he needed this as much as I did, so I just held him close, and we let the moment be.

Chapter 31
Jesse

I lay on my back and Hayden fitted himself against my side, our fingers clasped together on my chest and his foot absently running up and down my shin. His hair was damp against my skin after our shower, his skin warm. Neither of us spoke for a long time.

I had never been this wrung out and exhausted after sex. I was utterly drained and raw, like I would have broken down sobbing if I'd had anything left.

It wasn't the sex that had worn me out. If anything, it had brought me back to life and left me feeling like maybe I could get through everything that was crashing down on me emotionally. If not for the bone-deep exhaustion and the steady throbbing of my bruised cheekbone, I could *almost* pretend the party at my parents' house had been a nightmare. If I squinted hard enough, I could tell myself the whole night had been spent here in a no-name Joshua Tree motel with Hayden.

But the night had been real. Come Monday, Dad would have everything written up to remove me from his will and cut me off from his finances. The car would be gone. The condo would be gone. My family…

I closed my eyes and pushed out a breath. Aside from Alex and maybe Reanna, I doubted my siblings would ever speak to me again. Mom had stood up for me tonight, but I had no faith left in her. At the end of the day, marriage and family were for security, not sentiment, and while she'd call my father out on his bullshit, she wouldn't jeopardize her own place. She had money of her own as a Sherer, but the prestige that came from being an Ambrose couldn't be replaced, and that was the life she'd known for forty years.

I'd made my choice, my parents had made theirs, and the only family I had ever known—toxic or not—was gone.

My father doesn't love me enough to accept who I am and who I love.

My father doesn't love me enough.

My father doesn't love me.

I swallowed past the lump in my throat. No matter how much time I'd spent preparing for this, no matter how much the end justified the means, the truth was I *wasn't* prepared for it.

Absently running my fingers through Hayden's wet, disheveled hair, I blinked away tears. I wanted this night to be a dream because then my dad wouldn't have disowned me or hit me. Then all this pain wouldn't exist, and I could be like I was a few hours ago—sure that he would disown me, but with the faintest glimmer of hope that maybe he loved me. Some truths are like a punch to the face—even when you know it's coming, it still hurts.

So yeah, I wanted this night to be a dream, but at the same time, I prayed like hell it had been real. Hayden had told my father he loved me before he'd told me. I hated why he'd said it. I hated that my father had put him in that position—I would forgive my father for what he'd done to me long before I forgave him for that. But the words had come out, and now we were here, holding each other in a rumpled bed. The tornado had ripped through everything I'd ever known, and in the end, I still had Hayden.

I didn't think I'd ever been more grateful for anyone or anything in my life.

I pulled him closer and kissed his forehead. "I'm sorry I dragged you through all of this. I'm glad I met you, but I am so sorry for all the bullshit you've had to go through."

He lifted his chin and pressed a kiss beneath my jaw. "I don't know. I think everything shook out pretty well in my favor in the end."

I laughed, but it took some work. "Maybe, but I hope you know I never meant for you to get hurt."

"I know." His thumb ran along the back of mine. "None of it's your fault, though. It's those asshats who raised you, if one could call it that." He looked up at me, a cautious but playful grin on his lips. "And if it weren't for them, we never would have met."

The laugh came a little easier this time. "Yeah, I guess that's true." I kissed the top of his head. "That's a hell of a silver lining."

"No pressure, right?"

"No pressure."

We lay in silence a bit longer. I tried to concentrate on us and not everything that had gone down tonight, but it was hard. Thank God I'd fallen for the man I'd married; I had no idea how I'd get through this without Hayden.

"Tonight reminds me of the wedding," I said after a while. "When I was hoping Dad would come around and change his mind. Even though I knew there was no way in hell it would happen, there was that little glimmer of hope." I swallowed past the ache in my throat. "I guess some part of me still thought he'd love me anyway, and I even held out hope that he still might change his mind after the wedding." I sniffed. "After tonight…"

Hayden held me tighter and squeezed my hand.

I sighed, staring up at the ceiling. "God, I'm such an idiot."

"No, you're not. You're a son who wants his father's love."

"You'd think after all this time, I'd have learned to stop beating my head against that particular wall."

Hayden pushed himself up and kissed me softly. Caressing my unbruised cheek, he looked in my eyes. "You wanted your dad to love you. That's not something that's going to go away overnight."

"No, I guess it isn't. But the sooner I make peace with it…"

"Give yourself time."

I nodded. God knew how much time this would take, though.

The silence stretched on for a minute or so before Hayden quietly asked, "So what happens now?"

"I don't know." I touched his cheek. "You're the only thing I'm sure of anymore."

He smiled, closing his hand over the top of mine on his face. "I'm not going anywhere unless you want me to."

After everything that had gone down tonight, I believed him. The conversation he'd had in my father's office had driven that home, and I was still stunned. In a million years, I would never have dreamed of asking someone to choose between me and a career or a huge windfall, never mind both, but someone else had told him to choose, and he'd chosen me. Without knowing I had the same feelings for him, without realizing that I was listening, Hayden had stood up to my father, and he'd said no. For all he'd known, he'd had a lot to lose and nothing to gain by turning down my father's bribe, and he'd done it anyway.

I swallowed hard, stroking Hayden's hair. I could barely comprehend that he had feelings for me at all, but the idea of someone giving up so much... for *me?* That blew my mind.

"Those threats my dad made about doors slamming shut..." I closed my eyes. "I'd love to tell you those are empty threats, but in this business..."

"I know." He brought my hand to his lips and kissed my knuckles. "I never had any illusions that I could still have a career in Hollywood after this. Or, well, not many illusions. I knew that when I told him I wouldn't take his bribe."

"But you did it anyway?"

"Of course I did. I'm not taking his dirty, homophobic money, and I'm sure as shit not if it means..." He broke eye contact, biting his lip.

"What?"

Hayden rolled onto his back and sighed. Apparently it was his turn to stare at the ceiling now, and he was quiet for an uncomfortably long moment. "I guess it was one thing to lie to the world and say I loved you." He finally turned his head toward me. "But I couldn't stomach saying I didn't."

"Not even when you still thought it was fake for me too?"

Hayden smiled sweetly and caressed my arm. "Didn't matter. I had no idea how you felt, but I knew how I did. And I just… I couldn't."

I stared at him, then shook my head. "My own father is willing to disown me for sullying his name, but you? Jesus. You're willing to pass up a suitcase full of cash rather than saying you don't really love me." I kissed the back of his hand. "Even when you didn't know how I felt. That's… that's kind of amazing. You know that, right?"

Hayden smiled again, combing his fingers through my hair. "Yeah, well, if anyone had told me a few months ago that a guy would ever come along who was worth passing up five million bucks, I would have said they were insane." The pad of his thumb brushed over my uninjured cheekbone. "But here you are."

"Yeah." I kissed his palm and grinned. "You're stuck with me now."

He laughed, making my pulse do crazy things. "Oh no. Stuck with you." He put the back of his hand to his forehead and sighed dramatically. "How *ever* will I manage?"

"I'm sure you'll find a way." I winked. "If nothing else, I'll put out enough to make it worth your while."

"Oh well when you put it like that…" He grinned.

"Uh-huh. Figured you'd be on board."

"Of course. And what *do* we do now, anyway?" Hayden held up his hand and tapped his ring with this thumb. "I mean, we're still technically married."

I played with my own ring. "I don't know. What do you think?"

"No idea."

I thought for a moment, then shrugged. "I mean, I guess if we're going to do this, we could just leave the paperwork the way it is. Then if we decide we're in it for the long haul, we can stay married."

"Yeah, but what if we *do* decide we're in this for the long haul? We've already had the wedding."

I considered that too. "I guess we could renew our vows. Just have a ceremony with people we actually like and—"

Hayden snorted. "I like that last part, definitely." Sobering a bit, he added, "But you're serious? You want to just leave things as they are, and we'll renew our vows later if we want to keep going?"

"Yeah, I'm serious. You in?"

He smiled. "Hell yeah, I'm in."

I smiled too, but it faltered. "You know it's not going to be quite the high life anymore."

Hayden patted my hand. "We're not going to be living in a shoebox and tearing our hair out over putting gas into cars that barely run. I think we'll be all right." He ran his fingers up the middle of my chest. "I'm more worried about you than the money. Tonight was hell, and it's probably going to take you some time to deal with it."

Sighing, I rubbed my eyes. "Yeah. But I'll take that as it comes. Right now, I'm just glad people know who my father is, and by some insane miracle, I still have you."

He laughed. "You won't be saying it's an insane miracle after you've lived with me long enough to get annoyed by my bad habits."

"To be fair, I've been living with you for a while."

"Okay, true. But give it time."

"Eh, by that point I'll be annoying you too, so we'll just be an old married couple like everyone else."

"Hmm, I kind of like the sound of that." He kissed me softly, then propped himself up on his elbow and met my gaze. "So, you want to stay here the whole night? Or check out and head home?"

"That depends." I trailed a fingertip down the middle of his chest. "How many more condoms do you have in that pack?"

He twisted around to check, and as he faced me again, he said, "Enough to make sure we don't get bored tonight."

I laughed, gathering him in my arms, and God, it felt as good to laugh as it did to hold him. And now that I thought about it, I should have known Hayden was a godsend on the way home from my parent's house the very first time. He could make me laugh—really laugh and feel it—after being in the company of my family. That definitely should have told me something.

Maybe I hadn't figured it out back then, but here in this tiny motel room, as laughter turned to kisses, and we tangled up under the sheets again, I definitely knew it now. Hayden was everything I'd never known I wanted in a man.

The night had been a rough one, but I couldn't ask for anything more than landing in bed beside the man I loved. The future... we'd figure it out. It would take a while to deal with the fallout. I could live with the financial fallout, but the emotional shit was going to be rough. The throbbing bruise on my face would heal long before I did.

But I'd get there. Eventually, I'd be okay.

And I'd have Hayden. If there was anything in the world that could cut through the dark cloud hanging over me and make me believe things would be all right, it was the man I'd be holding in this hard hotel bed until the sun came up. He'd come into my life as exactly what I'd needed to keep my father from taking power, and he'd turned out to be all I could ever want in a man.

So I vowed right then and there that I would spend the rest of my life doing everything I could to make Hayden as happy as he made me.

L.A. WITT

Epilogue
Hayden

Almost a Year Later

I'd worn this tux enough times, it should have felt like a second skin. It kind of did, but there was still a part of me that couldn't get over the fact that I owned a top of the line designer tux in the first place.

One that probably needed a teeny bit of tailoring when we got back to Los Angeles since a year of having access to food on a regular basis had added a few pounds. I still ate well and I had a gym membership that I used religiously, but there was no way I wasn't going to see some physical changes now that I could actually, like, *eat*. No complaints here aside from the occasional tailoring bill.

I tugged at the sleeve and looked myself up and down in my parents' guest room mirror. I took and released a deep breath, but that didn't help my nerves much. And why the hell was I this nervous? Jesse and I were already married. We were just renewing our vows. We'd done this, and we'd done it in front of a hell of a lot more people and under a hell of a lot more pressure.

Just breathe. No reason to freak out.

Aside from the part where I was finally making a real commitment to the man I loved, anyway.

In an odd way, our arrangement made our relationship a breeze. We hadn't really bothered being on our best behavior right from the start because it had been a business arrangement, not a romantic relationship. By the time we gave dating a try, we'd already lived together and traveled together. We'd been completely domesticated, and none of that had changed. We still grocery shopped together once a week. Household chores were still unofficially but evenly divided. We still spent plenty of evenings kicked back in front of the TV with takeout kebab while he iced his wrists after a long day on-set. It was perfectly boring, and I loved it.

It probably didn't hurt that we didn't have my toxic in-laws lurking in the shadows anymore. Isaac had made good on his promise to cut off Jesse, but even if he hadn't, the damage had been done. His reputation plummeted once people realized he was not only a homophobe, he was willing to disown his son. A political career, especially as a progressive? Not in this lifetime, sweet cheeks.

That wasn't to say that whole fiasco had been easy for Jesse. Quite the opposite. In fact, it had taken him a lot longer to cope with all that than he'd expected. Financially, he hadn't done too badly, but emotionally, it had been hell. Thank God Los Angeles was teeming with therapists, and the makeup artist union's health insurance covered the weekly sessions that had been keeping him on a mostly even keel.

He still had bad days and rough patches. Sometimes it caught up with him in the most unexpected ways. He'd been kind of indifferent about it on his birthday when no one except his younger brother had called him. Christmas had been depressing, which we'd both expected, but New Year's had come out of nowhere and bitten him in the ass. It wasn't an occasion he'd ever been particularly sentimental about, but something about closing out the final year he'd spent as a member of his own family? Yeah, *that* had been a tough night.

Fortunately, Jesse's youngest brother had become a much bigger fixture in his life after the whole disownment debacle, and he'd been a godsend. They'd gotten a lot closer, bonding over both the heartbreaking isolation from their family and the relief at being away from that toxic wasp's nest. There probably weren't many people who could understand what they were dealing with—how much it hurt to be cut off from their parents, but also how liberating it was—so I was grateful every single day that they had each other.

And what could I say? I liked Alex. Whenever he was in town, we had Ashton and Luis over, and we all played Magic until no one could keep their eyes open anymore. Even Jesse was getting pretty good at the game.

Alex had been too estranged from the family to come to our first wedding, but he was here now. In fact, from the sound of it, he was engaged in an intense game of Magic in the next room with Ashton, Luis, Reanna, and Jay.

I smiled as I listened to them trash-talking. I was still

getting to know Reanna and her boyfriend, but she and Jesse had been making an effort to be closer, so we'd spent time at their place in Georgia, and they'd come to visit us a few times. They were getting there. And damn it, Jay really needed to propose already because the secrecy was killing me and Jesse. We'd taken him ring shopping like three months ago, and he was still "waiting for the right moment." Come *on*, dude.

I laughed at the thought and brushed some phantom lint off my jacket. Life was very different now than it had been the night Jesse and I met, that was for sure. We were closer to his younger siblings. Completely cut off from his parents and the older siblings.

And it wasn't just Jesse's family life that had been shaken apart. Needless to say, the movie role my agent had been negotiating suddenly evaporated. All the other auditions I'd done that week may as well have never happened at all.

I wasn't surprised. In fact, I'd expected to be blacklisted in Hollywood, but what did surprise me was that there turned out to be a quiet—and seriously large— faction of filmmakers who'd been waiting for Isaac Ambrose to fall from grace. Oh, he was still making movies and influencing Hollywood because God knew this industry was notorious for forgiving all kinds of bullshit, especially from white dudes who were wealthy, powerful, creative geniuses or whatever. And interviewers were all forbidden from asking him questions about his ex-son.

So on the surface, it almost seemed like business as usual, but there was a growing crowd of actors and crew members who refused to work with him. For every article praising him, there was at least one more reminding the world that he was a terrible father, and that he'd lied about being progressive so he could win votes.

There was also a growing crowd of filmmakers who didn't care about sucking up to Isaac, and they'd started calling my agent after things had gone down. New auditions materialized. Callbacks came. Before I knew which way was up, I was cast in three different low-budget films and a TV pilot. The roles weren't as big as some of the potential blockbusters and Oscar bait that Ambrose's cronies had been making, but they were something. They were getting my name out there, and more importantly, putting money into my bank account.

Speaking of money, the financial adjustment had been harder on Jesse than it had been for me. He'd been rich all his life, and even if he hadn't had direct access to the big money, it had been there if he needed or wanted it. He'd had an enormous—by my standards—allowance dropped into his own account every month.

Now that was gone, all that remained was the money he'd socked away and his paychecks from his work as a makeup artist. Not that his reserves were pocket change or anything. The dude had money that my former roommates and I could have stretched for *decades*. He just wasn't used to the idea that there was no more money coming in aside from his modest but respectable paychecks.

I know, I know—cry me a river, right? But I got why it was such a jarring transition for him. Jesse was used to having substantially more money than I could comprehend, and he'd never experienced life without it. The loss of the safety net fucked with his head. My family had gone through that, too, after my brother's injury. Even if there was still a decent amount of cash on hand, realizing there wouldn't be any more coming in was a scary feeling. So I didn't blame him for being nervous about the adjustment.

Fortunately for him, he'd saddled himself with a husband-turned-boyfriend-turned-fiancé who knew a thing or two about budgeting, and my expert-level prowess at being poor had smoothed his transition to middle class. What felt like a desperate financial state for him would have been like getting the keys to Scrooge McDuck's money bin for me. Oh, perspective. Like dude, maybe we weren't buying a condo in West Hollywood or a castle in Beverly Hills, but we were good. Even with me slowly grinding through that second Masters, we still had more than enough to drop a huge down payment on a small townhouse in Orange County and buy a gently used car for Jesse. After all, he'd needed something with good mileage to handle his long commute into LA, and anyway, we'd needed to replace the Porsche that his dad had made a huge production about towing away.

And in the end, I think that was the worst part—his dad's insistence on making a big show of disowning Jesse. We'd landed on our feet financially, but the emotional toll of severing ties with his family had been devastating for him. More than even he'd anticipated. Carolyn had tried to make amends a few times, but he'd finally had to cut her off after she'd made one attempt too many to get him to forgive his father. She knew damn well Isaac would never apologize for how he'd treated Jesse, but if Jesse could forgive him, then the family could move forward peacefully. Not happening, sweetheart. Fuck off.

She especially needed to fuck off because she knew—and had shamelessly capitalized on—how taxing this had all been on Jesse. How deeply it had hurt him to lose his father.

It was such a weird paradox, mourning a relationship with someone who was so toxic and terrible, but there it was. And really, I don't think he was mourning the relationship—more like the potential for a better one. At the end of the day, Isaac was Jesse's father, and Jesse had spent his entire life craving a loving, healthy, functional father-son relationship. Letting go of that dream—actively being the one to sever it—had not been an easy thing for him, and I predicted it would be years before he was fully at peace with it. If I had to pick one reason and one reason only to hate my father-in-law, that would be it.

But fortunately I didn't have to pick one reason and one reason only, and I could absolutely hate him for an entire laundry list of reasons. Seriously that man could eat a dump truck full of rotting hairy donkey dicks. *Nobody* treated my husband that way, and nobody fucking used his grief to try to manipulate him. Seriously, fuck his family.

And speaking of families—of course things had been awesome with my parents all along, but they were getting better with Brian too. We'd emailed and instant messaged a lot more in the last few months than we had in years, and recently we'd started doing some Skyping and Facetiming. It was a slow process, but it had taken us years to screw things up this badly. It would take time to unfuck it. There was finally hope of having my twin back, so I couldn't complain. At least we'd never been—and thank God, would never be—as toxic as the Ambrose siblings. Which meant I supposed I should be thankful I'd been exposed to that cesspit of dysfunction. Talk about motivation to repair my relationship with Brian. Silver linings and all that.

A quiet knock at the door pulled me out of my thoughts. "Yeah?"

The door opened, and Mom poked her head in. "You about ready, honey?"

Ready? Oh God, was it almost time?

All those nerves I'd sworn I didn't have were suddenly present and accounted for. I looked in the mirror, immediately deciding I was a hot mess from my hair to my bow tie and was that button straight? That button looked all wrong. Shit, we needed to just burn this whole thing and go with... I don't know. Togas or something because this tux was a wreck and—

"Hayden." Mom stepped closer and gently squeezed my shoulders, meeting my eyes in the mirror. "You look perfect."

"So why do I feel like I look like roadkill?"

"Because you're getting married." She kissed my cheek and flashed me a knowing smile. "It's just the nerves talking, baby."

"Nerves. Yeah." I tugged at my sleeve. "So much for having less performance anxiety when it's time for the real thing, right?"

Mom smiled knowingly. "Something tells me it's not performance anxiety. Everyone's nervous about their big day." She fussed with my bowtie. "You're not acting this time, but you're making a big commitment."

"Yeah. Yeah, I am. But I'm not worried that if I flub my lines, someone's going to figure out it's fake."

"Honey." She laughed, shaking her head. "You could get up there and forget how to speak at all, and no one would think for a second that anything between you and Jesse is fake."

The words almost moved me to tears. Choking back my emotions, I faced her. "Thanks. And, um, thanks for sticking with us. I know this whole fake marriage deal was—"

"It's fine, sweetheart." She patted my face. "You boys were doing it for a noble cause. Then you ended up falling in love anyway."

I couldn't help smiling. "Yeah. I guess we kinda did."

She hugged me, kissed my cheek, and then gestured at the door. "Everyone's downstairs."

Were they? Damn, the game in the next room had gone quiet. How long ago had that been? Probably while I'd been zoning out.

"Okay." I took a deep breath, pushing my shoulders back as I tugged at my jacket. "Let's go."

I followed her downstairs to where our small group of guests waited. It seemed oddly poetic, doing this at my parents' house after we'd done the original at the Ambrose house. There weren't as many people, and the living room wasn't nearly as big, and I wouldn't have changed a thing.

We probably could have dressed a bit less formal, especially since our reception was basically a backyard barbecue, but we'd worn our tuxes again. I mean, we had them, and they looked hot, so why the hell not?

As I crossed the room, Jesse turned around and met my gaze, and his smile made me warm all over. I'd thought he was seriously hot the night I'd met him, way back when I'd expected him to be a clown porn serial killer or something, but now that I knew him? Really knew him? Good God, I couldn't even look at him without getting all fluttery inside. And now he was dressed to the nines so we could say our vows again and *mean* them this time.

"Hey." He smiled as he pulled me into a hug. "You look amazing."

"So do you." I kissed his cheek. "You ready?"

Jesse exhaled and pulled back enough to meet my eyes. "Been ready for months."

"Well, then. Let's do this."

It didn't take much to get everyone where they needed to be. After all, we'd kept it simple this time. It was just the two of us and our officiant—the minister from my parents' church—with a small group of family and friends in mismatched folding chairs. So much less formal than our original wedding, but as Jesse and I joined hands in front of the big stone fireplace, it felt so much more real. After all, it *was* real this time, and that realization didn't help with my nerves *at all*.

The first time we'd done this, I'd delivered all my lines flawlessly, without so much as fumbling over a word or getting tongue-tied. This time? Not so much. My voice kept catching, and every time I met Jesse's eyes, my brain short-circuited.

We were doing this. We were doing it for real. Today wasn't about selling a charade and completing a mission— it was about committing to each other. Remembering my lines and speaking properly when, out of billions of men, I got to be the one promising to love Jesse Ambrose for the rest of my life? Not happening.

But I got the important line right. Smiling as I gazed into Jesse's eyes, I said, "I do."

His eyes seemed to well up a bit, and mine damn sure did when it was his turn to shakily reply, "I do."

We both exhaled with relief, and laughed because we were nervous and what the hell else were we supposed to do? We'd made it this far. We'd managed to articulate our vows, and neither of us had passed out, and now there was nothing left to do now but exchange rings.

I thumbed the place where my ring had been all this time. My hands felt weird—we'd moved our original bands to our right hands, leaving our left hands with room for the new wedding rings. For the *real* wedding rings. I swear half the reason I was looking forward to putting on the new ring was so my finger didn't feel naked anymore.

"So, um." Jesse cleared his throat. "I made a little bit of an executive decision about the rings. I know we'd picked out gold bands like..." He gestured at the one on his right hand. "But I wanted something a little more meaningful."

I swallowed. "Uh. Okay?"

In the front row of folding chairs, Alex pulled a small box from inside his jacket, and instantly the logo on top caught my eye—Hot Topic. He smiled as he stood to hand it to his brother.

"Did you..." I stared as Jesse opened the lid, and my heart skipped when he revealed the matching pair of matte silver bands. "Jesse..."

Facing me, Jesse took a breath. "When we did this the first time," he said, tugging one of the rings free from the foam insert, "you said you didn't need anything fancy. Just a couple of sterling silver bands that said *We're so Metal.*" He shakily took my hand and started to slide the ring onto my third finger. "You wanted a ring that said I'm not in this for the jewelry. And every time I thought about what our new rings should be, I just kept going back to that. So I hope this says what I feel about you—that I'm in this for you, not the jewelry."

My heart went crazy as I stared down at my hand, and when my eyes finally stopped blurring, I could see the finer details. Sure enough, engraved on the top of the band, were the words *We're so Metal.*

"Oh my God." I met his eyes again. "I can't believe you remembered that."

"Never forgot it." He handed me the box. "And now we'll match."

I laughed, and I fumbled with the box. Somehow I managed to get the ring out of the foam and somewhat gracelessly slipped it onto his finger, right over the top of the tan line from the one he'd been wearing before.

When I met his eyes again, his smile made my knees tremble. How the hell had I gotten lucky enough to be marrying this man? To be *really* marrying him this time?

The minister cleared his throat. "Well, gentlemen. Only one thing left to do. I'm pretty sure I don't need to spell it out."

Oh, no, he did not.

I stepped closer to Jesse, and as we both leaned in, he whispered, "I love you, Hayden."

"I love you too." I kissed him softly, then grinned against his lips. "We're *so* metal."

He laughed, wrapped his arms around me, and kissed me for real.

Our small group of family and friends applauded, and someone whistled, which made us both laugh, breaking the kiss. A camera flashed, and I hoped the photographer had really gotten that shot. I didn't care how I looked, but that huge smile on Jesse's face needed to be captured for posterity.

After Jesse kissed me once more for good measure, we

faced our small cluster of guests. They clapped, and everyone started getting up and coming toward us for hugs, handshakes, and congratulations.

"Congrats," Brian said with a big grin, and hugged me tight. "You didn't even have to mail order him."

"Shut up," I laughed. He chuckled, let me go, and gave my shoulder a squeeze as we exchanged smiles.

After Brian had moved aside, Dad hugged me, then extended his hand to Jesse. "Welcome to the family, Jesse."

Jesse stiffened, staring at my dad like that was the last thing he'd expected to hear. He recovered, though, and shook my dad's hand. The handshake turned into a hug, and as Dad let him go, Jesse surreptitiously wiped his eyes. When Mom hugged him, I thought he was going to lose it, but he held himself together.

I gave his elbow a gentle nudge. He turned to me, smiled, and nudged me back before we continued through the informal receiving line. Once we'd been through everyone, they trooped through the kitchen toward the backyard where dinner would be served.

For a moment, it was just the two of us, and I put my hands on his waist. "Well, we did it."

"Yeah, we did." He glanced down at my hand. "And the rings—you like them?" Self-consciousness creased his brow.

"Are you kidding? I love them. I just can't believe you remembered."

Jesse chuckled, but said nothing. He drew me in, and we shared another long, tender kiss before we joined our friends and family outside.

Everything was pretty casual after that. My dad and

brother were grilling outside, and it would be paper plates and Solo cups for our "reception." Fine by me.

While everyone waited for dinner to be ready, we all hung out in the backyard. Jesse and I stood by the railing on my parents' deck, watching our brothers and their kids playing together on the grass. Our brothers' wives were off to the side with Mom, wineglasses in hand as they watched too. My dad was chatting with Ashton about something over by the grill, and Luis was playing cards with Reanna and Jay on the deck.

"It's so weird," Jesse said after a while. "Having an actual family."

I looked up at him.

His gaze was still fixed on everyone, but it wasn't that distant, tense look he'd had when we'd been talking on our cruise balcony a lifetime ago. His features were relaxed, his eyes serene, and a subtle smile curve up the corners of his mouth. Without turning to me, he said, "When we first met, I had a goal in mind, and I really didn't think much beyond that. How my life would be afterward." Lacing our fingers together, he finally looked at me. "I definitely didn't think I'd come out of it with a new family."

"They're not all new. You've still got Alex and Reanna."

"Yeah, I do. And they're letting me in a lot more now that I've jumped ship from the rest of the family." He sighed. "Should've done that years ago."

I squeezed his hand. "Don't beat yourself up about the past. You got there."

He nodded. "On the bright side, even if things were messy with my family, I got you out of the deal."

"And now you're stuck with me."

"Oh, the horrors."

Chuckling, I let go of his hand and wrapped my arm around his waist. He folded me into a hug and kissed my forehead, and I just leaned into him and enjoyed the moment.

If there was one place in the world I didn't imagine anyone could find love, it was via an ad for a paid stand-in husband. Even now I still thought answering an ad like that was most likely to land someone in the company of a serial killer Nigerian prince doing clown porn.

But Jesse's desperate Hail Mary to end his dad's political career had driven him to post the ad.

My desperate financial situation had driven me to answer it.

And now I was married—for real—to the most amazing man on earth.

About the Author

L.A. Witt is an abnormal M/M romance writer who has finally been released from the purgatorial corn maze of Omaha, Nebraska, and now spends her time on the southwestern coast of Spain. In between wondering how she didn't lose her mind in Omaha, she explores the country with her husband, several clairvoyant hamsters, and an ever-growing herd of rabid plot bunnies. She also has substantially more time on her hands these days, as she has recruited a small army of mercenaries to search South America for her nemesis, romance author Lauren Gallagher, but don't tell Lauren. And definitely don't tell Lori A. Witt or Ann Gallagher. Neither of those twits can keep their mouths shut…

Website: www.gallagherwitt.com
Email: gallagherwitt@gmail.com
Twitter: @GallagherWitt